Veiled Skies

Jessica Santi

Veiled Skies

Identifiers:

ISBN: 979-8-9904263-0-6 (paperback)

ISBN: 979-8-9904263-1-3 (ebook)

TEMPLE
REYNES CASTLE
FIREBRANDS
COURTYARD OF ANTIQUITIES
COURTYARD OF SILVERSMITHS AND JEWELS
SHOPPING DISTRICT
PORT
QUEEN'S BAY
TO THE EVERLASTING OCEAN

TELACIEN MOUNTAINS
EASTERN QUARTER
FARMLAND
FAIRHAVEN FOREST
Arsaela
IN THE QUEENDOM OF LAEY

CONTENT WARNING

Veiled Skies may include content that is unsuitable for some readers. This novel includes mild profanity, death of loved ones, on page death, anxiety, grief, torture, gore, and murder. If any of these are triggering to you, please proceed with caution.

PROLOGUE

QUIET AS A MOUSE, and nearly as small, she peeled back the quilts
of her bed and crept on arched toes to the doorway. The door was
thick and heavy and took all her might to muster open. She accom-
plished the task painstakingly slowly and closed the door behind her
so gently not even the dust motes on the floor were disturbed.

Three calming breaths and a glance down the hallway to the right
to make sure her parents weren't stirring. Nothing. She suppressed
a giggle and snuck off to the left.

Although there were only a handful of torches lit sporadically in
the hallway, her steps did not falter. The castle as a whole, and the
path she would be taking tonight even more so, was as familiar to
the young girl as the depth of her father's laugh or the warmth of
her mother's smile. She lived and breathed the winding staircases
and grand ballrooms. She loved every nook and ivy-covered corner
as intimately as one could love anything at eight.

The stone underfoot cooled the soles of her feet, making her
realize that in the excitement to leave the comfort of her bed she had

forgotten her slippers. No matter. Feet didn't scuff against the floor the way slippers did, she would be quieter this way.

It did briefly cross her mind as she silently stole through the grounds of the castle that this was perhaps not something she should be doing.

The sneaking around in the middle of the night and all.

But high above her, shining light through the narrow windows carved into the walls of the corridor, was Selene, the Moon Goddess. And if one wasn't supposed to be wandering around in the cloak of darkness and starlight, why would one of the two High Deities grace the night sky with her presence?

The apothecary was located on the opposite side of the castle's courtyard as her room and down three floors. Often, she would sneak glances into it when its doors were open through her window, peering through the boughs of the willow at the courtyard's center and wondering what potions and tinctures the High Apothecary and his sister were brewing. Though not related by blood, her parents were so close to the siblings that they felt like family to the princess. She spent more time with them than her actual aunt and uncle.

She could cut through the gardens and save time, but that would risk being seen by the guards stationed on the turrets above. And besides, this was a grand adventure with no time restriction other than daybreak. Selene was high above, protecting and watching over her. No need to rush.

The castle was stunning at night, quiet and cool. In her personal opinion, all the bustling about and yammering on and on about coin and war and marriage that occupied the castle during waking hours took away from the beauty of it all. She ran her fingers along the corridor wall leading up to her destination, letting her fingertips fall into the grooves of the stone, and came to a stop in front of a set of the familiar double doors of the apothecary, carved from solid oak.

Two long windows of hammered glass lived on each side, resting just above the cold, steel handles.

Grasping one of the handles with both hands, the girl leaned back, throwing her weight into her heels and the stone floor. The ancient doors creaked loudly in resistance and panic chilled its way up her spine. Frozen, she counted ten bated breaths in and out before slinking into the apothecary with a sigh of relief.

Darkness greeted her. With only the hammered glass windows on the doorway, the apothecary was extraordinarily dim at night. She came prepared though, and fumbled around in her pocket for the candle and match she brought. A quick strike of the match and the wick of the candle softly illuminated her surroundings.

A contented hum rose to her lips upon seeing the organized chaos of the room. A glass bottle the size of her pinky sat next to one made of ceramic pottery the size of a small dog, a dichotomy represented in every corner of the apothecary. The wooden shelves lining the walls were jam packed with jars full of various flora and fauna from around the kingdom, and many more that came from far off shores. In the center of the room sat a huge workbench covered in parchment, ink stains, and sticky residue from the barrels of alcohol stored below.

She placed the candle on the workbench and walked along the edge of the room, gazing at her options. Someone without a plan may be overwhelmed. Not her. She had spent countless hours inside these walls helping the High Apothecary create magic, because that's what this was. Magic. No amount of reminders that this work was not akin to what mages or Fae were capable of could convince her that it wasn't magic.

One by one, she gathered her materials. Downy owl chick feathers. Water from a mountain spring. Painstakingly collected sparrow tears. Monarch butterfly wings. Snow melt from the highest point in the kingdom.

Bobbling the glassware in her arms and eager with anticipation, she pushed her items onto the workbench then pulled a rickety stool from the corner and clambered on.

With a mortar and pestle she ground the dry materials to dust and then added in the snow melt and water drop by drop until it reached a paste-like consistency she was happy with.

She peeled off her shirt and began the process of applying her magic to her shoulder blades. The wooden spoon was useful up until the very last dregs of her concoction, she couldn't quite reach the last edge of her back.

She arched her back, grunting in frustration.

Switched arms.

Stretched up onto her tiptoes.

She was reaching and squirming when her left foot slipped off the stool. She became a whirlwind of limbs trying to maintain balance, a chaotic dance that culminated in collapsing onto the stone floor.

She shook her head. Eyes stinging with tears from the impact. Feeling slightly embarrassed but glad no one had been there to witness her fall, she brushed the dust off her knees and palms and rose, taking slightly longer than she would have normally to notice that the room was brighter than it was seconds ago.

Confusion flickered across her face until she turned around to see that her candle on the workbench had tipped over in her fall and caught a thin stream of flammable liquid, remnants of some experiment earlier in the day. The flame licked across the workbench, slowly at first, then with increasing need to consume. Before she knew it the flames had leapt to the floor, following the trail to the barrels below.

The impending crisis snapped her out of the trance she had been in. Fear seized her heart. Her breathing became erratic and panicky. She took one step back, then another, eyes darting frantically around the room for somewhere to hide. The room was too small and the flames too hungry. She had to get out, had to leave. Was there enough time? Terror sizzled in her finger tips as she snatched up her shirt and sprinted to the door, bare feet slamming into stone.

Before she could reach the imposing oak doors, the barrels exploded and suddenly the flames were everywhere—floor, ceiling, doors—and she was in the air with no idea which way was up. Her body slammed into the ground, skull cracking on stone, and before the world went black her last thought was filled with disappointment.

Not magic then, that awaited her tonight.

CHAPTER ONE

THE HEAT WAS INESCAPABLE. It scorched her throat with every breath, filling her lungs with smoke and peeling the skin away from her bones from the inside out. Fiery tendrils danced across her closed eyelids as she opened her mouth to scream only to realize she was already a pile of charred—

Deming startled awake, eyes wide and hands flying first to her throat, gasping for air, then down to the scar that discreetly laced its way across her rib cage. She pulled her hands away before they could try and follow the trail of puckered skin to where it expanded across the whole of her back. Sweat dripped from the base of her neck, snaking down her spine as she labored to regain control of her body and mind.

"I am awake. I am alive. It was only a dream," She whispered the mantra to herself again, "I am awake. I am alive. It was only a dream."

Each repetition quieter and quieter until her chest was rising and falling slowly and she could no longer feel her heartbeat in her toes.

She leaned back against her silk pillows with a sigh, taking another pair of settling breaths with eyes closed. She rubbed her palms against her temples, noting the base of her hairline was soaked, too. Grimacing, she wiped the sweat onto her bedsheets. Julia would have to send them down to be cleaned.

Again.

For a decade these nightmares had plagued her and yet each one felt fresh and intimate, as if she was experiencing that night for the first time all over again. Mages and healers alike from across the queendom had been called to the palace to find cures but none had prevailed. Not that she necessarily wanted them to. Waking up in complete and utter panic was a small price to pay for what that night cost the queendom.

What it had cost her.

Deming rolled her neck and allowed the satisfying cracks to bring her back to her body. Her breathing slowed, but not nearly enough. She could still feel the blood pulsing through her temples.

She opened her eyes and began counting.

Five things she could see. The ceiling. The posters of her bed. The tapestry. The high-backed, patterned armchair in the corner of her room. The door.

Four things she could feel. The sheets, soaked. The pillow pushing into her hair. The breeze from the window. Her fingers intertwined.

Three things she could hear. The leaves rustling. The creak of the bed as she shifted. Handmaids' mumbled voices passing through the courtyard.

Two things she could smell. Bread, freshly baking for breakfast. Lavender sprigs in a small vase on her bed side table.

One thing she could taste. Deming reached over and picked a mint leaf from the tin placed close by for this specific purpose.

As always, dark thoughts swirled through her mind like foamy eddies in a current as the remnants of the nightmare slunk away. Was it worth it? A life filled with fear of tomorrow? A life spent worried sick that history would repeat itself?

Cheek to pillow and savoring the sharpness of the mint on her tongue, she blinked towards the bay window facing the courtyard. The early morning light was soft and gentle.

Her eyes drifted to the chaise next to the window where a barrel-chested, black dog stared back at her, head cocked and warm, brown eyes inquisitive. Deming could swear the dog was concerned for her. Animals were intuitive like that, after all.

Warmth spread through her chest. There may be a litany of terrible, torturous events waiting for her outside the walls of her bedroom, but there was also the unconditional love of a dog. And sometimes you just had to cling onto the smallest bits of good in order to get through the day.

"Good morning, Hollis. Hope that didn't disturb you."

Hollis leaned her head to the other side, let out a soft whine, and padded over to the bed, reaching up to give Deming a lick on her nose.

"Thank you," Deming murmured, nuzzling the dog in appreciation.

The tremors of the nightmare lingered in the early morning air, as they always did, but Deming was used to this by now and pushed the flames to a deep corner of her mind she refused to touch.

By the light sifting through the linen curtains adorning the windows, she guessed it was about time to get up anyway. Officially aware that her skin was disgustingly slick and sticky, she peeled off her slip and crawled out of bed.

The marble floors of her bathroom cooled the soles of her feet as she walked towards the basin of water waiting for her by the fireplace. She hesitated momentarily, debating whether or not to stoke a fire to life to warm the water, but decided against it. Too much effort. Besides, the water was room temperature. She wouldn't freeze. A cool bath was better for grounding herself in reality anyway.

She lugged bucket after bucket from the basin to the porcelain tub, heaving water over the rim until it sloshed somewhere close to full. She deliberately left just enough room near the top so her body wouldn't displace the water onto the floor when she climbed in.

Deming grabbed soap and a stopper of eucalyptus essence, squeezing in multiple drops of the latter and watching as the oil mixed into her bath.

Toes first and with a sharp inhale at the temperature, which was cooler than she anticipated, she entered the water. The water wasn't too shocking as it lapped up her ankles and calves, but as she squatted down to sit her thighs and chest seized and she lost her breath.

Perhaps stoking the fire would have been worth it.

Deming rested her head against the edge of the tub, nestling her neck and shoulders into the smooth porcelain. She slid down into the curved floor of the tub and closed her eyes. The water moved gracefully around her body as she shifted closer and closer to the rippling surface. Occasionally, the water lapped over her mouth and nose. She took a deep inhale and allowed herself to be pulled under.

She floated gently along the basin of the tub. Breath held, she slid her fingers into her hair, wrestling out the tangles from her restless sleep. Her lungs began warming, heart began beating fast, body begging for air.

Gasping, Deming breached the surface. Water splashed onto the floor at the disruption. She loved these morning wake up calls, as painful as they were. Nothing else has proven as effective at setting her mind right.

A gentle knock on the bathroom door turned her head, "Deming?"

"Mhmm," Deming mumbled in response, knowing by the voice who would greet her momentarily.

The door opened to show a willowy young woman with brilliant red hair in a neat plait resting over her right shoulder. Colette entered and found a seat on the cushioned bench along the wall. Concern filled her expression. Leave it to Colette to recognize the wake of a nightmare that quickly.

"Which was it this time?" She queried, hands folded neatly in her lap and legs crossed at the ankles.

"Not sure if you're aware, but you don't actually have to sit like that when no one is around to chastise you."

Colette flicked her plait to rest down her back and said nothing as the two women sat in silence. Deming massaged soap into her skin and inhaled deeply.

"Burnt to ashes. They're always worse this time of year. Today especially," Deming finally supplied. "The bath is helping."

Sorrow flooded Colette's pale blue eyes. She wrung her hands and let loose a weary sigh then stood, grabbed a bronze hairbrush from the counter, and knelt on the ground beside the bath. Deming shifted in the water so her back was to Colette. The bristles tugged at her scalp as her friend pulled the brush through the long lengths of her tricolored hair. What should be rich, red strands matching her cousin faded in and out across her scalp. Some swaths perfectly honeyed red, some swaths so light Deming considered them pink. Stark white strands wove themselves in and out of her hair too, including noticeable sections framing both sides of her face.

It was as if the gods ran out of color when she was born.

She loathed it and would have shorn off the lengths years ago were it not for decorum and the expectations of a woman in her position.

"Thanks for not vocalizing your pity."

"I know you hate that. Come on, let's get you dressed." Colette gathered her lilac skirt, full and heavy, and stood. She held out a fluffy white towel to Deming. "We need to get you down to breakfast if you want to visit the cemetery with Miriam before the High Steward holds formal court."

"He's your father, Colette. Honestly it weirds me out when you call him High Steward."

"That's what he is, isn't he?"

"Yeah," Deming said, rising up out of the water. She wrung out her hair and water splashed at her feet. "But that doesn't make it any less weird. It's like when you call me Heir Apparent."

"You are—"

"I know what I am." She rolled her eyes so hard the scene in front of her flashed out of sight momentarily.

Colette shook the towel at her. "Fine. Father is holding court this morning and you really should be there."

"I'd much rather go into the city with you and Paris. I need a distraction from… everything," Deming protested with a scowl. She took the towel and wrapped it around herself, fingers tracing the embroidery. The royal crest taunted her. A roaring animal, complete with menacing teeth and hackles wreathed in wickedly sharp quills, stared at her from the threads of the towel. The golden-furred leodin was an ancient feline beast that, when fully grown, stood nearly as tall as a war horse. Though scarcely seen, packs of them roamed the mountains surrounding the queendom and had been a symbol of the royal family for generations.

While she very much enjoyed the perks that came with being heir to The Queendom of Laey, access to the Great Library, beautifully ornate gowns, and luxuries like honeycomb and marzipan being a few of her personal favorites, the mundane tasks of royalty had always been a bore to her. Perhaps terrifying was a better descriptor. After the death of her parents, Deming had avoided anything that reminded her of them, including her responsibilities as heir.

Her mother should be sitting on the throne, not her.

No dosage of reality, no pressure from council, no veiled assurances from what remained of her family could tear away the delusion she hid behind.

Being a child when the crown fell to her, it was expected that her uncle, the last remaining Reynes-Elyachar pure blood besides Deming herself and his daughter, Colette, would take the role of High Steward until Deming came of age to rule on her own and Deming was more than happy to step aside.

More than a decade had passed however, and Deming was no longer a child. There was pressure from in and out of court in recent years for Deming to ascend the throne. Even the High Steward, Dresden Penrose, set aside his personal excuses for his niece and had been asking Deming to show more face around political events, but Deming was firm in putting off the responsibility as long as possible. Why would she choose to spend her days listening to the problems of a queendom and reading dull reports of grain and cattle when she could be traipsing around the city and beyond with her friends? Her uncle was better suited for the role anyway. He had been a primary advisor to his sister, Deming's mother, and had been playing an important role at court for longer than Deming had been alive.

"We can go to Firebrand's afterwards, is that an acceptable compromise? I've heard their cider may be on tap finally."

Deming smiled wryly. "Deal."

"Honestly Deming, you are truly a child sometimes," Colette chided half-heartedly. A few years older than Deming, her cousin had early on filled the missing older sister role that Deming often longed for and always needed.

"And yet, here you are, loving me all the same." Deming smirked back, tongue out to emphasize the point. The two women had made their way to Deming's armoire, Colette in the process of flicking through various dresses. "You know, I have handmaids to help with this exact task."

"Yes, but Noreen and Julia have terrible taste." Colette grimaced. "Don't tell them I said that."

Deming chuckled in agreement. Her handmaids were lovely and well-meaning, but the pair were severely lacking in the fashion department. Honestly, if Deming herself didn't have an intimate knowledge of fabrics and styles she probably would have replaced them years ago.

Guilt gnawed at her and she offered a compliment for the women that weren't around to defend themselves. "They are irreplaceable seamstresses though, and are wonderful at keeping the chambers in order."

Colette shrugged and turned around to offer an option. Deming considered the cornflower blue dress. Simple in design, the fabric was silky and allowed the mid-sized skirt to flow rather gracefully from the bodice. The sleeves would sit off the shoulder and end wider around her wrists. Navy embroidery embellished the edges of the gown. Knowing the color would compliment her hair and complexion she accepted the offering and stepped into the gown.

Pulling her hair into a soft bun at the nape of her neck, Deming stepped back to admire herself in the full-length mirror resting against the armoire. Colette threw an arm around her shoulder and leaned her head to rest against Deming's.

"What a vision we are," the latter commented.

"Indeed. Now let's get food. I am absolutely starving."

Whistling for Hollis to join them, the pair left Deming's bedroom and strolled across the living quarters to the door. Guards greeted them on the other side with a nod and courtesy salute. Hollis bounded ahead, the hound had free range of the castle and would likely spend her morning terrorizing the squirrels and rabbits in the garden. Deming made a mental note to take the dog hunting sometime soon to help burn off some of that energy.

The women walked through the corridors in comfortable silence, both appreciating the sound of birds chirping and the crisp autumn air winding through the occasional open window until they arrived at the Great Hall.

With its double doors wide open, the bustling activity within the hall was clearly visible even before Deming and Colette entered the fray. Various lords and ladies of court milled about, either finishing up their breakfast or else bothering someone who was trying to. A pair of young girls were whispering intently and giggling over their empty cups, no doubt reading the tea leaves, given the small book open beside them, and tittering about love and the rumor mill at court.

Against the far wall was a long wooden table where cooks had placed various baked goods for breakfast. Pumpernickel, rye, wheat, and white bread loaves in various shapes were placed in the center, with jams, butter, orange glazed scones, and lemon curd pastries placed nearby. The chocolate and almond filled croissants at the edge of the table seemed to be drawing the most attention. There was nearly none left on the display.

Deming saw Lord Dougherty with his rosy cheeks cramming the remnants of one such croissant into his mouth, crumbs coating his thick mustache. Another fresh one was gripped tightly in his other hand, ready to be consumed imminently. The buttery grease on his fingers caught the light, noticeable even from across the room.

Frustration bubbled in her gut. If she had the audacity to eat with such lack of decorum she would be the talk of court for weeks. Little would it matter that she was to be queen, or that women had always worn the crown in Laey. Deming's mother had sat the throne, and her mother before her, and so it had been for centuries.

Double standards were yet another part of the crown she very much relished delaying playing her full role in.

Deming took in the rest of the room. Large floral arrangements in the traditional colors of Arsaela, emerald and gold, were lined up against the walls and larger-than-life tapestries of the gods and goddesses hung from ceiling to floor.

Hanging closest to the giant stained glass windows on the back wall were tapestries of the High Deities - Kielle and Selene.

The artist who created the tapestry of Selene, the Moon Goddess, had somehow managed to capture her legendary discernment in her crystalline eyes, which took in the hall with a knowing gaze. A crown of stars perched atop the luminescent silver and white threads of her hair, which twisted around the goddess with effortless ease and caressed the eggshell blue skin she was said to have. Held close to her chest was a tome, representing her eternal wisdom.

Kielle, the Sun God, stood imposing and fierce, his likeness posed as if ready for battle. Skin such a deep brown it was nearly black only further emphasized his trademark solid gold irises. In one hand was his staff topped with an ornate gold globe clasped in the talons of an eagle with outstretched wings. In the other, a shield embellished with a depiction of The God's War.

Long ago, before humans or Fae or mages walked the land, a great evil had torn through the fabric of time, ravenous in its hunger to destroy. Kielle and Selene led the rest of the gods and goddesses against this evil, and while they were victorious, it came at a great cost. Many perished and the world they had come to love was damaged beyond repair.

In her sorrow, Selene wept endlessly. Her tears fell onto the scorched earth in such abundance that they created new oceans, lakes, and rivers. With water readily available again, plant life soon followed.

Seeing the wonder of the world Selene was rebuilding, Kielle decided he too would make his mark. Slicing into his palm, Kielle squeezed droplets of blood into the land and water, creating animal life. The Fae followed shortly after. Kielle imbued their souls with the magic of all living creatures, giving them their telltale animal aspects, to tie them intrinsically to the land and be immortal stewards of the new world. He created humans last of all. With short lifespans, they were to be a reminder of the delicate nature of the world.

Deming was pulled out of her reverie by a sharp tug from Colette.

"Are you okay? You look completely lost."

"Sorry." Deming shook her head to clear her thoughts. "I get sucked into those tapestries every time. Honestly, I don't know why we choose to decorate the Great Hall more lavishly than the throne room, or even the ballroom. You'd think we would want the places where we hold court or festivals to be the most beautiful."

"Well, maybe when you're queen you can change things up."

"Yeah right," laughed Deming, "You know as well as I do that even if I take the throne, your father would never let me move artifacts as ancient as those tapestries."

"When, Deming. When you take the throne."

"Yeah of course, that's what I said."

Chapter Two

Deming's breakfast had been a quick, bland affair. She had barely been able to keep her buttered toast down. Colette sat with her until Miriam arrived.

As her mother's best friend and confidant, Miriam had been a constant presence in Deming's life since her first breath. Miriam's brother and the former High Apothecary, Khalil, had been lost in the same fire that took her parents life. Since that fateful night, Miriam had helped Deming walk through their communal grief and return to some semblance of normal.

Deming loved her more than anyone else alive.

As way of greeting in the Great Hall, the woman who raised her had given Deming an embrace so full of knowing that tears threatened to fall, and then the pair departed for the royal cemetery.

Her parents' memorials were already littered with roses when they crested the final hill.

Deming now walked hand in hand with Miriam, past row after row of monarchs long gone, the latter giving a tight squeeze when the larger than life white marble statues of Silas and Samira came into view.

The bundle of light pink peonies that Deming held in her other hand swished softly in the breeze. Their existence was a testament to the skill of the florist who tended the greenhouse nearby. Miriam held waxy-petaled calla lilies.

Mourning doves flocked in the distance. Their song was haunting and beautiful as it echoed through the early morning light that filtered through the tall pines at the edge of the cemetery. Cold mist still hung to the blades of grass, unwilling to dissipate as day broke.

The two women laid their bundles of flowers at the foot of the statues as they did every year on this day. Always at dawn. Always peonies and lilies. Always only the two of them, hand in hand.

The queendom had lost their monarchs to flame and terror ten years ago today. Silas and Samira had been beloved. Their rule was peaceful and their hand benevolent. Despite the passage of time, the queendom still paid their respects to the lost couple during the week leading up to the anniversary of their deaths. Hence the roses.

The queendom had lost their monarchs, certainly. But the women standing silently before the marble likeness of the former king and queen had lost so much more.

For Deming, a mother. A father.

For Miriam, a relationship with Samira so deep they were more sisters than friends.

So the cemetery was closed to the public on this day, the day they had died, so the daughter and best friend could mourn the deaths privately.

The years may have dulled the sharp bite of loss, but grief still swam in their veins, still clouded their senses. Instead of the deaths feeling like daggers sinking into their skin and vices constricting the air from their lungs, they felt like being submerged underwater. Senses and emotions muffled. Smothered under the weight of reality.

Miriam handled her grief far better than Deming. The older woman felt the loss, recognized it, and tucked it away safely.

Deming hadn't possessed the wherewithal when her parents died to learn how to deal with the grief. The guilt. It suffocated her. Drowned her. Pulled her inwards until she no longer knew how to exist in a world where she was their daughter but they were gone.

Children weren't supposed to say goodbye to their parents that young.

A raven cawed, circling the highest tower of the castle that could be seen in the distance.

Miriam pulled Deming in close. She used a hand to guide the princess until the heir's head was resting on her shoulder. Her curls mingled with Deming's.

Their soft breath puffed rhythmically in the air between where they stood and the burial plots. They said nothing, they didn't need to. Their presence was soothing enough.

After a time, Deming straightened and stepped forward, closing the distance to Samira's statue. She caressed the cold stone, traced the inscription engraved on the plaque.

She kissed her palm then pressed it firmly against the marble.

Her tears fell like snow. Silent, steady.

The soil she kneeled in was damp by the time she rose.

CHAPTER THREE

SOFT STRING MUSIC PLAYED throughout the throne room as Deming milled about, speaking with the households that had been invited to court this season.

Siphoning away her emotions surrounding the anniversary of her parents deaths was something she was still horrendous at, despite the length of time since the accident. Unfortunately for her, court life proceeded regardless of how much the princess wanted to bury herself under heavy blankets and sleep the day away.

And so she found herself faking a smile to the lords and ladies that peppered the ballroom.

Some households, like Colette's, who was currently deep in forced conversation with a man her parents were trying to set her up with, were related to the royal bloodline and had been guests of the royal court since before Deming was born. Others were new invitees. Even though she knew every member of the court like the back of her hand, Deming was convinced she would still be able to tell the newcomers from the veterans without the knowledge the woman on her arm ingrained in her daily.

A perfect example moved about ahead of her.

She observed Lord and Lady Blackwell on the edge of the crowd with strained smiles, dressed in formal wear that was clearly out of place. Court had its formal moments, but it was certainly no occasion for a full ballgown and Deming was sure that Lady Blackwell was regretting her wardrobe choices this morning. She briefly wondered why no one had told them and made note to send a letter complimenting the gown and inquiring about the seamstress, with hope that would ease the lady's insecurities.

Just beyond Lady Blackwell, Deming saw Miriam politely parting ways with the governor of a small coastal town and moved to catch the older woman.

"Mir, doesn't this bore you?" Deming asked as she looped her arm through Miriam's.

"Not in the slightest. In fact, I find court to be one of the highlights of my week. Although that may be because it allows me to spend precious time with you," Miriam answered, giving her ward a warm smile.

Deming leaned into Miriam's shoulder and smiled back. Although she was sure it wasn't meant as a slight, Miriam's comment didn't sit right. Deming looked at the woman who taught her how to read, the woman who held her when she cried and encouraged her when she faltered, the woman who was as close to a mother as she has had for the last ten years, and felt a wave of shame wash over her.

"I'm sorry I haven't been spending as much time around the castle as I should lately. I promise I'll make more of an effort to be here," she whispered.

"Oh darling, that's not what I meant—"

"I know, I know," Deming said, forcing the wobble in her voice to level out before continuing, "But it's true all the same. I don't understand why this life feels so foreign to me. It's my birthright, I should be joyously anticipating my coronation. The people of Arsaela deserve a leader who knows and understands them and wants to better their lives with every fiber of their being, and I just don't think I can give them that." Her pace across the throne room slowed in conjunction with her voice softening. This crisis seemingly came out of nowhere and it was quite jarring to Deming, who, most of the time, was perfectly content not having a greater purpose.

For as long as she could remember, Deming had never wanted for the crown. When she was younger she would spend hours praying to the gods to send her a brother or sister who could take up the throne instead of her. It wasn't that she hated her responsibilities necessarily, it was just that they didn't seem as important to her as they should. After her parents died, the aversion to responsibility grew even more. Anything related to the crown or throne felt traitorous to Deming, as little as that made sense.

Her mother should be here. Not her.

Everyone told her that as she aged she would learn to appreciate the solemn duties that came with being heir. That she would come to recognize that by leading well, she could honor her parents legacy. But alas, here she was. Eighteen, nearly grown, and still digging her heels in at the thought of wearing the crown.

It felt almost certain that things would have been different were her parents still alive. Maybe they would have instilled a deeper sense of connection to her people than Miriam had been able to. Or perhaps they would have been able to impress on her the importance of structure and commitment when running a queendom that Dresden hadn't been able to. Maybe Deming would feel compelled if she saw the woman who had birthed her sitting on the throne.

But that felt unfair.

It was impossible to quantify the ways Miriam had stepped in and stepped up in the wake of Silas and Samira's death. She had never married, never entertained leaving Reynes Castle to return home to her small farming village to grieve in peace. She had stayed. Stayed in the place that held the ghosts of her best friend and brother. She had stayed and raised Deming with love and care as if she were her own daughter.

And Dresden had stepped up not just for Deming, but for Arsaela and Laey as a whole. He had carried the mantle of High Steward with grace in the wake of his sister's death. Only someone from the Reynes-Elyachar line was eligible to rule. He had no choice and bore the weight of a crown he had never expected to wear without complaint. He extended his hand time after time to Deming, trying to weave her into the fabric of political life.

It wasn't either of their fault she was a miserable excuse for a princess. A miserable excuse for an heir.

Miriam took in her adopted daughter's concerns and guided the two of them to a secluded corner of the room, coming to rest at a small bench nestled half in shadow. Miriam settled into the cushions, adjusting the skirt of her lavender gown so it looked regal even while sitting, and gestured for Deming to do the same. She turned to face Deming, placing one hand softly against Deming's cheek.

"Deming, my love," she spoke gently but firmly, "you carry with you a weight that no one else can relate to. A queendom, yours to inherit and care for, is more responsibility than anyone can imagine." Miriam's brows furrowed slightly over her honey-brown eyes. "It is no wonder you feel hesitation at the task. And to be honest darling, I believe that your resistance to the crown is a testament to you deserving it."

"I don't understand." Deming felt her forehead crease as she struggled to follow.

"Those who hunger for power are never the ones who should have it," Miriam continued. "Power is a drug, I have seen good men and women succumb to its attraction. To be lusting after it before you've even had a true taste would be to put yourself in a situation you could never win."

Deming considered Miriam's words. "You've made similar comments about my parents." She had memories of her parents, but they were mostly contained to family interactions like her father teaching her how to ride a horse or her mother bringing her into town to shop, not royal duties. And even those had faded with time.

"As you know, Samira was an only child, like you, when she took the throne. She certainly didn't shirk her responsibilities with the same ferocity that you do." Miriam chuckled and tucked a stray hair behind Deming's ear. "But she understood what her inheritance meant. She was a simple woman, her greatest loves being you and your father. And I think Silas's ability to empathize with the common folk allowed your parents' reign to be as peaceful as it was.

"And you, my love," Miriam finished with a smile, "will lead just as gracefully." She stood, extending a hand to Deming and helping the princess to her feet. "I know it doesn't feel attainable to you right now, but you will be the most wonderful Queen for many reasons, not least of which being that you do not want the role. Stay humble and kind, remember your roots, and take care of those who cannot care for themselves. Ruling well is not so difficult a thing when it really comes down to it."

Deming smoothed her skirt and, after a beat, said, "Thank you for your honesty and guidance. I don't know that I believe you, but I want to."

"I know, love, and that's perfectly fine for the moment. Now, we have spent far too much time worrying about your future and far too little hosting our guests. Let's divide and conquer the rest, shall we?"

"Yes, let's." Deming took a deep breath and entered back into the fray, almost immediately being pulled into a conversation with Lord Dougherty, crumbs from earlier still decorating his mustache. She was immediately reminded of what Miriam had just said. Stay humble and kind.

Easier said than done, but she would try.

An hour or so later, Deming stood near the open arched doorway to the throne room watching the last of the court trickle out. Her feet ached from her choice of heels, which were far too high, and skirt, which weighed far too much. While she was very much looking forward to getting on with the rest of her day, it hadn't truly been as painful as she anticipated. She was even able to connect with Lady Blackwell and compliment her gown, taking one thing off her to-do list for the afternoon.

Colette approached, one of the last to leave as always. Her eyes were bright and her hair was immaculate.

"How is it that you always look better after court than before?" Deming huffed in annoyance, the thickness of her own hair fighting its way out of the neat bun it had been placed in earlier.

"I know you don't love court, but I find it so invigorating! It's wonderful to speak to the Arsaelian nobility. Most of us live far outside the city, so the time we spend here allows us to mingle and find companionship."

"Speaking of companionship, where is Paris?" pouted Deming. "He almost never misses court. It's infuriating that he relishes in it as much as you."

As if summoned, hands snaked around her waist and twisted Deming into a dip. Shock melted into amusement and Deming smiled against Paris's lips before bringing her hands to his neck, deepening the kiss he greeted her with.

"If you could not snog so egregiously in my presence that would be great," Colette complained, faking a gag.

"Oh, come on, look how beautiful our future queen is! How could I resist?" Their childhood best friend smirked as he pulled Deming out of the dip and left an arm loosely held around her waist, running the other hand through his short, ash blonde hair. "I'm sorry I missed court today, I had a particularly fruitful hunting session going down in Fairhaven and didn't want to cut it short."

Deming looked up and admired him with a soft smile. No matter the heaviness of her emotions, Paris was always able to lighten her mood. She couldn't help but notice that the billowing white shirt tucked into deep emerald trousers he wore complimented her choice of dress.

"Quite a lot of buttons you have undone today, Paris. Feeling particularly roguish this morning?" she teased, running a finger down the open collar.

"I figured I might as well give the lords and ladies something to talk about other than Lyle's estrangement."

"How chivalrous of you."

"Did you hear he's run off with the barmaid? Lord Santano is beside himself. No heir, what a shame."

"Honestly, it puts their house at incredible risk," agreed Colette.

"You don't find it even slightly romantic?" Deming asked.

"Not at all! Santano is a widower, and not particularly young. If he doesn't want the throne to pass to his sister he'll have to remarry and produce another heir." Colette not only always had her finger on the pulse of court, but seemingly knew the exact right or wrong thing the parties at play should be doing. Deming envied her for it.

"What if he doesn't want to remarry?" Deming contemplated the concept of putting the fate of a reign ahead of her own desires. The thought of marrying someone for the sole purpose of having them quicken her womb made her stomach turn.

She was sure she wanted children, that was not the issue. Rather, the idea that her own timeline would be set aside, or even worse, that she may be forced into marrying someone she didn't desire was revolting to her. She looked at Paris. Being with anyone other than him was difficult to imagine. Surely if he were to die she could never take another lover.

"That's not a luxury someone in his position is afforded," Colette said solemnly. She gathered her skirts, began walking towards the corridor leading out of the throne room, and looked over her shoulder at her friend and cousin. "Enough of this, court has ended and if I remember correctly, I promised you we would go to Firebrand's. I would prefer not to get stains on this gown, it's rather new. Shall we change into something more appropriate?"

Deming grinned wide, eager to accept the offer. She turned to Paris who smiled in return, bowed low in jest, and said, "I'll follow you wherever you go, my liege."

Colette rolled her eyes and Deming let loose a full bellied laugh. The trio left the throne room with linked arms, joyous and carefree.

Deming, for what it was worth, had been ready to go soon after they split into their rooms. She had quickly slipped out of the gown and into leather trousers that hugged her hips and a loose white blouse, akin to what Paris had been wearing. Tall black riding boots and a loose braid completed the look.

Much to her chagrin, however, Colette had gotten caught up with her parents who had insisted they take afternoon tea with the Duke and Duchess of Wrenfast. Duke Lowell was notoriously long-winded and prideful, and he and his wife were relentlessly pursuing Colette as a match for their own son and heir, Theron.

He was also Master of Coin, and was too important to offend.

Due to the delay, it took them far longer than preferred for the three of them to reach the splintered door of Firebrand's. The stench of spilt ale and sweat hit them like a wall as they entered.

"Cassius should hand over some coin to the perfumery next door."

"There's not enough perfume in the world to cover this and you know it," Deming quipped at Paris, reaching back for his hand and pulling him further into the tavern.

They gathered around a hightop, not bothering with stools, and flagged down one of the barmaids.

"Three ciders?" Colette ordered hopefully.

"Sorry, not on the menu yet."

Paris flung a hand in the general direction of the door. "The leaves are changing color! The orchard must be ready by now."

"I can't quicken the fermentation process. Even for royals. Come back in a couple days." The barmaid lowered her chest in a quick bow, recognizing Deming and Colette as royalty from their telltale hair color, before darting away. "I'll bring you a pitcher of the ale we do have."

"And a glass of red, please!" Colette shouted after her. She turned back to the couple in front of her. "Now," she said, rubbing her hands together conspiratorially, "help me pick my poison. Theron doesn't have my hand yet."

Deming surveyed the tavern and its options.

The rail was full of young twenty-somethings, humans or mages she couldn't tell. While the offspring of Fae and human couplings had elemental magic coursing through their veins, mages physically looked human with rounded ears, no animal aspects to be seen, and a mortal lifespan.

Their very existence on the continent was a miracle even the gods hadn't expected. Fae and humans were never intended to mate. The cohesion that existed in Arsaela, as with many of the other larger cities in the continent where humans, Fae, and mages alike lived together, had been a recent development within the last couple hundred of years as the difficulty of traveling between territories eased.

Even now, human and Fae relations, while not unheard of, were not entirely commonplace. For many humans, sharing a bed with an immortal was intoxicating but terrifying. For Fae, there was a sadness in taking a lover only to have them blink out of existence once their mortal lives came to an end.

The Fae notoriously did not conceive easily, so most encounters with humans didn't result in anything other than pleasure. The rare occurrences where a child was born between the two, though, produced a mage.

Where does the soul binding, god given magic that was woven into the tapestry of the Fae go when muddled with mortal blood?

No one knew quite why elemental magic was the answer. Perhaps they were given control over air, water, earth, fire, or shadow because Kielle had intended for the Fae's magic to be linked with the earth. Perhaps the more explosive, expressive magic of mages was meant to be offset by their mortal lifespans.

The Fae, after all, had no control over their magic. It was in their bones, their breath. They may be stronger, faster, exotic with their animal aspects, but they could not wield magic like mages could.

Mages were beautiful and dangerous, powerful and rare. Colette very much enjoyed their companionship. Unfortunately, tonight everyone at the bar seemed to be coupled off. A weathered man old enough to be her grandfather sat at the very end, nursing an ale. That wouldn't do either.

Deming looked to the dance floor in the middle of the room and pointed immediately to a Fae male with golden skin and legs that shifted into thickly furred limbs and paws around his knee. "What about him? Looks leopard-y. He could be fun."

Colette scrunched her nose. "I just ended things with a male who had a bobcat aspect. Too predatory. No more big cats."

They mulled their options.

"What about her?" Paris pointed to a female with beautifully curved horns protruding from the sides of her head. Dark hair fell around them, framing an equally dark face with lightning blue eyes and full lashes that were already batting themselves in Colette's direction.

"Goddess," Colette said breathlessly, "Isn't she gorgeous."

The Fae female sauntered gracefully over to their table. "May I have this dance?" Thickly accented. Visiting from Runne, then.

"You may."

And with that, Colette was swept away as the female led them to the floor. She wrapped a hand around Colette's waist and pulled her in close, whispering something in her ear that had the red head giggling like a child.

The barmaid returned, setting down a pitcher of ale and a glass of wine as promised. Paris poured them both a stein and Deming took a sip. Decent, if a little mundane. She wiped frothy remnants from her upper lip.

"Care to dance?" Paris wasn't known for his love of dancing, but occasionally relented if Deming pushed enough. She seemed to be lucky tonight.

He stood and extended a hand. "For you, Deming, anything."

He pulled her upright and drew her on light feet towards the center of the room. The harp in the corner offered a dainty melody to sashay to, though it was nearly drowned out by the tavern's boisterous patrons. Paris led them around the wooden floors with the skillful expertise of someone who had grown up in ballrooms and royal courts and hallways laden with gold and pearl.

She smiled into his lips and he dipped her slowly and kissed her deeply. His grip on her waist tightened and warmth pooled below her navel.

This is what she was meant to do. Love and be loved.

It was almost midnight by the time the trio threw a handful of coins on the sticky counter and left. Selene was high in the sky, though most of her was hidden, leaving only a thin crescent nestled in plentiful stars to light the cobblestone path that led up to the castle. Most of the torches had used up their oil reserves, so only the shimmery natural light illuminated the way.

Deming hopped from one cobblestone to the other, pretending for a moment that she had no responsibilities to wake up to. How easy it would be to slip into an alleyway and leave Arsaela behind. Walk through open fields, fingers shifting through tall grass and flowers. Find Queen's Bay and then the ocean beyond and feel the waves lapping against her ankles. She could make a life for herself in some far off city, in some far off land. Maybe she would tend to a farm. No, far too much work. Maybe she would be a seamstress. Although she was notoriously bad at needlepoint.

She certainly wasn't suited for being heir or queen.

Deming slowed to a stop. She chewed on the inside of her cheek, contemplating. "What am I good at?" She asked, half serious.

Paris and Colette, mid conversation, didn't quite hear her.

"What?" Colette asked, still laughing, hand on his shoulder.

"What am I good at?" Deming repeated. "As much as Miriam, or Dresden for that matter, might try to persuade me otherwise, I'm not particularly suited for ruling the queendom. What else could I be? I'm a terrible seamstress and not nearly strong enough for any hard labor."

"You'll come into your own once the crown sits on your head, Deming, don't worry," Colette affirmed.

"Okay, sure. But indulge me, please."

Paris's brows knit together before teasing, "You're rather talented at pleasing me, perhaps you could come live in my bed chambers forever."

The glare Deming shot him could stop an army in their tracks.

"Well," he continued more cautiously, "you're just about the nicest woman I've ever met. And you're smart, you could probably pick up any trade if you put your mind to it."

Deming nodded, unpacified but also unwilling to press further at risk of coming across needy. "Thank you, that's very kind of you to say." She looked up the street, the looming castle greeting her gaze.

Arsaela, the capital city of the Queendom of Laey, rested in a crook of the Telacien mountain range and was perched high above the surrounding farmlands. With the mountains providing both protection from behind and a high altitude, the city was well secured and easily defended. The downside to being in such close proximity to the chaos of the mountains was twofold: winters were abysmally cold, and the streets were terribly winding and hilly.

Thankfully, there were still a few months left before winter set in and the autumn air that caressed her face still held a whisper of summer's warmth. Deming linked arms with Colette and Paris, giving the latter a chaste kiss on the cheek. They continued up the path to the castle and within minutes were at the front gates, indicating it was time to part ways as the royal wing of the castle was to the west while Paris and Colette's living quarters were to the east.

As Deming turned to head back to her own room, she caught a glimpse of movement out of the corner of her eye. A large black bird, perhaps a raven or crow, was floating across the sky. Its open wings blocked a portion of the moon as it moved through the night.

She watched it circle the north east tower, a candle still lit in the window indicating that someone was likely still awake and going over correspondence, before it landed gently on the stone sill.

Rather late for a letter to be arriving.

She watched it hop into the tower and, after a moment, fly back into the darkness.

Deming finished the walk back to her room, wasting no time slipping out of her clothes. Though she found that when she finally laid her head on the pillow she twisted and turned, unable to find comfort. The bed was too warm and the answer Paris had given bothered her something fierce, though she couldn't put a finger on why.

Sleep evaded her until the early hours of morning.

Chapter Four

WHILE THE BERRIES WERE ripe and sweet, they remained mostly uneaten. Deming pushed them around with her fork, mindlessly pressing a raspberry against the edge of the bowl and watching as the juices stained the ceramic a sharp magenta.

She had woken up feeling no better, and, to add to the mood, a dense fog had crept in, casting the whole city into greyscale and blocking Kielle so thoroughly that only a few of his rays were able to pierce through to warm the brick and stone of Arsaela.

Giving up on her sad bowl of fruit, Deming set the fork down and gathered her skirts to rise from the small wrought iron table on her balcony. Perhaps a ride through Fairhaven, the thick pine forest on the eastern edge of the city, with Hollis would lift her spirits and shake the odd start to the day.

She quickly changed into slim fitting trousers, riding leathers, and knee high brown boots, tying up her hair with a forest green velvet ribbon that complimented her shirt's lighter shade of green.

"Hollis, come," she whistled. The black dog trotted from the living room obediently to her side. "Want to go hunting?"

Hollis's ears perked up, clearly interested.

"Okay, girl," chuckled Deming, "Let's go."

They strolled through the castle, taking the long way through the maids' corridor and kitchen. Not only did their detour allow Deming to avoid as much Arsaelian nobility as possible, it also gave her the opportunity to snag a lemon pastry for herself and a piece of jerky for Hollis, who greatly appreciated the morning snack.

Brisk air greeted them as they entered the sprawling grounds through the back door of the kitchen. Autumn had claimed many of the trees already, whose red and gold leaves twisted precariously in the breeze.

The trees were not the only flora touched by the changing of seasons. Deming let loose a melancholy sigh at the sight of the gardens, which hugged the backside of the castle. During peak warm seasons the royal garden was a sight unmatched by anything Deming had ever seen, its gentle rolling hills a canvas for flowers. While many of the topiary accents remained full of evergreen needles, most of the floral sections had withered away to stalks and dirt meaning that the jeweled butterflies that usually flitted about were also gone, in search of warmer lands for the next six months. She was already looking forward to spring, when her favorite peonies would grace the gardens again with their pastel tones and beautifully layered petals.

Taking a paved stone walkway through the yellowing gardens, Hollis and Deming approached the stables. The heavy musk of horsehair and droppings hung in the air. Objectively an off putting scent, Deming still found it rather comforting. She had grown up on the back of a horse and spent more of her childhood riding her favorite ponies through the streets of Arsaela than inside the castle.

She came to a stop in front of a large dapple gray mare with an interrupted white stripe down its forehead. Quintessential whinnied softly in greeting. Deming had ridden every horse in the stables and enjoyed nearly all of them, but Quinn, having been specifically bred as a gift for her, held a special spot in her heart. Quinn was sired by High Standard, the warhorse her father rode into battle decades ago. Star Gazer, her mother's preferred mare, was Quinn's dam. Both older horses had since passed and the beauty of a horse that stood in front of her felt in many ways like one of Deming's last tangible connections to her parents.

"Hello sweet girl, want to get out for a ride today?" Quintessential nickered and shook her mane as Deming unlatched the gate and stepped inside the hay-filled interior. She hoisted a worn leather saddle onto the mare's back. "I know the weather is rather dull, but you're such a swift ride." Deming patted her broad neck. "I thought maybe we could outrun the mist."

She tightened the straps underneath Quinn's belly and chest and slid the harness over her head, giving her soft ears a scratch. At over seventeen hands, even Deming, who was far taller than most of her women counterparts at court, had to put in effort to pull herself up onto Quinn.

She settled into the seat of the saddle and grabbed the reins, leading the horse out of the stables and through the castle's side gate. Hollis padded alongside, tongue lolling and thick paws making indentations in the soft mud on the side of the pavers. Deming nudged Quinn into a gentle trot, relishing in the familiar pressure against her inner thighs and the bounce of the horse's step.

"Hollis, out of the mud."

The hound did no such thing.

"Hollis, heel."

Her ears perked, but not at Deming. A squirrel darted through the garden behind them and she bolted after it, never minding that she was far too slow to catch the nimble creature she wanted so desperately.

"Dothrum take you, you good for nothing dog." Deming huffed a sigh and rolled her eyes, leading Quintessential away from the gardens. Hollis would follow when she damn well wanted to and not a moment before. Deming had tried and failed to train her like the other hunting dogs the palace bred. She was as rambunctious as she was stubborn, and Deming loved her for it.

Even if it made going anywhere with her a pain.

They made quick work of the winding path leading from the castle and soon Quinn's hooves were clicking satisfyingly on the cobblestone roads of the city below.

Thick fog aside, the city was still beautiful. Towering stone buildings lined the road, enticing the citizens to come inside with various meats and tinctures. Deming preferred the shopping district, with its marble and glass facades showcasing reams of fabric and ribbons, but everywhere you went in Arsaela was lively and easy on the eyes.

She gave Firebrand's a warm smile as they passed the bar, already filling up even though it was still early morning. It was the melting pot of the city, drawing in humans, mages, and Fae alike.

Deming admired the combination of patrons both entering the bar and strolling through the streets. A particularly striking woman with raven black hair and a matching deepness to her skin who was speaking to a Fae male with curved antlers caught her eye. The woman had a sharpness to her eyes that made Deming wonder if she was a fire mage. The element gifted to a mage was often a representation of them in some way, similar to how the animal a Fae takes after represents their soul.

She led Quinn down the weaving roads, one hand on the reins and one resting lightly on her thigh. The fresh air held more of a chill than it would have had the sun been out and was numbing the tips of her fingers. Despite the briskness, she could feel herself loosening up with each step Quinn took away from the chaos of the castle.

Soon the tall brick and mortar of the busier districts gave way to dirt roads and spread out farm houses with thatched roofs. Deming waved to a farmer near the path, his dog bounding in and out of the field with Hollis, who had, in fact, left the garden squirrel alone and joined them shortly after.

There was likely one last harvest before the soil here lay dormant until spring. Deming wondered casually what the yield would be. They had never wanted for food during the winter, what with the ancient forest to her east and the vast ocean sprawling out only a few miles south providing ample game and fish to smoke and store, but it always seemed to be in the back of her uncle's mind.

The fog thickened as they approached Fairhaven. The forest seemed shallow, only a few rows of rotund trunks visible before a wall of mist withheld the rest from vision.

Quinn startled at the edge of the forest, pawing her hooves at the oak leaves littering the ground.

Mist tendrils creeped towards them.

"Come on Quinn, it's only air." Deming urged the horse into the forest.

They moved slowly, the mare clearly hesitant and Deming not wanting to spook her further. The ground seemed to shift underneath the thin layer of mist coating it. She glanced back and realized she could no longer see the fields they had come from, which was slightly alarming as they had only just entered Fairhaven. The mist had seemingly swallowed them whole.

"Hollis," Deming called sharply, not wanting to lose her in the dense grayness that surrounded them. "Stay close." This wasn't particularly necessary, as the dog had uncharacteristically not left Quinn's side since entering the wooded depths, careful to avoid the powerful legs but not straying further than a few feet.

Deming reached into the saddle bag and pulled out a compass. It showed them heading east, as she expected. They had started on the same trail Paris was hunting on just yesterday, one she had ridden countless times. It should take them towards an open glen that rested along a river.

Keeping the compass ready in hand, she had learned early on that navigating anywhere in dubious weather was not to be trifled with. Deming led her paltry party of three deeper into the woods. Quintessential was sure-footed and although the mare was clearly uneasy, she did not misstep in the tangled roots.

Deming glanced upwards, trying to no avail to find a patch of sun. Everywhere except directly in front of her was gray. She looked down at her compass. Still east. Just as she was beginning to worry, she saw the fog begin to lift ahead.

"There we are, ladies," she voiced confidently, sure they had arrived at the glen. However, once they breached the fog she pulled on Quinn's reins, halting her to a sharp stop in surprise. What in the gods...

They had emerged exactly where they started not ten minutes ago.

Deming looked down. Her compass was now tauntingly proclaiming they were facing west.

"That's impossible," she scoffed to no one. They had not turned off the path, she would stake her reputation on it.

Deming careened her head and eyed the woods over her shoulder. It appeared as it had before—cloaked in gray up until the first few rows of trees.

"This is ridiculous. I'm getting a new compass." She shoved the obviously broken compass back into the saddle bag, pulled the reins, and aligned Quinn's muzzle with the trailhead. "Let's go."

The three embarked into Fairhaven once more, this time with more pace. Deming held Quintessential to a canter, her own body fluid and moving as one with the mare. Hollis, able to keep pace, ran alongside. A branch whipped out of nowhere and cut Deming sharply across the cheekbone. The heir paid it no mind.

Again, she could see the beginnings of a brighter space ahead. She pushed Quinn into a full gallop and burst into what should be the glen only to curse when she realized they had once again been brought back to the edge of the gods-damned farmer's field.

Face flush and jeweled hair wild from both wind and ride, Deming once again looked back at the landscape of mist and trees. Her frustration melted into concern.

She whistled at Hollis to heel and backed Quinn slowly away from the dense wall of fog. What had been simply dreary and annoying this morning had turned ominous. Dread filled her chest. Sweat coated her palms. Was she going insane? Deming bit her lip and let out a shaky breath. What was happening in Fairhaven?

This wasn't naturally occurring. Whatever it was needed to be reported to her uncle immediately.

She pulled on the reins and urged Quinn towards the city proper, digging her heels into the mare's side to coax her faster and faster as they whipped through the streets that turned from dirt to gravel to stone as they approached the winding road to the castle.

Quintessential thundered through the open castle gates. Hollis dodged the gravel and grass that her hooves sent flying.

Deming pulled sharply on the reins, guiding the mare far fiercer than necessary towards the stables. She leaned forward in the saddle, trying to remain seated and not on the dusty floor, as Quinn reared her head and kicked the air with her hooves as they entered.

"Water her," she said, flinging the reins at the nearest stablehand as she vaulted off Quinn's back. "And a sugar cube." The last command was thrown over her shoulder as she sprinted out of the doors. A not insignificant part of her felt ashamed it was an afterthought. Quinn rode hard back to the castle. She deserved better than to be handed off so abruptly.

Nothing to do about that now.

Deming surpassed the garden and went straight to the entrance of the east wing. She threw open the door so hard it ricocheted off the interior wall. Not bothering to check if it closed behind her, she walked with purpose through the castle corridors, mind racing and theories flowing rapidly, each as unlikely as the next.

The realm was no stranger to magic. It coursed through the life blood of the Fae, giving them their deeply coveted immortality, grace, and strength. And mages, rare though they were, wielded the elements.

But whatever was happening in the forest was unlike anything she had seen before. What even was it? A shield? An attack? From one person or many?

Deming tasted a metallic tang. She swiped her tongue across her lips, clearing the blood from where she chewed through her skin.

She hesitated. What if she had made the whole event up? She only led Quinn in twice... Maybe she truly had gotten turned around. She was a talented rider but even the best make mistakes from time to time.

No, no. There was nothing natural about that fog. Malice had laced the air.

One thing was certain. She knew next to nothing other than that her uncle and his council needed to hear about this as soon as possible.

Deming approached the double doors of the council chambers, throwing up a hand at the protesting guards before barreling in. She was Arsaela's princess, she would go where she pleased. It mattered not that she had turned down invitation after invitation to have her seat at this particular table.

CHAPTER FIVE

THE CONVERSATION DRESDEN AND his council were in the midst of having was cut short at the disruption. Echoes of a sentence inquiring about ship size faded into the air.

Dresden, along with the four other occupants of the room, looked up at Deming from the excessively long and meticulously polished redwood table. Duke Lowell's fist was paused mid air, clearly ready to emphasize a point.

The High Steward's brows furrowed. "Deming? What is it?"

"Has anyone ridden out into Fairhaven today?"

"No," he drawled slowly, not understanding, "I don't believe so. Not on my orders, anyway."

Deming opened her mouth to speak again but paused after a beat to collect herself, realizing far too late that barging into a council meeting was not very becoming of a future queen. Immediately her cheeks flushed. This group did not need more reasons to dislike her. She tucked the loose strands of hair behind her ears and cleared her throat.

Every council member sitting around the table was focused on her, expressions ranging from incredulous to confused to curious.

Lady Brittan was clearly caught off guard. Her brows furrowed as her eyes flicked between Deming and the inventory of goods she had been tallying up. Her duties as Mistress of the Hunt were demanding around this time of year. Ensuring the city would have enough food to last the winter was no easy job.

Lord Nolett, High Marshall and in charge of the safety and security of the realm, looked displeased at the intrusion but intrigued at what brought Deming to council looking so ragged and out of breath. He placed a hand on the table and leaned towards her, eager.

The Duke, unsurprisingly, wore the same exasperated expression he always had when speaking to the princess. The most diligent of council members and a devoted Master of Coin, he was continuously perturbed by Deming's lack of ambition.

At least Miriam was a friendly face. As someone not of noble birth, it had been a shock to the court when Dresden appointed her Chamberlain. He was adamant that someone as integral in raising Deming and as close to the previous queen as Miriam was not only a smart addition to council, but a necessary one.

Worry was etched across Miriam's face. Not for Deming's lack of decorum, but for her well being.

Deming was flooded with a confusing mix of gratitude and anxiety. Miriam would hear her out, even if the others would not. Perhaps she should return later when she could make a better impression...

"Please forgive my interruption." Face flush and full of heat, she bowed her head in an attempt to save face. "I let my emotions get the best of me. Dresden, when you are finished I would request a moment of your time." Murmurs rumbled through the chamber—council members whispering questions and critique alike at the oddity of the situation. The high marble ceilings did nothing but assist in the echo of their words.

The High Steward was already standing up. "I can certainly step away for a—"

"No," insisted Deming, "please, finish council." She caught a scathing look of disapproval from Duke Lowell. Out of the corner of her eye she saw Miriam tilt her head in a silent question. Deming shook her head softly and turned on her heels to leave the chambers.

She cursed herself.

The doors closed behind her and within moments she heard the muted conversation pick back up. Sighing, she twisted at the sleeve of her shirt. Something fearful and cold coursed through her veins.

A glance out the window confirmed that the weather hadn't changed. Kielle often hid behind clouds and fog for days at a time, but with the accompaniment of her experience this morning, each passing minute without the bright rays of the High Deity caused Deming's anxiety to grow.

Unable to sit still, she paced down the hallway, no destination in particular in mind. She was so lost in her thoughts that she turned a corner and nearly collided with a thin mass of red hair and alabaster skin.

Colette was dressed pristinely, as always. A gossamer gown of pale yellow tulle unfurled underneath a brilliant orange bodice. Small jewels encrusted both the hem and neckline. Her hair, curled, was pinned up with bone hairpins topped with pearls.

It was quite a comical contrast to Deming's nest of knots and mud spattered riding leathers.

"By the gods, Deming! You nearly ran me over!"

"I'm so sorry, I am not in my right mind at the moment. Are you okay?" Deming, much to her annoyance, found her throat tightening and tears welling at the corners of her eyes as she apologized. The troublesome experience in the forest had thrown her in such a tizzy, she had given Dresden's council further confirmation that she wasn't fit to take the throne by barging in on their meeting unannounced, and now she had nearly knocked over her friend.

She reminded herself she didn't want the throne anyway. The only member of council whose opinion she cared about was Miriam, and Miriam would love her regardless of the mistakes she made or the title she wore.

Still, she was quite sick of the day and it was only just noon.

"Am I okay? Of course," her friend said. "It looks like I should be the one asking you that question. What in the gods has happened?"

Not knowing where to start, Deming stood mouth agape, looking like a fool for a moment.

"I cannot seem to do anything right when it comes to council," she said, starting with the most recent incident. "I just came from their session, having completely interrupted them without announcing myself at all. You should have seen the look Duke Lowell gave me."

"Well, a cat in heat has a better temperament than that man."

Deming cracked a smile. "You simply can't accept a proposal from Theron. I can't imagine the apple falls far from the tree."

"It doesn't," Colette confirmed with a scrunch of her nose, looking like she smelt something foul, "but you know as well as I that the decision has little to do with my opinion."

Colette waved her hand at Deming's attempt to protest, changing the subject back to the matter at hand. "Why were you at council anyway? You never attend. And you certainly don't look dressed for the occasion," Colette's eyes roamed Deming's rugged appearance with a grimace, "no offense."

"None taken," Deming replied honestly. "I needed to speak to Dresden about Fairhaven. I rode out with Quintessential and Hollis this morning and the strangest thing happened."

The pair had begun walking through the corridors again. The castle was bustling with servants preparing lunch for court. Thankfully, this meant that most noble women were putting the finishing pins in their hair and tightening their corsets so they could barely breathe, and therefore were either tucked away in their quarters or already in the throne room awaiting Colette's mother, who held a well attended tea regularly that provided an avenue for gossip to flourish within the castle walls.

"The fog," Deming continued, gesturing vaguely towards a window, "is much deeper the further away from the city you get. The edge of Fairhaven is only just visible through it."

"Okay," said Colette with skepticism, "and I assume something more happened than just bad weather."

Deming aggressively eye-rolled. "No, of course not. Clearly I barged into council in my riding leathers in hopes of pissing off Lowell and the rest, who already have reason enough to scoff at me, by the way, because I was bummed about dreary weather like a petulant child. Please, Colette."

There was a solitary beat of silence before Colette curled over in raucous laughter, causing the nearby servants to startle and look at the pair briefly before moving on with their tasks. One poor maid was spooked so badly she dropped her basket of linens.

"If you're finished," said Deming, one eyebrow quirked at her friend, who waved at her to continue. "When we entered the forest we rode for a while but suddenly we were back exactly where we entered. And no," she said, hand up in anticipation of what was about to come out of her friend's open mouth, "I did not get turned around. I checked my compass multiple times and we did not make any turns. We took the trail Paris hunted on yesterday! How many times have the three of us taken that route? Countless!"

"Countless," agreed Colette with a nod. "Perhaps it was a fluke. It's easy to get disoriented in this kind of weather. Maybe your compass was broken."

"That's what I thought," continued Deming, "so we went in a second time. I made sure to keep Quinn on the path. I..." she debated even admitting her hesitation. "Afterwards I thought maybe I had made the entire experience up. But that doesn't feel right. There is no way we could have strayed. That trail is so worn down any deviation would be obvious and you know how sure of myself I am when I'm riding. Even in thick fog I would be able to tell if we went from dirt to brambles."

Deming stalled her walk, needing to impress upon Colette how sure she was. "Within moments we appeared at the trailhead again facing the road up to Arsaela. It felt wickedly alive. Like something in there was playing a trick on me." The last flicker of amusement left Colette's eyes. "I swear to you. By all the gods. Something about this fog is... sentient. It almost felt like someone was watching me." She tried and failed to suppress a shudder.

Colette chewed on her lip, considering the information. Both women lifted their heads as the clock tower in the gardens rang out, one long peal to announce the first hour of the afternoon was over. It also marked the end of council.

"I need to go speak with Dresden, I'm sure he's looking for me." Deming bid Colette farewell, the last vibrations of the clock tower still humming in the chilled gray air.

The High Steward had found the heir on a wooden bench in the royal courtyard, the latter having decided to sit still after a quarter hour of wandering the hallways in search of the man taking care of her queendom. She figured it would be better to stay in one place so they wouldn't keep missing each other.

The courtyard was surrounded on all sides by towering columns covered in blue and white mosaic tiles that held up the mezzanine level above. Evenly spaced rectangular terra-cotta slates paved the entirety of the first floor corridor on the interior of the columns, in addition to paving the walkways that crossed throughout the grass.

It was both stunningly beautiful and deeply disorienting to see for the first time, as it contrasted so significantly with the overall aesthetic of the rest of the solid, gray, and resoundingly plain stone castle.

The Common Courtyard, holding rows of birch trees and located on the other side of the castle, was the larger of the two by far. However, in spite of its size, the Royal Courtyard was famously more enticing due to the ancient willow tree at its center.

The tree had a trunk so thick three men couldn't wrap their arms around its circumference and was tall enough that even on the mezzanine one had to crane their necks just to see the top. It was said that centuries ago, the location of the castle was chosen specifically because of the willow, great even then, and that the stonemasons laid the foundation of the castle brick by brick starting with this courtyard.

Of course, no one alive could confirm this and since there was no written recollection of it either, most believed the old wives tale originated as the ramblings of some romantic poet. Why would a willow be growing in a mountain range anyway?

During the fire that took Silas and Samira but spared their daughter, much of the tree had caught fire. It had continued to thrive in the years since, but a sweeping charred scar ran up its trunk as a physical reminder of what had been lost that night.

Years later and Deming still couldn't pass it and not touch her own winding scar. A mirror of the tree's charred bark.

The tree was a picture of resilience and grace and it thoroughly took one's breath away.

It was beneath the great boughs of the willow that Deming's uncle finally found her.

"There you are," Dresden said, "I'm sorry about council, I wish I could have been more helpful in the moment."

"It's okay, truly. I shouldn't have interrupted like that. It was inappropriate."

"Yes." He was not one to mince words, even when directed at the heir. "There were harsh words said after you left. No damage that can't be undone, though." The older man sat down next to Deming, close enough that the hem of her skirt covered his shoes. "So, tell me what happened? You mentioned Fairhaven."

Deming nodded and began her story, sparing no details. The farmer's dog playing with Hollis. The way the mist shifted across the dirt. How completely it seemed to swallow them up. And of course, the fact that she knew with certainty they did not stray from the trail and yet somehow ended back where they began. Twice.

They sat in soft silence after she finished speaking. Deming looked for any sign of distress on Dresden's face but was disappointed to find none. Instead, the High Steward wore quite a wistful expression, as if thinking of something else entirely. Even if council had been particularly challenging that morning, Deming was confused at the lack of immediate concern.

"Uncle? Aren't you going to say anything?"

Something snapped into place in Dresden's eyes. "Apologies, I was collecting my thoughts." He stood, clasping his ring-clad hands in front of her. "That is an odd occurrence, of that we can agree. I believe you when you say you are sure Quinn did not stray. I, as well as anyone, know your riding capabilities."

Deming stood as well, not liking where this conversation was heading.

"However—"

There it was.

"I am not sure we can consider foul play yet."

Deming stilled, deeply sorrowful for a brief moment at the realization that even someone as trusted at her uncle didn't believe her. "I..." Whatever shred of confidence she carried earlier disintegrated into the dense air. She willed herself to look her uncle in the eye. "I know something is wrong with this fog. It doesn't behave like any weather I have ever experienced. Please, believe me."

"You hold such strong opinions on the matter. It is unlike you, and of that I am proud. You should speak your mind, it is your right." Dresden proceeded cautiously. Regardless of his opinion on the situation, he was not one to speak down to Deming. "But you have only ridden in it twice and, really, it hasn't behaved differently than any other kind of bad weather. People get lost in storms all the time. Even those skilled in navigation."

Deming felt utterly defeated. "You say constantly that you trust me, how is this trust?"

"I do trust you. I trust that you experienced something concerning, and I trust that you are bringing it to my attention because you care for the queendom and want to keep it safe. I also know that trauma haunts you."

"This is not because of my parents," Deming said dejectedly. She wrung her hands over and over. This conversation was not going the way she had thought it would.

"More of yourself than you know can be traced back to that night. Perhaps the lack of control you felt in Fairhaven brought you back to the lack of control during the fire."

Her next words wiped out of her throat with a violence she didn't know she possessed. "I didn't come to you to be studied like a moth in a jar!"

Her outburst chilled the air. The world seemed to pause for a moment. Even the birds and the wind were quiet.

A shaking hand flew to Deming's mouth. "I'm sorry. I'm so sorry I didn't mean to yell."

Dresden wiped the shocked look off his face and within seconds he lifted a gentle hand to bring her own away from her mouth. He held her small hand in his and rubbed his thumb across her palm. "You do not have to apologize. It was not my intention to make you feel cornered."

The pair would have likely tabled their discussion for the following morning had it not been for a sudden shout from a royal guard on the mezzanine.

"High Steward Penrose, you are needed immediately. There is a large band of citizens gathered outside the castle walls. They are demanding to meet with you."

Chapter Six

The throne room devolved into anarchy the second the woman in front ceased speaking.

In her seat left of center atop the dais, Deming cringed away from the explosion of voices that sounded throughout the cavernous space as the third citizen, a seamstress and mother of five, finished her tale.

Deming had already forgotten her name. This caused the uncomfortable heat of shame to prickle across her skin, but it was not nearly the most important problem facing her at the moment and she soothed herself with the fact that no one here was concerned with whether or not she remembered their name.

They were concerned with the weather.

The seamstress had gone foraging early this morning in the outskirts of Fairhaven, relatively close to the trail Deming and Quinn rode on. She quickly became enveloped in dense fog and shortly thereafter she appeared at the trail head despite her insistence that she had not turned around.

The man before her had been hunting in the Telacien's when he was abruptly spat back to the outskirts of the wilderness.

The man before him was a fisherman who had rowed out into Queen's Bay seven times in an effort to enter the fog only to find himself, without fail, eventually facing towards Arsaela after each attempt.

"Silence!" Dresden's commanding voice boomed through the room, cutting through the chaos like a knife through butter. His hands gripped the crystalline edges of the gilded and jeweled throne he sat on with such vigor Deming worried he would crack the bones in his fingers. "I will have order!"

The cacophony of voices dwindled immediately, leaving only traces of echoing whispers in its wake. Some citizens shuffled anxiously from side to side. The fisherman's foot was tapping incessantly. The seamstress was biting her nails to the quick.

"Panic in the face of fear fuels only more fear. The crown will hear the rest of your experiences, but we cannot do so if we are yelling over one another." Dresden motioned for the seamstress to step aside.

A girl around Deming's age took her place. Her eyes were glassy and red. Her face, puffy. Despite this, her voice was strong and steady.

"My name is Rose. My older sister and I have been responsible for our younger brother ever since our parents died from sickness years ago. We always hunt in Fairhaven before dawn because the deer are more active. I—"

Her voice cracked. She cleared her throat and began again. "I slept in today. My sister said she could handle the hunt. When she left the sky was clear. Then the fog rolled in. I didn't think anything of it until she was late for her shift at the bakery. She is never late. She has never missed a shift. She always comes home." Her facade was breaking. A lone tear welled in the corner of her eye and dripped lazily down her cheek. She balled her hands into fists. "I tried to find her in the forest but I couldn't walk our normal trail. I tried so many times and I always ended up back where I started. I thought maybe I was dreaming but when I heard of others whispering about the fog I knew. She was taken. Or trapped. Or dead. It doesn't matter which it is, really."

Her voice took on a harrowing tone and her final words chilled Deming to her core.

"She's gone."

Rose's lip wobbled treacherously as she inclined her head to the dais, taking her leave. Another thick tear dropped from her lashes and hit the floor.

Dresden rubbed his temple. "There will be more and more accounts of missing people as the day progresses."

"That is the least of our problems," Duke Lowell said, earning him a glare from Miriam.

The members of council had stayed behind once all citizens had told their stories and been ushered out of the throne room. They hadn't bothered moving to the official council chambers before beginning their debrief.

Lady Brittan and Lord Nolett had crowded near the throne where Dresden still sat. Duke Lowell had snapped at a servant boy to fetch him a chair. Miriam was perched on the edge of the dais, resting her head in her hand.

Deming had vacated her smaller, symbolic throne. She couldn't bear to sit a moment longer. Her legs had felt like pins danced in them the last half hour. Instead, she was pressed up against the back of the throne, battling between the desire to be present and helpful and the anxiety roaring through her at speaking up in a room of people who, by and large, thought very little of her.

"The least of our problems?" Miriam questioned, a purely incredulous look on her face. "These are our people."

"I promise you more will die to famine than the fog if we can't get my shipments in. I have three boats scheduled to arrive from various ports this week and near a dozen more the week after. If our trading is cut off, our coin is cut off. If our coin is cut off, the city will fall into ruin."

"A person can survive without money for a time, Lowell," chastised Lady Brittan. "We had a good harvest this year. We'll be fine."

Lord Nolett spoke up, having been extraordinarily quiet up until this moment. "We are all jumping to conclusions too quickly. We need to gather information. No one here would suggest planning a war without knowing the enemy. We have a handful of accounts from the townspeople but no one in the room, other than the princess, have seen the fog work firsthand."

War. The word settled like ash in her mind. Laey couldn't be at war, could it? Her uncle scratched at his chin, pondering, then leaned back into the throne. Deming couldn't help but notice how comfortable he looked. How did he do it?

"You're right," Dresden said, "we don't know enough to decide on how to retaliate. We need to lead expeditions of our own. I will lead one first thing tomorrow morning into Fairhaven. Lord Nolett, as High Marshall I ask that you lead a second into the Telacien's." Nolett nodded stoically. "Do we all feel comfortable with this course of action?"

Murmurs of affirmation accompanied the four heads bobbing up and down.

"Then it's settled. We will reconvene tomorrow afternoon."

He waved his hand in dismissal and everyone made to leave.

The words flew from her mouth unprompted. "Can I go?"

Every pair of eyes turned abruptly to Deming, who was frozen like a deer, shocked that she had spoken at all. Shocked that the desire to participate in the exploration of the fog felt warm and strong and right in her gut.

"Deming." Her uncle's voice was laced with curiosity. "I'm pleasantly surprised."

"You're always saying that I should participate, this is me asking to participate." She hated the way her ask sounded like a plea.

"I appreciate your demonstration of commitment. It is wonderful to see you taking an active role in the care of the queendom."

"So I can join you?"

Before Dresden, who looked like he was about to agree to the proposition, could respond, Lord Nolett interjected. "Is it best practice? For the heir to go in addition to you, High Steward?"

"I must agree with Nolett," Duke Lowell said. "We don't know what we're dealing with and as such, must treat it like a threat. The princess isn't trained to defend herself if something should arise."

Miriam echoed their sentiment, shooting an apologetic glance towards Deming. "She is one of the last in the Reynes-Elyachar line. It is too great a risk."

Pity filled Miriam's eyes and Deming hated her for it. She didn't need pity. She was fine.

"Fine. That's fine. It was a stupid request anyway."

"Deming, don't say such harsh words."

She shrugged off her touch. "I said it's fine."

Deming's small flame of desire was quelled as quickly as it was stoked. They were right. What good could she do on a mission like that? What could she offer?

The answer sat like a stone in her stomach. Nothing, she could offer nothing. And wasn't this exactly what she wanted? What she had built her entire persona around?

For the first time since her parents died that fact filled her with sorrow.

A gentle breeze from the open window pushed a strand of hair onto her face. Before Deming could blow it away, Paris lifted a hand and brushed it aside.

"Tell me what you're thinking," he whispered.

Deming breathed deeply, exhaling into the crook of Paris's neck. Although hours removed from the scene in the throne room, she was still somber and quiet.

She picked at a loose thread on the cover of his duvet. With everything that had happened they hadn't seen much of each other all day.

By the time Deming found her way to Paris's quarters that night, the entire city had either heard the news or experienced the mystery firsthand. Dresden had ordered that no one enter the fog until the crown could determine more about its effects, but that did little to dissuade the more curious citizens. And it wasn't as if they could post guards at every trailhead. People would sneak in elsewhere. There wasn't enough personnel regardless.

Gossip ran through the halls of the castle like water through a sieve. Paris had heard from Colette shortly after she ran into Deming that morning.

"I've thought about nothing else for hours, as has everyone. There's nothing left to say," Deming addressed her partner with an exasperated sigh.

"There's still the chance that this is all a misunderstanding and that the fog will lift tomorrow."

"Don't be daft, Paris."

He pulled himself up onto his elbow, face and shoulders silhouetted by moonlight coming through the window so that when Deming looked at him, he was shrouded in darkness, only an outline of the man she loved. "Don't chide me for being optimistic," he said sharply.

"I'm not chiding you for being optimistic, I'm chiding you for not seeing what's in front of you," Deming said.

"I understand what happened today as well as you do."

"No, you don't." Deming rolled onto her back, away from Paris. "You didn't go into the woods, you have no idea what that felt like. It was completely debilitating. Every sense was turned against me, I couldn't trust anything I saw or heard or felt." A shiver ran up her spine. "And to find out it wasn't an isolated incident, to find out that our entire city is surrounded as if we are at war? But the war is with a wall of air?" She cut off her rambling.

Paris was silent for a moment. He lay back on the bed, resting his head on Deming's shoulder. Her hair was unbound, slightly damp still from her bath. She smelled like eucalyptus.

"Maybe you're right. Maybe I don't understand."

"You don't."

Paris closed his eyes, pinching his brow between his index finger and thumb. "We are on the same team, Deming."

They laid in bed, together yet alone in their thoughts, for long minutes before Deming said, in a precariously wobbly voice barely above a whisper, "I'm sorry." She shifted to her side, trembling and hugging her knees to her chest. She pulled herself into a ball as if the smaller she could compress herself, the smaller she could make herself, the smaller her problems would become, too. "I'm just... I don't know. Frustrated. Scared. Anxious. I finally feel compelled to do something, to help in some way, but I don't know what to do and the council said I can't join the parties tomorrow so even if I came up with something they probably wouldn't let me act on it."

Paris let loose a sigh and turned to curl himself around Deming. "I know. I'm sorry too." He leaned in closer. "I'm sorry they didn't take you seriously."

She exhaled heavily. "It's not even that. They're right, it's not smart to send the High Steward and the heir into something this unknown. Who would rule if we were to die?"

"Colette, I suppose."

Deming hummed softly. "Now, she would make a good queen."

"You'll make a good queen, too."

"Maybe some day."

CHAPTER SEVEN

DEMING FOUND HERSELF AWAKE just before dawn. Peering over the shoulder of a still sleeping Paris, she looked out at the hazy sunrise. Unsurprisingly, the fog was still present. A small part of her had hoped Paris would be right.

She pressed her lips to his forehead, thankful she hadn't woken up alone. Paris stirred slightly in response.

"I'm going to go back to my room," she said.

Paris mumbled something she couldn't make out, sleep-filled eyes fluttering open.

"What?"

"Don't go," he said more clearly, propping himself up in the nest of pillows and blankets. "I don't like how we ended things last night."

Her heart swooped with affection. "Paris, we're fine. I'm so thankful I have you as an anchor. I was frustrated and annoyed, but not with you. I'm sorry I reacted the way I did."

His blue eyes looked at her intently, worried. "Are you sure?"

"I'm sure. I love you so, so much. We're fine."

"Okay." He rubbed his eyes and made to get out of bed. "At least let me take you to breakfast."

"I really should make an appearance at my aunt's event this morning."

Althea Penrose had taken to royalty surprisingly well for someone who married into it. Even before Dresden was made High Steward, Althea's gatherings were renowned throughout the queendom. As Deming wasn't needed on the expeditions into the fog this morning, a fact that still made her feel squeamish and on edge and more than a little uncomfortable, she figured she could at least do her part and show face at tea. Perhaps quell some of the women's fears about their partners venturing out into the fog or the fact that they seemingly couldn't contact their children. Many families that came to Arsaela when court was in session left their children in their respective cities, cared for by nannies and brought up in their own courts and customs.

Besides, Miriam and Colette would be there. How bad could it be?

"You have time before Althea's gathering."

The playful pout he wore brightened her morning. Deming's lips curved upwards. He was nothing if not persistent. "Fine. But I truly don't have much time. I need to wash up and ready myself for the day. I'll meet you in the Great Hall in an hour."

"You got it."

Deming hummed her approval and slipped into her gown from yesterday. She recoiled at the amount of wrinkles that now threaded through the delicate fabric. Julia would faint if she found out Deming had left it crumpled at the foot of the bed. She smoothed the full skirt, willing the fabric to loosen. No luck. Perhaps she could find Noreen first. She was always more lenient than her counterpart.

"See you soon," Deming said, patting the bed as she turned towards the door. Over her shoulder on the way out she saw Paris shift onto his back again and rub his eyes with the backs of his hands. "One hour!"

Where was Paris?

Deming suppressed her mild annoyance and dipped her fork into the delicate lemon cake she was picking at. Delicious though it was, she could hardly focus on anything except the dwindling number of people in the Great Hall. Woman after woman had come, ate, or pretended to eat in many cases, much to Deming's disappointment, and left for the ballroom Althea was using to host.

She swallowed the last bit of tartness and stood. She had put off leaving long enough, any more dalliance and she would be late. And not fashionably.

Deming had just turned left out of the Great Hall, making for the sprawling staircase that would take her up to the ballroom, when she heard Paris shouting from down the hall.

"Deming! Wait!"

Surprised and exasperated, Deming turned.

"I'm sorry." He was out of breath when he caught up to her. "I fell back asleep, I didn't mean to miss our date."

"It's fine." Why was she always saying things were fine when they weren't? She should say she was annoyed, disappointed. Relationships didn't work if they weren't honest. She sighed and opened her mouth with the intent to say just that, then said nothing of the sort. "It really isn't a big deal."

"Do you have to go now?"

"Yes."

Paris cursed. "We'll see each other afterwards, then?"

"Dresden and the others are set to be back early this afternoon. I imagine I'll be tied up with them all day trying to figure out what's going on around the city."

"Tonight, then?"

Deming sighed again, shoving her emotions down and stepping forward to cup his face in her hand. "I'd love that." She kissed him softly. "I'll see you tonight." Maybe by then she will have gathered the courage to speak her mind.

He kissed her once more on her forehead and then turned to return to his rooms.

As Deming walked towards the staircase, each step brought another pang of nausea and discomfort. First she acquiesced with her uncle, and now with Paris. Playing the demure role she'd crafted for herself had never bothered her before. But now...

Is this the kind of woman her mother would have wanted her to become? Someone who rolled over at every slight? Someone who let others decide her fate? She didn't even have to consider the answer.

No, Samira would be disappointed in who Deming had allowed herself to become.

The thought brought tears to her eyes. She angrily wiped them away.

It doesn't matter.

This is the path she chose to walk.

She didn't want the crown.

Didn't want to be beholden to its responsibilities.

Her parents weren't here to chastise her. They were dead and any chance at Deming becoming who she was born to be had died with them and she was fine and she was fine and she was—

"Paris!"

Deming spun around and yelled down the hallway. Paris's blonde mop of hair whipped through the air as he turned towards her, curiosity sprawled across his beautiful face.

"I hate that you were late." She started walking back towards him with long, purposeful strides. He did the same, though far more hesitantly. He was walking towards someone yelling at him, after all. "I specifically told you I didn't have a lot of time this morning and needed to be somewhere. I know I usually don't care about whatever ridiculous event my aunt is throwing but I wanted to go this morning. I wanted to help. And you knew that. You knew I was feeling frustrated at not being able to go with my uncle or the High Marshall and you knew that this was my attempt at doing something, anything! And you couldn't be bothered to show up on time. It was rude. It really hurt me. It makes me think you don't care about what's important to me."

She stopped just in front of him, emotion making her face flush and her breath come out heavy. It was invigorating and terrifying, standing in front of him being so honest. She felt vulnerable and scared and powerful all at once.

Paris, to his credit, didn't so much as blink at her accusations. "I know, you're right. It was rude. I understand that my actions have consequences and while I didn't mean to hurt you, I did."

"Thank you." Deming brushed a stray hair out of her face. She nodded and looked around the hallway awkwardly. "Yes, thank you. I'm glad you see that."

Silence settled in the air around them.

The click of heels on stone could be heard vaguely in the distance.

He cocked his head, a smirk playing on his lips. "Is that all?"

Deming stammered, "Yes, yeah. That's all."

"Okay." He lifted her chin gently with his hand and kissed her nose. "I'll see you later then. Go, you'll be late."

"What has gotten into you?"

Miriam looked at Deming in confused awe as the two of them settled into plush chairs in the corner of the ballroom.

Deming had spent the better part of the last hour flitting between the various noble women of Laey, listening intently to their concerns and offering words of support and encouragement. Nearly everyone who spoke with her left feeling more hopeful than when they arrived.

"You walked with such grace this morning. You looked…" Miriam continued, pausing to find the right word and deciding on one that surprised them both. "Queenly."

Deming's eyes darted up from the steaming cup of tea she was nursing.

"Truly. It is no easy feat to assuage the worries of these women, and you have done so with the confidence I so rarely see you use. Is this all because of yesterday?"

The heir considered the question properly before answering. "I suppose. In part. But also… never mind." She shook her head.

"What?"

"Well, I kind of told Paris that I was mad at him. Loudly. In the middle of the hallway."

This made Miriam chuckle warmly, the corners of her eyes wrinkled with the laughter. "And yelling at the young lord helped because?"

"I don't really know." Deming answered honestly. "I think it just felt good to be in control for once. To be honest."

Miriam smiled softly. "I know the feeling. It took me a long time to be able to relay to others what I was feeling on the inside. You and I are alike in that way, I believe."

She set her own cup of tea down and turned to survey the opulent room before them. Women in gowns of every color and fabric imaginable wandered through the marbled space. Trickles of conversation made their way to the corner where Miriam and Deming sat, though only bits and pieces could be heard. Althea herself, with her perfectly coiffed brunette hair, was speaking to her daughter. Colette tilted her head back in laughter at something her mother said.

"You were born into this world whereas I was not, surely. But we are still cut from the same cloth. Knowing yourself is hard enough." She looked back to Deming. "But knowing yourself and then letting others know you too? That is work that can take a lifetime."

"It certainly comes easy for some people," Deming huffed, still looking at her cousin. Colette kissed her mother's hand and twirled away, sliding seamlessly into another conversation. Her ivory gown swished across the marble.

"Jealousy does not look good on you, Deming."

"I'm not jealous."

A pregnant pause. Then a switch of subjects. "I'm proud of you for asking to join in the exploration of the fog."

"It didn't matter, I wasn't allowed to go."

"I disagree. It mattered greatly. You showed the council you are willing and eager to help your people. That goes a long way. I spoke with Brittan afterwards. She was impressed with you."

That sowed a kernel of pride in Deming's chest. "I'm sure Duke Lowell wasn't swayed, though. He hates me."

Miriam laughed once more. "He doesn't hate you. He's old and curmudgeonly and his respect is hard earned. It's hard to get him excited about anything other than our treasury. And even you must admit you have been absent from your duties as heir far more than you have been present. He only wishes to see you take control more. You said earlier that felt good. Perhaps you can practice the habit in other areas of your life, too."

It had felt good to speak honestly with Paris. And it had felt good when she spoke up in council.

Somewhere deep inside her, a bundle of nerves and doubt and hesitation began to unravel.

Chapter Eight

Despite her measly prayers sent up to the High Deities, both parties were late arriving back to the castle.

The clock tower had chimed eleven. Then noon. Then one.

Deming peered through the window of the council chamber at the tower. Each tick of the clock's hand put her more and more on edge. The members of council who had not ridden out, Miriam, Brittan, and Lowell, sat in the thick oak chairs around the table. If they were nervous they hid it far better than her.

Moments before she was about to dash to the stables and grab Quinn, orders to stay behind be damned, the doors to the chambers opened with a crash.

She stifled the undignified yelp that came out of her and rose to greet her uncle, who stood through the open doors with purpose, swathed in amber fabric that highlighted the gold crown on his head.

Behind him was Lord Nolett and twelve guards.

Deming sighed in relief. Everyone had returned.

Though she wasn't required to, Deming joined the other council members in giving her uncle a bow, careful to mitigate her facial expression into the picture of queenly grace. The sting of embarrassment from the insinuation of the other members of council, however true, that she would be more risk than support on the recognizance mission still simmered in her. She would add no more fuel to that particular fire today.

Dresden motioned for everyone to sit as he eased into his own seat at the head of the table. "I apologize for being late. Let's begin."

Dread bloomed in Deming's stomach. This wasn't going to be good.

"High Steward and council," Lord Nolett began. "We've arrived back from the north east quadrant of Arsaela, where the city meets the Telacien's. I can confirm that the fog continues far into the mountain range, further than we could travel on horseback. I would feel confident in saying it wraps completely around the back side of the castle."

Dresden sat back straight, hands clasped neatly in his lap and eyes inquisitive. "Thank you, Nolett. Our patrol reached a similar conclusion. It appears that there is roughly a ten mile berth from the city center to dense fog in all directions."

Miriam leaned to Brittan, whispering something in her ear. Brittan nodded, solemn.

"What of the fog itself?" Dresden asked.

Lord Nolett gestured to one of the guards on his left. "I will defer to Raygar for that."

Raygar examined the room stoically, hand on the pommel of his sword. It was so silent one could have heard a pin drop as he began to tell his tale. "Much of what I have to say we heard yesterday, I'm afraid. We ventured into the fog at three different points in the Telacien's. Each time, two guards entered and four stayed behind with the lord. Each time, we were unable to continue on the trail for long before finding ourselves back where we started.

"What we found interesting," he continued, "was that time moved differently inside the fog than out, and even then it wasn't consistent. The first time we were traveling for merely a minute before being brought back, though the lord told us they had waited closer to ten.

"The second time, we traveled for longer, my best guess would be five minutes. When we returned, we were told half an hour had passed.

"And the third time." Raygar swallowed hard. Fear flickering in his eyes. "The third time we had barely begun walking before we returned to the trailhead. Seconds, it had to be. But," he sighed deeply, "over an hour had passed."

A chill ran down Deming's spine.

No wonder they had all been so late returning home.

"Were you harmed in any way?" Duke Lowell spoke up, leaning forward in his chair as if getting closer to Raygar would get him the information faster.

"No, sir. None of us were harmed. The fog is turning those inside it around, that is certain. But so far it has not harmed anyone who enters it."

The duke murmured softly under his breath then turned to Dresden, rubbing the rings decorating his fingers as he leaned back in his chair. "What of your team, High Steward?"

"Much the same. We similarly found time to be an enigma within the fog and similarly found that no harm befell anyone who entered."

Deming rallied herself and spoke before she lost the courage, every question on her tongue spilling out in a rush. "What does this mean for our citizens who reside in the farmlands further than the reach of the fog? Or the rest of the Queendom? Are we no longer able to correspond with our sister cities? What does that mean for the missing people?"

As Dresden had predicted, after the initial meeting in the throne room dozens of people had been reported missing. Every story was slightly different, but the crux of the issue remained the same. Someone's mother, brother, friend, or cousin had gone out past the city limits before the fog, the fog crept in, and they never returned.

Miriam gave her a nod of encouragement from across the table.

Dresden looked at his niece. "I am not sure. We can only go off the information we have. If the fog is not harming us, we can assume it is not harming others."

"Bold assumption," scoffed Lowell.

"Perhaps. But all the same that is what we will be telling the citizens. The fog is a barrier, nothing more. I will not have panic spread like wildfire through the city. That benefits no one and sows chaos."

"I don't like the idea of lying to our citizens," Lady Brittan said.

"We aren't lying. We don't know what has happened to the missing people, but we do know that every venture made into the fog since has been at least safe, if disorienting."

Lord Nolett rose from his chair and began pacing back and forth. His muddied boots making marks on the floor as he walked. "I'm more concerned with deducing the cause of this. Who or what has created this? The gods? A person? Another territory?"

Deming found room to slip into the conversation again, thankful that she had something to contribute. "Laey is not at war with any of our neighbors, nor are our allies in conflict with anyone. I am reluctant to believe any of them would attack us without cause. Barrier, sorry, not attack. They wouldn't put up a barrier without cause." She stumbled on the last words, silently cursing herself for her lack of eloquence.

No one seemed to notice. Everyone was too busy mulling over the possibilities to care about the princess misspeaking.

"The gods could certainly cause an occurrence such as this."

No one else in the room was pious enough to give Brittan's suggestion any real weight. The gods hadn't tampered with the working of the continent for centuries.

"We keep, correctly, in my opinion," said Miriam, "coming back to the fact that no one who has touched the fog has been harmed. Perhaps it is not an attack, but a preventative measure? What if it has fallen over Arsaela to keep something, or someone, in or out?"

"Interesting theory, Miriam. But no more comforting than an outright attack." Lord Nolett stopped his pacing, placing his hands flat on the table. "In that scenario there is still a threat. Inside the city being kept from the continent, or outside the city being kept from us. One way or another we will have to face it and I, for one, am uncomfortable with how little we still know."

His stern words cowed Miriam, cowed the whole room entirely. Whatever vigorous spirit they had when they initially gathered had vanished from the council chambers. They were no closer to figuring out what was happening to their city than they were before the parties left.

"We will explore every avenue for solutions," Dresden concluded heavily. "I will send messengers out to the city encouraging anyone with information regarding the fog to come forward. I have already sent for mages to advise on this as it is becoming more and more clear this is magical in nature."

With council dismissed, everyone slowly filed out of the chambers, none feeling remotely confident about the situation unfolding in Arsaela.

Chapter Nine

THE CIDER, STEAMING AND full of cinnamon and cloves, warmed Deming's palms through the ceramic mug. She lifted the mug to her lips and blew gently across the surface, watching the steam disappear into the musky tavern, before taking a careful sip and recoiling when she realized it was still far too hot to drink.

She set the mug down and pushed it to the center of the table, knowing full well that the foot of space would not be enough to restrain her from trying again in a minute. It wasn't her fault, she would insist to anyone who would listen, Firebrand's made the absolute best mulled cider. The apples from the orchard south of the city were the perfect combination of tart and sweet and the cider was only in season for a few weeks in the autumn. And only days after their last visit, it was finally available.

About time.

"I warn you every time to wait and yet you always insist on drinking the cider too early." Paris clicked his tongue from the stool next to her. "You're a glutton for punishment."

She stuck out her tongue, which was indeed throbbing from the burn. Colette laughed from across the table and took a sip from her chilled glass stein, something wheat based sloshing within. Deming hadn't been listening when she ordered.

"That's how you speak to the woman who shares your bed?" She flicked a crumb from the table at him, snickering when it hit him square in the forehead.

"You'll get no pity from me," he said, brushing a hand across his face. "Try your other friend. That one is bound by blood to love you."

Deming swung her head dramatically to Colette, who shook her head.

"No pity from me either. I do love you though," she crooned.

"Treasonous, the lot of you."

Deming turned her attention to the music winding its way throughout the room. To call the two Fae playing folk songs from one of the dank corners of the tavern a band would be a stretch, but the music was lovely all the same. A soft, melodic voice floated from the lead singer, a tall Fae female with delicate membraned wings dark as night tucked behind her. A stoic looking male with strong bull horns protruding from his temples strummed on a harp beside her. One of the horns ended in a jagged edge rather than a sharp tip, making Deming wonder what the harpist's story was.

It had been Colette's idea to come to Firebrand's and Deming was more than happy to oblige. After the chaos of the last few days, all three of them were eager to relax.

In fact, the whole city seemed to share the idea. The tavern was far more full than usual. It seemed that everyone wanted to drown their sorrows in Arsaela's best cider. Or worst ale. Either worked to dull their senses and help ease them into oblivion.

Though the wooden floor boards remained crooked and sticky, though the patchwork of bodies ranged widely as usual, from Fae to human to a fire mage with slick black hair twirling embers between her fingertips, the energy could not have felt more different than when they had been here days ago.

Nervous conversation had replaced rambunctious voices. Eyes flicked to and fro with chaotic energy. A dimness that had nothing to do with the poor lighting had fallen over the trio's favorite hole in the wall.

It didn't help that the fog had found its way into the city. Ghostly remnants of the dense wall of fog surrounding the city now wove through the streets of Arsaela. They kept to dark corners of the city. They shifted with slinky, feline grace. Though they were more tendrils of mist than anything else, they nonetheless stoked undiluted fear into the heart of the city.

Deming and her friends found their ease further stifled by the palace guard standing rigid beside their table. Dresden had demanded that they be accompanied by guards if the three of them were to venture into the city. Despite the acknowledgment that the fog seemed to be contained and not physically harmful, he was taking no risks when it came to his daughter and niece.

Deming supposed she should be grateful. They had originally been told they couldn't come at all. Then, that there would be a guard assigned to all three of them. The fact that they had talked him into sending only this one, stoic, silent guard was a miracle in and of itself.

At least the musicians were still playing, she reminded herself.

At least there was still dancing.

"Dance with me," she said to Paris. The sweet, slow song the duet was singing filled her with longing and she would be damned if she let the fog take away the joy of Firebrand's. She stood, the simple skirts of her dress sweeping against the floorboards.

"I danced with you the other night," he protested. He took a swig of his drink, then gave her an apologetic look and shrugged. "You know I don't like slow songs. All the swaying and leaning. Sorry."

"Fine. But if they play something more lively I'm coming to get you."

"Fair enough."

Deming pressed a soft kiss on his brow then turned to her next target.

Colette, unlike Paris, had no qualms with dancing and happily took Deming's outstretched hand.

"Do you want to lead or should I?" asked Colette once they had woven their way into the center of the dance floor.

Deming's eyes brightened. "Can I? I'm not very good. I never get the chance to..."

"Does it matter?" Colette retorted as they began to sway to the ballad, "It's not like we're at a Midwinter or Midsummer ceremony with thousands of eyes on us."

"Fantastic point."

Deming placed one hand on Colette's waist and held her friend's hand with the other. Colette in turn placed her open hand on Deming's shoulder.

The pair moved gently with the crowd and music. Deming mused that this was likely the happiest she had been all week, and was suddenly very thankful for Colette's friendship.

On the next turn, she made eye contact with a brooding Fae male in the far corner of the tavern. He leaned heavily into the wall. A shadow covered most of his face, his gray eyes mingling with the darkness and the glint of several daggers strapped along his thigh giving her pause. Behind him, an expansive pair of dark, feathered wings were tucked tightly behind his shoulders and blended seamlessly into the shadows.

As their eyes met, intrigue flashed across what she could see of his face.

Within moments the song ended and Deming, having completed another turn with Colette, lost track of the Fae male. She peered in between the bodies in the tavern, but the stool he had occupied moments before now stood empty.

The singer and her companion shifted seamlessly into a jaunty two-step, which was apparently the shift the bar needed to shake off the air of depression. A raucous roar of approval rose from the tavern members and a mass of Fae and human alike were suddenly pressing into Colette and Deming from all sides.

"What a change of pace!" Colette exclaimed with a laugh. She wasted no time spinning to the beat and within moments a brown haired man had a hand on her waist, whispering something into her ear.

Colette's eyes flicked to Deming as she listened to what he had to say. A sly smile grew across her face as she turned to him and said something with a nod. The music was too loud for Deming to hear her response. Before she could check in on her friend, Colette's shimmering red hair was whipping around the room and she was joyously enjoying the newfound company.

It was hard not to feel the tinge of jealousy creeping in. Colette was always asked to dance.

Deming lifted a hand and twisted a lock of hair. The red color that she and her cousin shared was passed down to her through Deming's mother's line. It had been a mark of both the royal family and the Queendom of Laey as a whole for generations and therefore made it nearly impossible for either her or Colette to achieve any level of anonymity.

Deming twirled the white strands near her face. The strawberry blonde and white sections that were purely her own marked her as other. No one in the royal lineage had ever been graced with hair that wasn't pure, brilliant, royally, red.

The whispers, though never said directly to her face, had found their way to her all the same throughout the years.

Disgraceful.

Diluted bloodline.

Shunned by the Goddess herself.

No one ever asked her to dance when they went into the city. She consoled herself with the fact that everyone knew she was courting Paris. Time and time again she reminded herself that they had no reason to offer their hand.

And still the shadowed, quiet, parts of herself believed it was because they thought her unworthy.

As slow and delicate as spinning glass, Deming drew herself out of her own mind. It did no good to dwell on those emotions. Why would she even care?

Shoving her insecurities deep down, she turned on her heels to head back to Paris who was sure to be right where they left him. He owed her a dance.

The upbeat tempo had drawn more people in, making the crowd thick and surging. Deming snuck her arm in between two couples and instantly cringed at the sweat sticking to someone's back. She rubbed the back of her arm on the bodice of her dress and tried to navigate around the edge of the dancers instead.

She neared the wall, far enough away from the throngs of people that she had space to breath. This far back, the tavern was veiled in shadows. Whatever light the lanterns hung by the bar emitted did not reach here.

Placing a hand on the wood to steady herself, she scanned the tavern. Although it was packed and dim, Colette was easy to find thanks to the positively sparkling dusty rose colored dress she wore tonight. She was twirling around the floor with reckless abandon, her dance partner smiling wryly as she spun.

Deming could also glimpse Paris sitting at their table at the far edge of the bar, back turned to the dance floor and ordering another round from the barmaid. She took a step towards him, but before her foot fell someone checked her hard into the wall.

Her head smacked against the solid oak. Stars and darkness blurred her vision. She slumped against the wall, ending up on her knees as her feet struggled to find purchase on the slick floor.

She briefly thought some drunk member of the bar lost control while dancing, but then someone grabbed a fistful of her hair from behind and pulled hard, tugging her further back into the poorly lit corner.

Pain laced her scalp and panic raced up her spine.

Scream, she needed to scream.

Deming opened her mouth but the second her voice sounded it was cut short by a cloth gag thrust into her mouth and pulled taut. Her head was sharply pulled back again, straining her neck. She thrashed against the binding but was unable to shift it.

A distant shout from the guard broke through the din of music and ringing in Deming's ear.

Whoever was dragging her writhing body towards the back entrance started moving quicker, alarmed at being spotted. Despite her best efforts to wrest herself from their grasp they held firm.

Night air flashed in from behind her. The back door was open.

There was no way the guard would make it here in time.

She was helpless and she was going to be captured and tortured and whatever else happened to kidnapped princesses and she would never get to tug at the strand of honor and hope that had begun blossoming around the idea of stepping into her mother's role as queen—

The dagger!

She reached into her boot with trembling hands for the small dagger her uncle had forced her to keep hidden there. The brief relief at having a weapon was smothered the moment her hand grasped the hilt. An ankle hooked her wrist and slammed her hand into the floor, sending the dagger skittering across the wood and nearly breaking her wrist.

She tried to turn around, to get a glimpse of her attacker but she found she couldn't focus her eyes. Everything had all happened so quickly the world was still spinning from hitting the wall. Through the dissipating stars Deming saw, too late, the heel of a black leather boot flying through the air at her. It made solid contact with her left temple and the world went black.

CHAPTER TEN

DEMING CAME BACK TO consciousness slowly.

Blood coursed behind her temples with every heartbeat. The light coming from the street lamps sent pain piercing through her skull. The left side of her face was so tender even the evening breeze caused her to wince, let alone the pain that accompanied each jostling movement as she rolled slightly back and forth atop something large, warm, and densely muscled.

Tucking the pain from her head away as best she could, Deming found herself bound, gagged, and thrown over the back of a large, brown, work horse like a sack of grain.

Her chest tightened and breathing became difficult. Though the gag was the primary reason for the latter.

She briefly closed her eyes and took as deep a breath as the cloth biting into her mouth would allow. There was no noticeable scent alluding to a poison or sedative coming off the cloth, but Deming wasn't naive enough to think that meant she was out of the woods in that department yet. There were plenty of ways to incapacitate or kill someone without alerting the senses.

A fact that was piquing Deming's interest. Clearly whoever had attacked her didn't want her dead, not yet anyway, or she would have never woken up.

Was there some sort of rebel uprising in the city that no one knew about? The citizens of Arsaela, the entire queendom for that matter, loved Dresden. Trade and prosperity had flourished under his rule. Who could possibly be upset at that?

Was it an outside hire? An assassin from Haimrath? The neighboring kingdom had always been friendly with Laey. King Bastion and his son, Bane, were regular attendees at Arsaela's Midwinter and Midsummer celebrations. There were even talks early on about a marriage between the two heirs. Thankfully her courtship with Paris put an end to those discussions. All in all it seemed unlikely that they would be behind this.

Who then? Runne? Though she hadn't gotten a good look at her attackers, they hadn't appeared to be Fae.

One thing felt certain. Whoever had bound and gagged her, whoever had stolen her away, was tied inexplicably with the fog. The two events were too closely timed and too similarly threatening to not be linked.

How? That was another question entirely.

Trying to suppress the rising panic, she counted to ten and then opened her eyes again to take in where she was.

Within seconds, it was clear she was still within the city. The hooves of the horse she was on trotted with urgency along paved stone streets. Buildings rose tall on either side of them. Rough brick shaded in tones of gray from the fog and cloak of night rushed by them. Wisps of mist hung to the corners of walkways and storefronts, clinging to the shadows and fading into nothing near the center of the street. The scent that so often clung to unused alleys hung heavy in the air.

Rotting food remains.

Rat droppings.

The musk of unknown fluids.

Although they were taking side streets Deming rarely found herself on, glimpsing through the alleyways she was able to make out the distant outline of store fronts she was familiar with. Glancing up she could see the outline of castle turrets peaking above the angled building roofs. She must have been unconscious for only a few minutes.

The rider was clearly eager to get them as far away from Firebrand's as possible. Deming closed her eyes and focused on the sounds of the evening. She filtered through the distant bar raucous and crickets chirping, hoping to hear something, anything, that indicated the palace guard was in pursuit.

Her heart sank as she heard nothing.

Had her attackers shaken him already?

He surely had sent word to the castle. Her uncle would have everyone available in search of her within moments, she was sure.

But for now, she was alone.

She forced the terrifying thought to steel her resolve rather than send her spiraling. If she kept her wits about her, maybe she could make it out of this alive.

On impulse and not waiting to lose the guts to do so, she threw her body weight as best she could towards the tail of the horse. She rolled off its back and let out a yelp through the cloth gag as she hit the ground squarely on her shoulder. The shallow puddle she landed in splashed what smelt vaguely like diluted urine onto her cheek and lips and began soaking into the part of her bodice touching the grimy stone.

"What the—" A gruff voice exclaimed from atop the horse. He dismounted and yelled towards someone Deming hadn't seen a few yards ahead of them, "She's awake!"

The companion, dressed in all black with a scarf wrapped tightly around the lower half of his face, hurled himself off his horse, quickly unsheathing a sword that, even in the darkness, had the coppery sheen of rust coating its length.

She strained against the bindings holding her hands and feet. The rope bit further into her already raw wrists. She tried to stand, but the rope around her ankles made her unstable and she only managed to hop pathetically once before falling over again, this time bearing the brunt of her fall on her elbows.

Her eyes widened at the sight of the two men stalking towards her. The man in black twirled his sword menacingly as he approached her. The other, whose horse she had been on the back of, whipped out a dagger from his belt.

Deming rolled over and began scooting back towards the edge of the brick building. Her dress caught an uneven crack in the stones and tore, exposing her upper thigh to the rough, wet ground and leaving ribbons of velvet trailing in her wake.

Fear bubbled up in her chest. She had not thought this through. She couldn't possibly outrun two men on horseback in normal conditions, let alone when she couldn't move her limbs properly. She was going to die and no one would know where her corpse lay. She was going to die in an alleyway in a urine soaked dress. She was going to die—

The panic reached a tipping point and poured out of Deming in the form of a blood curdling scream. Muffled slightly by the gag, it nevertheless echoed through the streets before a hand cracked against her cheek, silencing her immediately.

The pain shocked any and all breath from Deming. She nearly retched, heaving in fresh air to her lungs far too quickly.

"I suggest you shut your mouth," the captor growled. They were inches from her now. The man who slapped her bent down, resting on his haunches with his sword arm draped casually over his knee.

Deming marginally succeeded in rallying her senses. Panicking would get her nowhere. And again, she reminded herself, if they wanted her dead she would be dead. It seemed they were only brandishing the weapons as a threat.

Defining details, defining details. Her eyes darted back and forth between the men. Both were mid size, average height and build, brown hair and eyes. Scarves covered half their face anyway.

Not a unique quality to be seen. No scars, no specialty weapons.

A glint off the crouching man's shoulder caught her eye. Pinned on his chest—no, both of their chests, she confirmed with a quick glance—was an insignia of woven vines encircling an eagle with outstretched wings. An arrow was clutched in one of its talons. In the other... something small and round. She couldn't make it out. A sigil or crest of sorts. She had no idea what house or court it belonged to, but at least it was something to go off of if she managed to get herself out of this increasingly dire situation.

He looked to the other man. "What do you want to do?"

"She's going to be more trouble than she's worth now that she's awake," he responded. He tapped the point of his dagger with his finger, pulling it slightly and testing the bend of the metal. "I say we kill her now and bring the head back as proof. They want her dead anyway."

Well, there went her theory about them not killing her.

The masked man tsked and stood. "They won't be happy."

"They don't have to know."

"Are you that dense? Of course they would know. You know what, forget it. We can't kill her. They explicitly said to bring her to them alive. Our own heads will roll if we disregard an order that direct."

The man wielding the dagger nodded and tucked his weapon away. "Fine, knock her out again then. This time with force. I don't want her rolling off my gods-damned horse again."

His companion grasped his sword and raised it above his head, readying the pommel to knock her unconscious again.

Deming had reached the wall of the building, the brick pressed firm against her back. The cold of the stone seeped into her bones, though they were already frozen in fear.

She looked down the alleyway for anyone, but couldn't see a soul. A part of her had held onto hope that someone heard her scream. Apparently not.

She tried to find some small bit of fire or strength to fight back but the malice in the man's eyes stoked only horror and dread in her until she could feel nothing but the impending silence of death.

Sinking into despair, she looked past him to the moon. She closed her eyes and said a silent prayer to Selene, bracing herself in anticipation of the pain of metal pommel connecting with skin and bone.

A deafening crash assaulted her senses.

The horses whinnied shrilly. The pounding of their hooves grew more and more distant as they bolted from the scene.

It took a long, disorienting moment for her to understand that the pommel of the sword had not fallen.

Deming opened her eyes and saw a tall Fae male with pitch black wings fighting against her attackers. A wave of recognition hit her almost immediately. The Fae from the bar.

She watched in awe as he deftly handled the two men.

She hadn't seen how, her eyes had been closed in prayer when the Fae arrived, but he had disarmed one of the men. The rust-riddled sword of her captor lay useless on the ground ten feet from where he now swung fists at the Fae.

The winged Fae expertly dodged the swings. He was light on his feet and seemed to float across the ground. Deming realized with a jolt that it was because he quite literally was floating. He was occasionally lifting the arch of his wings ever so slightly to catch the breeze blowing through the alleyway, allowing him to move gracefully from side to side through the air, like a fish slipping through water.

He was armed to the teeth—smaller daggers were slotted into his belt and thigh straps and two large scimitars glinted in the moonlight from scabbards on his back—but had yet to pull any weapon out.

In one fluid motion, he kicked the dagger out of the hand of the man behind him and connected a fist to the chin of the first man, causing the scarf to fall and reveal the strong jaw of the man who had danced with Colette.

Deming's shock quickly dissipated into blood boiling anger. Though common sense told her it had been a distraction tactic and Colette was almost certainly fine if the man was here and Colette was not also bound and gagged on the back of a horse, fear for her friend welled in Deming's stomach just the same.

The Fae continued his assault on her attackers. He swung again at the man in front of him, the second punch landing hard in the center of his face. The man crumpled, knocked out, with blood pouring from his newly broken nose.

Her heartbeat sped at the sight of his limp body. In fear or pleasure, she couldn't say.

The remaining assailant had scrambled to gather his dagger and was now running at the Fae with intent to kill. The Fae's back was turned, his body still in motion from taking down Colette's dance partner.

Deming was about to release a warning cry despite the gag biting at her lips but before she could even attempt to yell, he bent low and swiped a leg around, sending the man sailing over his wings and landing face first in a shallow pile of leaves and mud.

Wincing in pain, he rolled over slowly. He ground out something Deming couldn't quite hear from across the alleyway. The way he held up his hands made it easy to assume it was a yield of some capacity. Bits of gravel clung to his face. Blood seeped from a wound on his head that Deming couldn't locate.

The Fae growled back before pulling the man up by the shirt collar and slamming his skull into the brick. Deming gasped and lurched back at the abrupt contact. Peering through near closed eyelids she saw his head lolled to the side, unconscious or dead she couldn't be sure.

He dropped the man unceremoniously. The body hit the ground with a thud. Then he turned to Deming.

Up until this point, Deming had not considered the possibility that he was equally as dangerous for her in the long run but now, as he strode towards her with his looming wings and gray eyes still holding feral ferocity from battle, she conceded that she may have gone from one horrendous situation to another.

She shuffled uselessly backwards, trying to press herself further against the wall as if it would somehow protect her from the male before her.

He crouched down and pulled out a small knife from a strap on his thigh. While no longer than her hand, it was dense and wickedly sharp, like the knives Paris used to gut deer. Perfect for carving away skin from muscle, muscle from bone. Her own skin prickled in fear.

Deming turned her face away from his, pressing a cheek into the rough red brick.

A smattering of seconds passed in which Deming held her breath, but the sharp bit of his knife didn't come. Instead, he spoke.

"I'm not going to hurt you," he said in the common tongue. "See?"

Deming slowly looked back just in time to see him using the knife to cut through the bindings on her feet. The rope fell off with ease. She stretched her legs out and flexed her ankles. Sore.

His gray eyes glanced towards her hands then back at her. Deming offered them up with intense hesitancy, but he once more cut through the rope. She gently rubbed her wrists. Very sore.

He gestured towards the cloth gag. "May I?"

Deming inclined her head towards him, allowing him access to the knot at the base of her neck. Rather than waste time untying the knot, he slid the knife in between her head and the fabric. The blade was flat and cool against her skin. With a gentle flick of his wrist, he cut the gag.

Deming pulled the cloth from her mouth and massaged her jaw. She began to speak but found her voice came out quiet and cracking, as if it had forgotten how. After clearing her throat she looked at the male in front of her and croaked out, "I could have done that last part myself."

He tucked the knife away and one corner of his lips pulled up into a smirk. "I know," was all he offered in response.

He stood and extended a hand.

She stared at it. Then at his face. His eyes were the same shade as the mist creeping along the alleyway at the edge of her vision. His posture was rigid and strong.

Who was he? He had disposed of the immediate threat, surely. And he had cut her free of her bondage. But to what end? Why? He did not radiate with justice or pure intentions.

No. He radiated power. It rippled off his essence like smoke from a fire.

And to have all of that hyper focused on her made her quiver in newfound fear over the fact that she had little choice but to accept his offer.

Deming took his hand, pressed her other hand into the ground, and stood on wobbly legs.

She retracted her hand from his once they were both upright and went to wipe the grime and gravel off the other on her bodice before remembering what was coating her dress. Her face scrunched up in disgust and was about to settle for brushing her hands together to knock the dirt off when the Fae pulled a handkerchief out of a hidden breast pocket.

Deming arched an eyebrow but took the handkerchief. "Do you always keep dainty clothing accessories in your fighting leathers?" she asked incredulously.

"What can I say, I enjoy the finer things in life." His eyes winked with humor. They were more than one shade of gray, Deming realized, and shifted in the moonlight, much like the feathers of his wings so neatly tucked behind his shoulder blades.

"So," she began, unsure how to proceed, "Who am I to thank for saving my life?"

The Fae bowed low and rose, dark hair swooping with the motion. The ends gently curled near the nape of his neck. "My name is Nikita," he said, "but you, Queen Deming, can call me Kit. Enchanted to meet you."

Deming balked at his use of the title. "I'm not queen."

"You will be."

He shifted his weight to his other foot, wings shifting slightly with every movement. They were an extension of him, just like an arm or a leg, and the way the black feathers shifted almost imperceptibly in the breeze lit something warm and rumbling in her chest.

She wrestled her eyes away, realizing with a flush of embarrassment she had been staring. Nikita smirked but let the moment pass without saying anything.

Though her wrists and ankles throbbed, with each passing breath her body was catching up with the fact that she was not in immediate danger anymore, however suspicious the male in front of her might be. Deming could feel her heartbeat slowing.

She looked around the alley. The horses had been spooked and were nowhere to be seen. The misty fog mingled with the dark cloak of night, obscuring the aftermath of the fight. A fact Deming was very thankful for. She was much more comfortable assuming the gleaming patches on the ground were damp with water and piss rather than blood.

Her eyes rested on the two assailants. Both bodies lay still on the cold pavement. They were too far away for Deming to see if their chests were rising and falling.

Nikita followed her gaze. "They're dead, if that's what you're wondering," he said as he turned back to her.

She felt a wave of queasiness. Her stomach threatened to empty its contents. Her eyes flicked up to the wall where the last man had met his end. Perhaps her eyes were playing tricks on her since she was looking for it, but it seemed like there was a rather large dark stain on the brick where his head had hit.

Nikita took a step back and ran a hand through his hair. He opened his mouth to say something then closed it.

The entire alley took on a more ominous tone as she fully came to terms with the destruction that had occurred. The men that had been mauled. The lives taken.

And life saved.

She tore her gaze away from the dead bodies and looked at Nikita once more. Questions roared through her mind, one after the other. How had he known where she was? Why had he saved her? What were his motivations? Who was he?

The ricocheting thoughts pounded against her head which was already throbbing in pain. And with the adrenaline wearing off she was quickly becoming exhausted. She could feel a bone deep ache nearly everywhere on her body. The sewage and water that had seeped into her torn dress was now chilling her so much she was shivering.

Questions later.

"I need to get back."

Nikita crossed his arms. "You are in no state to walk anywhere. Let me fly you." Confidence dripped from his words like honey. Here was a male overly familiar with getting what he wanted. Annoyance rolled though her. She was surrounded by arrogance enough as it was.

"Absolutely not."

He took a step forward.

Deming threw out a hand and was immediately frustrated at how much it was shaking. "I said no. Don't touch me."

He backed away and Deming sent a silent thank you to the gods. She was in no state to fend him off had he not listened.

Deming began walking out of the alley. In a matter of minutes she could see the worn wooden sign of Firebrand's in the distance. The closer they got to the bar, the busier and louder the city got. The noise did nothing to help her pounding head.

The wounds where rope had dug into her skin ached ferociously. Her mouth felt parched and dry. Every movement was a monumental effort as she pulled herself along the road.

The Fae had said nothing since they started walking. Deming was reluctant to breach the silence, both because speaking suddenly seemed too large a task and because her tongue felt like lead, but curiosity got the better of her as they approached the outskirts of the tavern. They wouldn't have much time left alone. "How did you know I was in trouble?"

"I had been watching you rather intently."

"I noticed," Deming said, "and I know you know I noticed."

Eloquent, Deming.

Nikita stiffened next to her. She waited for him to offer more information, but apparently she would need to ask something more specific.

"If you had been watching me, why did you wait to do something?"

He glanced down at his feet, then up at the sky. "I was tracking the men who took you. I needed to see where they were taking you." He looked at Deming, gray eyes burning with earnest intensity. "You were never in any real danger."

A laugh cracked out of her lips, sharp and harsh and immediately causing shooting pain to lance through her throat. She shook her head in disbelief. "What the fuck do you call real danger, then."

She waited for his response, but he never had the chance to answer. Just as he was opening his mouth a high pitched cry came from up ahead.

"Deming!" Her name, long, drawn out, and full of angst.

Deming whipped her head towards the voice and saw Colette running towards her, Paris close behind.

Sobs wracked her body as relief washed over her at the sight of her friends. The reality of what had happened settled on her and her body began shaking uncontrollably.

Colette barreled into her, knocking her back and spinning them slightly with the force of her hug.

"Ow, careful." Deming flinched, putting too much weight on one of her ankles.

"Oh my— what happened to you?" Colette said, eyes roaming her body, looking for injuries and gasping at the raw skin on her wrists. "Who did this? Where were you?"

"It's a long story."

Paris rested a hand on her shoulder and rubbed gentle circles into her skin. His other hand brushed a tear off her cheek, worry etched into every inch of his face. "Are you okay?"

"I'm fine now," she assured her friends.

Paris looked behind her. "Who was the Fae you walked up with?"

She turned to introduce Nikita, but he was gone.

Much later—after having filled in Colette and Paris, Dresden and Miriam back at the castle, the Captain of the Guard, and then finally the healer—Deming found herself back in her room.

The sky was losing the deep hues of night. In its place, the suggestion of dawn was beginning to break over the horizon. Had the fog not been dampening the normally glorious sunrise, Deming knew the light would be bathing her chambers in periwinkle.

She approached her bed, more ready than she had ever been to sink into the down comforter and forget the world for a moment, but paused mid step.

Her breath caught. She glanced out the window and then back at the bed.

Lying peacefully on one of her pillows, delicate and pristine and iridescent in the early morning glow, was a single black feather.

Chapter Eleven

"ABSOLUTELY NOT," DRESDEN SAID quietly but firmly, leaving no room for argument.

The High Steward sat in an oversized red velvet chair with bronze embellishments lining the arm rests and high back. Plush, cozy, and near the floor to ceiling single pane window edged with a diamond grille pattern that graced the north wall of the library. It was one of the most comfortable seats in the castle and Deming's favorite place to curl up with a good book.

Dresden, however, was doing nothing of the sort. Her uncle, regal as ever, sat with one leg casually crossed over his thigh, his well tailored pinstripe trousers accented his muscular frame. He had led an infantry unit in his youth and took care to remain in shape as he aged. His back was straight, but not rigid, and only gently caressed the velvet behind him.

Deming, sitting across from him in an older and much less comfortable couch, frowned and said, "But it's suffocating—"

"Deming, I love you very much," Dresden cut her off, "and I know how frustrating it must be—"

Deming let loose a sharp laugh.

"But this is for not only your safety, but the safety of the realm." Her uncle picked an invisible piece of lint off his suit and laid his hands back in his lap. He raised his eyes back up to meet Deming's. "Do you understand?"

Deming sucked on a tooth, trying to stifle the sharp words bubbling up in her throat.

The past week had been a whirlwind for everyone. In the wake of Deming's kidnapping, failed as it may have been, the entire contingent of castle guards and dozens of soldiers that remained stationed at the castle had scoured the city for any piece of information that could be found on the crest that Deming described.

To everyone's extraordinary disappointment, none such information surfaced.

As a final effort, priestesses had been brought in to show Dresden and a few select members of his council various records of the city that they kept in the Temple in the hopes that something remotely related to a vine encircled eagle would reveal itself. High Priestess Xiomara with her beady eyes and beak-like nose presided over those meetings with pious condescension but even her and her retinue of history rich tomes hadn't shed any light on the matter.

The men the crests had been pinned on were found and brought back to the castle the morning after the attack. Having been undeniably cold and dead, they were sent immediately to the morgue.

What had everyone still in a torment of unease and chaos was three fold.

First, the men had mentioned reporting to someone. They may be dead, but whoever organized the attack was still at large.

Second, and without a doubt intrinsically tied to the first concern, when their bodies were recovered, the crests had been missing from their uniforms.

Third, Deming's mysterious savior was at large. No one quite new what to do with the information that a winged Fae had been watching the heir with purpose at the tavern, killed two men in a back alleyway of Arsaela in order to save her, and then disappeared into the night and hadn't been seen since.

The air in both the castle and greater city was tense. Having been thrown the attempted capture of a member of the royal family so quickly after the mystery of the fog, everyone was in disarray. There were whispers of rebellion, of Dresden losing control of his court, of the High Deities Kielle and Selene turning their backs on the people of Arsaela and the entire Queendom of Laey.

In an effort to provide some level of comfort and stability to the heir, Dresden had commanded the Captain of the Guard, Vallyn Morgan, to personally protect Deming. She was not to leave her side. Breakfast, walking in the gardens, the library, visiting Paris and Colette. Wherever Deming went, so did Vallyn.

At the moment she was stoically poised at the entrance to the library, having just completed sweeping the perimeter.

The woman was blunt, fierce, and far younger than the other guards, only a few years older than Deming herself. Deming had caught her fighting back a snicker at some of the more obnoxious comments made by members of the court this week. She felt that under different circumstances they could have been friends.

Her presence had helped at first, but it quickly became a nuisance and, Deming felt, a huge invasion of her privacy. She had come to ask Dresden if she could be relieved of her assignment, but apparently her pleas were falling on deaf ears.

"What if she only accompanies me when I leave the castle grounds?"

Dresden inhaled deeply and opened his mouth to respond, only to be interrupted by Deming, who could tell he was about to shoot down her idea again and swiftly sweetened the pot before he could do so.

"I'll pick my training back up!" she blurted out.

Dresden paused, mouth agape for a moment. He leaned back into the chair, contemplating the compromise. While Deming was competent enough with small weapons and had been given cursory training in defending herself throughout the years, the heir had never shown any interest in becoming well versed in sword and shield. Her strengths as a leader lay elsewhere, and while her uncle sat the throne, no one had thought to force her into combat training.

"In light of recent events, I think that is a necessary precaution to take. Thank you for suggesting it. Vallyn will oversee your training." Dresden gave a curt nod, standing up to end the conversation.

Deming broke into a smile so wide her cheeks hurt and resisted the temptation to shout for joy. "Thank you so much, uncle. I promise I will take this seriously." She looked over at the Captain of the Guard, itching to dismiss her.

As if he read her mind, Dresden said, "She will remain."

Deming spun around so quickly the ends of her hair whipped her cheek. She angrily brushed the wisps away from her face and protested, "You just said I could train with her!" Her hands curled into fists at her side.

"Yes, you can. And even if you begin tomorrow you would not be able to properly defend yourself for weeks, put up a real fight for months."

Deming scowled and stalked towards the door, Vallyn following in her footsteps like a living shadow. Deming barked at her to give her space.

Vallyn paused for a breath, allowing the heir to put a few feet of separation between them as she exited the library before leaving as well.

"Deming," Dresden called after her, but she was gone.

If the future Queen of Laey heard the echoes of his voice trailing after her, she did not show it.

Later that day all members of council joined Dresden and Deming in welcoming mages to the castle. Deming's new shadow, Vallyn, hovered nearby.

She couldn't possibly be enjoying this situation the two of them found themselves in either. To go from all the duties that fall under the purview of Captain of the Guard to a glorified babysitter must be just as demoralizing to her as it was to Deming. Maybe she could convince Vallyn to talk some sense into her uncle. The compromise she proposed, only needing accompaniment outside the castle walls, seemed perfectly reasonable. If the Captain of the Guard suggested it, perhaps he would be amenable.

The aftermath of their argument in the library was still simmering in the air. Deming found it difficult to say anything to her uncle that wasn't malicious and sure to lead to another disappointing conversation. She opted to avoid saying anything at all, and gave only a shallow curtsy to the High Steward as they sat down in the high-ceilinged room. Her throat raged with fiery words clawing to escape.

Dresden had requested a mage's input on the wall of fog, as wielding magic was outside his, or anyone else in the room's, realm of knowledge. Though the call went out to the city immediately following the wreathing of Arsaela in fog, only two mages had responded. They had waited days before officially inviting them to the castle, hoping more would surface, but none had.

Both Lady Brittan and Lord Nolett had voiced concern over the small number, but Deming thought they had been lucky to get more than one. It wasn't like mages grew on trees.

The doors opened and the council rose from their seats to greet the mages, both women, Deming noticed quickly, that were ushered in.

The taller of the two had dark brown hair piled messily atop her head, some of the strands had loosened and lay in wisps against her forehead and neck. The skin on her face was wrinkled, crows feet firmly burrowed into the corners of honey-gold eyes that winked warmly as the light of the room bounced off them.

The other... looked far less inviting.

Short in stature but not in presence, the other far younger mage swaggered into the room with arrogance. Her thin lips, painted a vibrant red that was shocking against her snow white skin, did not move from the stone cold line they drew on her face as her eyes scanned the room. Short black hair hung free above her shoulders.

There was no way she wasn't a fire mage.

The guard accompanying them gestured first to the older, then the younger. "The Ladies Gisela and Yesenia."

"Neither of us are a lady of anything," snapped Yesenia. "You can keep your titles."

Deming smirked, amused. The men and women sitting around the table were in for a fight today, it seemed.

"Gisela and Yesenia, thank you for joining us." Deming caught Yesenia raising an eyebrow as Dresden lowered his shoulders slightly towards the women in respect. "As you both know, we are in the midst of troubling times."

An understatement.

Dresden continued, "Based on the evidence we have procured from the fog surrounding our city, we have come to the conclusion that foul play is involved." Gisela looked solemnly at the High Steward from her seat at the table, her mouth settled into a soft frown. "We currently believe magic to be the source and cause."

Yesenia leaned forward. "If I may," she said, blue eyes piercing the room. "Can you share the evidence you have supposedly found?" She gestured flippantly to her companion. "We have only heard rumors and hearsay. The gossip surrounding the fog has gotten quite out of hand in the past week. Two nights ago there was a drunkard telling everyone in earshot that the fog took the shape of a fanged beast larger than a horse and attacked him. No one believed him, of course, but it's been difficult to tell truth from tale regardless."

"Of course," said Dresden. "We've withheld information from the general public thus far in order to limit panic, but perhaps that was a mistake." Deming managed to suppress her scowl. She had told the council not three days ago that they needed to release as much information as possible. The commoners shouldn't be kept in the dark, it was bound to incite fear and lies. "Lord Nolett, if you could?"

The High Marshall, stoically and succinctly, recounted the experiences of his party's experience in the fog. Dresden followed. Both Gisela and Yesenia, in addition to the rest of council, listened raptly even though the second group had heard this information before. Duke Lowell scoured the room, looking for what, Deming did not know.

Gisela was the first to speak. "Those are concerning accounts, on that we can agree. Though I'm secretly grateful the mist has no shapeshifting abilities."

"For now," Lady Brittan interjected. "the fog has no shapeshifting abilities for now. We have no idea if or when the fog will morph into something else."

Gisela frowned. "True," she said, "but nevertheless, for now it appears to be harmless."

A thick fist slammed into the wood table with a resounding thud. "Harmless?" Duke Lowell stood, anger flooding his ruddy features as he aggressively rose from his seat. "What about an insidious fog that is not only trapping our citizens inside Arsaela's city limits but keeping all trade partners out, is harmless?"

"Duke Lowell," scolded Dresden, "remain in your chair or you will be escorted out of these chambers."

He reluctantly returned to his seat. "We must assume the fog works both ways. The shipment of pearls, silks, and dyes from Crenstead was supposed to arrive yesterday. You know as well as I there is only one reason for the delay. I'll have lost thousands," he snarled.

"I am sure," Yesenia drawled in a voice dripping with venom, "Gisela only meant that the fog is currently a victimless crime. It has not physically harmed anyone." Her hand lay steady on the table, fingers loosely intertwined. The words she said next were as pointed and lethal as any weapon. "I have no doubt you will find other ways to make up for the interruption to your cash flow. Perhaps you can expand your presence in the west side brothels? I hear Maiden Voyage is in need of new ownership."

The chamber stilled. Even Deming didn't dare breathe. To accuse a high bred lord of dabbling in financial debauchery was unwise at best, treason at worst.

Duke Lowell studied his opponent. Just as it bordered on too still a silence, he responded, voice cool. "Consider this a warning. The next time you speak deliberately slanderous tales against my name will be the last time you speak," he said, something dangerous steeling in his eyes.

Yesenia said nothing but refused to lower her gaze.

"I must remind everyone that this is an inappropriate use of our time," Miriam said pointedly, breaking the tension.

Always the peacekeeper. Deming wished she could reach across the table and squeeze her hand.

"Our apologies," said Gisela. Yesenia and Lowell remained quiet, but both slunk further back into their seats, hackles relaxed for the moment.

"If you could return to the matter at hand," Miriam said, "I'm sure everyone in this room would appreciate the two of you sharing your thoughts on the fog. As mages, you are intimately connected to magic and can offer insight otherwise lost to us as there are no mages appointed to this council."

Deming breached her silence. "It seems prudent to ask what kind of magic you both possess?" She did not want to make assumptions, though Yesenia seemed a rather obvious example.

For the first time, Yesenia met her eyes. "I am a fire mage." Deming sat a bit straighter, pride blooming in her chest that her assumption had been correct. "I find my temper as wild as the flames I summon." She glanced at Miriam, then at Lowell, and finally at Dresden. Everyone was well aware her claim was as close to an apology as anyone was going to get.

"And I am an earth mage," offered Gisela. She smiled at the dark haired mage sitting beside her. "We complement each other well."

Deming wondered what their relationship was. It was unlikely they were related by blood. Their age difference made them being siblings unlikely, and the fact that mages couldn't bear children meant they were not a mother and daughter. Though, the love warming Gisela's eyes spoke to a parental bond.

Dresden, taking back control of the room now that the duke was sitting silently, asked, "And your thoughts on the fog?"

The pair shared a look before Gisela spoke. "We agree that the fog is being manipulated with magic. Almost certainly a mage, as Fae magic works in very structured ways. The Fae are gifted with near immortality and animal aspects that help bind them to the earth as stewards, like Kielle intended. Their magic is not accessible to them in the way ours is. They cannot wield it. The closest they come to tangible magic is the bond that occasionally exists between them and the amphitheres."

Deming's breath hitched at the mention of the continent's most powerful being.

The Queendom of Laey may boast the leodin—the golden, sharp-quilled, big cat that prowled in the Telacien's and graced the royal crest—but even that fearsome animal would cower before the amphitheres of Runne.

The legless beasts lived in the eastern most edge of the Fae Territories. Scales as thick as armor and wings so broad they were said to block out the sun, the fanged and ferocious amphitheres were as good as myth to the people of Laey.

Serpents of the sky.

Winged death.

Legend made flesh.

And occasionally, if one was blessed, a life bond.

Upon coming of age, each and every Fae was brought to the amphithere nest high within the snowy peaks of their mountain home to see if they would be chosen as a rider.

Most were not.

Some were eaten.

The few who were deigned worthy enough were marked and allowed to accept the rider's bond.

Lady Brittan cut through Deming's day dream. "The amphitheres are awe-inspiring, to be sure, but even they do not control the weather." She twisted a gold bangle around her wrist. "There is no way a Fae could manipulate the magic that lives inside them? You're positive about this?"

"There is no way they can tangibly manipulate their magic," Gisela said at the same time that Yesenia said, "It would be near impossible."

All eyes swung to the fire mage, assessing her words. Near impossible was not the confidence with which they wanted to be handling this.

"And with the two of you wielding fire and earth, am I correct in assuming the manipulation of fog is not something either of you could accomplish?" Although the question posed by Lord Nolett was benign, it felt pointed. Accusation veiled in the calm tenor of his voice.

"Yes," Yesenia said, cleaning a fingernail. "Our magic is exclusively tied to our element. I couldn't till the land with a thought any more than Gisela could summon flame to the tips of her fingers." For the first time since she entered the chambers, Deming could hear a hint of affection in her voice. "And neither of us could create whatever monstrosity is currently afflicting our city."

As if to demonstrate, Yesenia cupped her palm towards the ceiling and a gentle flame curled into existence. The warm orange hues flickered as Yesenia quietly moved her fingers back and forth, extending and retracting. It looked like she was beckoning the flame to flex with her. Something calm and ironically cool drifted across her blue eyes as she gazed into the fire, as if letting the fire come out to play released some of the blazing tempest of emotions roiling beneath the surface of her facade.

Deming's breathing stilled. To see a mage and her element interact stirred feelings deep in her gut. The edges of flame winked in and out of existence. The whole room seemed to warm in its presence.

Yesenia closed her fist. The flames, and the brief lull in the woman's fierceness, were extinguished as swiftly as they had been lit. It was impossible to tell if she had been showing off for seconds or minutes.

"There is nothing of earth or fire in that fog," Yesenia said, raising her head to meet the eyes of everyone in the room.

Duke Lowell adjusted the broach on his jacket, an obscenely large ruby set in gold that rippled away from the jewel like a sunset. He interlocked his fingers and rested his forearms on the table, leaning forward as he spoke, "Another element, then."

Miriam spoke directly to the mages. Meeting their eyes with respect and curiosity. "Do either of you have an inclination towards whether water, air, or shadow is at fault here?" Serenity emanated from her every pore despite the tension in the room. "To me, air seems like an obvious culprit. Someone who could gather the wind to nudge someone off the path they were on."

"That is certainly possible," conceded Gisela. "For me, however, it seems a water mage would be the more likely answer. What are fog and mist but clouds that have drifted too close to the ground? Someone with an affinity to water could easily manipulate the water in clouds. Although, the scope of the fog still presents a problem. Even if I were a water mage, I would not be able to hold the fog for this long. To accomplish covering the entire city for only a moment would be an incredible show of force. Our magic may be more flexible than that of the Fae, but even we have restraints. The well of our power only goes so deep."

Dresden addressed Gisela as well with his next question, "And what of shadow magic? How does that express itself?"

"Neither I nor Yesenia," she gestured to the other mage, who gave a nod of agreement, "have ever personally known a shadow mage. If I were to make an argument for a shadow mage being responsible for the fog, I would say that shadow magic can often hide and shield. It would not be so farfetched to say that a shadow mage would be able to use fog to hide the city from the rest of the continent, so to speak. Again," Gisela finished, "this is all conjecture."

The room stilled, everyone trying to grasp the extent of a magic no one had seen or heard of. A well of power that seemed unimaginable. How does one fight such an opponent? How does one even find the opponent?

"Of course," Miriam responded kindly after a moment. "You were both brought here as advisors. We appreciate any information you're able to share, even if some is a thought experiment."

Dresden stood, acknowledging the meeting was drawing to a close. "Gisela and Yesenia, I cannot thank you both enough for your support in these troubling times. I will likely be calling on your services as we continue this investigation." He smoothed the wrinkles out of his well pressed suit. "I will also be recommending a public announcement of what we have discovered. I apologize that our lack of transparency has caused chaos."

The two mages, understanding their dismissal, stood and bowed. Yesenia didn't break eye contact with Duke Lowell and stayed bent slightly too low for slightly too long to be seen as anything other than mocking. She spun on her heels and stood in one motion, hair a striking curtain of jet black.

"Thank you for your time, my lieges," she said as they exited the room.

The double doors closed with a thud.

Chapter Twelve

Gentle rays of late afternoon sun shimmered through the smattering of stained glass windows adorning the wall of the library alcove Deming had sequestered herself in. The beams of light darted through the otherwise dim room, dust motes twirling in their glow before settling on one of the many, many... many open books that lay scattered on the desk.

Deming sat on a plush green armchair, cocooned in an oversized cream shawl, legs tucked under herself. A dense, leather bound tome lay open in her lap. One arm rested on the edge of the chair, propping her head up. The other ran a finger lazily against the soft edge of withered paper, then paused as she realized she'd read the same sentence three times in a row.

The library's temperamental orange tabby, Sorrel, wound himself around the legs of the chair before curling up in a patch of sunlight. Rumbling purrs sounded almost immediately.

Deming reached down to pet him, then thought better of it. He loved being close by whenever someone spent time amongst the expansive collection of books that Reynes Castle boasted, but rarely allowed the castle's inhabitants to touch him. She didn't want to scare him away.

Instead, she huffed a sigh and rubbed her eyes. She had been in the library since sunrise. Asked the librarian to pull as many books on mages as possible, and then spent hours combing the shelves herself for any lingering mention of magic. She even asked Vallyn to take a pass through the stacks earlier, their brief separation both a reprieve for her and an opportunity for more eyes to search for content.

She had pleaded her case to the Captain of the Guard, begged her to ask Dresden for a reprieve from their situation. Vallyn had relented, though almost certainly because she grew annoyed of Deming pestering her about the matter, not because she actually believed it was the smart thing to do.

It hadn't done them any good. Dresden would not be swayed. Vallyn would remain until the network of conspirators had been fully smoked out of whatever rancid hole they were simmering in.

And so the pair of them had come to the library together.

The stack of books collected was equal parts impressive and overwhelming and they were nowhere close to sifting through all of the information sprawled in front of them.

A creak of weight on floorboards. Deming looks up to see Colette smiling meekly at her, a paper bag speckled with grease in one hand.

"Would you mind some company?" she asked, lifting the bag slightly, "I brought biscuits."

"Cheddar and thyme?" Deming perked up.

Colette scoffed, not deigning her a response, and sat down across from the heir. She plopped the bag down on the desk, careful not to track grease too close to the ancient texts.

Deming snatched and peeled open the bag, paper crinkling, and a small puff of doughy warmth wafted to her nose. She let out a moan and pulled out a buttery herb biscuit.

"By the gods," Colette laughed, taking the bag back and retrieving her own biscuit. "Do I need to give the two of you some privacy?"

"Mhmm," Deming could only mumble as she savored the impeccably well-baked goodness, every bite better than the last.

"There's one in there for you too, Vallyn."

Colette's thoughtfulness clearly caught the stoic woman off guard. Her eyebrows raised, deep brown eyes sparkled with gratitude. She dipped a hand in and broke off a flakey chunk. "Thank you."

Far too soon, Deming brushed the crumbs off her hand and sucked the last flake of salt off her thumb. She peered behind Colette, then at the empty bag. "No more?"

"Next time I'll remember to bring an extra," her friend responded with a shrug. "You've been holed up in here for hours." Concern flitted across her silvery blue eyes.

"Have I missed anything important?"

"Unless you consider Lowell complaining more about his delayed shipments, no. Nothing important."

Deming frowned out of the center window. The stained glass depicted one of the lesser goddesses, Mirentia. A crown of tulips and brambles perched atop the Goddess of Spring and Fertility's golden curls. Two lambs lay serenely by her feet. If Deming focused, she could see the outline of the harbor through her gown crafted from pale blue glass. Could see the lack of new ships that should be bouncing in the waves.

She turned back to face Colette. "More are missing?"

"There are now two livestock, one luxury, and one passenger ship that have failed to arrive," Colette said.

Deming swore. "A passenger ship?"

Colette nodded. "Coming from Temrowe, a common route. Apparently it makes the trip every month. It was supposed to dock early this morning."

"Families were on that." Deming felt a swell of emotion rise in her chest. "Children."

"If no one has been harmed on this side of the fog, we have to assume no one is being harmed on the other side too."

"That isn't going to ease anyone's conscience."

"No," Colette acknowledged, "it isn't."

Though it couldn't be seen from this part of the library, both women lifted their heads at the sound of the bell tower. It was far enough away that only four echoing tremors of the resounding bell could be heard, telling Deming she had stayed sequestered in the library far longer than she anticipated.

Four peals for each day since the council meeting with Yesenia and Gisela.

Four peals for each missing ship.

"People are going to start getting restless," Deming said with a frown. "Midwinter is only a few months away. Snow and cold will come fast and hard after." She shifted in her chair, releasing her legs that had been tucked for too long. Pins and needles twinkled down her calves. She winced and stretched her feet, flexing feeling back into them. "Do you believe your dad that we have enough food to last the winter?" She asked, rolling her ankles as another way to get blood flow back into her lower extremities.

Colette paused to consider, one hand playing with a pleat of her dress. "I know you dislike lying, but if I was in his position I would say we had enough food regardless of whether or not that was the case." Deming hummed her concern. "However," Colette said after a beat, "yes, I do believe we have enough."

"Why?" asked Deming, curious.

"Everyone is emotional about this, understandably so. But it is coming at the cost of reality. When you look at what has actually happened to restrict our food production, it doesn't amount to much. I was speaking with Lady Brittan this morning. She isn't concerned about our food stores for the winter either. Yet, anyway." Colette scrunched her eyebrows together. "Surely she's mentioned that in council meetings?"

Deming sent an apologetic look to her friend. "I've only been attending the sessions regarding the fog."

"Deming!" she scolded.

"I know, I know. Everything else is just so boring! Especially Brittan's sessions." The heir threw her hands up. "How would you like to sit through a three hour meeting where the only topic is comparing the quantity and quality of our beef and dairy cattle?"

Colette winced. "Three hours?"

"Three. Hours." Deming flicked up her fingers. "One, two, three hours about cattle. When we have a killer on the loose and what amounts to, at best, a magical ward keeping us from communicating with the rest of the queendom. We should be spending every waking minute on those problems. Not tracking grain supplies."

"It's all related, Deming." Colette rubbed a temple. "We may have supplies to last winter but if the fog hasn't resolved itself come spring you will need to know things that will help your people. Things like how much food we need to ration. My dad is trying to prepare you as best as he can, you need to take up his offer to participate in all council meetings, not just the ones you think are interesting."

Sharp words that cut right to the bone.

Deming bit her lip. Colette never spoke that harshly to her. The truth stung and the fact that her friend was the one to deliver the blow only added salt to the wound.

The library was silent save for Sorrel's warm purrs.

Colette looked like she was about to apologize but Deming spoke instead, eager to change the topic. "Tell me why we won't starve this winter."

For a moment it seemed like Colette was going to push the previous conversation further, but eventually her face fell and she dropped it. "In an attempt to not overcomplicate things, the general gist is that we really only import luxury consumables from other countries. Lamb," she gestured to Mirentia's small, stained glass flock above them, "certain types of seafood like oysters or scallops. Things that the royal court and high society eat often enough, but the masses do not. Everything else—all our grains, dairy, meat like beef and chicken, we raise and grow in the farmlands that surround the city." She leaned back into her chair and conceded the next bit with a nod, "So the Midwinter feast might be less opulent than usual, but no one is going to starve."

"What would I do without your wealth of knowledge?"

"Make a fool out of yourself when some member of council asks you a question you should know the answer to," Colette said half jokingly with an eyebrow raised.

"Couldn't have said it better myself."

"So," Colette said, eyeing the desk that one could talk themselves into believing was visibly sagging under the weight of the books atop it, "what have you found?"

Deming shook her head in frustration. "Nothing helpful."

Indeed, in the hours Deming had spent secluded in her alcove today she had read more about the history of magic than she had in the entirety of her lessons growing up. Most of the books covered magic in a broad sense, explaining the difference between Fae and mage magic and the most common ways magic showed itself. The different authors occasionally had differing opinions on specific branches of magic. One particularly weathered tome detailed a theory that there was the potential for more than five elemental magics. Deming had found that idea intriguing, and, though purely theoretical, tucked it away for further thought.

For the most part, Deming skimmed the information, reading only a sentence or two on each page to ensure the topics discussed were ones she already had knowledge on. She wasn't interested in the broad scope of magic. She was looking for nuance and creativity. For examples of magic being wielded in innovative ways.

Over the millennia of history, there had of course been records of mages skilled beyond the normal capacity. Fire mages who could cause explosions, air mages who could float as still as silence, not being propelled by air currents. During the Thousand Year War that began the dawn of a new age eons ago, a water mage named Kristeth had been able to summon tsunamis so large they were said to have changed the coastline of the continent after they crashed into the land.

Vallyn had opted to help her look through the stack of books after the second hour had passed. The Captain of the Guard's searches had found more than one rumor that an earth mage, not the gods, had created the mountain range that Arsaela was nestled in. Though she was by no means a regular attendee at Temple, even Deming found that one rather blasphemous. However, it had cropped up twice so maybe there was a kernel of truth in there.

She told all of this to Colette, who listened attentively as book after book were brought out as examples and theories were strung together across the pages.

There was a lull as Deming finished, then Colette said, "That all seems very helpful, why did you say you hadn't found anything?"

"Because all of these examples are from ages ago, some quite literally from before the continent as we know it existed. I mean, come on, look at some of these pages." She curled a gentle hand underneath a page so old it had holes where bugs and time had eaten through the words, its coloring so tan it looked like it had been steeped in tea. "How are we supposed to know what is reliable and what is folklore?"

Colette hummed. "What is folklore if not altered reality?" she offered sympathetically.

"I don't need altered reality, I need facts," Deming said stiffly. "And besides," she continued, closing the book carefully so as not to further destroy the brittle pages, "even if all of these accounts were completely true, which is doubtful, I don't know that they are helpful outside of proving one person, not many, could possibly be behind the attack."

"I heard one of the maids this morning calling it a siege."

Deming tilted her head, considering. "Hmm," she murmured. "Interesting. That's actually quite a bit more accurate."

"I thought so as well. It's always fun when the staff have more nuanced opinions on public affairs than council members."

A scoff escaped Deming's throat and one corner of her mouth was pulled upwards into a smirk. "Happens more often than it probably should." She let loose a heavy sigh, taking in the mess she's made of the quaint sitting area. "Will you help me put these back?"

"I bring you food and then you put me to work?" Colette stood up with a smile and began stacking the books into neat piles. "Of course."

By the time the women had slid the last book snugly back into place, the afternoon light had fully faded behind the wall of fog and dusk settled onto the castle grounds. Too late to do anything meaningful, Deming said goodbye to her friend and retired to her chambers, Vallyn in tow.

Once undressed and inside her bedroom, she paused to eye the sleek feather resting on her bedside table. She hadn't known what to do with it and since the initial thought of throwing it away had made something in her ache in a way she didn't understand, it had stayed in the room, mostly untouched, since that first night.

Occasionally she felt a desire to run a finger across its surface, needing to know if the vane and downy tufts were as unnervingly soft as they looked, wondering what her mysterious Fae was doing—

Deming caught herself mid-thought. She sighed and let her hand fall to her side, ignoring the pull to touch that small piece of him. She crawled into bed, not bothering to remove the throw pillows before resting her head and closing her eyes.

Sleep came swiftly, a small gift.

CHAPTER THIRTEEN

FIRE LICKED ACROSS THE floor. Up the walls. Up the skin and sinew and bone that knit her body together. Soot and ash fell from the sky like rain. It coated her tongue though she hadn't opened her mouth. Light danced under her skin. The fire was in her. Coalescing the blood in her veins to stone that burned blue with heat.

Strong hands lifted her up. Panic. No, no, no, no her mind chanted at him. She was fire, she was death, she would kill him, she would kill him.

She wanted to close her eyes, wanted to rip and shred at the terror that sank into her chest, but she had no control. She was limp, scalding in his arms, burning his skin to ash just as her own became flame, forced to watch as the world, her world, burned around her. Forced to watch as the roof crumbled into embers and sparks and crashed down—

Everywhere was warm. Too warm, too warm. Heat suffocated her, stealing her breath, her life—

"Princess, please." A lilting voice beckoned in the dark. Hands, strong and steady, just like his had been, shook her shoulders. "It is only a nightmare. Come back to us."

That was not his voice… not his…

Deming clawed her way out of inky, thick, unconsciousness and forced her eyes to blink open, parched and panting.

Vallyn with her skin like midnight and eyes rich as soil, inches from her face, took up most of her vision. Her hands gripped Deming's shoulders with warrior's strength.

A nightmare. It was only a nightmare.

Deming opened her mouth to speak, but found words difficult to form. She cleared her throat. Vallyn reached behind her and offered her waterskin. Deming drank deeply.

"Thank you," she said, leaning back into the sweat covered sheets. "I'm sorry."

"There is nothing to apologize for, princess," Vallyn said, retreating from the bed. "I am glad you are awake."

Deep breath in. Deep breath out. No fire clawing at her skin. No heat other than the thick bedding.

"Vallyn," she said quietly, the walls still feeling like they were creeping in, "will you give me a moment to collect myself?" The Captain of the Guard paused, clearly not wanting to leave Deming alone. "Please, I…" She squeezed her eyes shut. "I just need a moment to myself."

The panic still echoing in her voice must have cracked Vallyn's resolve. She nodded curtly. "I will be just outside your door. I will return in ten minutes." She bowed low and left Deming in bed, still grasping for calming breaths.

Breathe in. Breathe out. Five things. Open your eyes.

Five things she could see. The open window. The tasseled edges of the rug. The mirror. The armoire. The chipped paint on the far wall.

Four things she could feel. The plushness of the bed. The cobweb thin nightgown. The tickle of hair against her cheek. The... She reached over, tentative, to the nightstand. The feather, soft as silk. A shiver of pleasure rushed through her.

Three things she could hear. Hollis whining on the ground near her. Vallyn's boots shifting beyond the door. The last song birds of the year chirping.

Two things she could smell. The tang of sweat. The decay of autumn leaves piling up outside.

One thing she could taste. Deming plucked a mint leaf from the tin and placed it in her mouth. Sharp. Crisp. Grounding.

The tightness in her chest eased slightly. She reached her arms above her head, inching towards the headboard, toes curling towards the end of the bed, and held the stretch for a satisfying couple seconds before releasing both her hold and her breath.

Deming wiped the lingering beads of sweat off her face and swung her legs over the side of the bed, letting Hollis lick her feet until she was present enough to nudge the hound's soft muzzle away.

"You can come back in," she said loud enough for the guard to hear through the solid oak door. Vallyn entered, no pity lingering in her gaze, of which Deming was eternally grateful. "Thank you," she continued, brushing loose strands of hair behind her ear.

Vallyn only dipped her head in response.

Deming looked towards the open door to the bathroom, her porcelain tub calling out sweetly with promises of skin slick with water and bubbles rather than sweat. She turned to Vallyn. She usually enjoyed solitary baths, and if the desire arose Colette would provide commentary and aid, but... "I need a bath. Would you accompany me?"

"Of course, princess."

Deming strode into the bathing chambers, tile cool on the soles of her feet. She built a small but efficient fire quickly, every passing second reminding her of Yesenia's demonstration the other day. How quickly the tips of her fingers lit with flame. Soon the trough of water was heated enough to transfer.

Though she was still flush from her nightmare, an icy bath did not appeal to her at the moment. Something warm would do. With bubbles. Lots of bubbles.

She noticed Vallyn standing awkwardly near the door. "When Colette joins me, she usually sits over there." She inclined her head to the cushioned settee along the wall. Vallyn walked over and sat, albeit uncomfortably. It appeared that she was unwilling to take off any of the weapons strapped to her person, so sitting was an ordeal in adjustment of steel and pinched leather.

Deming padded around the room, collecting the various soaps and oils she preferred from the cabinets.

"Couldn't you ask your handmaids to assist with this?"

"Yes, I could. Noreen and Julia are always available to help with whatever I need. Honestly, though, I enjoy doing most of those kinds of tasks myself. Drawing a bath. Picking out fabric for my dresses. Clothing alterations and laundry are usually what I ask them for assistance with."

Once the water was warm enough and the bath full, Deming pulled off her nightgown and slipped under the water, combing her fingers through her hair before breaching the surface and settling into the rounded corner of the bathtub that allowed her to face her guard. The water lapped against her chest.

"You're rather young to be Captain of the Guard."

Pride swept across Vallyn's eyes. "The youngest to be given the honor, yes."

"You really don't mind being my personal guard dog?"

"Whatever the High Steward asks of me, I do. It is an honor to serve and protect the crown. "

"The rumors don't bother you? Surely you've heard the whispers about all our time spent together."

Vallyn's face flushed. She had, no doubt, heard the whispers Deming alluded to. Despite Deming's courtship with Paris, despite Vallyn's commitment to her station, despite this appointment here being mandated by the High Steward, the gossip mill had been turning.

An affair between the two of them was just the kind of salacious piece of nonsense that court members loved to spread like wildfire.

"Unfounded rumors are the bread and butter of the weak minded. I would never dishonor either of us in that way."

"And here I thought I was rather becoming," Deming said in jest, twirling a strand of bright red hair that had turned closer to russet now that it was soaked with bath water.

"You are a vision, princess."

Deming smiled at the compliment, though she knew she had been fishing for it. "Back to the matter at hand," she said. "How did you work your way up the ranks so quickly?"

Vallyn paused, clearly contemplating how much to divulge. The gold decorations in her hair contrasted sharply with the stark white dreads. "I devoted my life to the crown when I was young, far younger than most when they join the apprenticeship program that feeds into the royal guard." Her voice was stiff, structured. "It is easy to rise in the ranks when you are dedicated and have the time to study those around you."

Deming hummed softly, maintaining eye contact and waiting to see if she would elaborate. She did.

"There was… It is…," Vallyn stumbled through the beginning of her story, then stopped speaking for long enough that Deming thought she would cease all together. Just as Deming was about to impress that she didn't need to explain herself, that it had only been an inquiry to pass the time, Vallyn broke the silence.

"I grew up on the east side of the city. As I'm sure you're aware, that is a harsh environment to survive in." She paused, cocked her head and pursed her lips slightly. "Or maybe you don't know. After all, it's not the kind of place you would bring delegations from visiting countries to. Most of the time we're ignored completely, forgotten by the wealth that sits higher up the mountainside."

Deming frowned. Vallyn was right, she had never seen it for herself except in passing. She knew it housed the poorer citizens, had heard stories about the cramped apartment buildings and dilapidated storefronts. Occasionally a resident wrote to council asking for support, but there always seemed to be more pressing ways to spend the money than fixing a broken lamppost or repaving a side street.

No, she hadn't spent any meaningful time in that part of the city. Not out of spite or disgust… it just hadn't crossed her mind to go. Deming felt her cheeks flush. The intimacy in the air of the room highlighting what she now understood to be a moral failure of hers. Were they not her citizens too? Had she really burrowed so far into herself these last couple years that, in an attempt to protect herself, she had turned her back on others so egregiously?

Vallyn recognized the thoughts flitting across Deming's face and chose to let her filter through them on her own. Rather than speak to the heir's actions, or lack thereof, Vallyn pressed on with her tale.

"It was just my parents and me. They found me abandoned as a baby and raised me as their own. I owe my life to them in more ways than one. We had a small one bedroom apartment above a store that sold a random assortment of things. Half of the floorboards were warped and what little remained of the paint chipped off daily in yellowing flakes. The water we had access to was rarely clear so we walked back and forth to the river every morning. But it was cozy, it was home. We were happy.

"One night, there was a robbery at the store. My father went to help the shop owner, they had been friends for decades. My mother tried to keep me upstairs, but I was young and quick and eager to offer assistance. I had no concept of life threatening danger. That quickly changed.

"When I got downstairs, the shop owner was already dead. Blunt force trauma. Probably from the metal pipe the robber was wielding. My father wasn't in much better shape. He must have heard me, because he turned his back to the robber to find me. I tried to call out in warning as the pipe rose once more, but it was too late. The thud my father's corpse made as it hit the floor haunts my dreams.

"The robber took the money from behind the counter, lit a match, and dropped it on the floor. There were enough smashed bottles and spilled liquor that the whole place ignited with ease. I escaped through a broken window in time to turn around and see our apartment go up in flames. I heard my mother's screams. I heard when they stopped."

Deming recoiled. Her own memories threatened to break loose. Flashing bright across the darkness of her consciousness in snippets.

Tumbling jars. Curious hands. Floors sticky with liquor. A tipped over candle. Flames devouring wood as fear devoured her—

She snapped herself out of it. Breathe in. Breathe out.

Vallyn was still speaking, unaware of the flashback her story incited. "No one came. Not one of our neighbors. Not a single guard from the castle, though I'm not sure it would have fallen under their jurisdiction. No one. So I sat across the street and watched my home burn.

"It rained, eventually. At the time I believed Selene sent it to comfort me. Now I think I just got lucky. It tamed the fire. Washed away my tears. The blood. When morning came I had resolved to never be helpless like that again. I would learn to fight, and fight well. The next time someone needed protection, I would be able to provide it. Though I had no love for the royal guards at the time because of their inaction, for a newly orphaned and newly homeless little girl, there were not many options. I applied to the training program that week. With nothing much to live for except the grind of the guard, I rose in the ranks rather quickly. And now I'm here."

Deming realized that at some point during Vallyn's story she had started crying. She quickly wiped the tears away. She didn't know what to say, knew there was nothing she could say that would fix anything. "Thank you for your vulnerability. It is an honor to have you serve in my court."

"The honor is mine." Vallyn's shoulders were more relaxed than before, as if she had never told the story out loud, and in doing so had eased some of the tension she carried. "We have both had vulnerable mornings, it seems."

Indeed they had. Deming's nightmare seemed ages ago, but one thought brought the fear rising back into her chest. She shoved it down before it had a chance to regain any of the control it had over her earlier.

Shared pain and hurt, both said and unsaid, hung heavy in the air.

Deming rose from the now cold water and wrapped herself in a plush towel. "I..." she hesitated, unsure how to broach the topic on the tip of her tongue. "I'm sorry that no one came to help." Not enough, no apology would be enough. She turned to face Vallyn, the strength emanating from the woman more nuanced now that Deming understood its roots. "And I'm sorry that I do not know enough about your home. I didn't realize its residents felt so disconnected from what I know Arsaela to be."

"You didn't know any better," Vallyn offered limply. "How would you know we needed attention if no one you surround yourself with believes it either?"

The peace offering sank like a rock in Deming's gut. "That doesn't seem like a good enough excuse."

"No," Vallyn said, her eyes mimicking the cool steel of the daggers in her bandolier. "It does not. The truth is rarely comfortable."

Deming murmured in agreement just as a knock came at the door to her bedroom, echoing through the open bathroom door.

"Princess?" Noreen's timid voice was almost too quiet to hear.

"We're in the bath, Noreen. You may come in."

The handmaid entered, slippered feet shuffling softly across the marble. Unassuming taupe hair neatly tucked into a low bun and deep brown eyes so large they invoked images of a doe in the forest met Deming's.

"High Steward Dresden has sent for you. There is a delegation from the Fae Territories of Runne here and you are to greet them in the throne room in an hour."

"A delegation?" Deming was convinced she had heard wrong.

Noreen only nodded her confirmation.

She asked once more, more so because she believed someone along the way had gotten the information wrong than because she thought Noreen had misheard. Quiet as she was, if she was given a message to deliver it was delivered correctly. "A delegation, as in visitors?"

"Yes, princess. From Runne. There are three of them."

Vallyn interjected, still seated. "How is that possible? No one has been able to breach the fog in either direction for over two weeks. Have they been sitting ducks in the city for two weeks and are only now deigning to come to the castle? Or have they somehow found a way through?"

Noreen shifted her feet. "I'm not sure. I was only told that they arrived at dawn and are to be formally greeted by High Steward Dresden and Crown Princess Deming as soon as possible. Julia is gathering gown options as we speak."

Thoughts swirled, each one faster than the last. Deming shifted through information as fast as she could. "Not many humans live in Runne." Not a question. Noreen answered regardless.

"Yes, princess. I am told that all three delegates are Fae. And," she paused, "and that one is their prince." She clearly saw the shock that darted through the room, through the eyes of both Deming and Vallyn. Before either had a chance to refute her claim, she spoke again. "I know, the Fae Territories of Runne do not have an heir. I am only passing along the message I was given."

Vallyn and Deming exchanged glances, the former shrugged and said, "Sounds like it's going to be an interesting meeting."

Noreen and Julia had pulled together quite the ensemble of options in what little time they had.

After choosing one of the gowns, Deming barely had to move a muscle other than stepping into it while they dressed her. Noreen secured the bodice and made small adjustments to the skirt while Julia dried, curled, and styled her hair.

Deming admired herself in the mirror. The gown she had chosen was full bodied and deep emerald green. The fabric seemed to be cut directly from a shaded thicket in the height of summer. Where light hit the skirt, jeweled jade tones shone. Where the fabric folded the color became a deep earthy moss. Thick gold thread dove in and out around the scooped neckline, met at the base of her neck, and trailed all the way down her spine to where the gown pooled gently on the floor.

A crown of opals and diamonds perched on her head, her hair woven into both the delicate gold band and the whalebone pins securing it away from her face.

Other than small diamond studs in her ears, the only jewelry she wore was a small ring on her right hand, the royal crest engraved into its surface. An heirloom of the family.

"You look lovely, princess," Julia said as the two handmaidens bowed and left the room.

Deming followed them to the hallway door, then split as they went off to the servant quarters and she was ushered through the castle by Vallyn and five other guards.

No one spoke as they entered the throne room, Dresden was already sitting on the dais in a vest of deep amethyst and crown of silver and sapphires. His guards peeled away from him, three down each side of the room, as Deming walked to her own seat next to the High Steward. He gave her a once over, then a nod of approval. Dressing in the royal colors was a deliberate decision Deming had made and was glad that the man she looked up to and admired approved of the decision.

There was just enough time to smooth the folds of her gown and slide a facade of authority over her face before the throne room doors opened wide.

One of the guards by the door announced the arrival of the three Fae, his voice echoing through the massive chamber. "Prince Nikita Magdalene and the delegation from the Fae Territories of Runne."

Deming's jaw dropped.

Chapter Fourteen

Her hand shot to her mouth, unsuccessfully attempting to cover the audible gasp that escaped her lips.

Dresden shot a look at her, but Deming didn't remotely register the silent reprimand. Every part of her was honed in on the male stalking towards her as if he owned the room.

Nikita had shed every brooding, bloody bit of him that Deming had seen that night. Wealth and grace, the kind that can only be amassed over centuries, walked towards her, not a warrior.

He wore a decorative rapier in place of the twin scimitars. The multicolored jewels on the hilt and guard glittered with each step he took. He had swapped fighting leathers for a formal suit of deep blue, coattails long and tapered.

Pinned on his chest was the crest of Runne's royal family, an amphithere with wings flared and body wound in a spiral. Its feathered tail at the center, its fanged mouth wide cresting the upper edge.

What hadn't changed was that wicked smile. She would recognize that lazy grin anywhere. Would remember the sweeping gray of his eyes until the end of time.

And his wings... she sucked in a breath. Those hadn't changed either. Even tucked neatly into his shoulder blades, Deming could sense how broad they were.

He stopped a few yards from the dais and gave a courtesy bow. He ran a hand through his hair as he rose, smoothing back the shoulder length waves away from his angular cheekbones.

"Welcome to the Queendom of Laey, Prince Nikita." Dresden, always the picture of decorum, wore a soft smile and inclined his head to the Fae.

"Thank you for having us, High Steward Dresden." A voice of velvet. He cocked a smile towards her, white teeth flashing. "Princess Deming, lovely to see you again."

It was a monumental effort to speak with any sort of collected presence. "And you, Prince Nikita," she managed through bared teeth, "I am positively enchanted to meet you. Again. Though you failed to mention your title at our last encounter." Throwing his words from that night back at him did nothing to quell the anger at being deceived that flashed through her, electric and hot.

"Ahh yes," Nikita said, far too nonchalant for Deming's taste. "I am sorry about that. We," he waved a hand behind him, gesturing to the two remaining Fae, both of whom had yet to say a word or move a muscle, "have been in the city proper for a few weeks now and were keeping a low profile. Especially once this very intriguing fog descended. It was a necessary omission."

Weeks! Weeks in the city without anyone knowing.

"Deming?" The clipped question from Dresden was so carefully laced with ice Deming may not have noticed had she not grown up under the High Steward's wing. A silent tell of his anxiety at the shift in the power dynamic. Hands gripped the edges of the throne tighter than usual, knuckles turning white with pressure.

It was unnerving to see him off kilter. Though Deming supposed that was the point. Nikita may have been the visiting party, but he had been smart enough to tailor his presence in the city so he had the upper hand. Secretly spending time in the city for gods know what reason, not revealing his status as heir to Runne until absolutely necessary. All subtle ways to tip the scales of this meeting in his favor.

It was politically flawless. Deming wondered how many years, centuries likely, he'd had to practice the art of court.

She answered without taking her eyes off Nikita. "He is the Fae who assisted in my rescue. I was unaware I was in the presence of Runne's prince." A beat between thoughts. "I was unaware the Fae Territories had a prince at all, in fact." A prodding statement.

Nikita clasped his hands behind his back. "Not many are."

The room waited for more information. None came.

"We are, of course, more than happy to have you and your court in Arsaela," Dresden said, trying another route. "To whom do we have the pleasure of hosting?"

Nikita's face warmed as he opened his stance slightly to introduce his small entourage.

"Ilysse Cane, my second in command and a captain in Runne's armies." The muscular female to his right stepped forward. Eyes that burned like molten amber met Deming and Dresden's gaze, lazily moving from heir to High Steward with predatory stillness. Thick gold hair was tied back simply. No animal aspect until—

"A pleasure," she purred, exposing long, sharp canines.

Nikita gestured towards the other body behind him. "And our emissary to the human lands, Hartford Harrow." The final Fae was a female of subtle beauty and full, feminine lips. Of the three of them, this female had the most expressive aspects. Sure, the wings and canines were impressive, but Hartford...

Her dark hooves clipped against the floor of the throne room. Had Deming not been so taken aback by seeing Nikita again she would surely have been drawn to that sharp, staccato sound when the delegation had entered. Soft brown fur coated delicate ankles and tall, sloping legs that disappeared beneath pants that had been cropped mid thigh. An unusual style, she noted. Popular amongst Fae, perhaps. Deming found herself wondering where Hartford's body transitioned from deer to female.

And atop the tight coils of her brown hair, perched as perfectly as Deming's own crown, sat a stunning pair of antlers. Deming counted fourteen points. She resisted the temptation to let out a low whistle. Paris had been proud to bring back a buck with—

A buck.

Deming dropped her gaze from the impressive set of antlers to the face below. Large hazel eyes dappled with dark brown spots greeted her. She must have sensed the contradiction Deming was working her way through because the edges of her mouth tugged upwards slightly. When she spoke, however, she only spoke to the role she played in Nikita's court.

"Greetings, High Steward Dresden and Princess Deming," the emissary addressed both royals on the dais in a quiet voice. "I have been Runne's emissary to the human-ruled territories for most of my life, though this is the first of my travels to bring me to your queendom. I quite enjoy my time among your kind and hope to continue to be a bridge between our people."

Dresden gave her a tight smile. "The world moves more seamlessly when we work in tandem."

"Of that we are in agreement," Nikita faced the dais once more, his hand now casually tucked into the pockets of his trousers.

The High Steward leaned forward slightly in the throne. The air in the room chilled as his tone grew serious. "Unfortunately, I must insist we move past pleasantries. We would normally be happy to host you, but your arrival is ill-timed and frankly, pardon my bluntness, suspicious. We have had threat after threat knock on our doors. I will not have another. To that end," Dresden's grip on the throne increased, his knuckles white with tension, "why are you here, Prince Nikita?"

Protective determination glinted in his eyes. He would not balk at cutting down the Fae in front of him if they posed a threat to the crown. To Deming. Diplomacy be damned.

The guards lining the walls tightened their grip on their swords. Vallyn stood straighter, her position near Deming deliberate.

None of this fazed the Fae prince or the women behind him.

"No offense taken. I would expect nothing less than careful scrutiny given the circumstances. Take my word as you will, but we come to Arsaela to prevent violence, not stoke it." He did not pause as he answered the High Steward, plunging the room into ice with his words. "A seer in our court had a vision of war. Bloody and deadly in ways most alive have never seen. One that wove strands of courts and kingdoms from all corners of the continent together. This city, Arsaela, was at it's center. We are here to mitigate damage and, if all goes to plan, prevent this future from unfurling all together."

He spoke the words calmly, as if he hadn't just told the entire unsuspecting audience of the throne room that they were fated to be pulled into a massacre.

Deming considered the male in front of them. How much of his word could they take at face value? Prophecies and visions were notoriously fickle and difficult to interpret, but there was almost always a kernel of truth in them. A Fae seer, especially one working for the royal family, would be more accurate than most. If this seer had indeed seen a war in Arsaela, and Nikita wasn't spinning lies straight to their face, it would without a doubt come to pass in some way.

Would he have reason to lie to them? If he or a member of his party was behind the recent attacks on the city and herself, would he parade himself through their castle? The idea seemed unlikely. They had been undetected within the city limits for weeks, if they were assassins sent to kill her, what was their motivation for revealing themselves now?

For that matter, if they were assassins sent to kill her, why would Nikita have saved her?

Thoughts ricocheted in her head, bouncing back and forth between wanting to trust the male and wanting to kick him out of their court.

"I assume you are able to provide proof of this vision?" Dresden asked.

"You will have to take us at our word."

The High Steward scowled. "Prophecies are preserved in Runne, are they not? Imbued into natural items like bones or gemstones?"

The prince remained still. All three of them did, in fact. Their lack of movement was beginning to set Deming on edge. It was unnatural.

"Yes, they are. We did not bring the prophecy with us for fear of it breaking. It's quite a long journey, traveling coast to coast. A conch shell would hardly have made it without incident."

This answer was deeply displeasing to Dresden. His mouth twitched. He stared the foreign prince down with daggers for eyes as if he could pry more information out of the male with intent alone.

After several tense seconds, he moved on, voice terse and clipped. "And your reasoning for coming to the castle now rather than when you first arrived?"

"We thought our presence would raise our enemies' alarms. The fog led us to believe that whoever intends to incite the war is here, in the city. The attack on the princess further confirmed our suspicions. When we could not find the organizer of the attack, we decided it was time at last to come to you and work together. Here, I believe you are missing these."

He grabbed something from within his breast pocket and opened his palm slowly, showing it was not a weapon. Two small gold items glittered. It wasn't until he tossed them towards Deming and she held them in her own hands that she recognized the crests from the men he had killed.

"And," Nikita drawled, reaching back to grab something the lioness appointed Fae held out, "I believe you'll be interested in this as well."

Everyone present ever so slightly leaned towards the center of the room to get a better look at the offering.

"What is it?" Deming asked, lifting her eyes from the bag to Nikita's eyes.

"The contents from the saddlebags of the attacker's horses," he replied. "We tracked the mares down that night and recovered what we could."

Deming's eyes widened in shock. This was the biggest lead they've had since beginning the investigation. It was incredible. And yet, she couldn't find it in herself to be fully thrilled. "You could easily have tampered with the evidence. Or be making this up all together."

One corner of his mouth pulled up. The expression was perhaps meant to be placating, but it came across devious instead. "You'll just have to trust us, princess."

Deming leaned back in her throne. Every bit of her felt taut and apprehensive. She buried her hands into the folds of her skirts so she could pick at the skin along her thumb without anyone seeing.

The High Steward surveyed the Fae in front of him with cold apprehension. "You'll find that here in Laey, trust is not freely given." The walls themselves seemed to hold their breath. "However, we will have the northern wing of the castle prepared for you." The tension in the room hardly alleviated, but the guards along the wall loosened their grip on the hilts of their swords. "You must accept our apologies, our furniture is not particularly accommodating for your wings. As your emissary mentioned, we have not had to host Fae for extended periods of time in quite a while. We will bring up chairs with appropriate backs up to the desks in all the quarters, though they are designed to sit at formal banquet tables and therefore do not match the decor. The couches and armchairs are, unfortunately, built by and for humans."

Nikita shook his head and waved him off. "Please," he drawled languidly, "we understand the consequences of our unprompted arrival. I am sure the furniture will be more than fine. Thank you for offering quarters at all."

"They are conditional on your cooperation and behavior, let that be clear."

"We desire the same outcome. To find the perpetrator behind the attack on the princess and a solution to the fog. We will be gracious guests and I hope an asset to the investigation."

Dresden merely dipped his chin briefly, unconvinced, and gestured for the guards to open the doors. Nikita and his companions left, the two females waiting for him to pass before turning on their heels and filing out. Each movement was regimented and clean.

The closing of the oak doors reverberated through the hall. When the only noise was their quiet breathing, Deming turned to Dresden. "Do you believe them?"

He shook his head. "I don't know."

"Since when does Trevelyan have an heir? He's ruled for longer than most history books go back and there has never been a whisper of him and Sabel having a child."

A second shake of his head accompanied the repetition of, "I don't know. I plan to find out, though." He looked at her, intensity burning in his eyes. "They are a mystery, but your safety is my first priority. Better to have them where we can see than send them off to roam the city unattended."

Chapter Fifteen

Paris's fingers, calloused from years of pulling bow strings, stroked mindlessly up and down the back of Deming's hand. Their roughness was a comfort after years of holding his hand, after years of feeling them trace patterns onto her skin.

"How long will they stay?" The question Paris posed were the first words either had spoken in the long minutes since they started strolling through the yellowed gardens towards the temple that resided in the northwest corner of the grounds. Neither of them minded the serenity of silence.

Crisp air nipped at their noses. Hollis bounded ahead, romping through the fallen leaves and snapping her teeth at whatever small mammals dared to dart in front of her. Vallyn stayed a glorious distance behind, granting Deming a smidgen of privacy to speak freely.

"I'm not sure, all Dresden said was that their stay was conditional on their behavior," she answered.

"How much will they interact with the court?"

Deming shrugged. "Apparently they will be welcome at all traditional court appearances." She absentmindedly pulled their entwined hands upwards and placed a soft kiss on the back of his hand. "For all intents and purposes, they are as much a part of court as you or Colette."

Paris silently took in the information, though Deming could sense his discomfort. "I don't trust them," he said quietly, as if saying it to himself more than anything.

"I don't think anyone does at the moment. They haven't exactly been forthcoming with information. And I would find it supremely coincidental if he just happened to be watching me at Firebrand's when I was attacked. There's something they aren't telling us."

"Likely many things they aren't telling us."

"Mhm."

Paris paused his walk and pulled Deming into his arms. She closed her eyes as her head found the familiar crook of his neck. She breathed in his floral scent, summery and warm despite the chill.

Paris lifted her chin. "I won't let anything happen to you." Earnest faithfulness coated each word. Deming leaned back and coaxed a smile to her face, weary of yet more unwanted protection.

"Paris, love," she said, "if he wanted me dead he would have left me in that alleyway. He is the only reason I'm standing here with you right now. You," she reached up to kiss his cheek, "should," the other, "thank him," his lips.

The kiss he returned lacked his usual passion. "You just said you don't trust him."

"I don't." Deming stepped away from him but extended a hand. "I don't know why they are here or what they want. I don't know whether to trust their story about seers and war and bloodshed. I don't know if they tampered with the evidence from the horses. But

I do know that it makes little sense for them to save me only to kill me later."

Paris took her hand and they continued their walk. "That, or they want to gain your trust. Lull us all into a false sense of security and worm their way into court to tear it apart from the inside."

"What a sour mood you're in," she teased, bumping her hip into his in an attempt to lighten the dark mood that settled around them. She was anxious enough about the immortals as it was, she didn't need Paris to add to that. "I have it on good authority that Kielle and Selene don't accept prayers in the form of grumbling nonsense."

"I don't grumble!" The protest eased his tone into playful banter, and soon a warm smile graced his face. He squeezed her hands in thanks. "And besides, I would take Hollis' word on the gods before yours. You hate temple."

"No," Deming held up a finger as she corrected him, "I love temple. It's beautiful and the songs bring me to tears. I hate the formality of it all. My issue is with how most practice their faith. It doesn't feel connected to our lives. Why do we have to go to a certain place and pray at a certain time for the gods and goddesses to hear us?"

She crooned her neck to the sky, frowning at the gray expanse that sprawled before her. Kielle himself was almost directly above, sending periodic rays of light through gaps in the mist filled sky. "The world is so vast and we are so many, I doubt they even hear us."

"Maybe," he acquiesced. Deming knew he didn't mean it. Paris was devout in his belief. She envied him for it occasionally. "But on the off chance they are listening, I will continue to reach out my voice."

She leaned into him, placing her free hand on his arm briefly in acknowledgement.

The temple appeared before them as they rounded the final corner of the garden.

Unlike the gray stone of the castle, the temple had been built with red stone imported from the center of the continent. According to legend, the oasis in the midst of those desert lands was where Selene's first tear fell. Every formal temple on the continent was crafted from stone hewn from deep beneath the surface of the desert in honor of the sacred land there and in an effort to be as close to the gods and goddesses as spiritually possible.

Despite the dampened sun, the temple shone with jeweled brilliance. Every facet of stone glistened as if it were filled with rubies and garnets and topaz. Two towering spires covered in silver extended from the center, in honor of Kielle and Selene. Eight smaller but just as dazzling spires rose from the circular outer wall, representing the lesser gods and goddesses. Silver bells tinkled from each spire, sending a gentle twinkling melody out across the gardens.

Deming sighed. Beautiful was too common a word for the resplendent building that stood before her.

"Greetings, princess." The priestess at the door bowed and opened the door to let Paris and Deming inside.

Though the temple had smaller chambers for study and prayer, and there was a rather large library underneath the temple dedicated to religious texts and records of the Queendom, no one outside of the priestesses rarely ventured beyond the yawning chamber on the other side of the door.

Deming had prayed here for her entire life, but to this day she was stilled by the reverence the room demanded. The high ceilings were dotted with hanging chandeliers, each lit with a multitude of candles that were so far away they looked like stars. Floor to ceiling windows graced the walls parallel to the aisle. The stained glass inside mimicked the tapestries from the Great Hall—eight windows for eight lesser gods and goddesses.

Deming thought Dorthrum, Goddess of Death and Truth, had the most impressive depiction, even more so than the two looming statues of Kielle and Selene, carved from pristine white marble that stood behind the altar. Dorthrum's pale figure in the stained glass was thin and willowy with wisps of wind and mist and darkness shrouding most of her. Each curved line was a different shade of gray and black, creating a far more intricate piece of art. The darkness coalesced in a bright white orb that she held in front of her stomach.

She was the black sheep of the gods, being the bearer of death tended to isolate you. Deming had always thought her rather comforting, though. For a Death Goddess, at least.

The reddish-brown pews, solid mahogany, stretched wide on either side of the aisle. This temple, the largest in Laey by far, could seat upwards of a thousand. The only time it was ever filled, however, was during coronation ceremonies.

Today it was roughly a quarter full, as it had been for the last few troubling weeks. More and more members of staff and court had been visiting the noon service at the bequest of Dresden.

Miriam was nowhere to be found.

Deming frowned but strolled to the front row, where it was expected she would sit, and pulled Paris along with her. The service hadn't yet started, so people were still milling about, having quiet, casual conversations with those around them as they waited for the High Priestess to arrive.

And arrive she did. The High Priestess certainly knew how to make an entrance. Drums began beating a steady rhythm from where the instruments lay behind the altar. Everyone took their seats.

The wall behind the statues of Kielle and Selene, deceptively solid, opened in the middle to present High Priestess Xiomara to the masses.

Dark lines of kohl swept from her lips to her forehead, the curves highlighting the sharpness of her face. She wore a flowing gown of white and red that kissed the floor when she walked. Her dark hair was unbound but not unruly. Though they were hidden, Deming knew from past encounters that her feet were bare to the floor.

When preaching, priestesses were expected to have both head and feet unrestricted, to better let the word of the gods pass through them.

From behind her came a steady stream of lower priestesses, dressed similarly though their kohl was applied far lighter. They spread out in a wide arc behind Xiomara, hands clasped and softly singing the opening hymn.

Beside her, Deming could hear Paris as he began singing along, the familiar, soothing timbre of his voice blending in with the rest of the temple-goers. This is what she loved, the community that could be felt in her bones. Perhaps it didn't matter so much if Kielle and Selene were actually paying attention. Perhaps all that mattered was the peace of mind that their stories brought.

She opened her mouth to sing.

Curls of steam rose through the air as Deming brought the cup to her lips. Her breath rippled across the surface of tea as she blew, attempting and failing to cool down the soothing herbal drink.

It was long past dusk. The windows would be letting in little light even if the fog wasn't obscuring most of the moonlight. Candle wicks had been lit throughout the room, making every shadow waver slightly.

Miriam's room had no balcony to be worried about threats with and as such, Vallyn had been relegated to stand guard outside. Deming was savoring the feeling of having a conversation without anyone else in earshot twice in one day.

"Your absence at the noon services has been noticed."

Miriam arched an eyebrow. "Really?"

"Well, I've noticed, anyway. I suppose the priestesses haven't said anything. Or my uncle."

The older woman leaned back against the chaise she was elegantly perched on. Miriam's suite of rooms were well appointed if not as ornate as the rest of the suites occupied by members of council. The door opened to a small living room with one large couch, a chaise, and two elaborately carved wooden accent chairs. She slept in the adjoining room, which was set up uniquely with bed and bath coexisting in one large, circular space.

This had been where Miriam resided for the entirety of Deming's life and she had always been rather fond of the oddity of it all. Anything out of the ordinary in the architecture department spiked her curiosity.

"That makes more sense. Dresden has too much going on at the moment to worry about my attendance at run of the mill religious services."

"Where have you been?"

"I have been taking my prayers here, in my chambers. Just as the priestesses keep the crown of their heads and the soles of their feet bare in order to better commune with the gods, I have found that my prayers are more often answered when I commit to a routine. I feel more in touch with my spiritual side when I am surrounded by my own copy of the sacred text and am able to sing the hymns that align most closely with my prayers for the day. Plus," Miriam added, as if just now remembering, "I am keeping the Holy Hours, so for continuity's sake it's easier to pray from my bedside."

Deming shook her head, she must have heard wrong. "You're keeping the Holy Hours? Only the acolytes pray at both noon and midnight."

Miriam nodded, eyes twinkling with mirth at the sight of her ward in such disbelief.

"Xiomara doesn't even get up to pray at midnight!"

"I think we are in agreement that Xiomara may not be the end all be all for morality."

Fair.

"Well," Deming's mouth pulled downward into an incredulous grimace, "more power to you, I guess. I hope Kielle and Selene hear you."

Momentarily satisfied, the heir moved on to the other topic of conversation she was eager to have with the woman before her.

"The Fae delegation..."

Miriam's face instantly soured. "Yes?"

Deming set her cup down and tucked her hands neatly into the folds of her dress to hide that the tips of her fingers trembled. It frustrated her to no end that she could not shake the feeling of unease about the newest guests of the castle. Despite everything she shared with Paris about her confidence that they meant her no harm, and she was still vaguely sure of that, she was not yet convinced of their motivations. With her city seemingly shrouded in more mystery by the day, her nerves were frayed and her body would not let her forget that she hadn't slept well in weeks.

"We haven't had a chance to discuss their arrival. Privately, at least."

Miriam shook her head, curled hair shining in the light of the thick candle burning on the table beside her. Its warm sandalwood scent wafted through the room. "They are hiding something from us."

"Yes," Deming said quickly. Everyone was in agreement on that. "Did you know the king and queen of Runne had an heir?"

"I did not."

Deming cursed and Miriam chastised her. A familiar song and dance.

"Sorry. I was just hoping you'd have more knowledge than my uncle since you and your brother had traveled the continent more than the rest of the court."

"Khalil was well-traveled, that's true. But I only went with him occasionally. Perhaps he would know more if he was here."

Deming opened her mouth to apologize weakly for the thousandth time, but clamped her lips shut instead. Miriam had made it clear long ago that she did not fault Deming for her brother's death just as she did not fault her for the death of Silas and Samira. That night was a travesty, but one Miriam tried to convince Deming she didn't have to bear. It had taken years but Deming was finally in the habit of not voicing her guilt whenever Khalil came up.

It simmered beneath the surface instead. Called out to her in her nightmares.

"I just don't understand why no one would know about him. How ashamed of your son do you have to be to keep him a secret for decades? Centuries maybe." Her head tilted to the side as she looked again at Miriam. "He didn't say how old he was?" Miriam shook her head. "Didn't think so."

The older woman set her tea down in favor of the piece of parchment laid out before them. "Have you had a chance to look at this further?"

"I mean, I've looked at it," Deming replied, frowning. "No insight into what it is, though."

The contents of the saddlebags had been sorted through immediately following the arrival of the Fae delegation. Most were pieces that they discarded quickly—a waterskin, spare socks, dried meats, a handful of quills, a wobbly compass. But this piece of parchment had thrown every member of council for a loop.

At first glance, it appeared to be a map. There was a compass rose in the lower left hand corner. Thin, overlapping lines that seemed like roads covered most of the parchment. Occasionally, locations were noted with small dots. An eight pointed star sat almost dead center, taunting them.

The issue was it wasn't a map of anywhere on the continent. They had all stayed up late into the night cross referencing any map in the Temple's archives and found nothing that even remotely resembled the tangle of roads and marked locations inked onto the parchment. Something about it felt vaguely familiar, but it was impossible to pinpoint what.

Someone had protected their whereabouts well. And although every member of council had been given a copy of the map, so far no one had been able to break the code.

Deming sighed, swallowed the last dregs of her tea, and joined Miriam in hunching over the map.

No one had been able to break the code, yet.

It was only a matter of time.

CHAPTER SIXTEEN

ONE DOES NOT START out with the fun, twirling and jabbing aspects of swordplay, apparently.

Deming hissed at the burn that radiated through her thighs. She had been pressing her back into the wall of the training pit, squatting so her thighs were directly parallel to the ground, for only thirty seconds and she was already at her breaking point. As the last physical exercise of the morning, it did not take long for her legs to fully give out.

She slid to the ground with a pathetic thud and heard Vallyn stifle a mocking laugh.

"If I had the energy, I would remind you that I outrank you and..." Deep breaths to regain some sense of normal heart rate. "Gods, this is exhausting." She stretched her legs and winced at the tightness in her legs. "That I outrank you and it is disrespectful to make fun of me." She laid down, hand above her head and eyes closed. Layers of sweat made her hair cling in greasy strands and chunks on her neck as she breathed to no one, "Dorthrum, take me."

"Sorry to disappoint, princess," Vallyn said with a grin, "but there's no rank in this pit. Only you and your training."

"Me, my training, and you." Deming opened her eyes and blinked away the stars that sparkled across her vision.

"I am here as a conduit for your strength." Vallyn offered a hand, and pulled Deming to stand. "And as an occasional jester when you are incapable of holding a squat for a measly minute."

A grunt of acknowledgement was all Deming could offer this time.

They had been working every morning at daybreak for an hour for the past week and still Deming was woefully weak. Vallyn had reminded her time and time again that building up her strength would take months. The sentiment was extraordinarily akin to what Dresden had told her.

To make matters worse, she had yet to touch a weapon, wooden or real. Apparently there was an intense amount of work to be done on her muscles before she was ready to learn the steps of swordplay. Not that she could argue with that, given how she felt at the end of their lessons. Most days she was barely able to hobble back to her room.

"Here," Vallyn tossed her a waterskin, "drink."

She gulped the water down messily, not caring that most of it ran past the corners of her mouth and down her neck in small streams.

"Now finish with your breathing exercises." Noting Deming's reluctance, Vallyn added pointedly, "Breath work is essential to both battle and the more mundane aspects of life. I would expect that you of all people would understand that."

"You're right, I'm sorry."

She closed her eyes and began.

The breath work that Vallyn had taught her was more complicated than what she did after a nightmare. Breathing in and breathing out in steady beats had given her a good base to start from, though, as that idea was at the core of these new exercises. They were movement sequences that she flowed through, each movement attached to either an intake or release of breath. The exercises started out slow and easy, stretching her sore muscles gently. As she worked through the repetitive movements though, they gained pace and deepness. She had started doing only five minutes of this cool down breathing, stretching combination, but each day Vallyn had instructed her to add another movement addition.

Arms arc above the head, inhale.

Fingers guide the body into a dive, exhale.

Palms to her shins, inhale.

Palms to the floor, exhale.

Deming lost herself in the movement, could feel the connection between body and breath with each new position. Time meant nothing until she found herself in the final pose—back flush to the ground, one hand over her heart and one over her stomach.

This part of training came far easier than the strength training, however interconnected Vallyn claimed them to be.

She wiggled her toes, stretched her legs, worked feeling back into every part of her, and then rose.

Only to find the Fae prince peering down at her from the upper ring.

The lioness gifted Fae stood next to him.

"You certainly have a habit of showing up where I'm not expecting you," she called up to him, wiping sweat from her brow.

"May I come down?" A cock of his head. A very birdlike behavior, Deming mused.

She glanced at Vallyn, who shrugged before returning to sharpening her blades. Deming said nothing but waved him over. He likely would come down whether she wanted him to or not.

He put both hands on the railing and heaved his body over and into the three story drop to the pit's floor. Deming felt panic surge for a moment before his wings swung open and brought him down to the ground with two huge beats. She coughed to cover up the stifled scream that was still caught in the back of her throat.

"I make it a point to fly whenever possible." His smile was lazy and wide. This was a male who got what he wanted, when he wanted. He rustled his wings to draw attention to them. "Wouldn't you?"

"That seemed less like flying and more like a guided drop," Deming said, ignoring the question. "For what do I owe the pleasure?"

"I heard that the Crown Princess of Laey had started to train in earnest. I had to see for myself."

Deming rested a hand on her hip and arched her eyebrows. "And?"

"You are—" He fell into a fit of laughter, then began again, "You are not good."

Heat, first from shame then quickly followed by anger, flooded her face. "And I suppose you were a prodigy from the second you touched steel," she seethed.

Something wicked gleamed in his eye. He opened his mouth to respond, but decided better of whatever had been about to come out. Instead he turned to Vallyn and said, "When did you train with Fae?"

Deming's brow furrowed in confusion. Luckily, her unasked question was answered by Ilysse, who had prowled her way to their small circle.

"It's rare indeed for humans to know the ways of Fae breath work," she said in a husky voice, "and rarer still for those humans to be well versed enough to teach others."

Vallyn did not rise from her bench, nor did she halt her sharpening. The whetstone sent rhythmically ominous tangs through the room. "I spent a year in the outskirts of Naeryll," she said. "For those of us who complete our training to become royal guards, we are given an opportunity to study outside the castle walls. It's an attempt to broaden our skillset and provide diplomacy through the realm as armies train together."

Ilysse narrowed her eyes, her golden hair bound back with a thin strip of leather. "I've never heard of humans coming to our realm to train."

"You wouldn't have. Almost everyone chooses to train with the armies of Monstakar. The kingdom is our closest ally and the border is not far from here. It's an easy decision, especially for those with families."

"A few choose to train with the Artaxian Assassins," she continued, "and a few sail to the island nations. I was the first to choose to study with the Fae in centuries." She examined her sword, pressing a thumb gently to the blade to test its sharpness and wiping away the blood that surfaced. "A combination of fear and inaccessibility, I suppose."

Nikita looked thoughtfully at the warrior. "So what made you choose to venture over?"

Vallyn shrugged. She stood and sheathed the sword. "Your warriors are legendary."

Approval rippled across Ilysse's face. "Well, that's certainly true," she said, raising her hand and choosing that moment to showcase the miraculous unsheathing of five sharp-as-daggers claws from the knuckles of her fist. She curled them toward her, a movement that reminded Deming of what one does when they admire their newly painted nails. "I don't need a whetstone for these," she said to Vallyn.

Vallyn went still as death. "I would think twice about threatening the princess in my presence."

"Not a threat," Ilysse threw up her hands innocently, retracting the claws, "just a brag."

Nikita turned his attention back to Deming, deeming the sizing up that was occurring between his second and the human not worrisome.

"I was hoping that you could show me around the grounds," he said.

The sweat on her skin only enhanced the chill that swept over her. Her body's instant, visceral reaction at spending prolonged time in his presence came as a shock. Had she not spent nearly every moment since the prince's arrival convincing Paris that the male was not a direct threat?

Fear of the unknown was a powerful thing.

"Didn't my uncle arrange a tour already?" She willed her voice to keep her insecurities hidden.

"Oh yes," he brushed an invisible piece of lint off his tunic, "he had that insufferable know-it-all trot us around the morning after we arrived. I believe he's a lord of sorts. A duke? The one that prattles on about himself incessantly."

"Duke Lowell?"

Nikita snapped his fingers. "That's the one."

Apparently the duke's unlikability transcended race.

"I am tied up this morning," she said, "but Vallyn and I are happy to take you on a walk around the grounds after that."

A cocky grin of triumph graced his face. "Wonderful."

Chapter Seventeen

Deming looked out a window as she made to leave her chambers. The pines that created a natural barrier beyond the edge of the garden swayed in gusts of wind she couldn't feel but knew held the biting promise of the change of seasons. The Goddess of Winter and Respite, Descette, had today in the palm of her hand. She was letting everyone know that her cold and barren landscape would be gracing the queendom soon.

On a whim, Deming picked up a wool overcoat and a matching pair of gloves and then began walking towards where the castle's newest guests had taken up residence.

The northern wing was underutilized most seasons. Full of turrets and winding stairs, it was one of the oldest wings of the castle and because of that, was drafty on its best days. It did offer access to the highest points in the castle, though, which Deming guessed was why Dresden had offered it to the delegation from Runne, the prince being winged and all.

Not to mention it put them far away from the rest of court. There was no doubt that most of Laey's lords and ladies would find it uncomfortable to be in such close presence to three immortal Fae with secrets brewing beneath their guise of diplomacy. They would have to share space eventually, but easing into that relationship seemed smart for everyone involved.

After the fifth flight of stairs, Deming was deeply regretting her insistence that she meet Nikita at his room. She took a break at the next landing, leaning into the cool stone walls.

"Don't get any ideas," she breathed to Vallyn. The Captain of the Guard, while usually silent as she followed Deming around like a shadow, was now doing a poor job of hiding her mocking snickers.

"Sorry, princess," she said, "stairs are on the training plan already."

She handed a kerchief to Deming, who smiled in thanks and wiped away the sweat that had begun beading on her forehead.

Nikita and his court had been appointed the entirety of the seventh floor, only one level below the ultimate peak which held the owlery and messenger ravens.

She raised a fist to knock on his door but before she could make contact the wooden entryway swung open.

Nikita filled her vision. Arms crossed, he leaned casually against the doorway, wings slightly flared behind him. His thin lips were pulled into a smirk that reached his eyes, gray and shining and far more expressive up close than Deming remembered.

The air was suddenly full of cardamom and sea salt. Crisp and warm at the same time. The scent unlocked a memory of running across the beach as a child, wind whipping at her hair and laughter filling the air. Her mother and father warning her not to wander too far.

"I was just about to knock," she stammered out, choking down the emotions that had flooded her senses. She shoved the memory deep, deep down.

She lowered her hand and smoothed the pleats of her black skirt. What would have been a rather morose outfit was brightened by the yellow flowers threaded into the bodice.

He pushed against the doorway to right himself, then stepped into both the hallway and Deming's personal space. She stumbled back a step and shot him a withering look.

"If it's alright with you," he said, ignoring her glare entirely, "I would have my court join us as well. They were equally disappointed with the Duke's rendition."

"Of course, the more the merrier."

As if summoned, the next door down the hall opened and both Fae poured out with immortal grace, silent save for one set of hooves.

Nikita must have picked up on the shock Deming felt at their sudden appearance for he explained without prompting, "Ilysse's lioness aspect grants her heightened hearing, in addition to her retractable claws and canines."

"How fortunate," Deming said breathlessly.

He looked her up and down with lazy confidence then cocked his head to the side and said, "You know, as royalty, you really should be better at hiding your emotions. Those beautiful eyes give everything away."

She glared at him again. What an infuriating thing to say. "I'm so sorry I haven't had half a millennia to master my expressions," she snapped.

"Nor have I."

She raised an eyebrow.

"The three of us have only been around for two decades. Give or take a year." A wink, then he walked to meet his court. He grasped Ilysse's shoulder and patted the stag appointed Fae on the back.

"Twenty? That's impossible," Deming stammered out. There was no way the three Fae in front of her were only couple years older than her. They spoke with such confidence. They seemed full of such purpose.

"Did you think Fae came out the womb grown?" Ilysse raised an eyebrow, unimpressed.

"No, I—That's not what I meant." Deming clutched the fabric of her dress in her hands, then released it. "I'm just surprised. I expected you to be older."

"You'll find I'm full of surprises," Nikita said, pulling the tone of the conversation back to lighthearted. "Ilysse was with me in the training pit. And I presume you remember Hartford?"

Deming turned her attention to the stag appointed female. Her tanned, bone antlers were a crown upon the tight coils of her brown hair.

Hartford spoke, "You've been curious since you saw me." A statement, not a question.

Deming stiffened. "I did not mean to offend. The duality of your spirit was a surprise, we in Laey so rarely have interactions with those who walk both paths."

"Humans have such strict rules about these things, it truly is a shame," the Fae said, amusement playing in her eyes. Not offended, then. "I contain multitudes. You may address me as female."

Blunt and to the point, but said not without kindness.

"Thank you," Deming said. Her curiosity was not quite satiated, but now was not the time.

She turned back to Nikita, buried the flutter of uncertainty his proximity caused, and smiled wide. "Shall we?"

"Lead the way," he said, "unless you'll allow me to fly you down myself?"

Vallyn rejected him before Deming could. "That would be highly inappropriate and certainly not sanctioned by High Steward Dresden or her guardian, Miriam."

Both extraordinarily true statements.

Deming, happy to play the part and make him think she had been seriously considering it, shrugged innocently. "My hands are tied. Apologies, Prince Nikita."

"Please, call me Kit." Mischievousness danced in his eyes.

She tucked the thought away and mustered all the courage she could, letting her gaze give him a once over. Hoping her voice came across as lazily sure as his had, she said sweetly, "I'll consider it."

The grounds were vast and the Fae, for all their supposed speed and strength, moved languidly.

Deming had led the Fae court as they meandered through the kitchen, the library, the living quarters except for the royal wing, and both courtyards. Hollis had joined them halfway through and hadn't left her side. The hound seemed to know that Deming being able to reach down and spread her fingers through sweet, soft fur was a wonderful deterrent for the rolling feelings of inadequacy in her gut.

Each stop had been accompanied by some sharp-witted comment or sarcastic snicker from one of the Fae, usually Nikita. Deming didn't think he meant harm, the three of them shot quips to each other almost as much as to her, but she was on edge all the same. Colette, Paris, and she had never had the kind of give and take rapport that the present company seemed to have.

She had been pleasantly surprised to find that the Fae also preferred the more intimate courtyard. She had presumed that with immortality came a disdain for the simple and plain, much like she saw in the wealthy companions of court, but the Fae in front of her seemed to appreciate the willow's history more because of their long life, not less.

Ilysse in particular had been affected by the ancient tree. She looked up at the grand willow and spoke with reverence about a similar tree in their own kingdom. When Deming downplayed the willow by saying the Fae counterpart was likely far older and imbued with magic, Ilysse had only shook her head and placed a tanned palm on the willow's bark, eyes bright and full of emotion before snapping back to her usual abrasive self.

The sun had dipped below the horizon, barely visible through the haze, by the time they entered the gardens.

"I must apologize," Deming said to the group as a whole, "I should have brought you here first. Dawn or early morning is when the gardens shine."

"Even if we had started here, without a doubt neither the fog nor time of year would have helped the viewing pleasure." Another back-handed comment from Nikita, supplemented by a smile that would have made weaker women buckle at the knees.

A chuckle from Ilysse, quickly followed by a glare from Hartford and a hushed chide. The quietest Fae seemed the only one of the bunch to not revel in sarcasm at the expense of the heir.

Deming swallowed a vulgar retort and said diplomatically, "You're right. The fall is not the time of year to enjoy the gardens." She led them through the winding stone paths, guiding them to the stables. "I'm sure the gardens here pale in comparison to your realm. With centuries to dedicate to them, it would only be expected."

"You usually spend time out here?" Hartford's question caught her off guard and hung in the air.

"Yes," she replied, blinking away her surprise. "In late spring, this entire swath of land is filled with peonies. And the butterflies come back from their migration. It's absolutely beautiful. I'm almost always found reading on one of the many benches or strolling through the labyrinth of walkways with my friends or Hollis."

Ilysse voiced a more pointed question. "As heir you have time for that?"

Deming scowled. "No," she said, trying to keep the bite out of her words, "not really. I have to make time for what I enjoy, though, or else my days would feel endless."

Nikita hummed, lost in thought. "You would enjoy the gardens at Bascade. Since the Fae realms are closer to the center of the continent, our gardens often act out of step with the seasons. The palace where the King resides has a garden as large as this entire estate that is locked in eternal summer."

King, not father. Interesting.

"Perhaps one day I'll get to see them."

"Perhaps." What looked like a wave of pure ambivalence washed over him.

Deming cleared her throat, eager to let the moment pass. "And last but not least," she said as they approached the massive barn, "the stables."

Nikita grunted and rolled a kink out of his neck.

Soft nickering and the heavy scent of horses greeted them as they entered. Deming was so caught up in the spirit of the room that she almost missed Nikita's subtle cringe as a roan mare reached out to affectionately nip his shirt.

Warm delight spread through her.

"You aren't…" The smile plastered to her face spread wider with each syllable. "You aren't afraid of horses? Are you?"

Nikita whipped his head to her. "Absolutely not." Both Fae behind him buckled over in laughter, confirming his lie. He spun to them. "I'm not!"

Fighting for breath, Hartford righted herself. "He was given a nasty stallion to ride when he was young," Deming gave Nikita an exaggerated pout and let out a soft whimper dripping with sarcasm. "Got completely bucked off."

"Avoids riding horses at all costs now," Ilysse said, eyes gleaming.

"I have a scar!" Nikita pulled up his sleeve and showed off a moderately sized scar on his forearm.

Ilysse patted him on the back. "You've gotten scars from much worse, friend."

Nikita growled. "You never know what they're thinking! And nobody seems to care how large they are. And the hooves…"

"Your emissary has hooves," Deming pointed out. Hartford clicked into the pavement in emphasis.

"It's different," he insisted.

"Poor, immortal baby," Deming cooed.

The laughter settled and smiles turned into a slightly uncomfortable silence as everyone realized they had all come very close to a semblance of camaraderie.

"This way," Deming began walking to the middle of the stable. "Come meet Quintessential. She's gentle, I promise."

The dapple gray mare whinnied as the group approached. Deming grabbed two apples from the bucket near her stable door and offered one to the mare. She stroked down her forehead as she ate, tracing the white mark from tip to tip.

"She's beautiful," murmured Hartford.

"Thank you. She was a gift many years ago." Deming let herself briefly swim in the golden memories before turning to Nikita. "Here." Without asking permission, she grabbed Nikita's hand and placed the second apple in it.

He hesitated but let her bring the apple to Quinn's muzzle. The horse took the offering, gently as if she could sense his nerves.

As Quinn munched on the second treat, Deming again took Nikita's hand in her own and coaxed him to pet her. Softly on her broad neck, her mane, her cheeks. Then once, twice, a third time down her forehead just as she had done.

On the last pass Deming let their hands drop. She curled her fingers into her palm to fend off the chill that his absence left.

She lifted her chin to find his eyes already on her. "See?" she said softly. "Nothing to be afraid of."

He inhaled deeply and remained quiet, though his eyes sparkled with a story she couldn't quite decode.

A loud thud jolted her from thought. The wind had slammed the barn door closed, ensconcing them in near complete darkness.

"Well," Deming chuckled, "apparently the tour's over."

She walked to the door, sure-footed even in the darkness, and ushered the Fae back into the garden. The walk back to the northern tower was quiet but comfortable and soon they arrived at the seventh floor once again.

Ilysse and Hartford retired to their rooms almost immediately, thanking Deming for her time. Vallyn had remained at the bottom of the stairs, waiting to escort Deming back to her room.

Which left only the prince and princess in the dim hallway.

Nikita crossed his arms, leaning against the doorframe just as he had been when she arrived hours ago to pick them up.

His entire countenance softened as he took her in, admired her. "You have quite the spine of steel to put up with my court all day."

"Your court or you?" she countered, "Hartford is lovely."

His warm laugh filled the air between them, the movement jostling his wings and sending a waft of his sharp-soft cardamom and salt scent to her. She shivered.

"Fair." The remnants of laughter danced from his smile to his eyes.

They stood there for too long, neither wanting to break the silence or the eye contact first. A power play, Deming convinced herself.

Finally, Nikita said, "Thank you for the tour. Yours was far more satisfying than the Duke's. Perhaps if queendom doesn't work out you could pursue that."

Deming bowed her head and let a closed lip huff of laughter out. "A tour guide? Yeah, I'm sure that conversation would go over really well with my uncle."

She looked up to find all playfulness gone from his face. The hazy starlight from the window backlit his form and made it difficult to make out anything other than the curl of his hair. The arch of his wing. The gleam in his gray eyes when he cocked his head.

He reached forward, as if to tuck the loose strand of hair tickling her face behind her ear, but stopped. His hand stayed suspended in mid air for only a second before falling slowly to his side.

"Goodnight, Deming."

"Goodnight, Nikita."

The corner of his mouth lifted slightly. "I told you," he said, "it's Kit."

"And I told you," she said, stepping back into the hallway. Immediately clear headed with the absence of his scent. "I'll consider it."

They stood for a moment longer, then in the same motion Deming turned towards the stairs and Nikita closed his door.

The whisper of his laughter followed her through the castle as each footfall carried her away from him and toward her empty chambers. Echoes of cardamom and salt settled into bed with her.

Her dreams were blissfully quiet.

CHAPTER EIGHTEEN

ROW AFTER ROW OF the same gold crown perched delicately on top of subtle variations of the same curled, red hair, the same freckled skin, and the same amber eyes. All features that mimicked her own. Save the hair.

Deming subconsciously twirled a strawberry blonde strand as she wandered down the hallway that led away from the Grand Ballroom and towards the royal wing, looking at the portraits of past Queens of Laey. Each one was time stamped underneath in gold filigree with the duration of their reign.

There were missing years here and there, times when the Queen and King Consort had produced only sons and the crown skipped a generation, the son becoming High Steward until his own daughter came of age and took the throne, but for the most part the Reynes-Elyachar line had been blessed with first born daughters.

Deming stopped in front of her mother. Samira looked out at the world, regal and sure, the depth of her empathy somehow captured perfectly with only brush strokes and paint.

She rubbed the tears away with the back of her hand as guilt and self-loathing pooled in her gut. "You should be here, not me."

"Don't say that. You are our future." A soft, feminine voice from behind her.

Deming turned around, revealing Colette. Paris followed closely in her wake.

Deming sucked on a tooth, praying her next words wouldn't come out wobbly. Though it didn't matter. The three of them had never been a pair to hide emotions from one another. "She would have known what to do. She would have already fixed the fog and found the assailant and known how to pry information out of the Fae delegation."

Paris found his place by her side. Calloused fingers stroked her cheek. "You don't know that."

"I do. She should be the Queen of Laey. I'll never live up to that title. I can't even get myself to take it."

Not wanting to fight, Paris changed the subject. "Why don't we walk by the apothecary? It could be cathartic."

"I thought we were going to the stables?" In the chaos of the Runne delegation, Deming had seen very little of her two favorite people. She had specifically carved out time today to ride with them, even if just around the paddock or through the city. The horses needed exercise and she needed Paris and Colette. Two birds, one stone.

"I know, we still can." Paris took a step back but moved his hand down to lock with her own. "You looked so forlorn just now, though. With everything that's happened recently, I know you haven't been able to honor the anniversary of their death in the way you usually do."

That was true enough. The weeks after the anniversary of their death was usually a time of introspection and grief for Deming. With the fog sending Arsaela into crisis so quickly after her and Miriam visited their graves, she'd abandoned her usual routine.

The last thing Deming wanted to do in this exact moment was be further reminded of that night, but perhaps Paris was right. She had been such a bundle of tumultuous emotions this month. Maybe she needed to pay her respects.

She let Colette loop an arm through her own and guide her down the hall.

The three spoke little on the walk. A comment here and there about court the other day. Lady Blackwell had finally found her footing around the upper echelon of Laey high society. Lord Dougherty was impossibly dull, as usual. The Fae had managed to keep a low profile despite sticking out like a sore thumb with their wings and antlers and claws that sprouted from between their knuckles.

They quieted as they approached the massive double doors that gated the entrance to what was once the pinnacle of magic and innovation, both within Laey and elsewhere on the continent.

Charred burns covered most of the oak paneling. Some parts were so mangled that the rest of the ruins inside the doors could be seen. Ash and soot still stained the walls and columns lining the hallway. What had begun as a week-long mourning vigil in honor of the lost lives had long since turned into a calamity that seemed too far gone to do anything about. Even all these years later, the bodily remains of the king and queen long since buried, no one could bear to touch the place they died.

No one ever mentioned Khalil.

Miriam's brother had been the third casualty that night, entering the fiery fray to try and save his king and queen. No one in Laey, not even within the city limits of Arsaela, it seemed, ever remembered Khalil. When the Queen and King Consort die in a freak accident, any other citizen casualties fall by the wayside. Deming knew it pained Miriam deeply to this day.

She could feel Colette's eyes on her, watching for any sign of distress. Paris squeezed her shoulder. "I'm fine."

"Do you think it's time to air out the apothecary?"

Deming turned to her cousin. "Excuse me?"

"I just think that, with everything happening lately, it doesn't do anyone any good to have the traumas of our past haunting the air so visibly."

Deming tugged her arm out from the crook of Colette's elbow. "That's not how trauma works, Colette," she snapped sharply. "It's not like I can just clean up a room and suddenly I won't wake up in terror after being burned alive in my dreams."

"Deming," Paris said, reproachfully, "that isn't what she meant."

The silence that followed felt thick and heavy, stifling like a quilt thrown over a body in the height of summer.

Colette tried again. "I can't begin to know how much you miss them, how much you hurt for their loss and your part in it." Deming flinched. "What I do know is that my best friend hasn't been the same since that night and I want more than anything for her to stop clinging to the past. Maybe the chaos Arsaela has been thrown into is a sign. Maybe the gods want us to carve our own path. For you to use this as a stepping stone to healing."

Deming considered her friend's words. Even she had to admit there was something in the air recently, and not just the clinging mist. Something was shifting deep within the bones of the queendom. Perhaps Colette had a point.

Rather than admitting that, Deming gave a half answer. "Another time, perhaps."

Colette sighed in disappointment but didn't push the issue further.

In the hazy time between evening and true night, where the sky would be inky blue but not quite backlit with stars had it not been for the fog, Deming sat alone on her couch.

Or at least, she was trying to sit. Every couple minutes she unfolded her legs from their tucked position beneath her and stood, paced around the couch, occasionally opened the curtains and peered out into the empty courtyard below, and then plopped herself down on the couch again.

This had been going on for nearly half an hour when Vallyn finally got fed up.

"Would you please, for the love of the Goddess, stop that."

Deming turned, eyes wide in surprise as if she had forgotten the guard was leaning against the far wall, or in the room at all. "What?"

"The pacing. Stop it."

"I wasn't pacing."

Vallyn scoffed. "If you want to go visit the apothecary so badly I'll take you right now."

Deming looked offended. "First of all, I don't need you to take me, like I'm a child. I am perfectly capable of going without a babysitter."

"First of all," Vallyn retorted, "you do, explicitly, need a babysitter. The High Steward hasn't lifted his order. Though I like to think myself more of a murderer repellant than babysitter."

"Second of all," Deming said, raising her voice slightly and ignoring the very factual statement from the other woman. "I don't want to visit the apothecary."

"Okay."

"I don't."

"I said okay."

Deming picked at dirt that didn't exist beneath her fingernail. She looked towards her bed, where she wanted more than anything to be able to lay down and fall asleep, and then at the Captain of the Guard. "I don't have to go in."

"No, you don't have to go in."

"I could just walk by and pay my respects."

"You could just walk by and pay your respects."

Deming crossed her arms. "Are you always a parrot?"

Vallyn pushed off the wall, not waiting for the heir as she headed out the door. "Only when the recipient needs to hear the stupidity of their own words."

And that was how Deming found herself, in the darkness of a sleeping castle, close enough to the blackened door that all she would have to do to touch the ash would be to reach out her hand.

This was as close as she had been to the inner chamber of the apothecary since that night. She could easily turn around now and consider this venture successful. And yet, something pulled at her fingers, drawing them closer and closer to the closed door until, at last, the pads of her fingertips touched the door.

Deming exhaled, relief flooding her lungs. She hadn't realized she was holding her breath.

The wood was rough, not smooth as she remembered, but the weight of the massive oak doors had withstood the test of time and tragedy.

She leaned in, pressing her palm flush against the door. Her heart skipped a beat when it yielded to her touch and swung open, albeit on creaking hinges that hadn't been used in over a decade.

Then she stopped breathing all together.

The apothecary was a graveyard.

An ashy, apocalyptic graveyard.

The bones of the room were barely recognizable. The walls remained, thanks to the stone the castle was built out of, but nothing else was recognizable.

There used to be wall to wall shelves full of books and tinctures and bottles full of anything you could possibly dream of. Candles would be lit on every surface, casting the room in a warm, buttery glow as Khalil and one or two of the young mages that traveled from across the continent to train under him worked and studied. Chairs and stools once rimmed the edge of the grand workbench that was situated directly in the middle of the room. All underneath a sweeping iron candelabra that, while beautiful, was never lit because the candles had long since melted down to nothing and no one cared enough to replace them.

None of that remained.

If Deming hadn't known she was walking into the same room, she wouldn't have recognized it.

Piles of charred wood littered the floor. The workbench was split down the middle. A fallen candelabra sunk into the grain of the wood was seemingly the culprit. Broken glass sparkled across everything, the only hint of light or color against the expanse of black and gray.

It was simultaneously too much to take in and nothing at all.

A hand on her shoulder made Deming jump.

"Princess," said Vallyn, "you need to breathe."

Right. Breathing.

She inhaled deeply, the whoosh of air on the exhale disturbing some of the ash nearby. Her heart felt jittery. Her eyes, too, darted around the space too quickly. Seeing and not seeing. She didn't know what to do with her hands, she just kept clenching and unclenching her fists.

"Do you want to return to your rooms?"

Instinctually rejecting the idea, Deming stepped into the apothecary.

Her footfalls were silent, sinking into the thick layer of ash and dust on the floor. Vallyn followed in the indentations her shoes made out of respect for the dead.

When Deming reached the middle of the room she stopped and turned around. Though the scene before her was gruesome, she couldn't fight against the flurry of memories that came rushing back to her. Every corner of this room held a piece of her, a moment in time with Miriam or Khalil or her mother and father.

And what struck her the most, she realized with a pang, was not the sadness that always accompanied thinking about that night but rather an unexpected, mournful emotion. One that hung on the fact that they had squandered any chance of future memories being born in this room by keeping it a crypt.

Eyes bright with tears, Deming turned to Vallyn, a soft, calm smile tugging at her lips. With a sense of peace she hadn't experienced since she was a child and confidence she didn't recognize at all lacing her words she said, "They deserve better than an ashy grave. They would want this place to be alive."

Dresden had agreed emphatically with her proposition.

Miriam even more so. She had broke into tears and wrapped Deming in a fierce hug when she heard the news.

After hours of labor, buckets of sweat, and more than a few bouts of emotionally charged exchanges when the occasional surviving bowl broke in transition or a disagreement bubbled up about whether the swept up ashes should be saved or thrown away, the apothecary was nearly unrecognizable to the one Deming had stood in nearly a week earlier.

She looked around, pride swelling in her chest. Unable to suppress her grin she reached out and squeezed Colette's hand so hard her cousin yelped and pulled away.

"Sorry," Deming said, "I'm just so proud. Look at this!" She swept her arms out wide.

Indeed, the apothecary looked immaculate. There was still a lack of stores, since many of the items that were usually stocked in these walls were procured from other territories and the impending fog crisis had yet to be resolved, but on a whole, the room glistened with hopeful promise.

Deming did a lazy lap around the room, relishing in their hard work. She stopped in front of the workbench and placed both palms on the dense wood. Her cheeks hurt from smiling so wide. She couldn't remember a time she had felt more like the Crown Princess she was supposed to be than this moment.

"You should be proud, Deming. You saw a wound no one else was willing to look at closely and transformed it into something joyful."

"I would never have had the will to come here if it wasn't for you and Paris. Everyone should be thanking you both."

"No, no," insisted Colette, one hand raised in protest, "this is your win and your win alone. Want to celebrate the completion? Paris has been aching for a night out."

If at all possible, Deming lit up further. "Sure! I'd never say no to Firebrand's." To everyone's surprise, including her own, Deming had no qualms about returning to the scene of the crime. Perhaps because the plethora of positive memories of the tavern outweighed the terror of that night. Perhaps because Vallyn would, without a doubt, be hyper vigilant and eager to let blood flow from any one who so much as looked at Deming the wrong way. Whatever it was,

Firebrand's remained one of Deming's happy places. A celebratory night out sounded wonderful. Maybe they could cut the sharp pine of the gin and tonics with a glass of sparkling wine afterwards.

Deming walked back around the work table and yelled out in surprise as she tripped on the lip of a tile quickly followed by a rapid firing of swears as her knee then elbow slammed into the hard ground. Pain lanced up her body, the sharp, tingling sensation seemingly ricocheting through the very marrow of her bones.

She shifted to a sitting position, pulling her leg to her chest and massaging circles into the hurt knee. She stretched her jaw and shook her head. How did the shock of the impact reach her teeth?

Colette rushed to her. "Oh my gods, Deming are you okay?"

"Yeah, I'm—"

Her words cut off as she took in the sight before her. She cocked her head to the side, squinting her eyes and forgetting any remnants of pain.

"What is that?"

"What are you talking about? It's a slab of tile. Poorly laid, apparently. You sure you're okay?"

Deming ignored the question. She pulled herself over to the tile and leaned down so she was nearly eye level with the ground. So close she could feel the chill of the tile pressing against her cheek.

"It's not just poorly laid," She said quietly. "It's not secured at all." Deming stood abruptly. "Help me move this."

"It's heavy." Colette's nose crinkled. "And dirty."

"We just cleaned this entire room from top to bottom, Colette. This is as clean as this tile is going to be."

Her cousin grumbled a few more soft protests but ultimately relented, brushing swaths of curled red hair over her shoulder and leaning down to lend a hand.

The tile, while cut quite large, turned out to be far lighter than either of them expected. The trickiest part of moving the slab had been finding a large enough lip to squeeze their fingers under. Once they had purchase on the tile it shifted across the floor with ease, revealing, to Deming's utter delight, an incredibly small, incredibly dark tunnel leading into the bowels of the castle. A rickety ladder was attached precariously to one side.

"A secret tunnel!" Deming nearly squealed. "Vallyn!" She called to the guard, who was stationed outside the apothecary. "You're going to want to see this."

Dark skin and brilliant white hair appeared from beyond the double doors instantly. Vallyn surveyed the two women before her, the shifted tile, and the ladder leading into darkness and subsequently hissed out a string of words so vulgar that Colette's eyes widened in embarrassment.

"Was that necessary?" Colette chided.

"Yes. What in Kielle's name is this?"

"An adventure!" Deming piped in. "Come on, let's go."

Vallyn was in front of Deming before she could move a muscle towards the secret passageway. "Absolutely not. We need to report this to the High Steward."

"We can report it to him after we explore. He won't mind, right, Colette?"

The red head shifted from foot to foot. "I don't know. Normally, no. But I think the attempt on your life really got to him. He was wracked with guilt over that. I don't think he would want you taking the risk."

Deming bit her lip. Shifted her weight from one foot to the other. "Fine."

The pair of women in front of her both relaxed, thankful she wasn't pushing the issue, and turned to leave the apothecary.

Deming waited with bated breath, sure they wouldn't make it far enough away for her to execute the impulsive decision she had just made, then sighed in relief when they both made it to the far end of the room.

"Tell uncle I say hello," she said and swung herself down into the tunnel to nowhere.

CHAPTER NINETEEN

SHOUTS OF PROTESTS AND frustration from the two women went in one ear and out the other as she hauled herself down the ladder, cursing herself for wearing a skirt today. Riding leathers would have been much more appropriate, but how was she supposed to know that she would be plunging into unknown darkness when she woke up this morning?

The shaft was small, barely enough room for an adult. Deming's shoulder's brushed the damp wall occasionally as she stepped down, rung by rung, unidentifiable slime slowly coating her sleeves one layer at a time.

To Deming's surprise, the scent wasn't unbearable. There was a general blanket of must, similar to how the dungeons smelt, but weaving in and out of that were hints of clove and lemongrass. Something vaguely medicinal hung heavier in the air the further down she traversed.

Above, she heard angry footfalls and incessant muttering. Vallyn was following her.

To be expected. Deming hadn't been naive enough to think the guard would let her go in alone, she merely hoped to distract her enough so that she could slip down the ladder.

Where all this spontaneity was coming from, she couldn't say.

Far quicker than she expected, a tall ceiling opened up around her as her foot touched the floor.

She spun from the ladder and took in the cavernous room before her.

Unlike any other room in the castle, the walls in here were roughly hewn. It looked like they were walls of a cave deep in the Telaciens, not walls of a secret room underneath the floors of Reynes Castle.

Shelves and bookcases filled the outer edges of the space. Glass containers in all shapes and sizes were stacked on the racks. A multitude of contents filled them. Liquids ranging from crystal clear to opaque and hazy. Bundles of grasses and flowers. There was even a smattering of vials full of what looked like blood, dried flecks crusting the cork stoppers. A huge tapestry of Arsaela hung on the far wall.

And bones. Everywhere there was space, bones.

Bones so small and hollow they looked as if simply breathing on them would turn them to dust. Bones so thick and tall that Deming racked her brain to think of an animal alive whose body would house them and came up short. There was more than one jar of bones that looked eerily like they came from human fingers.

Realization hit her like a sack of bricks. With the exception of bones in excess, it was a near replica of the apothecary above them.

What was this space? Who had used it? It didn't appear to be in use. Dust coated the table and clung to the parchment filled shelves. Yellowed plants hung limply from pots of dry soil.

Mouth agape and still as a statue was how Vallyn found her when the Captain of the Guard's boots landed solidly on the floor.

"You are a pest." Her voice betrayed the rage roiling beneath the surface of her skin. "Did you think for a single moment about the consequences that could have come from jumping into an unknown, unsanctioned, clearly nefarious hole in the ground? In the current political climate? It is highly possible this is where whoever is behind the fog or the attack on your life or both has been hiding out, evading capture. Did you think at all about your safety? The Reynes-Elyachar line? The future of the Queendom of Laey? You have no heir, Deming."

"No one is using this space. It's probably leftover from when Khalil was alive. Extra storage or something." For the first time since prying open the tile Deming felt the excitement ebbing away and a hint of shame slithering in to take its place. She tried to spin the sequence of events that led her here positively. "Someone needed to look into the passage. Why not me? I'm taking an active role in protecting Laey, as a queen should."

"Queens don't throw themselves into harms way. Queens are not impulsive. You can't even *be* queen if you're dead," Vallyn snarled.

Deming had nothing to say to that so she kept her mouth closed, an apology bubbling to her lips and then melting away just as fast.

Vallyn shouldered past her and completed a quick sweep on the room. Any immediate danger was deemed nonexistent. The guard returned to the ladder, peering up towards where they came suspiciously and crossing her arms. "Well," she said, eyeing Deming, "we're here. You might as well look around. You have a quarter hour before I'm dragging your petulant royal ass up this ladder."

Deming tucked a white lock of hair behind her ear and began a slow stroll of the room. It really was a near identical copy to what the above apothecary used to be in its prime. There was a not inconsequential part of her that was concerned at the prominence of bones. In all her time sitting and learning from Khalil and his apprentices, they rarely touched bone.

Animal pelts, yes. Blood, often. But bones? Only on extraordinarily rare occasions had she seen Miriam's brother deal in the ashy white, morbid object.

She ran a hand absentmindedly on the table in the center of the room, its surface smoothed with time and touch, and came to a stop in front of a stack of papers laying haphazardly on top of it.

Rifling through the pages proved relatively unfruitful. They were almost entirely comprised of lists of ingredients and various methods for creating tinctures, most of which Deming herself had used and even made on occasion.

She lifted the giant tapestry of Arsaela along the wall thrice, hoping desperately that a secret passage would magically appear there every time she pulled its weight to the side. All that ever stared back at her was stone.

She moved on to the second to last bookshelf. A thick tome about fire magic rested at eye level.

Her finger tip paused on the book directly below it.

The leather spine was soft with wear. What had once been an embossed title was worn so much that only a few letters remained readable.

She pulled the book from the shelf and examined the cover. Like the spine, the title was illegible. She flipped through a few pages. Most were filled with detailed drawings of what looked like anatomy, both human and animal. A few held drawings of mechanisms that Deming had never seen before. Notes were scribbled down in any empty space in penmanship that was, to put it generously, chaotic.

"What's that?"

"I'm not sure. A notebook of Khalil's most likely." Deming shifted slightly so the Captain of the Guard could look over her shoulder as she flipped through the pages. She stopped on another foreign diagram. A long cylindrical object was drawn front and center. A sharp needle protruded from one end while a rod with what looked like a hook extended from the other. "Most of it is familiar. But these things? Have you ever seen this?"

The gold clasps in Vallyn's hair tinkled together softly as she shook her head. "No, I haven't. Bring that with you."

Guards and court members and royal blood alike had all scoured the hidden, second apothecary since its discovery. Outside of a curious amount of foreign substances and the comically large stash of bones, however, nothing of note had turned up. For all intents and purposes, it appeared to be a simple center for healing and potion making.

No one had known what to make of Khalil's notebook, but Miriam pointed out he was always working on something odd. She had taken the notebook to her room to study further.

Unfortunately, none of this did anything to mitigate Deming's current situation.

Deming expected to get yelled at for her actions, but the verbal assault that her uncle was in the midst of raging through was unexpected.

She had resolved to sit through the entire speech, but as it dragged on she found herself slipping inward, focusing on her breathing, picking at the threads of her skirt, anything but facing the brutality of her uncles words.

It seemed impossible, the thin line of expectations she was meant to walk. Don't shirk responsibilities but don't ask to ride out into the fog. Don't be quiet but don't be argumentative. Don't let life slip by but don't take action without consulting others.

She balled her fists together then flexed her hands.

Her uncle wanted her to step up and be queen but only if it looked like his version of ruling. What if Deming wanted to be a different type of ruler? How was she supposed to figure out what kind of queen she wanted to be if she wasn't allowed to make mistakes? To try?

She almost wished whatever seed of purpose had taken root in her would die.

It was easier before, when she didn't care.

Vallyn occasionally caught her eye, her expression looking slightly empathetic but mostly like she was trying to say I told you so.

Dresden abruptly stopped pacing. He sighed heavily, rubbed his temples, and turned to fully face Deming. "Do you understand what you've put at risk?"

"Yes." Short, meek answers were all she had dared to give during this conversation.

"I don't like to yell."

"I know."

"I was happy to see you start showing some interest in ruling. An interest in helping the queendom. But this..." He slumped into the chair across from her. "This kind of impulsivity is not conducive to someone sitting on a throne."

He looked at her like he expected her to say something, but what was there to say? The small part of her that still felt that excited spark from leaping into the shaft wanted to point out that the second apothecary was clearly unused, and had been so for years. A decade, if her hunch that it was last used by Khalil was right. She was never in any real danger.

The logical side of her, however, knew now was not the time to bring that up.

If her uncle wanted her to play the part of demure princess, if he wanted her to attend council but not enter the fray of chaos surrounding the city, then she could pretend. She would be quiet and soft spoken. Attentive but not disruptive.

She would not quell whatever ember of passion had been lit within her. It was the only part of her that felt like her mother. She would simply pursue it off the record. Vallyn might be difficult to evade, but she could manage.

She would figure out a way to help Arsaela without asking for permission from her uncle.

It was clear that he would not support her methods.

She was to sit still, look pretty, and apologize.

So, with the best rendition of repentance she could muster to her face, that is what she did.

CHAPTER TWENTY

DEMING RELEASED HER BOTTOM lip from her teeth, relishing the remains of sharp pain as they eddied away. Fighting the urge to reclaim her bottom lip, if only to feel something to distract her from the weight of the last few days, she focused on the journal in front of her.

Nothing.

Not one helpful bit of information.

Same as the last journal she read through, same as the journal before that.

She and Vallyn had holed up in an alcove of the library after dinner, once more looking for anything that might help shed light on how or why the fog acted the way it did. It had been hours. Her patience was wearing thin, her eyelids hung heavy. It seemed about time to call it quits for the evening.

"Vallyn?"

"Mhm?" The Captain of the Guard did not look up from the large tome she was analyzing.

Deming closed her journal and leaned to peer over her shoulder. "What are you looking at now?"

"A history of Arsaela." The brittle pages rustled as she flipped to a new chapter. An expansive map of the city sprawled across the page.

"Anything helpful? I think I'd like to turn in soon."

Vallyn leaned back in her chair, shrugging but not taking her eyes off the map. "Helpful? No, not really. Interesting, though." She brushed a finger across the page. "Arsaela is such an old city, it has such a rich history. Did you know the roads of the city have been rebuilt multiple times?"

Deming shook her head.

"I didn't either. Each version is layered atop the one before, almost maze-like."

The comment unlocked something deep with Deming, a key she didn't know she needed. She whipped her head to the Captain of the Guard, eyes bright with tentative hope. "Say that again."

Vallyn cocked her head, tearing her eyes away from the open pages. "What?"

Deming's heart pounded in her chest. "What you just said, about Arsaela and the roads. Say it again."

Vallyn's forehead was wrinkled in confusion, but she obeyed. "Arsaela is one of the oldest cities on the continent. It's been rebuilt over and over again. Each rebuild added another..." Her voice trailed off as Deming completed the sentence.

"Layer, like a maze." Deming balled her fists tightly, trying and failing to restrain her excitement. "The map from the saddlebag. It's an overlay of the different versions of Arsaela."

The pause that filled the air was quiet and thick with realization. Only for a moment.

"We need to get to the archives," Vallyn rushed out at the same time that Deming abruptly stood and began running out of the library.

She could feel her heartbeat in her fingertips, in her toes. The blood rushing through her veins was a roaring river too loud to ignore as Deming ran through the castle then the gardens.

With each footfall she felt more and more sure she was right.

Vallyn followed close on her heels as the two women burst through the Temple doors and whipped around to find the first priestess they could.

"Hey!" Deming yelled, waving her hand wildly at a waif-like girl with long brown hair who had just disappeared around a corner. "Excuse me!"

The priestess popped her head back around the corner, confusion flickering across her plain face at the sight of the princess and Captain of the Guard breathing heavily in the entrance of the Temple at this late hour.

"Yes?" Her voice was so soft it barely carried across the room.

"We need all historical maps of Arsaela, immediately." Deming knew she must look unkempt. Her breathing was erratic from energy and sprinting through the castle. Her hair was a mess, tangled and wild.

Nevertheless, the priestess nodded to her princess and ducked once more behind the corner.

The minutes she was in the archives felt like weeks.

When she finally returned, Deming barely had the wherewithal to mutter her thanks before kneeling on the cool stone and spreading out each one in a flurry of limbs and huffed breath like a mad woman.

She pulled her crumpled copy of the map from the saddlebag out and placed it directly in the middle, smoothing out the edges and only leaning away from the piles of parchment when everything was laid out before her.

She felt Vallyn kneel beside her, but neither woman said anything as both sets of eyes frantically roamed the information in front of them for any sort of connection.

"There!" Deming's exclamation was so loud she covered her mouth instinctively, though one hand remained outstretched, pointing to one of the newer, crisper renditions of Arsaela.

She lifted the map away from the floor and pulled it into her lap. Its edges crinkled as they settled on her thighs.

"See?" She traced a long, winding road on the map in her lap, then went directly to the map Nikita had brought them. The line there matched exactly. Every curve mimicked with painstaking accuracy.

Deming relaxed onto her heels, jaw hanging open in awe. Every muscle in her body loosened as a wave of relief and pride crashed into her.

She was right.

She reveled in the feeling for only a second before hunching back over the maps with renewed vigor to figure out which crossroads the enigmatic star was drawn between.

Chapter Twenty-One

Deming laid awake, listening to the soft, sleepy snuffles of Hollis and the rhythmic breathing of the man beside her, and contemplated how to get away without waking either of them.

Finding Paris slumped against her door in the middle of the night and subsequently asking to sleep with her had been a slight wrinkle in Deming's plans.

She could have turned him away, but she didn't want to see the hurt that would certainly flash in his eyes if she said she would rather sleep alone. He had been woken, as many had, from the commotion Deming caused upon returning to the castle. She had dragged every council member from their beds to show her discovery, and had not been quiet as she did so.

Paris heard secondhand about the reason for the nighttime disruption, and had come to her room to wait for her return even as the evening hours turned long and cold.

He looked so much like home when he smiled at her as she arrived back to her quarters. She missed the comfort of a warm body in her bed, so she said yes.

The coziness of being beneath blankets with Paris was slowly diminishing though as the room began to lighten, minute after minute, with the approaching dawn.

A dawn that would bring six palace guards leaving to investigate the starred location on the map.

A dawn that would see Deming triumphantly sneak off her balcony and follow said guards into the city.

From the moment she and Vallyn had deduced where the star was located in the current layout of Arsaela and presented their findings to council, she knew her uncle wouldn't have allowed her to go. He hadn't allowed her to explore the fog. He had chastised her for exploring the hidden apothecary. He certainly wasn't going to willingly send her into the clutches of someone who wanted her dead.

So she hadn't even asked.

The moment Dresden had declared his intent to send palace guards to investigate the location, Deming got to scheming.

She didn't know what kind of queen she wanted to be, but listening to the kernel of fire in her gut urging her to do something, anything, meant that she didn't want to sit around the castle waiting for others to fix her queendom's problems for her.

Perhaps this wasn't how queens were supposed to act.

Perhaps that was a good thing.

Ever so slowly, she shifted her weight to the edge of the bed. The frame creaked and she froze.

Paris stretched his legs and rolled over, burying his face into the pillow and draping a hand over his side of the bed. Hollis opened her eyes, but merely yawned before tucking her nose back into the crook of her overlapped paws.

Deming let out a quiet sigh of relief. She placed her feet on the chilled floor and stood, careful to take pressure off the bed slowly so as not to disturb Paris or the dog further, then padded on bare feet over to her wardrobe.

Stealthier than she'd done anything in her entire life, Deming dressed. Plain clothes so as not to attract unwanted attention, but warm and thick. The boots she chose were lined with rabbit fur and laced halfway up her calves. The cloak was dense and black, with an overly large hood that settled in loose waves of fabric on her shoulders when she threw it over her telltale hair.

She had gotten all the way to the balcony doors in absolute silence when a voice from the bed sounded, groggy with sleep.

"What are you doing?"

The curse that left her lips was breathy and quiet.

She turned, placing what she hoped was a believable smile on her face. "Just for a walk. With Hollis." She added in a panic.

Hollis picked her head up at the sound of her voice.

It was the wrong thing to say. Paris sat up in bed, the downy comforter and silken sheets falling off his bare chest and pooling around his hips. "And you were planning on leaving through the balcony?"

Her mind spun in circles trying to grasp any thread of an excuse but it was too late. Her delay in answering cemented her lie.

"Deming," Paris's head fell into his hands, "we talked about this."

Yes, they had. At length. Until Deming had a headache and begged to go to sleep.

"I need to do this."

He lifted his head. Confusion and worry and something close to anger clouded his eyes. "What has gotten into you lately? Throwing yourself into danger?"

"Quiet," Deming hissed. "Vallyn will hear."

"Good! I hope she does! You're being so irrational. You throw yourself down a shaft to nowhere. You were lucky that turned out to be nothing." His stare grew cold as he went on. "You seem to seek out the Fae prince. Offering to give him a tour of the grounds? Come on Deming. And now you're actually trying to throw Vallyn off your trail and wander into the city alone? Helpless? With a killer on the loose who has a vendetta against you specifically?"

He threw his arms up and scoffed. His hands hit the bed with a sad thump.

"I need to do something to help my people. If the council won't let me leave, I'll do it on my own."

"You can help from inside the castle."

"I don't want to sit in council meetings doing nothing!" She broke her own request and raised her voice. How could he not see that this change in her was good? That she was taking control of her life? That she was doing something meaningful?

Deming closed her eyes. Bit her lip. Then lifted her head to meet Paris's gaze. "You can either come with me or go back to bed."

"If you think I'm doing either of those things then you don't know me very well."

"Well, if you don't think I'm leaving out that window with or without your permission then you don't know me very well."

His shoulder dropped. He leaned back against the headboard. After a long, quiet moment he said, "I know you better than anyone."

"Not anymore, apparently."

She didn't wait to see the hurt on his face before opening the balcony door, lifting herself over the edge of the railing, and shimmying down the thick, ancient vines.

Wildflower Lane, Deming decided, gagging as she nudged what seemed to be the rotting carcass of a rat away with the toe of her boot, was not a place she wanted to spend more time in after this mess was sorted out.

An hour had passed since she successfully snuck out of the castle. Her hands were a mess of scrapes and bloodied skin thanks to the thorns on the vines that scaled the wall outside her room. That was a fun surprise. But she had made it out all the same.

Having followed the palace guards from a safe distance as they meandered through the city, she was now finally trudging through the street they had deciphered housed the eight pointed star from the map. The street whose whimsically bright name egregiously led Deming astray with what to expect.

There were no wildflowers to be found anywhere.

No greenery at all or even living things, in fact, save for a handful of residents jumping into apartments and bolting the door to avoid the procession of royal guards at all costs.

Just rat corpses and yowling street cats with yellow eyes darting in and out of the fog that eddied in corners and alleyways.

Deming wondered off handedly how many of the dodgy-eyed men shifting in the shadows had committed crimes against the crown.

From behind the heir a husky voice said, "Petty theft is the most common offense in this district."

Her pulse jumped to her throat and Deming unsuccessfully stifled a scream as she pressed herself against the nearest wall.

Her heart slammed in her chest and she whipped her head to see the white-haired Captain of the Guard standing in the middle of the street, three paces back from her, looking very, very unamused.

"What the fuck, Vallyn." Her words came out jittery and high pitched.

"I should ask you the same thing."

Deming opened her mouth to respond but Vallyn cut her off.

"Save it. We're here now. Keep walking and don't touch anything. If I say stop, you stop. If I say leave, you leave. I am not messing around with your safety. Understood?"

Deming nodded. She peeled herself off the wall and willed her heartbeat to slow before continuing down the road.

Both women watched their step, careful to avoid any mangy animals, alive or otherwise.

Sooner than she expected they were at the address she clutched tightly in her palm.

"Apartments?"

The palace guards were already searching the surrounding streets for anything out of the ordinary when Deming and Vallyn stopped across the street from the building.

"What were you expecting?"

Deming shrugged. "I don't know. Something more interesting, I guess."

"More interesting than the living quarters of the person behind a large-scale magical atrocity and an attempted murder?"

"Well, when you put it that way."

A light winked out in one of the windows higher up.

"Was it smart to bring such a show of force?" Deming asked. "One look at the armed guards circling the place like wolves, forget the fact they bare the royal crest, and whoever we're looking for will bolt."

Vallyn shook her head. "I told the High Steward the same thing but he was insistent."

Deming pursed her lips.

Just then, a tremendous crash followed by shouting echoed from around the corner.

Before Deming had a chance to even look towards the direction of the crash, Vallyn shoved her into a nook around the corner and pressed a dagger into her palm. "Do not leave this location."

"I can hold my own!" Deming pulled against Vallyn's grip on her arm, her own grip tightening on the weapon.

Vallyn leaned in close, intensity burning in her eyes. "You cannot. You've been training for a handful of weeks. This was the deal. Stay, or I will knock you out and carry you back to the castle. Use that dagger as a last resort only."

Deming wrenched her arm free. "Fine."

Before the word finished leaving her mouth Vallyn bolted towards the sound of clashing swords.

Deming found it near impossible to stand still. Adrenaline coursed through her veins. Her twitchy, high-alert state was the only reason she was able to leap out of the way with cat like reflexes when a body launched itself from the second story window of the building across the street. Glass shattered into a thousand glistening shards and the person rolled into a crouch right where Deming had been standing moments before.

A scarf was wrapped tightly around the person's head, obscuring any hair and facial features other than dark, near black eyes.

They burst into a sprint, lowering their shoulder and connecting with Deming so painfully hard the wind was knocked out of her before she even hit the ground.

Gasping for breath, she scrambled to her knees, trying and failing to find the dagger she had let go upon contact.

There! She lunged for the hilt and raised her arm to throw, still half laying on the ground, when she saw a guard apprehend the assailant by tackling the shrouded person around the waist. They collapsed into a pile of flailing limbs and desperate screams. The muffled voice behind the scarf sounded like a woman.

Instantly, two other guards appeared and within only seconds the entire company that had left the castle was encircling the pair, ensuring the woman was quickly bound and had no chance at escape.

Deming lowered the dagger and shifted so her hip was resting on the rough cobblestones rather than her knees, sighing in equal parts exasperation and disappointment.

Vallyn appeared and offered a hand, pulling Deming up and scanning her body for injuries. "What was that about you holding your own?"

Chapter Twenty-Two

Deming took a deep pull of the stale air. Floral notes, predominantly rose and lily, could be picked up, if only faintly, thanks to the wilted bouquet sitting atop the tall, six drawer dresser threatening to fall over in the corner of the room. Petals and pollen were scattered across the wood, some had made their way to the floor as well. Candles with wicks in various states of usability were perched on nearly every possible surface, though the windowsill held the bulk of them.

Deming was fairly certain no one in the castle had remembered this particular room existed until yesterday morning. She supposed that was bound to happen from time to time with a castle as large as this one.

After the woman had launched herself from the two story building and been subsequently restrained, she was immediately brought to the dungeons where she awaited interrogation and then trial. So far, the only information the guards had been able to pull from her were filthy curses, spittle, and a name.

Sasha.

The belongings of her incredibly cramped apartment were brought up hours later and dumped into the nearest available room. Dresden and Deming were taking a first pass at examining the contents, which were mostly comprised of an alarming amount of notes scrawled in messy penmanship and books that no rule-abiding citizen would have the wherewithal to even know existed.

Deming turned to her uncle. "What do you have there?"

"Looks like a record of her comings and goings. Nothing particularly damning, but I would be very interested to see where these meeting locations are and who frequents them." Dresden looked to Vallyn, handing the notebooks to her. "Post one of our own at every location listed here. Have them report back with names and associates."

"Yes, High Steward." Vallyn tucked the book into the folds of her jacket and dipped out of the room, thankful to have something to do besides observe the two royals.

It was easy to be overwhelmed with the extent of clutter and literature that occupied most of the room. Deming chose not to focus on how much needed to be reviewed. Stacks and stacks and stacks of volumes pulled from sanctioned libraries, royal stampings on their spine, and volumes bound in secret, notable by their lack of title or general ominous aura, covered any floor space that wasn't necessary to walk.

She picked a towering stack of text at random and selected the top most notebook.

The slight, soft-covered novel she picked up first was bound in dark blue, so dark she thought it was black at first glance. Given its size, Deming assumed it was another schedule keeper, like the one Dresden had handed off to Vallyn. As she flicked through the brittle pages, however, it became increasingly obvious that it was a diary of torture techniques.

Deming grimaced and closed the book. Nausea rolled in her gut. "She certainly had dark taste in reading material." Dresden didn't look up from her stack. "Torture. Lots of it."

"I suppose that is to be expected. One doesn't have resentment build up for years, culminating in an attempted kidnapping and magical ensnarement of an entire city, without delving into the sinister arts of getting people to do and say what they want."

Deming's mind turned a thought over and over like a stone in the waves before voicing it. "What are the crown's policies on—"

Dresden cut her off before the question came to fruition, the older man knowing exactly where his ward was heading. "We do not use torture techniques." He folded the worn book he was flipping through over one hand and turned to meet Deming's eyes. "We have had a period of unprecedented peace, this is true, but even if we were at war I would not fall to such levels of degradation. Even when you are only giving the order and not wielding the knife, harming another human in that way does as much emotional damage to you as it does physical damage to the victim."

Deming nodded. The violence in Nikita's eyes as he slammed her attacker into the wall flashed before her eyes. Blood stains dotted her vision like stars in the night. She wondered how scarred Nikita's soul was.

That was protection, though, not torture. Right?

She shook the thought away. Nikita had no place in her mind when the abundance of evidence piling up before her demanded her time and energy.

She moved to sit on the bed, leaning back into the flat pillow that did nothing to cushion her back from the metal headboard, and pulled what was less of a book and more a collection of paper bound by frayed string from the middle of a short stack on the dresser. It was surprisingly thick for something so unofficial.

It appeared to be a collection of dates and short descriptions of events. Wanting to look at the most recent entries, she flipped to the last page. No names were written down, but as Deming combed through the notes a chill crept up her spine. Each entry became more and more achingly familiar as she realized what this was.

A record of her movements in the city.

Every movement.

Every Firebrand's visit. Every outing to the shopping district. Every ride on Quinn through the countryside. Notations in the wings of the pages highlighted her favorite haunts, times and days she was more likely to be in one place or another. Even the details of what she purchased were present. The perfume she preferred. How often she got scones or pastries. The drinks she ordered at bars and how long she nursed different types of alcohol.

She stopped reading each word and skimmed the dates until she reached the end of the horrifyingly thick collection of pages and stared, too shocked to speak, at the initial entry.

Five years ago. Five years this woman had been tracking her. A stickiness that had nothing to do with the musty air coated her skin as she broke out in sweat. Deming felt the weight of hundreds of eyes settle onto her.

This woman had been watching everything she did for years. They saw her dance with Colette and try her first sip of tavern beer. They saw her steal trinkets from street carts during the Moon Festival when she was still too young to understand the thrill of it did not outweigh the consequences. They—

Oh, gods.

They had seen her first kiss with Paris. Her first coupling with him too. Rushed and heated against an alley wall only a year ago.

Deming leaned back against the bed frame and closed her eyes. Took a deep inhale to steady her beating heart and shaking fingertips.

She returned her gaze to the page detailing her and Paris. Ran a finger gently over the text and mourned the loss of a memory she once thought was private and joyous and theirs. Then quietly tore the page out, folded it, and tucked it into her bodice.

"Dresden."

"Yes?"

"You're going to want to see this."

The High Steward paused at Deming's tone, warm eyes full of concern. He smoothed his trousers as he stood and extended a hand. Deming swung her legs over the bed and reached to place the makeshift notebook in the hands of the man before her. "They have been watching me for years."

Deming watched as Dresden flipped through the pages Sasha had devotedly written down. It was eerie, seeing the horror she knew had just been on her face spread across someone new. Like watching an echo of a memory.

"I had my doubts about her guilt, running away from the guards is not a crime in and of itself," Deming spoke softly. Dresden vocalized affirmation, not looking up from the dates and description. "But this is..."

Her uncle was too immersed in poring over the pages and pages of intimately detailed notes to ask where her sentence had trailed off to.

Deming lay as still as she could. Willing her body, at least, to be calm since her mind was unable to do so at the moment. It would have been difficult for Deming herself to write a more accurate account of her life if she had tried. They knew her better than she knew herself.

"I need to leave." Deming lifted herself off the bed and maneuvered around Dresden.

He glanced up, Deming's voice breaking the trance he had been in. "Yes," he said. "Of course. That's understandable. This is a lot to take in." He flipped the pages of Sasha's handwriting closed but did not put it back atop the dresser. With as damning of evidence as the writing there held, Deming was doubtful if he would let it out of his sight. "I will come with you. We're almost out of time anyway."

He motioned for two of the guards standing near the door to take over and work through the rest of the recovered evidence.

Any remaining strength was suddenly out of Deming's reach. She was so, so tired. It was all she could do to walk out the door and follow her uncle back to the main wing of the castle. Thankfully, he took the hint and did not attempt to converse with her as the pair made their way to where Miriam and the three other members would be waiting for them.

Council waited for no one.

Not even their bone-weary princess.

CHAPTER TWENTY-THREE

SASHA'S FORMAL TRIAL WAS going extraordinarily poorly for her.

It took little convincing to get all council members to agree to a trial. After Deming and Dresden presented the evidence they found and the remaining four members were given access to peruse her belongings on their own, it was simply a matter of scheduling time for the accused to stand trial.

Held in the Grand Ballroom, each member of council was sitting straight-backed in their chairs, every set of hands clasped stoically in their corresponding laps. Even Duke Lowell wasn't so much as twitching his mustache as the litany of evidence against the scraggly woman before them was listed off one at a time.

A few members of court who were not specifically on council were sitting on a bench across from the larger dais where Deming and the High Steward presided over the trial. Their purpose was to provide a semblance of oversight to whatever decision the council landed on. If they were unanimous, the bench could overturn the council's decision.

Colette, as a member of the royal family, was always awarded a spot on the bench during trials. Sitting alongside her today were Lord and Lady Blackwell, an older woman whose name Deming didn't remember, and, much to Deming's chagrin, Lord Dougherty.

The woman in question was currently in chains from wrists to ankles, far more than was necessary to restrain her brittle frame. She was also gagged. The gagging was not a normal occurrence at trials. The Reynes-Elyachar line had been consistent in their pursuit of fair trials and free voice for both victim and accused. However, the woman being charged had been incessantly screaming her innocence since the second she was anchored to the chair facing council, not letting up in ferocity despite multiple attempts to wrangle her into submission.

And so Vallyn had been sent to retrieve a cloth strip and bind her mouth shut.

It looked painful. Deming winced once again as she looked at the aggressive shade of red the corners of the woman's mouth had turned over the course of the afternoon. Her mind constantly fluttered back to how her own gag had felt the night she was abducted. It was distracting and confusing. She had hated the feeling of being speechless. Hated how the gag took away her voice in such a demeaning and painful way. Hated how her jaw had hurt for days afterward. It was a terrible feeling she wouldn't wish on anyone.

She knew she shouldn't feel bad for the woman being accused of murder, but here she was, cringing when the skin near the corners of Sasha's mouth split and blood began trickling down her chin.

The trial was nearing its end. The handwritten journal had been the crowning piece of evidence, but by no means was it the only red flag on her record.

After investigation into her correspondence, schedule, and history within Arsaela, it was clear that Sasha had numerous connections to the shadier aspects of the city. She had met with three drug lords in the last year, one of which was known for distributing a drug that pulled anyone who inhaled its fumes into unconsciousness for short amounts of time.

Exactly the kind of drug someone would give their henchmen in order to silence someone long enough to drag them out of a bar, tie them up, and throw them on the back of a horse.

She also had a history of penning anti-royal petitions and letters, citing a disdain for the monarchy and a belief that Laey would be better off as a republic, as some of their neighboring countries were.

The nail in the coffin was that within the book of addresses that Dresden had seen earlier were the names and known associates for the two, now long dead, men that were in the bar that night.

"We have heard the evidence brought forward against the accused," said Dresden. "Now, we will hear from the accused herself."

He nodded to Vallyn, who hissed some unintelligible threat in Sasha's ear and then untied the knotted cloth.

The first thing she did with her vocal freedom was spit, venomously, at the foot of the dais.

Murmurs of disapproval rippled through the ballroom.

On the bench, Lady Blackwell shook her head.

"I told your filthy guards when they apprehended me, I screamed it so loudly that the walls of your dungeons know the truth, and I say to you now. I am innocent of what I stand accused of."

Hatred unlike anything Deming had ever heard dripped from each syllable.

"What evidence can you provide to vouch for your innocence?" Dresden kept his tone calm, though Deming could tell by his grip on the chair he was itching to rid the ballroom of this woman who had almost succeeded in ending the royal bloodline.

"How am I supposed to provide evidence to counter what has clearly been planted?"

"Clearly planted? Tell us more."

The woman's eyes darkened. Her dark hair hung limply in greasy strands. She looked deranged. "The journal and the pin are not mine."

"You do not deny your connection to the three drug lords?"

"No," she sneered, her tone verging on condescension, "I do not deny my connection to the drug lords. I have been a mule for them for over a decade, spreading their drug of choice throughout the city. To that I will admit. But I have never plotted to overthrow the royal bloodline and I am not responsible for the attempt on her life or the fog. How could I possibly be responsible for the fog?" She added incredulously, as if she still could not believe she had found herself in this position. "I am not a mage."

"It seems there are no depths to which your connections to the underground markets in Arsaela cannot reach," Dresden pointed out. "We will find out in due time if your reach into the underbelly of the city provided you with an opportunity to cast magic. If not, well, at least we have one assailant out of our way. In regards to your claim that the journal and pin do not belong to you..." He made a show of mulling the thought over before continuing. "It is plausible that the pin was planted. But we have cross referenced the journal to numerous of your own writings, writings you have owned up to and many of which, if I may point out once more, spew vitriol about the crown."

"A replica of my handwriting. Anyone could copy it."

"That is a thin defense. It is particularly difficult work to mimic another's writing so precisely."

"So this is what a free and fair trial looks like to you, High Steward?" The title held no respect when it slipped from her mouth. She addressed Deming with her next words when Dresden did not deign her a response, the first time anyone had directly spoken to the heir during the trial. "And you, Crown Princess? This is how you think your ancestors would treat one of their people? Blind accusations and decisions about guilt clearly made before the accused even opens their mouth?"

"I would hardly call these blind accusations." Deming's voice didn't come out nearly as strong as she had intended. She cleared her throat. "If you have nothing else to offer, we are done here."

Vallyn placed the tip of her sword in between the woman's shoulder blades and guided the accused to stand.

Dresden rose as well, voice echoing throughout the high ceilinged room. "We will now vote. All in favor of acquittal via proof of innocence." The bodies in the room were so still they seemed frozen. "All in favor of conviction via proof of guilt." One by one every member of council raised their hand. Dresden turned to the bench. "Council has voted to convict the accused. Is there any member of this body who disagrees with the decision?"

No movement. Not a whisper or twitch from anyone on the bench.

"Then get her out of my sight." Dresden waved his hand flippantly. "Her sentence will be decided at a later date. The dungeons will do for now."

Vallyn led the chain-bound woman away from the ruffled council members.

The last words the mangy woman ground out as she was led from the room rattled Deming to her core and stayed with her long into the evening, keeping her from sleep.

"Death to the crown."

CHAPTER TWENTY-FOUR

EVEN THE BRITTLE PAGES of ancient text that Deming was flipping through seemed to have relaxed slightly in the wake of the trial.

Much remained to be sorted out, including the sentencing, but her uncle had promised that the deliberation for that would be swift. Unless an extenuating circumstance of irrevocable evidence in her favor surfaced soon, she would never see the light of day again.

With one crisis halfway smothered, Deming had gathered Paris and Colette early the following morning and dove headfirst into the library to research solutions to the fog with a renewed sense of purpose. She had been picking through texts periodically throughout the fall, but with winter fast approaching, the mages back at the castle, and all three known accomplices in her murder attempt dead or in the dungeons, she suddenly found herself with more time and energy to devote to lifting the magical barrier around Arsaela. Her friends had been more than happy to help, though they were less confident in their ability to be useful to the mages' efforts.

For the third time in as many hours Paris gently pleaded for respite. "Let's take a break. Everything in this text is something the mages already know." He closed the dusky blue cover of the book he had been poring over and set his quill down. The parchment he had been scribbling notes on had a few lines of copied text and associated commentary but was primarily full of jaunty sketches of the three of them. There was one particularly scandalous depiction of him dipping Deming low, her leg hiked up his thigh so far her dress pooled around her hips.

"What a wonderful use of your artistic talent. Your parents must be so proud." Upon seeing the drawing, Colette faked a gag, rolled her eyes, then burrowed deeper into the cushions of the wing backed chair she was curled up in.

Deming ignored them both. She licked a finger and flicked to the next page of her text on the history of magic.

"Seriously, Deming," He gestured to her book, "do you really think anything you find in that will be something Yesenia or Gisela don't already know? The fog is a magical malady. It only makes sense that it will be solved with magic. Which you and I don't have."

She answered without looking up. "We won't know if we don't try."

Paris pulled his fingers through his hair, ruffling the thick, blonde into a roguish mess, and mumbled something unintelligible before picking up a new book from the stack beside him.

Another hour passed before Deming reluctantly stood from her chair, twisting her back and reaching her arms to the sky as her muscles stretched and her joints released tension with a series of satisfying cracks.

She was collecting her rolls of notes to bring to the mages when the clipped, sharp sound of hooves echoed towards the alcove they had sequestered themselves in.

Deming put the parchment back down on the table and took a step towards the aisle, leaning forward to peer down it. Antlers like an elegant crown of bone filled her vision.

"Hartford, hey." Deming took a step back into the cozy nook as the Fae emissary approached. Paris stood and meandered over to Deming, wrapping his arm around her waist.

"Hello, princess. Colette, Paris." Her voice was downy soft, warm brown eyes inquisitive. She addressed Deming directly. "How are you feeling in the wake of the trial?"

"I'm sure you heard it was a volatile encounter." Hartford nodded. Paris kneaded small circles into the skin on her stomach. "It was difficult to hear how much hatred she has for the crown. But I'm relieved that she isn't spewing vitriol in the streets anymore. My uncle said the sentencing should come shortly."

"Good." Hartford reached a hand into her cloak and pulled out a small book with a black cover embossed with gold foil. "I was hoping to find you here and give you this."

Deming took the book from her outstretched hand. "What is it?"

"We traveled from Runne with little in the way of literature, but we did bring a handful of texts that we thought would bring insight to the seer's prophecy. Recollections of past wars on the continent, histories of various royal families, that sort of thing. This particular text was written by a human healer from Laey during his journeys abroad. I believe he is of importance to you?"

Any words Deming might have said were trapped in her throat. She traced the spiky signature on the inside cover and thought only of bringing this to Miriam as fast as she could.

Colette, who had stood to inspect the offering and was now peering over Paris's shoulder, said, "Khalil?" Her eyes whipped up to Hartford. "How do you have this? Khalil was the Reynes Castle apothecary for years. He died in a fire." Her last words faded out quietly, as if she was just remembering how sensitive a subject his death was.

"It was in our archives, that's all I know."

"And why are you giving this to her now?" Paris glared at the Fae, trepidation dripping from his voice. He tightened his grip on Deming's waist.

"I only just put together that the author was someone meaningful to her and her guardian. It belongs with them."

Without any further explanation, Hartford turned and retreated back down the aisle.

Only once the Fae was out of sight did Paris release his hold on Deming's waist. Even then, she had to initiate the separation, kissing his cheek before peeling herself from his side.

"I can't believe she found this." Deming looked up at Paris through long lashes. "I didn't think any of Khalil's research still existed. Anything we didn't already know of, anyway. This is incredible. Hartford is incredible."

Paris scoffed. "That's being generous. I'm sure she only did this to further her own agenda. Fae are conniving."

Deming frowned and ran a hand down his arm, entwining their hands.

"That's rather reductive," Colette said.

Paris pinched his nose and inhaled deeply before letting out a weary sigh. "I know," he murmured. "I just wish they would be more transparent about their intentions."

"Isn't wanting to give back a piece of our history enough?" Deming agreed that the Fae had been far from transparent, but they had yet to show any sort of malice or ill intent.

"No," Paris said staunchly. "Not when they showed up right when our city went to shit. You don't think it's slightly concerning that the fog appeared so soon after their supposed arrival? Which, by the way, we can't confirm the timeline of because they didn't report to the castle right away. For all we know they had been mulling about our city for months, picking up information to use against us."

"Well, I—" Deming began defending the Fae but Paris interrupted before she could get anything meaningful out.

"And what about your capture? I know we have whoever that woman is behind bars for masterminding that, but she clearly wasn't working alone. Nikita," He spat the name out as if it tasted like dirt in his mouth, "had been watching you in the bar, you said so yourself, and then he serendipitously shows up to save you? And killed two people who might sell him out? I'm telling you, it's all a ploy to get you on their side, which is a mistake. They are not to be trusted."

A lock of blonde hair had fallen out of place in his ranting. He pushed it back, emotion thick in his eyes. Anger far beyond the simple exchange of a notebook flushed his cheeks. It was as if he had mulled over every step the Fae had taken since arriving in Laey so much that his distrust became malicious and tightly wound. And for reasons Deming couldn't place, Hartford's act of kindness today snapped his patience.

"You are too quick to judge them," Deming began. "If you would only—"

"And you are too naive." Anger flared across his features. Colette made to pull him away, bring him back down to earth, but Paris rushed out words laced with hatred unlike Deming had ever heard from him. "You have avoided politics and the crown your entire life and now is the time you choose to make a stand? It's pathetic. I have done everything in my power my entire life to keep you safe and loved and protected and here you are throwing it all away for some new shiny toy you think you have the right to play with. I'm sorry I don't have gods-forsaken wings, Deming, but for the love of the Goddess you have got to start acting like a queen, not a child."

The room collapsed in on the two of them. The stacks of books beside them became an inconsequential blur. Even Colette seemed in another world. Deming knew nothing except the beat of her heart and the heavy breaths escaping Paris's lips as he delivered the final blow.

"You are sheltered. You know nothing of the world, Deming. Nothing."

Deming pulled her hand away from his, cradling her own close to her chest. Breathing was difficult. Tears welled and threatened to fall, but she steeled her nerves.

Instant regret flashed in his eyes. His next words seemed far away, as if she was hearing them under water. "Deming, I'm so sorry, I didn't mean..."

She was already moving.

Through the towering shelves of books. Through the dust motes swirling across her vision. Through the air that felt heavy with desperation.

Air, she needed air.

If she stayed inside these stone walls any longer she feared she would never claw her way out of the hole Paris's words had buried her alive in.

CHAPTER TWENTY-FIVE

MIRIAM FOUND HER IN the stables.

Deming wiped the tears from her eyes as the woman approached her with empathetic eyes.

Miriam walked up next to Deming, watching as she brushed Quintessential in slow, methodic strokes. The mare kicked a hoof, sending hay and dust motes swirling into the air. "I heard you've had an argument with Paris."

Deming nodded. Verbally responding to anything felt monumentally difficult. The swoops of the bristled comb through Quinn's short gray coat were the only thing tethering her to the world at the moment. Time and space still felt odd, as if she were far away from the castle.

"Word travels fast in Reynes Castle," Miriam continued. She grinned wryly. "The librarian said it sounded like two mountain cats brawling."

Deming hummed and offered a tight smile that she knew looked as forced as it felt. She knew Miriam meant to lighten the mood, but her heart wasn't quite ready for that.

She glanced away from Quinn and took in the empty barn. "No mountain lion here."

Miriam came closer, placing a hand on the heir and rubbing gentle circles onto Deming's shoulder. Wind whistled through the stables. "I know you would likely prefer to be alone right now," she said tentatively, "Colette told me the details of what transpired. If you'd like to talk about what Paris said to you…" She trailed off, only wanting to take what Deming was willing to give. She had always been like this, even before she stepped into the matriarchal role Deming was missing after the fire. She had always been there for Deming, always offered whatever she needed. Nothing more, nothing less. Some had skills in politics or weaponry, Miriam had skills like a healer. Her expertise lay in deep understanding and comfort.

"Not right now." All Deming could scratch out.

Miriam nodded. "You won't want to hear this, but his heart is in the right place. Delivery, not so much. We all want you safe. Paris is no exception."

"He doesn't trust my judgment." The next words wavered treacherously. "No one does."

"Oh, my love. You are finding your voice and it has been the most magical blessing to be around to see. Continue to use it and soon others will follow your lead." She pressed a kiss onto Deming's forehead, then stepped away. "Come, my love. There is the unfortunate matter of council. Midwinter and its festival is to be discussed this afternoon."

Deming sighed and squeezed her eyes shut tight in an attempt to force the tears back inside her. She balled her fists and let her fingernails dig in deep. The sharp pain brought clarity back to her mind and quelled enough of the panic that she was able to turn around and face Miriam.

She steeled her nerves and put the wild emotions roiling inside her into a tight box and shoved it deep down. "You're right. Let's go."

It was a massive effort to focus on anything anyone was saying.

For the third time in as many minutes, Deming found her mind drifting back to the cruel, icy words that Paris had thrown at her. She snapped herself out of the memory and returned her proper attention to her uncle.

"I know many of us are eagerly anticipating the decision regarding the Midwinter festival. I would like to begin the planning process, as we are only a month out from Midwinter and it will take more time than usual to gather the necessary supplies given our situation."

Rumbles of discontent began rippling throughout the room, at odds with the budding interest that bloomed in Deming's chest, a star against the darkness Paris's words had cast on her. There had been a large part of her that expected Midwinter to be canceled, even with Sasha's arrest.

No one spoke initially, then Duke Lowell took up his usual mantle of confrontation. "Do you believe hosting the festival is appropriate, given the circumstances we have found ourselves in?"

"Clearly I believe it is appropriate, as I have just given the directive to begin planning." The High Steward waited for the remaining protests that were sure to follow.

Lowell continued, face reddening at the dismissal, which was far more direct than Dresden usually got. "With respect, High Steward,

I am not confident in our ability to host the event with the proper measures to keep Princess Deming safe."

An appeal to her well-being, that was new.

"I agree, the safety of our heir is the top priority. However, I believe she is and will continue to be well protected thanks to Vallyn, wouldn't you agree, Deming?" Dresden turned to his niece, warm eyes sparkling and dark hair weaving in and out of the crown sitting atop his head, not a strand out of place.

"Yes," Deming agreed, "I have found Vallyn to be far more than necessary to keep me safe." She then turned to address the room as a whole. "Besides, I believe the city is in need of some levity. This season has been unprecedented in its challenges. Our people need to feel hope and joy once more, even if only for a night."

"I couldn't have said it better myself," Dresden said. "I have already begun preparing the royal guard for the event. Not a single soldier will be unused and there will be limitations on where myself, Deming, and other members of this council will be allowed to wander."

Deming grimaced at that particular revelation... but a limited festival was better than no festival at all, she supposed.

The rest of council concluded shortly, which was a blessing since she was unable to concentrate on anyone speaking for long enough to hold a conversation.

There was a moment where the idea of all the fabric and jewels and shoes that would be necessary for the ball tugged at her heartstrings, but the flicker of joy was fleeting. No amount of beautiful things could distract her from the fact that her relationship was crumbling around her.

She felt as though she were a dress in need of mending, something discarded and old. Something coming apart at the seams.

CHAPTER TWENTY-SIX

DAWN BEGAN CREEPING INTO the room, as much as it could through the fog anyway. The delicate morning rays of the sun had not been visible in months, but their light persevered nonetheless. It had begun to seep into the air and break apart the darkness of night. Through the haze, one could imagine the blackness of night easing into navy, melting into pink and yellow and rich crimson.

Deming cringed away from the light and curled deeper into the duvet, only to find the warmth emanating from Colette stifling rather than comforting, as it had been all night.

She had been unable to fall asleep last night after her earlier fight with Paris. Every time she closed her eyes, her mind filled with everything she and Paris had done in her bed, spinning memories like silk as soft as his touch had been on her skin. And just as quickly, his words came crashing in, chasing away any fondness and leaving her wracked with sobs. The ricocheting back and forth felt chaotic enough to drive her mad.

So after failing to face the evening alone, she walked solemnly through the castle in her nightgown, Vallyn trailing after, to Colette's apartments. Colette took one look at her friend's haggard appearance and pulled her inside. The pair sipped chamomile tea in silence and then cuddled into each other's warmth until the time dipped from late night to early morning.

Colette's heavy breathing had signaled her sleep hours ago, but Deming had found no such solace. She had relegated herself to a sleepless night, and had more than once found herself debating whether she preferred this torturous insomnia or her nightmares. There was a certain comfort in knowing the pain that awaited you.

Realizing she had scraped as much relief as she could from the confines of her friend's bed, Deming crawled out from under the thick bedding, careful not to disturb Colette, and padded out the door. To her pleasant surprise, the guard who took Vallyn's night shift was slumped over an armchair, uncharacteristically having fallen asleep on duty. She had the early morning free of a chaperone, it seemed.

She scribbled a quick note thanking Colette and apologizing to the on duty guard for not waking her, then ducked into the quiet hallway.

The corridors of the castle were utterly still. There were surely cooks and kitchen maids beginning preparations for breakfast dough and pastries, but she was far away from that wing of the castle and found that the quiet of morning blanketed her with each step, like dew on grass.

She passed by an arched door that led to the gardens and paused to consider the cold for only a moment before embracing the sharp bite of winter air. There would be the season's first snowfall soon, she was sure of it.

She wandered through the gardens, void of their usual jubilant life, and settled down on an iron chair nestled deep within the maze of pathways.

The steel was hard and cold as ice and Deming leaned fully into it. The sting of discomfort banished the clouds in her mind, leaving only the very real fog visible in front of her. She closed her eyes and that, too, disappeared for a moment.

"Everything will be alright," she whispered, breathing in the cold air so deep it burned her lungs then exhaling and opening her eyes to see the cloud of warm breath that hung in front of her.

"Seems a bit cold for a nightgown, no?"

Deming jerked forward and twisted in the chair to find the owner of that velvety soft voice.

Nikita touched down behind her. She had turned around just in time to see the expansive length of his wings beat one last time before folding themselves neatly behind his shoulder blades, iridescent feathers winking between black and something somehow deeper as they shifted.

He trailed a hand along her back, an overly familiar gesture that she was in too much shock to protest, as he walked around her to the chair opposite her.

Deming shivered.

"You look like a trout," Nikita said, suppressing a grin.

She snapped her mouth closed.

He crossed one leg over the other, resting a hand on his upturned knee, and leaned casually into the back of the chair. A tight fitting royal blue shirt was tucked into equally tight fitting black trousers. A small but ornate dagger sparkling with emeralds hung by its hilt from his belt, the only visible weapon. Whatever meager sunrise the fog let through shone behind him, painting the illumination of a crown atop his loose curls. Even here, in the winter gardens of a human castle thousands of miles from his realm, he looked the picture of immortal royalty.

Her wispy nightgown was suddenly the only thing she could think about. She discreetly pulled at it and crossed her arms to cover her chest, knowing full well what the chilled air would be exposing.

He chuckled and tossed a soft shawl at her. "Here."

So much for being discreet.

She accepted it without comment, cocooning herself in the soft, if a bit flimsy, fabric. Instantly the skin on her shoulders warmed.

A sigh of pleasure escaped her lips.

Nikita let the smile that bloomed across his face warm the air for only a moment before saying, "Nightmares again?"

"No, I couldn't—" Deming cut herself off. "Again? How do you know I have nightmares?"

Storm clouds flooded his gray eyes, hesitancy shrouding any other emotion. He frowned. "With a past as full of trauma as yours… death of a mother, a father. The monarchs of your queendom. I only assumed."

The casualty with which he brought up her parent's deaths felt like he plunged Deming into ice water. Everyone tiptoed around the topic so carefully with her. Even Miriam tended to pad Deming's emotions before bringing them up.

She blinked at him. It was… refreshing to have someone speak about them without preamble. Almost like the icy baths she loved. It grounded her quickly and cut through the guilt that weighed on her consciousness like a knife.

The realization was all at once surprising and familiar. Terrifying and intriguing. Much like Nikita himself.

"Everyone has trauma."

Nikita said nothing.

"Anyway, it couldn't have been a nightmare since I haven't slept at all."

"Do you want to talk about it?"

Deming considered the Fae before her.

Logically, she had no reason to share the details of her personal life with him, a relative stranger even though he had never really felt like one. There was something about him, though, the inquisitive cock of his head, the earnest line of his expression, that made her open her mouth and say, "Paris and I got in a fight."

A muscle in his neck twitched. "Oh?"

"He doesn't like you."

"He would be in the majority."

Deming chuckled softly. She hugged the shawl tighter around her shoulders, regretting her decision to venture into the cold but simultaneously not wanting to leave the conversation. Not when she finally had the male in front of her alone.

"What will you do? Once Yesenia and Gisela figure out how to lift the fog."

"You and your friends were hard at work in the library earlier, who's to say you won't be the one to figure it out."

Deming scoffed, then eyed him incredulously when she realized he was serious. "We all know the mages will be the one to break the barrier. I just keep going back to the library to assuage my own guilt at being utterly useless."

He considered her words, considered her. She couldn't read his expression. She never could. He locked so much behind those steely eyes of his. Deming imagined that if she pressed a finger to his temple all his hidden words and thoughts and schemes would burst out of him, like water from a crack in a dam.

"You underestimate yourself," he said. "You let others do it, too. Think of what you could become if you only took the leap."

"What do you think I've been trying to do since things went to shit?" She hissed. "I haven't exactly been holed up in my room."

He shrugged, unbothered by her biting tone. "Pretend all you like, but the winds are changing. You need to change too. War is coming and the arrest of that woman may not be enough to hold back what has been written in the stars. We must prepare for the worst."

What was she supposed to say to that?

She rubbed her hands together, dread coiling like a serpent in her gut. The friction did nothing to bring feeling back to her fingertips. She stood to leave and made to take the shawl off.

Nikita interrupted, hand up. "Keep it."

Deming's hand paused mid-air, gripping the shawl. She did briefly consider pulling it back over her shoulders but opted for tossing it at him instead.

He caught it easily.

He smirked before spreading his wings wide and shooting into the sky.

Deming twirled to watch him soar through the dawn to the north tower. He turned in the air to look back at her frigid form once before dipping gracefully through his open window.

The chill creeping across her skin was not from the cold.

Deming hissed as she lowered herself into the tub. The water was scalding and each inch of skin that sunk into the silky depths wailed in pain and turned a splotchy red.

When her rear finally settled at the bottom of the basin and she relaxed her shoulders enough to lean back, Deming was reminded of why she had requested the heat. It was all encompassing. Even the parts of her that remained above the water level felt the warmth. Her face was coated in steam and sweat in seconds and other than taking deep pulls of air into her lungs, nothing else penetrated her senses.

Until a gentle knock on the door pried her back to reality. Deming lazily looked to the door to find large doe eyes peering in, clearly hesitant to disrupt the princess. Which was to be expected as Deming had explicitly requested privacy for the next hour.

Deming closed her eyes again and tried to restrain her annoyance as she said, "What is it, Noreen?"

The door opened slightly, just enough for Noreen's thin frame to be exposed. "I am so sorry to disturb you, princess. There was a request for your audience..."

Deming rubbed the bridge of her nose. "I am indecent at the moment."

"Yes, princess, that is what I told him. I'm afraid he is insisting on speaking with you." Noreen fiddled with her hands. "He said it was urgent."

"Who is it that feels the need to drag me out of the one part of my day I have been looking forward to since I awoke?" No need for the handmaid to know she hadn't slept a wink.

"Paris, princess."

Deming froze. The only movement was the water gently lapping at her skin. She hadn't spoken to Paris since their fight. Could it even be called that if she said nothing in return? Though it had only been yesterday, it felt like she had lived lifetimes since she ran out of the library.

And he had the audacity to come to her bedchambers unannounced? As if they would patch things up and fall into bed together as if nothing happened?

"Send him in."

Noreen hesitated, fumbling over the command. "Send him..."

"Please, Noreen." Deming met Noreen's eyes. "You know as well as I he has seen me in far more incriminating positions. No need for decency now." Noreen blushed a bright fuchsia. "I won't be disrupting my evening for that man. If he wishes to speak with me he can do so here."

Noreen bowed and left the room.

It took only moments before his familiar frame and blonde hair graced the doorway. Paris looked calm and collected. Ever the picture of courtly composure.

Deming said nothing and remained as still as she could as he approached. Her arms were perched on either edge of the tub, one knee peaking above the water. She knew the lengths of hair that moved with the waves did little to cover her chest.

Paris walked over to the edge of the bath and dipped a finger in, skimming the surface of the water and gently caressing Deming's knee before clicking his tongue in amusement and finding a seat in the armchair.

"You don't always have to take baths in extremes, you know," he said with far too much nonchalance for Deming's liking. "Try a mild temperature sometime, you might like it."

Deming scowled, not giving him a response. He at least had the good sense to wince at that. And it seemed that her lack of response was cause enough to break whatever show he had been attempting to put on to save face.

"I... I'm sorry that was..." Paris crumpled before her as his arrogant charade fell. He slumped over himself, elbows digging into thighs, palms covering his face. She could hear nothing except the gentle water licking her skin and the sides of the tub, but if she looked closely...

She cocked her head. Yes, there it was. A nearly imperceptible shudder ran across his shoulders. Trying to stifle the evidence of tears.

A pinch of pity nipped at Deming, but she remained resolute in her silence. She cleaned beneath her fingernails and avoided looking in his direction while waiting for him to complete his thought.

After a moment, Paris sucked in a breath and righted himself. He ran a hand through his hair once, twice. Then began to speak.

"I am sorry for what I said yesterday." The words were as stoic as his face, he had done a gods-damned good job of collecting himself so quickly. "I was wrong to say all of those hurtful and untrue things to you. I was wrong to think I know anything about ruling anything, or what it must feel like to take the helm of a queendom as young as you did while mourning the loss of your parents. I am sorry for letting my anger get the better of me. You have never been unfaithful, nor given me any reason to believe you would be. I was blinded by jealousy and fear of losing you, and I will not let that happen again." He finally lifted his gaze, nothing but somber acceptance peered out. "Please, can you forgive me?"

It was difficult to breathe. The heat of the bath had turned suffocating. How could she forgive him? How could she not? They were two sides of the same coin. They had done life together for years. They were no stranger to a fight. Why did this one feel so different?

Deming let loose the breath she had been holding and lifted her eyes to meet his. Her heart sang with sadness when she saw the wetness welling in their corners. Knew how the tears would feel as they fell. Knew how the warmth of his skin would soak them up. Knew how meaningful it was that he allowed them to show their face at all.

She knew all of this just as she knew from the moment he opened his mouth he was genuine in his apology. And it broke her heart that much more as she realized that although she could accept it, this was still the end of what had been.

Deming broke her silence. "I appreciate your apology, and I forgive you for losing your temper." Just as his countenance had changed the second he spoke, hers did as well. The anger that had welled up against Paris within her melted away like a snowflake on skin. She leaned forward, shifting into a sitting position that felt less dismissive of his presence. "Though if I'm honest, I don't know that you needed to apologize at all."

"Don't be ridiculous, Deming. I was completely out of line. As my friend and partner and future queen." His head hung low again, shaking slowly in disbelief as if he was relieving the movement over and over again. The shame felt tangible, Deming could almost taste the bitterness and regret as it mixed with the rose essence of her bath water. He fixed his gaze on her once more. "No one should ever speak to you that way."

"Yes, your tone was hurtful. But the content of your anger, while not eloquent or as pointed as you probably would have liked to be, was true." Her voice broke as she stumbled over the admission that came next. "I... I am naive. I don't know what it takes to run a kitchen, much less a queendom. I have avoided my responsibilities my entire life, and in doing so might as well have been spitting on the...," she swallowed the lump in her throat, "on the grave of my parents and the legacy they built."

"Deming—"

"Stop. I don't need your pity or your false comfort. I know my faults." She took a breath to steady herself, willing the emotion stuck in her throat to loosen. "I wish you had presented them more kindly. But I know my faults."

She looked up. Her heart turned to stone as she saw the pain that had begun to brim the edges of those beautiful, wonderful, sea blue eyes of his. Deming hated what was coming next and sent a silent prayer to Selene to give her the strength to do what needed to be done.

"So," he whispered hesitantly, "does that mean you forgive me? We can go back to normal? I miss you so much, Deming. I miss us."

Deming winced. "Paris…"

Realization did not come as quickly as Deming would have hoped. Instead, confusion rippled across his face. His eyebrows furrowed in question. "What?"

"I do forgive you for the outburst," she reiterated, "and I appreciate everything you have done to keep me safe and protected and loved the past couple years."

Where the conversation was going finally dawned on Paris. Deming could see the exact moment his eyes shifted from curious to crushed. "You don't want to be with me anymore? Do you not love me?"

"It's not that simple, Paris—"

"Then make it simple!" His raised voice made the hairs on the back of Deming's neck stand up. "It's the Fae prince, isn't it? I was right, you two are fucking—"

"Paris, stop!" The exclamation came out less as a plea and more a command, to the surprise of both of them. "Do not speak to me that way. I would never dishonor either of us by going behind your back with another man. You know that as well as I do. Nikita and his delegation are a puzzle I am piecing together for our queendom, not an opportunity to make a harlot of myself and embarrass the crown."

Paris's breathing was ragged. His eyes darted frantically around the room, jumping from one thing to the next, looking everywhere but at her. "Then what… I don't…" He scrambled to find the right question to ask and finally landed on simply, "Why?"

Deming's stomach curdled as the word escaped his mouth. Why indeed. How was she supposed to put into words the last couple months? The hiccups in communication. The misaligned priorities. The shift in expectations. The slight unease that had begun creeping in whenever he was around, warning her something was off kilter. The issue wasn't that there was this grand reason for needing to separate, it was that there were a million little reasons that had been brushed aside until suddenly there was no more space to brush anything.

"I don't know, there isn't one thing to point to…"

The sigh Paris let out was full of weariness and exasperation. "Can you try? For me."

Deming bit her lip, trying to compose herself enough to explain what she hadn't fully realized until moments before. "We have known each other our entire lives. You and Colette were the only kids who didn't pull bullshit niceties to me growing up." Both Deming and Paris smiled at that, albeit limply. "I loved that. And I loved you both because of that. We were always together, always the three of us. And when my parents died—"

Deming swallowed the lump in her throat, tears pricked at the corners of her eyes. She felt one escape, and quickly wiped it away. Why was it always so gods-damned hard to talk about them after all this time?

"When my parents died we became even closer. You and Colette were the rock that allowed me to weather the storm. The only people I truly leaned on. I cried in front of you and no one else. You were safe. Comfortable. Home." She smiled softly at the memory of them huddled together underneath her covers after Silas and Samira's death. She hadn't come out of her room in days so Paris took it upon himself to shelter in place with her. He didn't leave her side for weeks. "You've been a safe space for me ever since."

Paris took the momentary pause in Deming's speech to interject. "So you're breaking up with me because I was too nice to you? That's a bit of a cliché, don't you think, Deming? I thought you had more depth to you than that."

The memory crumbled. Her smile faded. The insult was cracked like a whip, but she ignored his crassness. He was hurting. Let him take it out on her. Fine.

"No. I am not breaking up with you because you are too nice. I'm breaking up with you because nice is all we are together." She waited for her words to sink in, but Paris clearly wasn't understanding, so she continued. "Do you remember at the very beginning of autumn when the three of us were walking back from Firebrand's and I asked what I was good at? What I offered to the world?"

Paris sighed again, exasperated. "No, Deming, I don't."

"You said I was the nicest person you knew."

He lifted a hand, waving her on. "And that insulted you because…"

"It didn't insult me, not in the moment at least. I couldn't even pinpoint why that comment bothered me until our world started falling apart. These past couple months have been so hectic and so much has been thrown at me that I never expected. I always thought I hated the crown and everything that came with it. But suddenly, I was thrown into an ocean of responsibility and instead of sinking, I swam.

"Our relationship is built on comfort and ease. It's nice. But that's it. There is no depth. Neither of us push each other to be better, do better. You protected me for all those years, but at what cost? I don't want to be comfortable anymore. I want to figure out who I am. And I can't do that with you."

The clock tower rang out, breaking the silence that had pooled in the room. As the last peal echoed out, Paris stood and spoke. "Well, I'm sorry that I'm not good enough for you."

The warmth and pride that had grown in Deming's chest as she had explained herself deflated immediately. He didn't understand. "Paris, that's not—"

"Save it." He looked at her longingly and Deming could swear she saw the exact moment that he closed her out. Years and years of their lives dismissed. Panic began bubbling in her chest. He gave a curt bow. "Your Highness."

The formality broke her. A whimper escaped her lips as he strode confidently away from the sitting area. Away from her.

What had she done?

He lingered in the doorway for long enough that she almost called out to him. Then, in a voice so soft Deming wondered if she had heard it at all, Paris said, "I would rather you be sleeping with the prince. At least that would have made sense."

And then he was gone.

Each second that passed felt longer than the previous one and Deming had the disorienting feeling of waking up from a dream.

Her and Paris were over?

That couldn't possibly be right. They were best friends. They were made for each other.

How long had it been since he left? Minutes? Hours?

All at once the only emotions she could feel were thick and heavy. She pulled her knees close to her chest and rested her head against their knobby surface, relishing in the sharpness of bone on bone. Something to anchor her.

She tried to remember what had happened.

She tried to remember how to breathe.

Loneliness crept in as she sat in the bath long after the candles burned out and the water turned cold. There was nothing she knew how to do better than mourn the loss of a loved one. So in the darkness, shivering and alone as silent tears etched canyons into her skin, that is what she did.

CHAPTER TWENTY-SEVEN

SHE WATCHED FROM ABOVE as her body burned. She watched as her small frame twisted in agony, mouth wide open in the midst of a scream that threatened to tear the skin from her throat, her mind aware of the pain but not yet aware of the black char that had replaced most of her skin.

She watched as a man and woman appeared. She watched as they broke down what remained of the crumbling apothecary door and manically searched the room for her body, taking licks of flame to their own skin. She watched as one of the support beams fell, trapping them both with sickening cracks.

She watched as a third form forced his way through the chaos and carried her out to safety, only to turn around and go back for the man and woman.

She watched as life left their eyes moments before the ceiling came crashing down on top of them.

The fire roared on.

Deming woke with tears wetting her face.

She wiped them away, banishing the scene back to her subconscious.

Her heart felt freshly ripped out. She hadn't had a nightmare where she saw her parent's face in years. To see them again... a gift. A horribly terrible, gut-wrenchingly painful gift. One that threatened to unravel her sanity now that she was awake and back in the land of the living.

She shifted up in her bed with trembling arms, leaning back against the pillows and carved wooden frame. The iron tang of blood and stench of scorched skin filled her lungs instead of the crisp edge-of-winter air she knew should be filling the room. Each breath was shakier than the last. She could feel the panic bubbling under the surface, threatening to break her if she couldn't stay grounded.

Five things she could see. The edge of her bathtub through the doorway. The hairbrush on her dresser. Her father's spine bent at an unnatural angle.

Deming gasped. She shook her head, flinging fresh tears through the air.

Five things she could see. The edge of the bathtub through the doorway. The hairbrush on her dresser. Sunlight streaming through the window. Her mother's eyes caked over with blood and dust.

Deming covered her mouth to try and stifle the cry that escaped. She curled into the blankets, making herself as small as possible.

Breathe in.

Her whole body was shaking.

Breathe out.

She was too hot and too cold all at once.

Five things she could see. The bathtub. The hairbrush.

An achingly sorrowful sob burst through.

The sunlight. The balcony.

Why wasn't she the one dead? She should be dead.

Feathered wings.

The sight shocked her out of the free fall. She blinked away tears and rubbed her eyes, certain the dampness had clouded her vision, but, no. Wings indeed.

Nikita had just touched down on her balcony.

Concern flooded every pore on his exquisite immortal face, though his features were warped slightly by the glass. His hand paused midair, only for a second, before he pushed open the window and stepped into her room.

The icy morning air grounded her, giving her space to take in a few gulps of air uninterrupted by the heavy sobs that had been wracking her body.

Nikita moved slowly towards her, then thought better of it and backed off. Like she was a wounded animal. Dry humor whispered that the comparison wasn't far off.

He settled instead for the embroidered chair against the wall. Deming watched as he tried to hide the grimace that stole across his face as his wings pinched and arched uncomfortably around the armrests and high back.

Finally, in a voice raw from sobs, she cracked out words to him. "Why are you here?"

"You're in agony," he said as if that explained everything, emotion flooding his words in a way that made Deming very aware of their proximity and isolation. "I don't want you to be."

"Yeah," she scoffed, wiping a tear off her cheek and cringing at the puffiness she felt there. She must look like a mess. "Me either." Deming took a breath and closed her eyes. "You need to leave. You shouldn't be here." After a beat she added, "Vallyn will have your head."

"Vallyn's job is to protect you from threats." He cocked his head in that same, bird-like motion she had noticed him do countless times. "Am I a threat?"

Deming said nothing. At first, she was simply taking a moment to calm her breathing, but once she could no longer feel the pulse of her heartbeat in her throat and skull and fingertips she pondered his question and realized it was already answered.

He hadn't felt like a threat, a true threat, since the very first night. She had only backed away from him in fear after she had watched in awe as he took out her attackers. Her first instinct was to admire him. And since then? Since then he had been a thorn in her side. He was an enigma. His motivations as befuddling as they were enraging. He never seemed to be fully transparent. And yet.

He wouldn't hurt her.

She held the thought carefully, turned it over in her mind looking for cracks or faults and found none. She was certain.

Perhaps she'd be made a fool. Only time would tell.

She couldn't trust him yet. Not quite. But she could trust in herself.

She met Nikita's gray eyes. They were storm-like and wild right now, betraying his calm demeanor as a facade. He hadn't been lying earlier, seeing her distressed put him on edge. He cared for her well-being.

"No. You aren't a threat," she conceded.

The muscles in Nikita's shoulders noticeably loosened at her admission.

It was more than just not being a threat. For reason's only the gods know, his presence put her at ease. Only a stray tear leaked from her bloodshot eyes. Her chest was rising and falling in a regular rhythm once more. The remnants of the nightmare washing away with the dawn breeze.

His aura was a better balm to her tattered soul than any grounding exercises she had learned.

A soft smile graced his face. "I didn't think I was either." He put his hands on his thighs and made to get up. "I can still go, though, if you want."

Deming shook her head gently. "Please, stay." The ease at which the words slipped from her lips surprised her.

"As you wish, princess."

Her eyelids fluttered, lashes suddenly heavy. Sleep beckoned her and she went willingly, knowing that it would be dreamless as long as he was here.

Before she was pulled completely under, she whispered, "How did you know I needed someone?"

Nikita took so long to answer that she thought he hadn't heard her. Then, in a voice filled with such longing it felt built from sorrow and more gently than she could ever remember being spoken to, he said, "I've taken on the trauma of those around me since I was born. Pain calls to me like a moth to a flame."

Too tired to query further, she murmured incoherently, nestled into the warm embrace of exhaustion, and was soon fast asleep.

CHAPTER TWENTY-EIGHT

"FOLLOW MY LEAD." THE warrior began moving through their warm up.

As always, it started slow and built in both pace and intensity. Having worked on these stretches and motions for months now, Deming knew the movements by heart and watched Vallyn not to know what comes next, but to try to pick up on the nuance of the forms that only came from years of work and dedication to her craft.

It was a dance. Bending, arching, twisting. The fluidity of their movements were punctuated infrequently by holding periods where Vallyn instructed Deming to stay still in a certain form. Balance and strength as two sides of the same coin. Both necessary for success.

The warrior used her own hands to adjust the heir when words were insufficient. Pride bloomed in Deming's chest every week as the adjustments became less and less frequent.

When they reached the final form, Deming's blood was pumping and sweat beaded on her brow and the nape of her neck.

"Water." A clipped command from Vallyn.

Deming obeyed, careful not to drink too much. Early on in her training she made the mistake of drinking half her flask before the full workout began and ended up keeling over in pain halfway through as cramps plagued her sides. She shuddered at the memory. The pain rivaled her monthly cycle.

Deming was late to wake up, having slept soundly for the first time in ages. By the time they arrived in the pit they no longer had the benefit of privacy. Small clumps of soldiers and royal guards dotted the vast training grounds, getting a workout in before their shift began.

Paris was sparring with another court member's son across the pit.

Deming was not ready for that conversation.

She turned away, rubbing her palm fiercely against her eyes in an attempt to banish the prickling sensation. How did she still have tears left to cry?

Out of sight, out of mind.

Focus on the task at hand—hydrating.

The water coated her tongue and cooled her throat as she took a deep pull.

She wiped a trickle of water away from the corner of her mouth, then wiped the sweat off her forehead, all the while watching what Vallyn was setting up.

Normally, strength training followed their warm up. The past couple weeks they had even been working in hand to hand combat, which, to no one's surprise, Deming was terrible at. To say her skills were embarrassing was an understatement.

She cocked her head inquisitively as she looked at the gear Vallyn was bringing to the mat. Forearm braces. Wooden training shields. Breast plates, though these were made of thick hide, not the traditional metal worn into battle. For hand to hand, they usually worked only in their loose fitting clothes so they had full range of motion. Which meant...

Giddiness bubbled from head to toe as a squeal of delight rippled out of Deming. "Are we using swords today?"

Vallyn smiled. "Yep." She tossed one blade out to Deming, who yelped and dodged the sword only to realize when it hit the mat she had nothing to worry about. "Wooden ones."

"I suppose that makes sense," grumbled Deming, picking up the solid wooden sword that lay by her feet. She tested the feel of it in her hand. It was heavier than she expected. She could feel the length and weight of it putting pressure on her wrist as she held it upright and took a couple playful jabs at her friend.

Vallyn laughed and flicked her sword, disarming Deming in seconds.

"Hey!"

"If you can't keep hold of a wooden sword, you're going to be in a world of pain when we start using steel."

"Which will be..." Deming picked up the training weapon and knocked the dust off with her heel.

"A very long time from now." She gathered the protective clothing that had been pulled out and handed them to Deming. "Put these on."

The heir did so, and quickly. The gear was heavy, grounding. She took a couple buoyant hops from one foot to the other to get used to the weight and gave a joyful pretend parry in the direction of Vallyn, who was taking in the princess with crossed arms and a shake of her head.

Deming eyed the shield, then arched an eyebrow at Vallyn.

The warrior swept her hand, motioning for Deming to pick them up. "Go ahead, you can't fight without a shield."

Deming smiled and coughed to suppress yet another exclamation of eagerness. She rolled her shoulders and picked up the shield. The straps on the interior of the shield made holding the substantial weight of it slightly easier, but Deming quickly realized that though the last couple months had indeed made her stronger, she had a long way to go before she would have the stamina to wield these weapons for longer than a couple minutes.

She took a moment to familiarize herself with the feel of the wooden extensions of herself and then stilled her feet and looked at Vallyn for instructions.

The warrior only settled herself into a defensive stance and said, "Attack."

Deming needed no convincing. She launched forward and swung hard at Vallyn's mid section. The warrior dodged left and swept a leg low to destabilize Deming. Before she could get her footing back, Vallyn spun, knocked the sword out of Deming's grasp, and laid her own sword into Deming's unprotected ribcage.

She fell hard and fast, yelping as she hit the mat flat on her back.

Pain lanced through her abdomen. She winced and held a hand against the throbbing impact spot. She knew that if she lifted her shirt there would already be a bruise blooming across her skin.

Light dimmed through her closed eyelids. Prying one open she saw Vallyn standing over her, extending a hand.

She scooted into a sitting position and took a few steadying breaths before taking the hand and rising.

"What did you do wrong?"

"Aren't you supposed to tell me that?" The warrior said nothing, so Deming wagered a guess. "I... moved too slowly?"

"Get this one into the war room," Vallyn chuckled under her breath.

"I heard that."

"You were meant to." Vallyn walked around Deming, moving her body into position with gentle touches and guidance. She talked as she adjusted. "You moved too fast, actually. You charged with reckless abandon. You neither took time to assess my position, nor ready yourself for a counter attack. Your grip on your sword was flimsy. Your wrist would break the second you made contact with armor, if you even got that far without someone disarming you. And finally, you might as well have left the shield on the rack for all the good it did you. Your shield arm dropped the second you stepped forward. Your core was completely exposed. If we were using steel you would be dead."

"Is that all?"

She handed the sword and shield back to Deming in favor of responding.

"Slow down. Strong grip. Shield up." Deming ticked off a mental checklist. "Got it."

"Good." Vallyn reclaimed her own weapons. "Again."

An hour and countless bruises later, Deming wiped her face with the towel Vallyn handed to her after their cool down.

Though the warrior seemed impressed with the past hour, Deming didn't feel particularly proud. She had been knocked on her ass over and over again. A handful of times she managed to bear the brunt of Vallyn's first counter attack, but she was disarmed within seconds after that without fail. It felt like she had spent more time on the mat than on her feet.

"If this was easy, everyone would do it." Vallyn gave her a pat on the back, slick with sweat and hot with exhaustion. "It was a good start."

Deming nodded and took a sip of water. The hair on the back of her neck prickled with a sudden sense of being watched. Before turning around she knew the culprit would be a pair of storm gray eyes.

Nikita was leaning nonchalantly against the railing of the second floor, smiling at her softly.

Anxiety spiked through her, hot and fast. She had been such a mess last night. She wouldn't be concerned if she had broken down in front of Colette or Miriam, but Nikita? His proximity had provided some level of comfort to her that she didn't understand, but there was still so much unknown about him.

She had been so alone, so lost after ending things with Paris. Surely that was why she felt so strongly about him staying the night.

Thankfully he didn't seem as embarrassed as she felt.

Ilysse was a shadow behind him, back pressed against the wall and wearing an expression that bordered on exasperation. Her eyes felt seconds away from rolling at the fact that she had found herself yet again watching Deming work through training exercises she had mastered years ago.

The pair of Fae were frequent observers of the training pit. Deming specifically. More often than not Deming felt his winged presence appear sometime during her training. Outside of the first time, they always stayed a level above everyone and always left when Deming and Vallyn did.

Deming couldn't find it in her to be particularly bothered by it. If they wanted to waste their morning watching her get her ass kicked, more power to them. Nor did she pay much mind to the fact that she was so attuned to his presence that she didn't need to see him to know he was there. Like today.

Vallyn began cleaning and organizing their gear, methodically wiping the leather free of sweat and hanging them back in their place piece by piece.

Deming wiped a lingering bead of sweat from the side of her face. "I can't get myself to dislike him. I know I'm supposed to but I just... can't. It feels like I've known him for years. Like a friend I met ages ago and has come back into my life."

Vallyn glanced from the weapon's rack, clocking the immortal pair on the second floor. "You know he can almost surely hear you. Fae hearing is far more acute than our own."

The heir shrugged. "I know." Even if he couldn't hear her, she was looking him straight in the eye as she spoke and knew he could read her lips.

Vallyn shot a glare up to Nikita, who smirked in their direction and twinkled his fingers in a delicate wave, and then sighed. Her next words were accompanied with a shake of her head, as if she didn't quite believe she was uttering the syllables. "I'll admit, the judgment against them from members of the court feels overly aggressive."

A jolt of surprise shot through Deming as Nikita stretched his wings out to their full length, covering nearly the entire wall and completely obscuring his second in command behind him, and propelled himself over the guard railing. In two massive wingbeats that sent dust flying through the air and more than one weapon to the ground, he landed in front of her.

"Was that necessary?" she asked. "Look at the commotion you've caused."

Indeed, nearly everyone in the training pit had stopped their sessions to grumble at the show of talent. Was it talent if you were born with the ability to fly? Show of strength? Knowing Nikita, it was more likely just plain showing off.

Either way, no one seemed particularly pleased to have had their weapons whisked out of their hands by the force of his wings. She caught Paris staring daggers at the male, then at her. He flipped over his hands, palm up, and shook his head as if to say, *see, I told you so.*

His words came rushing back.

You are too naive.

You have got to start acting like a queen, not a child.

You know nothing of the world.

It didn't matter that he had taken it all back last night. The words were out there in the world and would likely stick in her consciousness for a long time.

She sucked on her lip but looked away.

"Do you think I care?"

She scowled at the insufferable male before her. "I was just telling Vallyn that I don't particularly hate you."

That wicked smile. "I know. I heard."

"Do you want me to take it all back?" She crossed her arms, ignoring the strands of hair she could feel plastered to her forehead with sweat.

"I'm not concerned about you doing that, princess." He had the audacity to wink at her. "Have you used a bow before?" Changing the subject, he walked over to the rack of weapons against the wall and plucked a longbow from the selection. He strung it quickly, without fault. Deming hadn't expected him to struggle with that, but the ease with which he pulled the string taut was astonishing. It was as if the weight meant nothing to him.

She swallowed. "Yes."

He looked at her knowingly.

Deming sighed and shifted her weight to her other foot. "I hunt with Paris sometimes and he uses a long bow. I've tried recurve bows before but I still couldn't pull it taut." The admission frustrated her to no end.

"You're stronger now than you were."

"Deming is not practicing with a bow. The purpose of her training is self defense. Hand to hand combat with swords, shields, and daggers are what she needs." Vallyn stepped forward, arms crossed. She may have admitted to almost trusting the Fae before her, but that sure as shit didn't mean she had to like him.

"Hmm." Nikita shrugged noncommittally. "A shame." He plucked an arrow from one of the quivers and nocked it. Without breaking eye contact with Deming, he drew the bow and released, sending the arrow shooting across the training pit to a target so far away she had difficulty making out the multicolored rings.

Not such difficulty, though, that she couldn't see it bury itself dead center.

She glared at him. "There are other people training. You could have hit someone."

"Please," Nikita said, smirking. He returned the bow to the wall and flared his wings in preparation for flight. "You and I both know that's not true."

CHAPTER TWENTY-NINE

FOR THE FIRST TIME in weeks, council was lacking the ever present air of tension and aggravation that had plagued the chambers since the fog descended.

Sasha's arrest had given everyone a sliver of peace.

The fog was still a priority issue. It's tendrils snaked in and out of the city streets incessantly and the sky was cloaked in swirling shades of gray. The sun had been absent from the sky for so long many people had taken to building makeshift shrines dedicated to Kielle. Orange peels and small yellow flowers decorated window ledges and doorways, hoping to bring his energy into the city.

No one quite knew what to make of the longevity of the issue. On one hand, no one was going to starve. For a few months at least. Once the grain stores and cattle had been counted, double checked, and compared to the population, it was clear that they would be more than fine to feed everyone until the beginning of next summer.

On the other hand it was immensely upsetting to the families who were separated from loved ones. Losing contact with the outside world had been jarring for many. Those who lost someone to the fog the morning it descended on Arsaela had it the worst, they truly had no idea what to make of their loved ones's fates.

Dresden sent word out repeatedly that the crown was doing everything they could to lift the magical weather, but patience was wearing thin.

A morale booster for Deming was that, in lieu of Sasha's arrest, her uncle had lifted restrictions on her. Most notably, there would no longer be a guard on night duty within her chambers, just the normal guards outside her door. Deming felt a profound sense of individuality and freedom again. Vallyn would, however, stay appointed as her personal guard. Though that was more for convenience than anything since the pair spent so much time training together anyway.

All in all, an overwhelmingly welcome change of pace.

A morale booster for the city at large was the impending Midwinter festival. Neither war nor weather it seemed could interfere with one of two Holy Nights.

Deming saw Lord Nolett elbow Lady Brittan, jesting that the latter's suggestion of masks for Midwinter was because of her husband's notoriously scarred face. The baron himself had made it clear many times before that the battle-earned warped scar that ran from temple to chin was indeed a joking matter, so the laughs that ensued rolled down the length of the table.

Miriam chuckled through closed lips. Duke Lowell went so far as to crack a rumbling, full-bellied laugh that echoed deeply through the room, his antagonistic presence dimming for a moment. Deming liked him much better when he didn't have such a stick up his ass.

Dare she say this council session had been... fun?

A smile tugged at the edges of her mouth as she entered the conversation. "Masks would be an intriguing addition, but would the clothiers have time to make enough? There is less than a month until Midwinter."

"Yes," Brittan answered from across the table, "I've already been in conversation with several seamstresses from across the city. Martha, who I believe is making the dresses for both you and Miriam along with many other court members," she trailed off briefly, waiting for confirmation. When Miriam nodded she continued, "And she is confident that her team can put together masks for the royal court and council members with plenty of time to spare."

"And the rest of the city?"

Brittan leaned forward slightly, eyes still dancing with laughter. "I'm sorry?"

"The rest of the city," repeated Deming. "Will we be able to offer masks for the rest of the city? The castle residents are but a small number of the attendees of Midwinter festival."

Duke Lowell chimed in. "They don't need masks, we're providing cheap beer, they'll be far too drunk to notice." There's that sparkling personality. "In fact, you bring up an interesting idea, princess. Let's cut them out all together and host the ball here in the castle."

Murmurs of consideration rippled through the chamber.

"No, that wasn't what I meant."

"I know, but I enjoy the thought all the same."

Dresden interjected. "We will celebrate Midwinter in the courtyard as tradition requires." His voice held no room for discussion. Deming flashed him a thankful look. "After all, we are but conduits for the celebration of Selene and the life she brought back into our world. I'd be curious to know how you would properly thank and cherish the goddess when you can't even see her through the stone ceiling of our ballroom."

Lowell grumbled and waved off the pointed comment.

The High Steward turned to Deming. "You bring up a thoughtful consideration. As you seem to be passionate about the equality of the situation, I would like you to find a solution. Martha and her seamstresses will be at capacity with their creations for court and council."

Deming dipped her head. "I will head into the city this afternoon and make inquiries."

Her uncle nodded, then began addressing the council as a whole once again about the less fun, more logistical considerations for the occasion.

The princess beamed.

A fun council indeed.

Hours later, after a small lunch that consisted of a delightfully playful herbal tea that left notes of cardamom dancing across her senses and a smattering of nuts, crisp apple slices, and sharp cheddar, Deming rode side by side with Colette through the winding cobblestone streets of the city.

She had asked her cousin to accompany her and Vallyn. The latter, not being nearly as familiar with Colette as she was the heir, rode a respectful distance behind the pair.

The red-headed waif of a human knew the ins and outs of the shopping district better than anyone else in Arsaela. Deming was fairly sure that Colette knew every shop owner personally, and had purchased enough fabric, sweets, trinkets, and jewels to rival anyone.

Deming tightened her grip on Quinn's reins and used her free hand to adjust the fur-lined collar of the thick cloak draped across her shoulders.

Small snowflakes fluttered around her face. The clouds they fell from were fully obscured by the fog. Winter in Laey, Arsaela especially because of its northern position in the queendom, was often blanketed in grayness, with Kielle hiding away behind dreary skies for many months. It was easy to pretend that today's grayscale was simply a sign of the season officially turning and not a menacing magical threat.

Easy to pretend, that is, if one ignored the layers of ice coating nearly every surface.

It seemed that, due to the water based nature of fog, when the air fell to freezing temperatures any surface that the fog touched found itself suddenly shimmering in a thin layer of frigid ice.

The effect was beautiful and harrowing.

"Who is this one, again?" The trio had visited half a dozen clothiers ranging widely in size and scope. Some were small shops run by one or two women with creaking doors barely peeking out of alleyways. Others were storefronts with block-wide presences and immaculate stitching exhibited in windows so clean Deming didn't believe there was glass there until hot breath from Quinn's nostrils steamed up the surface.

Frustrating patterns were emerging from the conversations with shop owners. Both small and large shops alike were open to the idea given the price the crown was willing to pay, but everyone was voicing the same concerns.

Fabric stock for the winter.

If they were to use their reams for the masks, there would be an extreme shortage of resources to use for making clothes for what was sure to be a harsh winter. Without alleviating the fog, there was no way to replenish anyone's supplies.

Deming gritted her teeth during those conversations. She couldn't in good conscience ask the city to choose one night of revelry over the safety and shelter of quality winter clothes. It bothered her to no end that no one during the council session had thought of that particular issue.

After the third time someone brought up the concern Deming was ready to head back to the castle, cut their losses, and try to figure out something else but Colette was insistent they finish their routes.

"Meredith is next," Colette chirped from the back of her chestnut mare. "She made the gown I wore to my father's regency coronation. Sweet girl. Nimble fingers. I've gone back to her throughout the years for random dresses here and there."

Deming laughed in disbelief. "Dresden's coronation? How could you possibly remember the details of that day? It was ten years ago, we were children!"

"Don't you remember that day?"

"Well, sure." Her uncle's coronation into High Steward had occurred less than a month after the death of the king and queen. Deming's memories from that time either felt etched permanently into her skull, each wisp of hair or chip of paint in crystal clear resolution, or non-existent. There were weeks and months of that year that were completely lost to the yawning pit of loss and darkness.

When Dresden was crowned, Deming remembered nothing of the day except the exact moment the delicate silver crown was placed on his head. The jewels winked in the multicolored light that poured through the stained glass windows of the temple. His hair like fox fur. His head bearing the weight of the crown so easily it felt like betrayal. The whole room roared in celebration, but all Deming could think of was how the dust motes in the air looked like ash.

She blinked away the memory. "I remember certain parts of the day but certainly not what I was wearing."

Colette shrugged. "Well, I do. It was a wonderfully tailored peach colored number with a tulle skirt full of flecks of diamond stitched in that made me feel like you. It's not often a little girl gets to feel like a princess."

"Being a princess isn't all it's cracked up to be."

"Yeah, Deming, I know," she said with an eye roll. "Tie up Quinn here, Meredith's shop is just around the corner."

They swung off their saddles and knotted all three horses to the wooden post near the end of the street. Deming pulled sugar cubes from her saddlebag and gifted each of them a treat, conscious of the fact that Quinn grew anxious when left alone in the city.

A small bell tinkled as they entered. Meredith's storefront was quaint but well appointed. The walls had been painted a blush color that reminded Deming of the peonies that would bloom in the royal garden in the coming months. Curtains of fabric in every color and texture one could imagine hung gracefully along one wall. The shop was narrow and long, the deeper they walked in the more eclectic the surroundings got. Small tables were cluttered with needles and thread, beads and bobbles. A set of three mirrors hung across from an equal number of carpeted pedestals. A small, teacup sized jewelry holder with a latched emerald green lid caught Deming's eye. Her fingertips itched to reach over and see what lay inside.

"Meredith?" Colette pulled off her gloves and tucked them into the pocket of her overcoat. Her cheeks were flushed from the crisp winter air and the color looked out of place against the rest of her pale skin. With a few strands of hair out of place, she looked about as wild as she ever had.

Deming hid the laugh that bubbled up at that thought with a cough. She elbowed her friend and gestured generally to her face. Colette's eyes widened briefly. She quickly pressed a hand to either side of her head, smoothing down all stray hairs and tucking longer pieces back into the tight bun at the nape of her neck.

Just in time, too. A rosy-cheeked woman with soft features poked her head out of the back room and gave a wide, toothy grin at the sight of the trio. "Colette! To what do I owe the pleasure?"

"Hi, sweetness!" Colette walked forward with open arms, embracing the seamstress with genuine happiness. Deming was reminded, as she frequently was, about how easy it was for Colette to connect with others. She had a gift. "We have been hopping around to all the seamstresses in town trying to figure out a creative solution for a Midwinter issue that crept up in council this morning." Colette turned to Deming, letting the heir take hold of the conversation.

"It's lovely to meet you, Meredith." The woman bowed far lower than necessary as Deming began to speak. "It was suggested that we add masks to the Midwinter festivities this year and while everyone seems to love the idea, we have run into an issue with capacity. Our seamstress at the castle, Martha, is not able to provide masks for the general citizens of Arsaela. We are hoping maybe you could help us."

Meredith looked quizzically at Deming. "You are looking for someone to make enough masks for everyone in the city?"

Deming winced. "Yes, that is the hope."

The woman gave her a pitiful look and smoothed the ruffled edges of her dress awkwardly. "Princess, I am terribly sorry but I am afraid your search will likely prove fruitless. To offer that kind of service would deplete the fabric stores of even the most well-stocked clothiers in the city. Even for a hefty price, I'm not sure anyone would be willing to limit their supplies in such a way. Especially with the state of things. Winter is coming, you know. Bodies need to be kept warm."

Deming hadn't gotten her hopes up but the confirmation stung all the same.

"I understand." Frustration gave an edge to the sigh that escaped Deming. "Thank you for your time and input."

She turned and began walking back to the front of the shop. Colette did not follow right away, too busy catching up briefly with the seamstress and congratulating her on something that drifted out of earshot as Deming reached the entrance.

Vallyn waited for her by the door, leaning on its frame casually as if she wasn't armed to the teeth. "No luck?"

Deming shook her head. "Same story, different shop. Product is too valuable right now, no one is willing to part with it for masks when it could be used for winter clothes."

"You could suggest scratching the mask idea altogether to the council."

"Maybe." Deming looked back at Colette, who was wrapping up her conversation with Meredith with another warm embrace. "It's such a fun idea though, and it's so rare for fun ideas to come out of council."

"To the High Steward's point though, at its core Midwinter isn't about having fun. It's about celebrating Selene and her gift of life."

"You're right." After a beat Deming added, "We're lucky my uncle decided to go through with having the festival at all."

Vallyn pushed off the door frame and agreed.

A need for levity and joy aside, Xiomara and the temple priestesses would have had a conniption if Midwinter had been canceled. An affront to the goddess that egregious would have caused more problems than it avoided. Deming thanked the gods for the arrest and sentencing for a multitude of reasons, but the fact that it allowed for the celebration to be held as usual was higher on that list than she cared to admit.

"All right, ladies, ready to go? I've got a couple more options we can try." Colette laid her arm around Deming's shoulder and leaned her head in so their hair mingled.

Deming shrugged off her friend, not unkindly. "I don't think I can take another rejection to be honest. Everyone is right, masks aren't a good use of material right now. I'll just have to think of something else."

They found their way back to the horses. Quinn nickered in welcome, and Deming cuddled close to the mare's warm neck before sneaking her another sugar cube.

"Don't tell the others," she whispered as she pulled herself into the saddle. Quinn's ears flicked away new flakes of snow.

Deming adjusted her cloak so that it was snug around her neck and flowed neatly down her back to lay gently against Quinn's rump. She had always thought it was easy to romanticize riding in the winter, and one look at their reflection in the nearby shop window confirmed her theory. They looked straight out of a story book.

She gave Quinn a nudge with her heel and led them away from Meredith's store front and back up the winding roads to the city center.

Colette trotted beside her, sitting a smidge lower since her own mare was a hand shorter than Quinn. "So," her cousin began, "I spoke with Paris this morning."

Deming winced. She hadn't told anyone yet that her and Paris had ended things. At first, she could hardly remember her own name, let alone attempt to explain what had happened to someone else. Getting through that night had been agonizing and when she had finally got to sleep... the worst nightmare she's had in ages. And Nikita... The whole situation had left her feeling all sorts of emotions and she hadn't had the chance to sift through them on her own yet.

"How mad is he?"

Colette shook her head. "He isn't mad."

"Are you sure? He was certainly mad when he was talking to me."

"Deming." Her tone of voice made Deming look over. Colette had pursed her lips. "I would think that after all the years we've spent together you would know him better than that. He isn't angry. He's terribly sad. And confused."

Deming sighed and rolled her eyes. Deep in her bones she knew that was true. One truth didn't change the other, though. "He didn't handle it well."

"Did you expect him to?"

"No, of course not. It's just that... I mean," She paused, feeling the knowing deep inside, "I guess I thought he would have at least some understanding of where I was coming from. Some kind of recognition that things have shifted. Both inside me and between us. Nothing I had been feeling the last couple months resonated with him."

She flexed her fingers, gripping the reins tightly and lowering her eyes. Concern fluttered in her stomach. It was one thing to lose a partner on her own terms, it was another thing entirely to lose her closest friend if Colette decided that blood was not thicker than water. Unlikely, sure... but stranger things had happened recently.

Colette looked at her expectantly, patiently waiting for the rest of the story.

"I didn't realize I wanted to stop seeing each other until we were in the middle of talking. It was just this sinking feeling that even though he was apologizing so earnestly and saying all the right things, I didn't feel happy or comforted. And then when I explained myself and everything seemed like it was going over his head I realized that we had been living completely separate truths for months, which was depressing in its own right. We were together, but not really together. This fall has been full of so much change and challenge and growth for the queendom and myself and yet nothing had changed with our relationship. We were one dimensional.

"It was a wonderfully safe relationship. And I love him so much. But what we built is not sustainable for me in the long term. It's not what I want or need out of a partner." Deming bit her lip, then added, "It's not what Paris wants or needs either, even if he doesn't realize it yet. To stay together would have been a disservice to both of us."

Satisfied with her answer, Deming nodded curtly to herself. Speaking the words out loud loosened the grief in her chest. The right choice is rarely the easy one.

The pair rode in relative silence for a few moments. It was late enough that many of the streets they rode through were quieting. The rising moon cast a pearlescent glow through the air, highlighting the still falling snow in a more peaceful way than the daylight had.

"I love Paris as much as you do, albeit in different ways. And to be honest, I don't know that my relationship with him is going to change because of this." Colette spoke softly, as if she wanted to disturb the night as little as possible. Deming braced herself for an emotional blow. "But your friendship is the greatest gift life has given me. I am so proud of you for knowing yourself so deeply and honoring what your heart knows to be true."

A whimper escaped Deming as her vision blurred. She hadn't realized just how much she needed to hear those words. After nearly a decade of avoiding the responsibility of the crown and in doing so, teaching her body and mind to avoid their own knowing, feeling aligned and in control was more emotional than she could have ever predicted. She felt reborn.

"You are my best friend," she managed in between trembling lips, "I couldn't do any of this without you."

Colette gave her a smile that warmed every corner of Deming's soul. "I'm not going anywhere." Deming grabbed her outstretched hand, bridging the gap between their mounts as they approached the last road leading back home.

Chapter Thirty

Burning incense filled the air with opaque smoke and a thick smell of sandalwood. Not unpleasant, per say, but certainly overwhelming.

Deming sat in a rickety chair, both arms hugging the one leg she had pulled in close to her chest and chin resting on her knee. The chair, which was hanging on for dear life and felt as if it was one inopportune shift from collapsing into a pile of kindling, was placed in the far back corner of the apothecary and was one of only two options for sitting down. The other option was a cushioned two seated bench, which, superficially, one might assume would be the better choice. Lucky for her, Deming knew intimately what occurred in this room and was deeply uninterested in sitting on a cushion that had surely soaked up spills rivaling the vileness of even the dankest sewers.

The mages may have moved into the castle only a few weeks ago, but that was more than enough time for the couch to become home to a wide array of messes.

It wasn't that Yesenia and Gisela were messy themselves, it was just that the nature of their experiments lent itself to explosions and concoctions that bubbled over. There was only so much the two mages could clean. Sprayed and splattered tinctures were bound to slip through the cracks.

So the chair it was.

"Are you sure I can't help?" She offered for the third time. "I spent a lot of my childhood in here with my uncle. Well, not my uncle. That's misleading. We weren't related by blood."

"Yes, I'm sure." Yesenia said without looking up from her work. She stood a few feet away, leaning against the long workbench that stood stoically in the middle of the room. One foot was kicked out slightly behind her, the toe of her boot tapping rhythmically in a steady pattern that Deming had noticed on her second visit down here. "A close friend, then?"

"Yes, Khalil was Miriam's brother. He was like family."

Yesenia hummed in understanding, then followed up with a single, loaded word. "Was?"

Though she was expecting the question, a familiar pang of regret nevertheless resonated in Deming's heart. Her response was flat and practiced. "He was also lost in the fire that took my parent's lives."

For the first time since she started working, Yesenia looked up. Interest sparked in her eyes, along with condolence and understanding. To Deming's great surprise, there was also a lack of pity in her gaze. She was thankful for both that, and the next words out of her mouth.

"What was he like?"

A smile toyed at the edges of Deming's lips. "He was warm and effusive, you always knew how he felt about you and it was always something positive. His hugs were the best because he was so strong and tall. His beard tickled the top of my head as I was tucked into his embrace. I can still smell the rose oil he used in it. He was like a second father to me.

"I didn't have the comprehension to realize it at the time, being as young as I was. But as I grew up and Miriam shared bits and pieces about his work with me, it was clear he was also the most innovative man I've ever known. If he was still alive, he would have had the cause of the fog figured out within the first week." A glance to the mage. "No offense."

"None taken," waved off Yesenia, who simultaneously turned back to the workbench and began crushing the yarrow root with pumice and stone once more.

"He had spent years studying with the Sisters of Maidenhall."

Yesenia raised an eyebrow at that, impressed. Understandably so. Maidenhall only recently began accepting men as acolytes. Khalil had been the first, studying within the storied halls well before the change was made official.

No one had believed him that he had studied in Maidenhall when he came back after a three year hiatus. It was only through the miracles he worked with new tinctures and salves that they had begrudgingly had to admit it was unlikely he made the story up. Deming had a crisp memory of a morning in early spring shortly after her eighth birthday when Khalil had burst through the sitting room doors waving a piece of paper and demanding an official apology. His mentor, Sister Cristelle, had written inquiring about his endeavors since leaving the Sanctuary, and would he please send word if his experimental procedure on bone setting had been a success. It had been, but that was beside the point.

King Silas had laughed deeply and profusely apologized. Three Sisters had come for the Midsummer festival that year and that had been the end of anyone not believing Khalil when it came to healing practices or his travels.

"He is the reason Arsaela is so respected in the realm of healing, and why my mother's reign had been so peaceful and uncontested. Sicknesses were few and far between and any major injury healed twice as fast under his watch."

Yesenia put the yarrow root paste aside and began strolling through the room, considering each shelf and its contents carefully before moving on. "I only arrived in Arsaela a handful of years ago, I never knew him or his work. But it sounds like he had a mind that only comes along once in a generation," she offered, picking up a small jar of something thick and black.

"Some compared him to a mage. No offense, again. I wouldn't dare to claim that myself."

"No, I completely agree." Yesenia placed the vials she had collected, six in all, in a neat row in front of the yarrow root. "I would go so far as to say it's more impressive, what he was doing, than a mage's magic. He had to work hard for his miracles. Ours are passed down through blood."

Deming considered the compliment and found it lacking the nuance she wanted. It had always seemed odd to her, the comparison of her uncle's practices with the elemental magic that mages wielded. Both were uniquely powerful. But they were so different it seemed a disservice to hold one against the other.

She settled on vocalizing her agreement noncommittally. "Thank you for asking about him." One of the vials caught her eye. "What's that one?" Yesenia peered over, then held up the small black jar. "No, sorry, the corked one."

Second from the left was a tall cylindrical glass stoppered with a spongey, tan cork. The contents were a couple shades darker than the cork, and ground up so finely that the dry substance looked like sand.

"That," answered the mage, "Is hickory root. Ground as finely as possible and left to age for a few years before use."

"I've never seen it used before. In fact," the heir admitted, releasing the hold her arms had around her knee and leaning back into the chair, which responded by letting out a high pitched, splintering creak, "I am fairly certain I've never seen it in the castle at all before."

Yesenia offered a grin with her response as she methodically opened each container and began measuring out their contents into a bowl. "You would be correct, princess. This particular plant is not part of your local flora, though I don't doubt that historically most of your stores here are not local. It also happens to have little to no effect on humans, other than bland sustenance and a mediocre tea. Very few human kingdoms bother with harvesting it at all, and even fewer still have it stocked in apothecaries.

"For mages, though," she continued, "it is the most effective tool we've found to tamper down our gifts." Deming tilted her head, not having to vocalize the question that was begging to be asked before Yesenia answered. "Young mages, especially powerful ones, can take a while to master the inherent link between their gifts and their emotions. Sprinkling in even a little hickory root into our water gives us a bit of a reprieve from the unyielding waves of whatever elements we've been blessed with." She looked curiously at Deming. "It works in a similar way to the tincture you sometimes take in evenings to help with the nightmares. It's a shield of sorts."

Deming crossed her arms, wanting to piece together why something with those kind of effects would be valuable to their efforts before Yesenia told her. She cursed under her breath when the explanation evaded her.

Having watched the thoughts play out across Deming's face, Yesenia snickered and shook her head as she continued the conversation. "We're hoping to create a balm of sorts using hickory root as the base that, when applied to the skin, allows the wearer to become immune to the fog's magic."

"A more amplified version of easing the weight of your powers," mused Deming.

"Correct. It took us far longer to come up with the idea than either Gisela or I would like to admit, but we're both convinced that this is the right path to explore. The last attempt allowed Gisela a few seconds of safety before burning from my flame."

"Ouch." Deming's face recoiled in pain. Then, "We're going to need something that works a lot longer than two seconds."

A sneer as sharp as any dagger Vallyn carried. "Obviously," said Yesenia.

Deming raised her hands in submission, a wry grin pulling her lips into a smirk. "Just wanted to make sure you knew." She stood and walked towards the closed door. "If you don't need any help here, I'm going to go to the library."

Yesenia nodded and said goodbye to the heir, tone already cooled off. She didn't look up from her work, though, as Deming pushed open the apothecary door and into the hallway beyond.

Since her and Paris's breakup, Deming had been spending more and more time in the library researching elemental magic. Call it a hunch, a vindictive streak, or plain stubbornness, she was determined to find something useful within the shelves. The itch to prove Paris wrong had driven her to the library for five straight afternoons.

Today, she was sitting at a small table at the end of an aisle. Unlike many of the study spaces within the library, today's space was unremarkable in every way. The window behind her was simple glass, no sign of the intricate stained glass work that could be found elsewhere. The table itself, while a rich mahogany color with no knots to be seen, was small and unassuming with a chair that matched.

Deming was hunched over a text that detailed the rise and fall of the Illaesian dynasty of Monstakar. The neighboring kingdom had been a tenuous ally throughout the years and was known for their higher than normal population of mages due to their shared border with the Fae Territories.

As with many history texts, it was dense and dry and Deming found herself on more than one occasion rereading a passage for the second, third, fifth time in order to comprehend what was actually being said. To make matters worse, she had yet to come across any useful tidbit of information. The Illaesian dynasty had employed a number of mages, but if they had asked the mages to research the edges of what their magic could accomplish this wasn't the book the information was recorded in. After what seemed like the hundredth reference to the political climate within the long dead King Horan's court, Deming closed the cover with a huff and massaged the back of her neck.

Retracing her steps through the corridors of the library, Deming placed one book after another back on their appropriate shelves. As she slid the fifth and final book into its resting place, a thin memoir style document authored by a commoner fire mage, she sighed in disappointment and retreated to her rooms.

Chapter Thirty-One

"Only a moment more, princess," Julia trilled from the room adjacent to where Deming stood, arms spread away from her core and spine held straight.

She took a shallow breath and exhaled slowly so as not to disturb the many, many, many pins stuck throughout the navy fabric wrapped around her as she looked at herself reflected in the mirror before her.

The structure of her gown for Midwinter was mostly complete. Noreen and Julia had been working around the clock on Martha's insistence to create the impressive ballgown Deming would wear during the formal ceremony that marked the beginning of Midwinter. There was a far more casual gown she would change into once the social part of the evening began, but this first dress was for the more culturally significant portion of the evening and therefore was taking up more of Noreen and Julia's time.

Every stitch had to be perfect.

"Noreen," the heir said, "do you think we can take up the hem as well?"

Noreen peeked out from behind the skirt. Her brows furrowed as she lifted the hem of the dress, fluffed it, and observed where it settled as it fell. She pulled the pin from her mouth. "Sharp eye, princess. The hem should be just a touch shorter." She picked a quill up from the floor and jotted down the note.

"Here we are!" Julia had returned, nearly tripping over the fabric that had been cut away from the gown in the initial sewing weeks ago. She caught herself before falling, thankfully, and saved the basket full of ribbons in her hands from spilling onto the floor. Her face reddened as she continued, clearly flustered, "We have plenty of options, I'm sure one of these will suit your fancy."

Deming considered the options carefully and Julia presented them one by one. Plenty of options, indeed. There were ribbons of thick velvet, slippery silk, airy tulle, flowering lace. Some were so thin Deming could hardly see them unless the light caught them at the right angle.

"This is to embellish the waist, correct?"

"Yes, princess," Julia responded, tucking away a wide, white option and pulling out a sky blue strand of lace. "The neckline as well."

Deming lifted her eyes to the mirror once more. The gown would consist mostly of a satin, navy shell supported by hoops and layers of tulle underneath. The bodice would be a few shades lighter. "Silver will be best," she decided. "The satin one, please. It will tie in nicely to the silver in my second dress."

Julia bowed in acknowledgment before placing the selection on the table beside them and hurried to put the rest of the options back.

The room fell into a contented silence, broken only here and there with Noreen's humming as she finished pinning the dress for its final alterations.

Deming's mind wandered. Preparations for the ball were well underway, all that was left to do was begin setting up the following week. Midwinter would take place in just over a week. This was a source of excitement for her, with the exception that she hadn't been able to derive a solution to the mask issue. Colette had taken her out again, as promised, though the results were just as fruitless as the first venture. No one was willing to part with their fresh rolls of fabric.

Fresh fabric. The seamstresses had not wanted to cut up their fresh reams of fabric for the masks because they needed to keep stock in place for winter clothing orders.

What if they didn't need whole reams?

What if they didn't need matching swaths of fabric at all?

Deming's heart leapt to her throat.

"Princess!" Noreen exclaimed as Deming swung her head so sharply to the back corner of the room that a few of the pins on her shoulder dug in sharply. The pain did not register.

A wide grin blossomed on her face as Deming beheld the behemoth pile of scrap fabric.

"Creative." The compliment was accompanied by a warm smile and a gentle hand cupping her face. "So creative. I'm glad to see your uncle's faith in you was not misguided."

Miriam looked at her ward with a look of love that was at once a mother proud of her daughter and a court member proud of the queendom's heir.

Deming had rushed to Miriam's chambers the second she was able to step out of the gown without disturbing the pins Noreen and Julia had painstakingly placed. Thankfully, she was exactly where Deming expected her to be—nestled into one of the large chaise lounges that bookended the towering window in her sitting room, sipping tea.

"Do you think it will work?" Her breath was labored, having quite non-royally sprinted through the castle corridors.

"Yes, I do. Though, before we present your idea as fact to council we would do well to run it by Martha first. She should be with the other seamstresses, I believe they are putting the finishing touches on Lady Blackwell's gown this afternoon."

Despite the matter at hand, Deming asked the following. "What do you think of her request?"

Miriam chuckled, rising from her seat and waving one of her handmaidens to remove the tea. "Bold, but a marked improvement from the fashion she favored when she arrived at court. Come, let's find our Royal Seamstress and see if you have indeed brought access and joy to every citizen of Arsaela."

Deming followed Miriam out of her chambers. The pair walked leisurely through the halls and Deming was reminded of strolling through the gardens with Miriam as a young girl. Her heart warmed at the memory and looped her arm through Miriam's without thinking. As her forearm rested into the crook of Miriam's arm, she winced and suppressed a cry of pain.

Deming immediately pulled away. "I apologize, Miriam." Concern replaced the warm memory almost immediately. "What's the matter?"

Miriam immediately shook her head, face back to its normal regal expression. "No, my dear," she reached back to Deming, coaxing their arms together once more, "no need to apologize. I have been spending too much time on correspondence and journaling as of late and have developed a strain on my arm. Nothing to worry about, I promise." Seeing the look of concern did not retreat from Deming's countenance, Miriam leaned over and kissed her brow. "Truly, it is a silly ailment for those who have far too much time to write and far too little for active movement. I am sure you have sustained substantially more aggressive wounds from your training with Vallyn."

They rounded a corner and descended down the grand staircase.

"I am no stranger to a bruise, that's for sure." Just the other morning she had walked away from the training pit with a stroke of molten blue and purple gracing the side of her upper thigh. Walking had been a challenge for days. Riding, impossible.

"Are you still enjoying it though? The training?" Though Miriam didn't give voice to her real question, whether or not Deming felt it was necessary to continue training now that the threat on her life had been, for all intents and purposes, subdued, the princess heard it all the same.

"Yes," she responded, "I love my time with Vallyn, even if I don't share the sentiment with the soreness that plagues me after our sessions." The women approached the doors to Martha's workshop. Deming knew Miriam wouldn't press the issue further, but felt the need to add more. "I think," she began, hesitant at first then with building confidence, "building my skills with a sword has given me a sense of purpose and pride that I didn't know I was missing. I'm not sure if I would feel the same if the threats against the queendom had not come to be, but as it stands, I feel like I have a deeper understanding of my station."

They paused before the closed doors. Miriam turned to face Deming, taking the latter's hands in her own. Tears pricked the corners of her eyes. "I hope you know how proud I am of you. The crown is not for the faint of heart. I have always known you were capable of shouldering the burden of the crown gracefully. It brings me joy nevertheless to hear you have discovered that for yourself."

On instinct, Deming leaned into Miriam who instantly wrapped her arms around her. Deming buried her face into the crook of Miriam's neck and breathed in the cinnamon and clove scent of her. "I love you," she mumbled into the curls she was crushing.

"I love you too," affirmed Miriam. "Now let's get this mask deal sealed."

They peeled apart and entered the room.

CHAPTER THIRTY-TWO

ARSAELA WAS A SIGHT to behold.

Dusk had finally fallen over the city. Even if the skies had been clear, its citizens would have needed the thousands of colored lanterns that bejeweled the city with their candlelight. The glass and paper of the lanterns were a cacophony of shades of midnight, plum, silver, and gray. Traditional colors to honor the deep eddies of Selene's celestial queendom.

Deming leaned against the railing of her balcony, taking in the view. This far away, the city below looked like a dollhouse, or a mirage. Something small and magical and distant. The light of the lanterns, flickering in and out with the cool breeze whispering through the air, looked like fireflies.

She knew that festivities had already begun. The din of those celebrating, both piously with temple hymns and heretically with copious amounts of beer and wine, rose all the way to where she stood. Later in the evening even the priestesses would imbibe. But it was frowned upon by the High Priestess to pray to Selene without a clear mind and as such, those who took Midwinter seriously only muddled their senses after midnight, when the official ceremony had ended.

She shifted her gaze closer, towards the castle gates. Members of court had already congregated there in preparation for the procession. She searched for only a moment before finding the bright copper shine of Colette's crown of hair. She stood next to Paris.

Deming's stomach wavered. It was unlikely she would be able to continue avoiding him tonight. So be it. They would have to build their friendship up again brick by brick. Their positions in court demanded it.

Her eyes drifted to another. Nikita's broad wings were hard to miss on any occasion, and tonight was no exception. He stood to the side of where more entrenched members of the court had gathered. Ilysse and Hartford stood near him. Deming was certain she could see Ilysse's hand tight on the hilt of her sword, ever the warrior.

"Princess, I would kindly ask that you stand straight, so as not to wrinkle the fabric of your gown." Julia interrupted her thoughts.

"My apologies," she said, pushing off the railing and turning to face her handmaiden. "I was not thinking clearly. I would hate for all of your hard work to go to waste."

Julia curtsied in appreciation. "It is time to gather for the procession."

Deming took one last glance at herself in the mirror. Julia and Noreen had outdone themselves. The gown was regal and stately, with a high neck and long sleeves that hugged her arms all the way to the cuff. The bodice and corset underneath, in conjunction with the overflowing skirt that spilled out from just above her hips, gave her a well defined waist. Every inch of the satin fabric had been dyed varying navy shades of the night sky. Dusky blue near her neck transitioned to midnight navy at the skirt which pooled into such a deep blue it was nearly black at the hems. The silver ribbon they had chosen earlier had clearly been the correct choice. It wove in and out of the waistline, swelling up above her hips and diving into a point at her core that followed through to the edges of the dress.

The mask that Martha had designed was intricate and ornate. Impossibly small emeralds, sapphires, and diamonds were set in whorls throughout the fabric. It sat on the bridge of her nose, covering only the top of her face and tied back with a silver ribbon that matched the one sewn into her dress.

A gold crown with peaks replicating each phase of the moon sat atop her curls.

Noreen had vied for a heavy layer of rouge and paint for her face, but Deming insisted on a lighter application. What good would a heavily done face do underneath a mask? Similarly, she had opted for little jewelry. Small pearls studded her ears and a thin chain with diamonds interspersed lay around her neck. With a gown this intense, it would be best to let it speak for itself rather than compete for attention with other adornments.

Her heels set off crisp staccato echoes as she made her way through the castle and outside to the gates that opened towards the winding road down to the city. She was nearly the last to arrive, only Miriam arrived afterwards in a gown of radiant egg-shell blue that was encrusted neckline to hem with chips of sapphire and diamond.

"You look positively queenly," she said to Deming as she approached.

"Likewise." Deming gestured to the ensemble Miriam was in. "You are... impeccable. Selene incarnate."

Miriam offered a soft smile. "The color was a nice touch. I was worried Xiomara would think it heretical, with it being the same shade as the Goddess herself, but she gave her approval."

"Unlike her to be so flexible."

Miriam laughed in agreement.

Deming hesitantly asked about the remainder of the morning. She had been in and out of fittings all day and therefore had missed the most recent council session. There had been some talk about whether or not to include the visiting Fae delegation in the ceremony. "How was Lowell at council?"

"Oh, he was about as prickly as normal," Miriam said reproachfully.

"He put aside his asinine complaints about the Fae participating in the ceremony, I assume, seeing as the delegation is here?"

Miriam winced. Something she wasn't saying, then.

Deming groaned. "Just tell me."

"The compromise was that the Fae could partake in the ceremony but will be escorted back to their tower afterwards so, and I'm quoting our favorite member of council here, the citizens of Arsaela can celebrate joyously and without fear."

Deming saw red. "That makes no sense," she seethed. "We have Fae citizens. Humans and Fae and mages all live within our walls. No one is this threatened by them except for Lowell." It was a challenge to keep her voice from rising.

"I know that, my love. We change the world one step at a time. Focus on what surely is a win—they will be present for the most important part of the evening."

Deming mumbled something that the older woman chose to ignore.

Miriam brushed a stray whip away from Deming's face, careful not to smudge the rouge on her cheeks. "Now, do try and enjoy the evening."

She supposed she had no choice.

Ahead of them, members of the court were mounting their horses. Quintessential was brought over, along with Miriam's own horse.

Even the equine members of court were subject to special finery on this night. Swaths of fabric depicting Selene, in and out of her moon form, had been attached to Quinn's saddle and her reins tinkled with tiny bells.

Deming mounted, sitting side saddle for the formal occasion, and the processional began.

Throngs of people greeted them as they made their way from the castle gates to the courtyard. Deming felt a swell of pride as she beheld the faces in the crowd.

Everyone she could see was masked.

Patchwork, flimsy, fabric masks tied with scraps of string. But masked all the same.

Martha had balked at first when Miriam and Deming approached her about the idea to use scraps as the base for masks for the general population. Thankfully, she gave in soon after Deming suggested that the actual work be done by individual households. All Martha, and the other seamstresses throughout the city, would have to do would be donate the fabric scraps.

While there was only a finite amount of professional seamstresses in the city, nearly every household had a mother or daughter that could sew well enough to fix small tears. Cobbling together cloth masks was well within their capabilities and when the missives had been sent and word of mouth traveled, Deming was blown away by how quickly masks had begun popping up in the streets. Some with more capacity had even gone so far as to offer extra masks at street vendors.

All their efforts had resulted in a wonderfully chaotic slew of masked citizens. She may not be able to run a queendom quite yet, but she was capable of enacting some change, however minute, and that gave Deming heaps of comfort.

The path to the courtyard was direct, using the main street that was wide enough for court to ride through four abreast, and soon enough the processional had arrived.

The Courtyard of Antiquities, commonly referred to as Arabella's Courtyard thanks to the love that one of Deming's distant ancestors had for it, was, if nothing else, eye-catching.

The circular space was paved with round, white stones laid in concentric circles radiating out from a prominent fountain made in the likeness of Selene herself, an additional reason the formal ceremony was held here. The water that arched out of her upheld hands sparkled.

The cracks in between the stones had been filled with a mixture composed of mostly crushed conch shells from the Everlasting Ocean giving the ground the shimmery effect of walking on stardust.

The courtyard was the first space outside of the castle to have been built in Arsaela, and as such the surrounding buildings were made of limestone, a testament to how old everything here actually was. Age also played a factor in height. All of the storefronts sitting immediately against the courtyard were only two floors high at most. The city beyond the limestone walls towered over, giving those mulling about inside the courtyard the sense that they were inside an arena rather than a communal city space.

On its own, Arabella's Courtyard was dripping in history and beautiful. During Midwinter, it brought tears to Deming's eyes.

Glittering glass lanterns hung from every possible nook. The light that looked like fireflies from above blazed like small stars up close. The flames refracted each tinted color. In the duskiness of near darkness, the effect was painting the skin of those present in waves of mauve and cerulean. Deming knew that the smooth silver that danced in everyone's eyes was a product of this too, and not the mead. Drunk eyes dulled. The ones she saw here shone.

The light was particularly beautiful this year because the balls of flame were enchanted, brought to life by Yesenia. Not only were they incandescent, they also emitted warmth strong enough to stave off the bite of winter in the air. Those in close proximity to the magical lanterns needed no coat. It would only last for a few hours, but it was a wonder all the same.

The sight of snow drifting through the misty air and the ice coating the cobblestone coupled with the warmth from the lanterns was ethereal.

Thanks to the crown's greenhouse, endless strings of flowers connecting lanterns to walls to doors to windows added to the colorful ambience. Long lavender sprigs wove into long stemmed white roses. Delicate bluebells were nestled in-between. The scent would be intoxicating enough without the incense that had been lit at intervals from the castle gates to the courtyard, but alas, Temple always insisted on including the heady smoke. It was meant to guide the spirit of Selene to the ceremony.

Were it not for the ever present unnatural fog, this might be the loveliest Deming had ever seen Arsaela.

A curved table raised a few feet above the ground had been built near the far side of the fountain. This was where the High Steward, Deming, and their council would sit. The rest of the court would be seated at one of the many circular tables that nestled into the half moon shape the head table created. A small portion of citizens who had arrived early enough filled standing room space on the other side of the courtyard. A small aisle led from Dresden and Deming's chairs to a dais at the fountain where the High Priestess already stood. A prestigious selection of priestesses arched around the dais, forming another half moon that echoed the table shape.

They dismounted their horses at the entrance to the courtyard, where a collection of stable hands and servants waited to bring the barrage of hoofed animals back to the castle.

Deming's hand brushed gently over Quintessential's braided mane as she dismounted and fell in step with Dresden. As they began walking to their seats, a hush fell over the crowd. On Xiomara's cue, the priestesses raised their voices in chorus.

All members of the procession walked to and stood directly behind their seats. Dresden and Deming followed suit, but instead of stilling their feet by the table they continued down the aisle to the fountain and joined the High Priestess at the dais. The lilting voices of the priestesses stopped sharply at the exact moment Dresden and Deming turned to face Xiomara. The echoes of their song trilled through the courtyard for long seconds. As the final note disappeared into the night and the only sound remaining was the gentle bubbling of the fountain, Xiomara spoke.

"Welcome." Ever an authority figure, her voice was strong and steady and reached every corner of the expansive courtyard. "We are gathered here, in the midst of the longest night of the year and on the precipice of High Night, to acknowledge and honor the gift of life that Selene, Goddess of Eternal Wisdom, Holy Mother of the Midnight, Turner of Tides, and Queen of the Continent, gave us at the creation of all and continues to bless us with. On this one of two utmost Holy Nights I offer you all a prayer from the lips of the Goddess. May the water in your veins run clean."

Deming added her own voice to the chorus that responded. "And yours as in Selene's."

Everyone other than those on the dais sat.

Deming breathed in the scent of florals and night air. She suppressed the desire to turn around and look at the court behind her.

Xiomara continued with the ceremony. "High Steward Dresden." She bowed low, then turned to Deming and did the same. "Princess and Heir Apparent Deming. As a reminder that Crown and Temple are and will alway be two twin branches that uphold the Queendom of Laey in Selene's name, I now ask you both to recite the Vows of Sacrament."

Dresden went first. His voice was as sure and captivating as a stone from the sea that had been made smooth through years of waves lapping at it. "I, High Steward Dresden, offer myself as a conduit of Selene's will as I rule the Queendom of Laey in the heir's stead."

Xiomara reached to the upheld hands of one of her priestesses and dipped a finger into the clay mixture before her. She returned to Dresden and marked three half moon arches on his forehead, each one slightly smaller than the one before. The effect looked like a crude rainbow.

"I bestow upon you the marking of Goddess, Crown, and Temple. May you honor the Goddess in all you do."

Deming felt every pair of eyes in the courtyard shift to her. Her throat felt suddenly dry as sandpaper. She took a steadying breath before speaking clearly into the evening. "I, Princess and Heir Apparent Deming, offer myself as a conduit of Selene's will as I prepare to rule the Queendom of Laey."

Xiomara once more dipped her fingers into the clay and marked three arching lines on Deming's brow.

"I bestow upon you the marking of Goddess, Crown, and Temple. May you honor the Goddess in all you do."

On cue, the priestesses once more lifted their voices in song. Rather than another choral vocalization like the one they opened with, this one detailed the history of the world and Selene's role in it. A full bodied priestess with thick black hair braided into a knot atop her head sang the lyrics. It was a common song that Temple often highlighted, and members of court and council as well as commoners joined in if they knew the words.

Tears leapt to the corners of Deming's eyes. Something about songs from Temple lifted her in a way that other court music couldn't. She wished she could add her voice to the swell around her, but formality predicated that she remain silent during the ceremony unless directly spoken to by the High Priestess.

The final refrain ended, and Xiomara once more turned to the royals standing before her. "I now ask both of you, as stewards of the Goddess, to take a moment and bow your heads in silent prayer." She turned to the court and council, then the other half of the fountain and asked the same. In waves, everyone bowed their heads and a soft silence settled over the courtyard once more.

Deming closed her eyes. This was her least favorite part of the ceremony, even more so than her minimal public speaking. She had a healthy respect for Selene, all of the gods and goddesses in fact, but she had never felt comfortable praying directly to them. What were you supposed to say to someone who never spoke back? She settled on trying to find a small sliver of inner peace through breath work and sending grateful thoughts up to the Goddess for allowing herself and Dresden to maintain some level of stability in these troubling times.

The back of her neck prickled. The High Priestess had not asked the courtyard to raise their heads, and yet Deming found herself straightening. As if drawn together like the moon to the earth, her eyes slid immediately to the only other person not bent in prayer.

Slate gray eyes met her own. Her heart skipped a beat.

Nikita was night incarnate in a pitch black doublet and matching shirt with billowing sleeves tucked into well tailored trousers. His wings were resplendent. Even tucked in as they were, the shimmering undertones of color matched the light refracting from the lanterns. It looked like he had been created just for this moment. A puzzle piece that fit perfectly into this space.

He smiled at her from across the courtyard. She smiled back. She ached to go to him. It felt ages since they had last spoken, though she knew that wasn't true. She missed his insight and banter. When had he become someone whose companionship she not only tolerated, but craved?

He inclined his head in a bow, made infinitely more intimate by the fact that he did not break eye contact as he did so.

Before she could sketch a bow in response, Xiomara stirred out of the corner of her eye, rising from her own prayer. Deming snapped forward, eyes closed, and hoped her transgression hadn't been noticed by the High Priestess.

"The Goddess receives your prayers. Please rise."

Deming fought the urge to look at Nikita as everyone focused their attention back on the dais. Xiomara continued guiding the courtyard through the ceremony. She spoke more about Selene and how we are all connected through the life-giving water she gifted the earth. There were recollections of her travels through human cities at the dawn of time. Dresden and Deming walked in concentric circles throughout one particular retelling that documented the first Midwinter festival, during which Selene danced with the first human queen, Antelline. Song mingled in the night air.

As the ceremony drew to a close, midnight was upon the courtyard.

"High Night draws near." Xiomara's voice echoed through the lantern-lit evening. "While our physical honoring of the Goddess Selene culminates as she rises to her full height in the sky on the longest night of the year, we know that her light and life live within us always. Take joy in the warmth of the Goddess's embrace. May the water in your veins run clean."

Voices young and old melded in response. "And yours as in Selene."

Cheers erupted throughout the courtyard at the concluding line of the ceremony, marking both the Holy Hour and the beginning of the less structured portion of the evening.

Deming made to walk to their seats down the aisle, but Dresden touched her shoulder before she took a step.

"I know this has already been said," the High Steward began, "but I hope you know how proud I am of you."

"I know," Deming said earnestly.

"And maybe," her uncle continued with a prodding lilt in his voice, "next year you will be standing up here on your own."

Queen Deming Sofia Reynes-Elyachar. Not princess, not Heir Apparent.

She let the idea settle in her soul and found that it didn't invoke fear in the way it always had. "Maybe." That was as much as she could give for now, but standing there she knew that it would only be a matter of time before she took the throne.

The tides were changing.

CHAPTER THIRTY-THREE

IF THE COURTYARD OF Antiquities was steeped in history and demanded those inside to remember where the seeds of Arsaela began, the Courtyard of Silversmiths and Jewels was soaked in booze and demanded those inside to forget they ever existed.

The second location for the Midwinter festival was smaller than Arabella's Courtyard and square rather than circular. Those who wished to partake could dance and laugh in fellowship from High Night to dawn. Thanks to the coffers of Duke Lowell, cheap wine and cheaper beer flowed copiously from the tapped wooden barrels propped up in the alleyways radiating out from the courtyard. No one mingling through the streets seemed to care about the quality.

As long as it dulled their senses and made them forget about being trapped in a swirling dome of fog, the citizens of Arsaela would drink it.

The construction in the Courtyard of Silversmiths and Jewels was newer, and therefore looked no different than the other areas of the city. Cobblestones of tan, gray, and brown filled the ground and buildings built of stone and brick towered around. In place of a fountain, a handful of musicians stood in the center playing tunes ranging from romantic to bawdy.

Metal from the bench Deming sat on bit into the backs of her thighs. Crisp, cool. A perfect compliment to the heat flushing her skin from both the enchanted fire flickering in the nearby lanterns and the wine she swirled around in a thin-stemmed crystal glass then tipped back to swallow.

However smooth the ceremony had gone earlier and whatever flicker of praise she had received from her uncle mattered not in this moment. A queen she may become, but at her heart she was simply a girl who loved her city. This was the Arsaela she felt she belonged in.

Casual. Honest. Human.

The ting of nails tapping on iron made Deming blink.

Colette pulled her hand back, wrapping delicate fingers around the stem of her own wine glass, and tilted her head in question. "Hello? Deming? What has you so entranced?"

Deming looked around the courtyard. The center held bodies dancing to the string instruments plucking a tune. This particular song had a fast tempo and required one to jauntily step in between, out of, and around their partners legs, so many citizens had taken a moment of respite from dancing to explore the offshoots of activities that lay scattered in the surrounding streets.

There was a small contingent of shop owners who had brought a variety of their goods and set up along the street that led from the Courtyard of Antiquities to the Courtyard of Silversmiths and Jewels. Hand blown glass ornaments in any color imaginable hung in one stall. Another offered jewels set into bracelets and necklaces on chains so thin it seemed invisible. Many of the artists in the city took the opportunity to make extra coin and painted roses and swords and soaring amphitheres with vibrant feathered wings onto the faces of customers.

Food vendors stationed themselves on every corner. Smoked meats here, smoked fish there. A suckling pig roasting on a spit over a raging fire could be seen in the distance. The cloying scent of burnt sugar hung in the air, a remnant of the platter sized fried dough balls that had only seconds ago run out. A small boy with floppy hair, much too young to still be awake, ran off into an alleyway carrying the last golden brown, buttery treat with both hands.

Couples whispered sweet nothings into each others ears. Friends hugged and mingled. The din of laughter came from every corner of the courtyard.

A swell of pride for the resiliency of her people filled Deming's chest.

No threat of anarchy or destabilization could shatter their spirits. Every single person joyously partying the night away—citizen or visitor, young or old—refused to let the ever present cloak of fog take away from the one night a year that brought the world a little closer to the Goddess.

The light of the moon may be dim, but the light of their joy was not.

"Nothing in particular, I guess," she said, sighing deeply and smiling softly to herself. "Just admiring the view."

Colette harrumphed. "Does admiring the view preclude you from listening?"

"Oh, sorry. What did you say?"

The red head looked down the street, waving and smiling brightly at someone before turning back to her cousin and saying in an urgent, hushed voice. "Paris is heading this way."

Deming groaned. The warmth of the scene before her was no match for the sudden chill of dread that curdled inside her like sour milk.

"It won't be that bad, just smile and—"

"Hey, Colette. Deming."

Deming turned to the familiar voice and Paris's golden profile filled her vision.

He was resplendent in cobalt, his highly embroidered velvet doublet complimented the sky blue of his eyes. A stack of thin gold chains hung around his neck, twinkling in the light of the lanterns. He smiled at her and her heart cracked wide open.

It was infuriating to her that she didn't despise him.

Hate was an easy feeling. Sharp. Hot. Pointed.

Whatever was halfheartedly fluttering in her chest was not easy. The confusing mix of sadness and longing and hurt all laid against a backdrop of knowing beyond a shadow of a doubt that the decision to leave was correct was a duality she did not have the wherewithal to comprehend.

"Hi," Deming said, willing her voice to take on its natural tone. "How are you?"

Paris bit his lip. His chest rose and fell a few times before he said, "I'm fine. You?"

"I'm fine."

It felt as if a shimmering bubble coalesced atop them, drowning out the noise of the partygoers, the noise of the music, the noise in Deming's head. The world seemed to fade out until it was just the two of them.

Deming could see memories swimming in the depths of his eyes, just the same as she knew he could see in hers.

How was she supposed to reconcile who they were together and who they will be apart?

Was there a world in which they could make it back to the place of deep friendship that existed in their relationship? That friendship had existed on its own, long ago before either of them fell in love. It had laid the foundation for their love to grow. But overtime, romantic love wove its way into that foundation like roots seeking soil.

Deming didn't know if she could peel off the vines.

"The ceremony was beautiful," he said, taking a seat across from her. "You looked—" He cut himself off, cleared his throat. "You looked regal."

Deming ducked her head. The tiny wrinkles on the skin of her knuckles never looked so fascinating. "Thank you."

"I mean it," Paris continued, "you spoke so eloquently."

"Yeah, well, she should," Colette interjected, amusement lighting up her face. "She was speaking from a script."

Instantly the shimmering bubble around Paris and Deming popped.

Paris laughed. Deming smiled wide, eyes darting between her two friends.

"I'm serious," Colette continued. She took a sip of her wine. "A parrot could have done that ceremony."

Their whooping laughter drew no attention from the crowds who were deeply invested in their own lives and heartbreaks and humor, but it did ease the ache in Deming's chest.

She reached over to Colette and squeezed her hand, a silent thank you for breaking the tension.

Colette squeezed back, then let go and clapped her hands together. The sound crisply cracked through the air. "All right! Now that we have that awkward encounter over with, who wants another drink?"

CHAPTER THIRTY-FOUR

DEMING STOOD ON THE edge of the dancers, sipping on an amber ale that, given its tang, had soured far before being tapped. She cursed Lowell under her breath. Those around her may not care, but this truly was more swill than beer. The gods-damned cheapskate.

It was already two and a half hours past midnight, a little under halfway to daybreak. Dresden had retired not long ago, followed closely by most members of council and the more senior members of court who took his departure as an invitation to leave as well. The deeper the royal ties ran, the less people tended to spend at this second half of the celebration. There was only so much time amidst the commoners a lord and lady could take, after all.

Paris and Colette had gone back to the castle with them, leaving Deming and Vallyn alone in the throngs of people.

Deming took another swig of her beer.

"Want another?" Vallyn leaned against the brick wall behind her. The warrior had been relaxed all night, but Deming knew she was surveying every party goer for potential threats. The decorative uniform she wore similarly did little to dissuade onlookers of the idea that she was anything but strapped to the teeth with weapons.

She peered into the dregs of her stein. "No, two mugs of this is two too many. Thanks though."

Vallyn scoffed in agreement, having abandoned her first drink after only a few sips.

Deming returned to observing the crowd. She had spent the first couple hours dancing with Colette and by the grace of the Goddess had managed to avoid any awkward conversations with Paris. They were sure to come, but not tonight. A Midwinter gift.

Her friend had left the dance floor in exchange for the company of a burly, mustachioed man who had offered her a glass of merlot and stimulating conversation. Both were sure to be subpar, but Colette had never been one to turn down an intriguing proposition.

Deming was about to tell Vallyn they could return to the castle when the latter stiffened and turned towards someone in the alley-way behind them.

A melodic voice sounded from the shadows. "No need for alarm, Captain."

Hartford emerged, deep brown eyes glinted in the dim lantern light. The ambience of night highlighted the intensity of her gaze, no detail escaped her notice. Her hair crowned her head in tight curls as always, highlighting the pointed edges of her ears. She, like everyone else, had changed after the ceremony. Her formal gown was gone in favor of a well appointed but simple shirt and trousers. A satchel hung at her waist.

Deming had kept the pearl earrings and thin diamond necklace, but had changed out of the full-bodied ceremony dress in favor of the more slim-fitting one she had designed for the hours after midnight. Her current iteration was slippery gray silk, the fabric cascaded over her skin like water over fish scales. The neckline was scooped modestly then draped over her shoulders where the fabric hung in low, loose waves, showing most of her back. It was a rare occurrence for her to show off the mauled and scarred canvas of skin covering her back, but the dress Noreen and Julia had crafted was too tantalizing to pass up.

Her hair was curled and tied behind her with a matching gray ribbon. Because of the copious amounts of dancing that had occurred, more than a few pieces had fallen out of their confinement and now framed her flushed cheeks.

Suddenly aware that the female's presence was not only unexpected but breaking the rule Duke Lowell had laid down, Deming asked, "Aren't you supposed to be inside the castle?"

Hartford scoffed, head bobbing in a motion full of more disdain than Deming thought the stag-appointed Fae was capable of. Certainly more than she had shown thus far. "As if the petty squabbles of a human court could contain us."

Deming raised an eyebrow. Hartford waved her concern away.

"What that pompous man doesn't know can't hurt him," the female said flippantly.

This was not a good enough excuse for Vallyn. "The Duke may have arrogance and hatred fueling his gripes with you all, but he is not the only one to have qualms with how little information you are providing us." She took a step towards the Fae, utterly unfazed. "I should report this indiscretion to the High Steward immediately."

Hartford pulled a stone fruit out of her satchel and bit into it. She smeared the trail of juice that dripped from her mouth away with the back of her hand. "That is truly unnecessary. We told your court and council why we graced Laey with a visit as soon as we arrived. Aiding in the prevention of a cross continent war. We cannot do that within the confines of the castle."

Vallyn scoffed. "As soon as you arrived seems a bit gratuitous. You were snooping around the lower city for weeks before requesting an official sitting with the High Steward."

Hartford didn't seem to think the discrepancy was worth noting. "A week here or there is irrelevant."

Vallyn mumbled a curse under her breath. Hartford pretended not to hear.

The three of them listened to the merriment of the courtyard. It was deep enough into the night that the density of people had thinned marginally, but the intoxication had dramatically increased. It was loud and raucous, as Deming knew it would be for hours still. She mused that it may even last longer than normal, since the fog made the approach of dawn more subtle.

Hartford broke their silence. "We are not your enemy."

Deming waved her off. "That's besides the point. You can't expect us to trust you when you are being cagey with your information. We can't be expected to sacrifice the safety of our queendom just because you don't want to tell us what you're up to."

"You have no idea about sacrifice." Her voice dropped an octave. Her shoulders tightened with tension. "You can't begin to fathom how much some of us have sacrificed to be here."

Her abrupt change in tone shocked the two women enough to pause their queries into the Fae movements and motivations.

"We had not expected the fog any more than you," she continued, "And just as many of your constituents have been cut off from loved ones, so have we. My mate remains in Runne. We had been sending regular messages back to our own court. That has obviously been put to a stop thanks to this gods forsaken fog. She will have assumed we've been captured by now. Tortured and imprisoned in a far off court." Hartford stood, discarding the stone fruit and wiping her hands on her trousers. She cleared her throat, trying to regain some semblance of control over her emotions and failing miserably.

"The mating bond, it's like a sixth sense. There is this... deep knowing of rightness. I swear I can actually feel my mating bond with Soraya right behind my heart, as if when we accepted the bond she literally became a part of me." Her eyes glazed over with longing. "The bond can't fail unless one of us dies... but it certainly feels like that is what's happening. My second heart is barely beating. It's a shadow of itself. I can't imagine what Soraya must be thinking. To feel this too and not know where I am." She touched a hand to her chest. Tears welled in her eyes at the last admission. A singular drop rolled down her cheek before she snapped herself out of it and brushed the proof away.

Deming was quick to respond. "Thank you for sharing that part of you. It takes a strong woman to admit her vulnerabilities. Female, sorry."

Hartford exhaled loudly. Deming wondered how long she had been carrying her worries about Soraya around. If Nikita or Ilysse had thought to ask. She hoped they would have.

Her thoughts circled the idea of a mating bond. It wasn't unheard of for humans or mages to find their mate, though those instances were rare. The bond was harder to sense the further away one was from an inherent course of magic, so Fae found their mates more often than mages, who found their mates more often than humans.

When they were young, her and Paris would dream about the day their mating bond would reveal itself.

The thought sobered her.

Just as the three settled into a comfortable silence, a strong wind from behind them whipped more of Deming's hair out of place.

Wing beats. The scuff of shoes on cobblestones. Salt air.

As if born from the shadow and mist, Nikita prowled into the alley. "Hello, ladies. Hartford." The long drawl of someone unbothered.

"Any news?" All memory of the previous conversation fled Hartford's countenance like a thief in the night. Gone was the mourning lover and in its place, the Fae emissary.

A curt shake of his head. Black waves ricocheted off sharp cheekbones. Nikita leaned against the alleyway wall casually, dark curls framing his jawline elegantly.

Deming looked up to meet his eyes. "Are you more forthcoming than your emissary with the motions of your court?"

"Princess, we are merely trying to find a solution to this dastardly fog. As are you and yours."

"You were already in our city before the fog descended," she countered without missing a beat.

Nikita shrugged. His wings lifted and fell with the motion. Deming's eyes tracked with them. "Consider it a secondary priority."

"And the first priority?" Vallyn asked, voice clipped.

Nikita didn't miss a beat. "Preventing the war."

A non answer, one that had Vallyn clenching her jaw so tightly Deming feared her teeth may crack. Neither the heir nor the Captain of the Guard believed the Fae to have malicious intentions, but their tight lips were beginning to grate on them. Vallyn especially. It was hard to maintain trust in the foreign delegation when they refused to let anyone in on the details of their stay.

Nikita shifted on his feet. Cloud colored eyes darkened a shade as they drank in the sight of her. "Is that dress appropriate for the Heir Apparent of Laey?"

"Is your attitude appropriate for the Prince of Runne?"

Nikita chuckled. "More than fair, princess." He tilted his head and extended a hand. "Dance with me."

"I've danced plenty tonight and my feet are rather sore."

"Indulge me. A dance with you would be the finest thing life has to offer."

An echo of a memory rose with the warmth of blush to her cheeks.

"Do you always keep dainty clothing accessories in your fighting leathers?"

"What can I say, I enjoy the finer things in life."

She found herself accepting his hand. Rough calluses years in the making tugged against her own budding ones. "You're lucky I find your company enlightening. Though, as of late it's leaning towards infuriating."

Nikita smirked in acknowledgment of his win. "I won't argue with either point. Come."

He led her to the edge of the courtyard, then further into the mass of sweaty bodies. Outside of Nikita, there were only a few easy to pick out Fae. A female with the black tipped ears of a fox. A furred tail whipped to and fro. Deming saw reptilian eyes flash at her. They weaved through the throngs of people hand in hand until a small, unoccupied circle of stone appeared in front of them.

Nikita spun her around him, switching their grip with all the grace and ease of someone who had been spinning beautiful women around a dance floor for years. He guided her other hand to his shoulder while his own settled onto her hip. The slippery silk of her dress meant that she felt every twitch of muscle, every adjustment.

They had entered the fray in the midst of a fast paced number. Deming had danced to this particular one many times at court functions but as she made to fall into step with those around her, Nikita held her in place.

"We use different steps to this kind of tune in our territories. May I?"

She shrugged noncommittally. "You were the one who wanted to dance. Far be it for me to withhold part of the experience. I must warn you though," she said with a teasing edge, "I have danced with some of the most talented men Arsaela has to offer. I hope you lead well."

Conviction stole his features. "Oh, you'll find I can lead a female through a song as well as anyone."

"Woman."

"Elegance, grace, poise. Beauty." The hand on her hip flexed ever so slightly. Warmth pooled below her navel. "Woman or female. It's all semantics."

Deming cursed the waver in her voice as she responded. "Well, lead away then, prince."

As she expected, he was a ridiculously skilled dancer. The tempo of brass and drum was quick and left little room for error, but he pushed and pulled and guided her so flawlessly in step with the music that Deming realized after a moment she was no longer making conscious decisions about where her feet went. He played her like a harp and her body sang the tune.

She was spinning around Nikita, around herself, around the courtyard. The cobblestones blurred together. She knew that if the stars were visible they would be swirls of bright white indistinguishable from one another against the backdrop of the black sky.

Deming laughed as loud and free and joyously as she had when she was little and her father would heave her off the dock and into the warm waters of their summer estate.

She was breathless as the end of the song drew near.

With the final note, Nikita pulled her in close. It took a handful of rushed blinks before the world steadied itself again. Their heavy breath mingled in the sliver of air between their mouths. For a second they stood still as the ground beneath their feet. Hand in hand, smile to smile. His eyes flashed quicksilver.

"Can I help you, princess? You're rather flushed."

Suddenly she was hot and cold everywhere, all at once. She was not naive enough to blame it on the vigorous dancing.

Pull yourself together, Deming.

The musicians transitioned into a ballad.

"You lead well." Ignoring his question and its implications. She took a steadying breath and pulled herself away from him slightly. Her hand remained in his.

"I'm glad my claim proved true." Then, too casually, "A necessary skill I developed for the part I play back home. You understand."

Deming only nodded, still catching her breath. She hadn't spent time considering the weight his own crown might carry. Perhaps they had more in common than a shared intrigue for each other.

They swayed slowly in a circle to the new music floating through the air, both grateful for the change of pace.

When Deming was no longer fighting the need to gulp in air to her lungs, she posed a question, trying and failing to feign innocence. "Who's the lucky Fae that gets to claim you as their dance partner at your own court?"

"I have dallied with my fair share of eligible females. None have stuck thusfar," replied Nikita, an undercurrent of annoyance laced each word. "Speaking of partners, where is your darling Paris? I haven't seen him since the ceremony."

The mention of Paris doused Deming in ice water. "We are no longer together," she answered curtly, then added as an afterthought, mostly to herself, "And he wouldn't stay to dance even if we were."

Nikita let the information sink in. "How long ago?"

A pregnant pause. "The night you came to my room. I ended things before I went to bed that night."

Nikita chose his next words carefully. "You were... very upset. Distraught."

Deming jerked her head back and met his eyes. "Of course I was upset. He is one of my oldest friends. One of my only friends. And we were together for years. He was my confidant and protector. He is the only person I've…" She cleared her throat. "We shared many firsts."

A muscle twitched along his jawline.

"I don't think I've ever asked," Deming said, changing the subject, "how are you finding Arsaela?"

His feet hadn't skipped a beat the entire conversation. In fact, he was so light on his feet Deming rather felt like she was more air than muscle and bone. A stray breeze cooled her skin. They twirled gently around the cobblestones as he answered. "Arsaela is charming and quaint, frustrating and beautiful. I have loved every second of my existence here more than the last."

"Such elegant words for just a city."

"A city is a shell without its people."

"Ahh, so your praise is for my people."

The song ended and Nikita dropped Deming into a shallow dip, fingers splayed across her back and dark hair falling like a curtain around them. "My praise is for you," he mused softly.

Before she could attempt a response, Nikita pulled them out of the dip and took her hand in his once more. Already walking away, he said, "I'd like to show you something."

CHAPTER THIRTY-FIVE

DAWN WAS DRAWING NEAR and with it, the quilted beds of Arsaela beckoned her citizens home. Humans and Fae alike stumbled into apartments and corridors in various states of disarray. They passed a young couple consumed in a drunken lover's quarrel, their voices echoing off the alley walls. A tearful woman with limp hair after hours of festivities sat crossed legged on a bench, cradling her shoes. Two men with matching beards touched with gray held hands and whispered softly to each other before disappearing around a corner.

The aftermath of Midwinter never disappointed.

Nikita and Deming wandered in comfortable silence through the city. Nikita had plucked a lantern full of one of the enchanted flames from the streets. It's warmth kept them from shivering as they wandered further and further north.

"I'm surprised Vallyn let you out of her sight."

"I think she trusts you more than she lets on. And more than that, she knows how much the constant presence of a guard grates on me. Not her, personally. It's just nice to be alone sometimes."

"You aren't alone right now." Nikita nudged his shoulder into hers and scanned the sky. "I'm not convinced she doesn't have eyes on us somewhere."

"I'm not either," she conceded. Keeping a watchful eye on her from the shadows seems like something the Captain of the Guard would do. Deming could practically hear what Vallyn would say.

Even if it was fake, the semblance of privacy was delicious.

"It's strange," Deming spoke softly, "how quickly the magic of the evening melts into reality."

"Lucky for you, princess, dawn is not quite here and thus, a smidge of magic remains." Nikita stopped in front of a rather tall if not unassuming brick building. They had walked towards the castle, but veered left until they were at one of the uppermost corners of Arsaela that wasn't part of the castle grounds. There was a layer of dusky pines behind the building, but Deming knew that the exterior castle wall rose up not far beyond them. She could almost make out the pale stone of the wall from where she stood. Though serene and hidden away, their surroundings appeared otherwise ordinary.

"I appreciate the walk through town, but this hardly seems like a magical destination."

"That's because we aren't there yet, you wickedly impatient woman."

Deming looked over her shoulder to the left. Endless rows of pines. She looked to the right. The worn trail they had climbed up. She looked at Nikita and raised an eyebrow.

Nikita's grin only widened as he jerked his chin up.

Deming's eyes followed the action, up and up and up the solid wall to where she could see the top of the building weaving in and out of the edges of the fog. Her stomach clenched.

"You don't mean to tell me we have to climb this monstrosity?"

"I do not."

She pulled her eyes down to his. Her retort fell silent as she saw him reach out a hand, wings flared slightly in preparation for flight.

Her heart fluttered then stopped completely. She stumbled back. "Oh no. No, no, no."

"Fly with me." Either he hadn't heard her, or chose to ignore the weak protests.

"I couldn't possibly." She tried a more detailed response when it was clear her first explanation fell flat. "It wouldn't be appropriate."

"There is no one around to see, and my lips are sealed."

Deming broke their eye contact and glanced back at the open air above them. A shiver ran through her at the thought of touching the clouds, however foggy and mist-filled the sky might be at the moment.

"Only this once," she said meekly.

He echoed her words back to her softly. "As you wish. Only this once."

She stepped forward and took his hand.

Before she had a chance to breathe, Nikita pulled her close, far closer than they had been while dancing, swept her legs out from under her with his other arm, and launched into the sky. Deming yelped in fear and pressed herself further into his body, welcoming the tightness of his embrace and the warmth emanating from his core that was in sharp contrast to the bite of winter's air.

As suddenly as they had vaulted into the sky, they stopped. Eyes still closed, Deming felt their bodies undulating gently with the beat of Nikita's wings.

"You can open your eyes now."

"I don't know what you're talking about," she mumbled grumpily, flicking her eyes open.

The sight took away what little breath she had left.

They must have been a thousand feet in the air.

It was difficult to gauge height once the tips of the towering pines ended. Before them lay Arsaela in all her glory. The city lights were few and far between in these transitional hours. Not quite morning. Not quite night. Something in between. Lantern light still flickered from the courtyard. Candles lit only a handful of windowpanes. The castle rose regally above the city. The Telacien mountains reigned supreme above even the castle. The natural hierarchy of the world displayed poetically. The mountain range existed long before Deming's people, and would remain far after they faded into the ether.

"It's beautiful."

Nikita hummed in agreement. She was so closely nestled into his frame that the vocalization tickled her cheek.

They remained suspended in the air for a few moments more, hung like stars in the sky. Cold wind tugged at Deming's mass of curls. Her throat tightened. A singular tear fell from her lashes and winked out of existence as it dropped to the mass of green below.

Deming opened her mouth to protest as he began descending, then she realized he wasn't taking them to the ground but rather the top of the building they had walked to.

What she hadn't been able to see from below was that the building was topped with an open air perch of sorts made up of white pillars and crowned with a small, copper dome. As they approached she could see the copper was engraved, but time and weather had worn down the etchings to no more than vague lines and shapes.

Nikita touched down just outside the pillars. His landing was so soft Deming wouldn't have known his feet were on solid ground once more had he not begun to loosen his grip on her.

She stepped out of his embrace and immediately the weightlessness of flight dissipated into the dawn air. Her fingers itched to reach out and pull back whatever semblance of that feeling she could, but settled instead for brushing the wayward curls of her hair away from her face. Her heart pattered inside her chest.

"I didn't peg you as someone afraid of heights." Nikita had taken a few steps away from her, as if wanting to give her more space than necessary in the shadow of the intimacy of flying together.

He leaned a shoulder against one of the white pillars that held up the copper dome. What little rays of light that found their way through the fog backlit his features so Deming could only see the outline of him. She wondered if he was as flush as she felt.

"I'm not." The truth came out too wistfully, tangled up in nuance.

The winged male shoved off the pillar and walked to the edge of the building's chipped roof. He sat casually, dangling one leg over the ground below and tucking the other close to his chest. The muscles in his shoulders lifted to keep every feather off the roof. "Your heart rate certainly told a different story, princess."

Deming sat near him, but far enough away from the drop off that she didn't feel at risk of a deadly tumble. "You can tell my emotions from my heart rate? No, sorry," she corrected incredulously, "not the right question. You can hear my heart rate?"

He gestured towards his gracefully tipped ears. "Perks of the biology."

Deming cursed under her breath.

"I'm sorry," Nikita laughed, turning his head to face her, "what was that?"

"Gods-damned bastard with your Fae perks." Deming retorted, enunciating every word.

Nikita whistled. "Foul words for such a pretty mouth."

Deming pulled her knees in close and rested her chin on them for good measure. "I was not afraid of the height." She waited there, unsure how to continue. To his credit, Nikita seemed to sense her hesitation and waited too. When she found the courage to voice the words, they tumbled out of her. Disjointed and tentative at first, but with increasing ease as she let go.

"My first memory is of the sky. I remember flying through the air, feeling the tendrils of wind nip at my skin and hair and clothes. Feeling free and grounded and buoyant all at once. Nothing else existed except that feeling. No expectations. No pressure. No fear. Nothing. Only weightlessness and joy. It was the most pure and honest feeling I have ever felt in my life.

"Of course, I wasn't actually flying. My father was tossing me, a few years old at the time, in the air as high as he could, as father's do. But that feeling stuck with me. I became a girl obsessed with any and everything that had to do with the sky. I studied the cloud patterns and the weather. I can still tell when thunder is coming sooner than anyone else in the castle.

"When that didn't satiate me, I moved to birds. I spent hours upon hours, days upon days, in the castle gardens, finding anything with wings. I collected feathers in a pressed leather bound notebook my mother had specially made for me. I made note of beak shapes and eye colors and flight patterns. But the wings held my attention most of all. A few flaps and they were in the sky. They could go wherever they wanted. Be whoever they wanted. Birds bow only to the wind.

"Observing others fly wasn't enough either. I wanted to be in the air with them. To placate me, my parents hired the best riding instructors in Laey and taught me to master horseback. In their defense, riding Quintessential bareback through an open field is as close as I've ever gotten to matching the feeling I was looking for. She's a gods-damned fast mare."

Nikita chuckled beside her, his laugh jostling the pristine feathers of his wings.

"Despite this," she went on, "I got it into my head that all I needed to be happy in life was a pair of wings. Fae had them commonly enough, why couldn't I?" Here she paused to look at Nikita's wings. Glorious and powerful. Jet black. Alive with emotion. Jealousy reared inside her.

Deming tamped it down.

"I was young enough to turn a blind eye to the fact that Fae attributes are gods-given blessings, not the result of a doe-eyed child's wishes. I thought I could create wings for myself. My uncle was a once in a lifetime talent in healing and mystic offerings. I knew the ins and outs of his workplace better than my own bedroom. One night, when everyone was sleeping, I stole into the apothecary.

"Looking back, it's painful to admit how little I thought through my plan. How was an eight year old girl with no formal training going to make a tincture that would do anything successfully? Let alone the biologically impossible task of giving a human functional wings?" Deming cringed even now, a decade later. It was hard to give grace to her younger self knowing how much pain and destruction her actions caused.

"I didn't clean the workbench appropriately, and I didn't take the proper precautions for using fire in the apothecary. There are very specific sections made of mortar and stone to put lighting candles. I put mine directly on the wooden workbench. It fell over into a spill of alcohol, which lit the entire bench on fire. The contents of the apothecary are essentially a collection of kindling, and there are caskets of various flammable liquids stored in there as well. One caught fire and exploded. Within seconds the whole room was in flames.

"I was thrown against the wall and knocked unconscious. I can only remember bits and pieces of the rest of the night. I remember my father trying to find me. I remember the pain of my burns." She subconsciously brushed light fingertips against the puckered scar along her collarbone. She traced it down her stomach to where it disappeared behind her back, accented by the low back of her dress. She cleared her throat, continuing. "I remember hearing the screams of my parents as the ceiling of the apothecary collapsed.

"Apparently, my mother had rushed in first, only to get caught beneath one of the cabinets as it fell. My father saved me, then went back for her with my uncle. But the structural integrity of the room was too strained by that point.

"Three members of the royal guard. Two castle staff. One brother. One king. One queen. Quite the death toll I racked up in the matter of minutes. All because I couldn't get my head out of the clouds." She hugged her knees closer to the point of pain as her joints and muscles stretched, as if the smaller she made herself the smaller her crime would be.

Nikita reached over and placed a hand on the small of her back. It was a simple motion. It held no expectations, the touch barely noticeable. It was merely a gesture from one soul to another saying, I'm here. I understand. You are not alone.

"Since that night, it's been so hard to reevaluate what I want. I've avoided the crown because the responsibility is paralyzing. I've avoided exploring my passions and the impact I want to provide during my reign because of the trauma around my last passion. It was easy enough to shove the silly desire to be in the sky down, but then you and your," Deming huffed and shook her head, "you and your beautiful wings showed up and threw that out the window and the ache returned full force." Nikita's wings fluttered involuntarily at the compliment, but the rest of him remained respectfully still.

"I've been chasing the sky my whole life. So no, I was not afraid of the height. I was terrified of having my deepest hope realized. It was wonderful and magical and... Gods this is so stupid." She palmed the free flowing tears roughly away. "And everything that I ever thought it would be and now that I know all of that I have to live with the fact that I will never be able to do it on my own."

Deming laughed darkly and laid her back down on the crumbling stone. She flung an arm over her face in exasperation and shame. "I'm just a stupid girl who got her family killed over a childish desire and now has to somehow run a kingdom alone while living with the fact that she is superbly average in every way."

Neither one of them said anything for long moments. Birds chirped across the wooded expanse between the old lookout tower, for that must be the original purpose of the decrepit building, and the city below. Soft morning light filtered through the thick fog and danced atop the waves from the river as it emptied into the sea. The horizon was too far away, shrouded in gray, but dawn had finally arrived.

Nikita shifted his weight to lay on his stomach beside her. He reached over to pull her arm away, which she allowed but offset by turning her head to face the castle. He lifted a wing and covered them both in a canopy of feathers. "Deming." His voice was so soft and so full of emotion she indulged him and turned her tear stained, puffy face back.

Warm amber eyes met cool gray.

"Yes?"

"Nothing will bring your parents back. And time will never take away the pain of your loss. But life continues to grow even in the darkest of places. You know the power of loss in ways that most cannot begin to fathom. This makes you uniquely qualified to lead your people. You may not want the crown, but the crown needs you.

"And as for your last comment. You are a great many things, but average is certainly not one of them. You have a fire inside you, a light that shines so brightly even in the face of loss. I don't think you realize the power of it, or that it exists at all. I wish you could see yourself the way others do. Vallyn. Colette. Myself."

He reached over and brushed a calloused thumb across her cheek, taking the last of her tears with it.

Deming blushed, warmth pooling in her core. She found herself leaning into his touch and subsequently regretting its absence when his fingertips left her skin. Her eyes hadn't left his since he started speaking. She didn't know quite how to respond to his beautiful words. All she knew was that they felt like coming home.

"Thank you," she said softly. An inadequate response, but the only one she seemed capable of giving at the moment. "You speak of loss and pain..." She searched for the right word. "Intimately." She knew her eyes conveyed the question left unsaid.

Nikita's sigh was heavy and Deming instantly regretted bringing the topic up.

"You don't have to share," she sputtered, embarrassed.

"I know, I want to. You deserve honesty from me." He was silent for long seconds, then shifted his weight around so he was facing Deming fully, legs crossed beneath him. "It might be easier to show you."

Without further commentary, the Fae prince unbuttoned his shirt and peeled the clinging fabric away from his skin. Sprawled across his chest was a mass of intricate, intersecting whorls.

They were exquisite. Delicate and demanding and utterly beautiful and as soon as Deming processed what she was seeing her hand leapt to her mouth to cover the gasp that escaped. "You're a Rider?"

"No." His expression soured. It was only then that Deming realized there was something off about the pattern imbued across his chest.

The marking given to a Rider by an amphithere when chosen was supposed to be bold and defined. Nikita's was not. It was a ghost of a marking. A scar, almost. Thin and milky, there was no semblance to the opaque and ferocious examples she had seen in texts over the years. Deming had never met a Rider in person, but even she knew that what lay before her on Nikita's chest was wrong.

She looked up from his chest. Even the wind seemed to die at her hesitant next question. "What happened?"

He buttoned his shirt up slowly. "No one knows." In his voice was every emotion imaginable. A tangled mess of buried trauma. "The blessing was routine, as unexpected as it was. I was the first Rider to be chosen in decades but centuries could have passed and our people would remember the ways of the ritual. As soon as the Crest Major touched his snout to my chest, the mark appeared. My father, the whole realm, was so proud. I would live up to my birthright, rule Runne with an amphithere by my side. It would be the start of a dynasty unrivaled by any that came before."

Nikita closed his eyes and leaned back. His wings splayed out under him, the expanse of feathers covered nearly the width of the roof. "A week after being Marked, it began fading. It happened nearly over night. One day it was there, prominent and proud, and the next it was a flimsy excuse for the historic honor it is supposed to bestow. A shadow of what should be. Still, we tried. I went to the nest hundreds of times over the next three years. I met with every living amphithere. Meditated over every clutch of eggs. Nothing. It was unprecedented. Not that that made it any better.

"When no amphithere bonded me, my father banished me from the capital city. He would rather have no heir at all than the stain I had become. He said I can return when my honor is intact again." His hands were interlocked over his chest. They tightened so fiercely when he finished that Deming was worried his fingers would snap. "I was six years old."

Deming's pulse thundered through her veins. To be chosen so young was a burden to bear in and of itself, but then to be cast out at only six years old? Who had taken care of him? Had he ever spoke to his father again? His mother? How could a child that young possibly comprehend what was happening to him? Her blood began boiling at the choices the King of Runne had made. The sheer audacity.

She bit her tongue to stop the expletives on the tip of her tongue from spilling out. Anger did not seem to be what the weary Fae sitting beside her needed right now. He only needed an ear to listen to him.

Perhaps specifically, she realized with a jolt, her ear. Someone who could understand the soul twisting pain of loosing parental figures. Someone who, though their circumstances were different, shared a similar guilt gnawing at them from the inside out.

Nikita's admission weighed heavily in the air. To be rejected from one's family so completely was unimaginable. Especially over something no one had any control over. Deming's heart hurt intensely for the young prince all those years ago.

"Your father was wrong for..." She frowned. "Everything. All of that. You were just a child."

"I know," he said, pulling himself up off the ground and back into a seated position. "Time and truth doesn't make the pain any less sharp."

Deming nodded solemnly. She knew that well. How many nights had she been torn from sleep within the last few months because of nightmares? Her parents had died a decade ago and the wound still felt fresh.

She had so many questions for him, but now seemed not the time. They were both raw and vulnerable. This night was fragile, tenuous. And though Deming was sorry to see the carefree air they shared while dancing go, she still wanted more than anything to distill the feeling of being here, right now, with Nikita.

He made her feel known, down to the marrow of her bones.

And then it hit her.

"You're the first friend I've made in a long, long time." Her voice was full of both sorrow and awe. "I didn't realize that was something I had been missing."

Nikita tilted his head in that familiar way of his. There was an ever so slight tug upwards at the corner of his mouth. "You have Colette."

"Blood relative, doesn't count."

His face twitched, relaying his desire to argue, but he left it alone. "And Paris."

Deming sighed and buried her head in her hands. Her response came out mumbled. "Don't remind me. The one honest friend I've made now hates me."

"He's hurting, he doesn't hate you."

Colette had said as much to her, too. Deming sucked on her teeth. They were right, of course.

"I haven't made many friends, either," he went on. His barely there smile was full of quiet gratitude. "I'm glad you're one of them."

Happiness bloomed in her chest like a garden in spring. "I'm thankful to know you, Kit." The name he had asked her to call him all those weeks ago felt foreign on her tongue. Odd, but... satisfying. "Kit." She tested it again, more to herself than to him. It felt the way a drop of water hitting a puddle sounded. She turned her gaze to him. He was looking at her with an intensity she rarely saw in him. "I'm sorry," Deming fumbled, "You had asked me to call you that but I don't have to—"

"Never stop saying my name." His voice was husky and raw.

Her mouth was suddenly so dry any attempt at responding was impossible. She opted for a shaky bob of her head.

A rooster crowed in the distance, long and screeching and loud, and just like that, the insular ecosystem they had existed in momentarily dissolved.

Nikita cleared his throat, raised his wings, and stood.

Deming tore her eyes away from him and took a handful of steadying breaths while looking out over the shrouded city.

The suggestion of dawn was permeating through the clouds. A sudden desire to see the beauty of Arsaela bathed in morning light panged in her chest. The fog had taken so much from them. Although the heart stopping, buttery glow of dawn caressing thatched roofs and cobblestones and the evergreen needles of Fairhaven Forest was not high on the list of reasons to break free of its grasp, Deming longed for the sight all the same.

When her fingers had stopped trembling, she brushed off the rubble and grit from her dress and cringed. Noreen and Julia would have a conniption when they saw the state of the gown they had painstakingly put together. She'd have to make it up to them somehow.

Nikita held out a hand. "To the ground?"

"Mm... It really would be such a waste of time to walk back to the castle." She let the insinuation hang in the air.

Nikita loosed a low laugh. "As you wish."

She did wish. She had tasted the wind and found it to her fancy.

Deming restrained herself from jumping into his arms when he held out a hand. She couldn't quite hold in her squeal of glee though as he opened his wings and launched them into the sky.

If at all possible, the view was even better in the buttery light of early morning. Even the tendrils of fog that snaked around the tallest spires of the castle looked less menacing.

They approached her balcony far too soon, though the disappointment was muffled by the sight of Hollis licking the multi paned double doors with an exuberance only a dog welcoming her human home could have.

Nikita brought them down right next to the iron railing and lingered only slightly in letting Deming out of his arms.

"Your dog is happy to see you."

Deming opened the door and slipped inside, leaving it ajar for Nikita to follow. "Don't let her fool you, she gets this excited for everyone."

The huff he let out made it clear he very much doubted that statement.

Hollis bounded underfoot as they entered. Furred paws slapped against the floorboards, her tail whipped through the air so quickly her entire rump shook back and forth. Deming collapsed onto the ground laughing and let the black hound lick her face like the pup's life depended on it.

Once Hollis settled, Deming, still on the floor, leaned against her bed and pulled the pup into her lap to scratch the soft fur behind her ears. Nikita watched the pair with shimmering amusement from just inside the balcony door. His hand rested on the frame, keeping it propped open.

Her lips turned down into a soft frown. "Are you leaving?"

"We both need to rest. The castle will be awake soon and I doubt a hangover coupled with only an hour or so of sleep makes running a queendom any easier."

Running a queendom.

The shimmering bubble they had existed in for the past few hours had put enough space between Deming and the crown she had nearly forgotten all there was to do tomorrow.

Today, actually.

Neither said goodbye, though. Only when the clock tower chimed morning in the distance did Nikita compose himself and exit through the balcony doors. He gave Deming a wink that sent her heart fluttering and then swan dove off the ledge into the breaking dawn.

A chill crept into the room that had nothing to do with the winter air and everything to do with the Fae's absence.

Deming gave Hollis one last kiss, the dog's brow soft and warm, then left her to curl up on a mass of blankets in the corner of the room. She padded to the bathroom and peeled off her dress. Laid the necklace and pearls gently on the counter. Pulled every pin out of her hair until it cascaded down her back in gentle waves. Washed off the rouge and kohl with cold water.

As she wiped away the last of the droplets, Deming paused to look at her naked reflection. She traced the scar down the smooth column of her neck and across her chest and ribcage to where it dovetailed. The larger swath disappeared to her back, out of sight. The smaller tendril wrapped itself around the supple curve of her breast. A grotesque shadow of the way a lover's hand might cup it.

Her finger traced that, too. The rippled scar tissue forever pink and puckered.

Deming cut off the thought that threatened to turn her world upside down before it fully formed.

She sighed and returned to bed.

She dreamt of the full moon and starry skies and cold air nipping at her face high above the clouds.

CHAPTER THIRTY-SIX

AN HOUR OF SLEEP is definitely not enough to run on, but the gods give their hardest battles to their strongest warriors. At least, that's what Vallyn had reminded Deming as the latter stifled a yawn for the fifth time in half as many minutes.

Deming's eyes shot daggers at her companion, who merely shrugged as if to suggest this is what she deserved for disappearing for hours with Nikita.

Turns out Vallyn hadn't been following them after all. They had indeed escaped her gaze and had true moments of privacy in the early hours of the morning.

She knew that Vallyn would be marginally upset that the pair had left the Courtyard of Silversmiths and Jewels without telling her or Hartford, but the defense Deming kept coming back to was that if Nikita had wanted to kill her he would have done it by now. Vallyn could at least agree with that train of thought. The guard was more miffed that she lost sight of them than anything.

However, surely unrelated to her escapade last night, Vallyn had pushed Deming particularly hard this morning. Training waited for no one, especially not a terribly exhausted princess.

The white-haired woman apparently had hardly anything to drink last night and, after a cup of black tea, was perfectly awake and in no mood to go easy on the princess.

Deming wiped the sweat from her brow and rolled her shoulders, relishing in the stretch it provided the unbearably sore muscles protecting her spine.

"You're improving."

Deming lifted an eyebrow at the compliment. "Are you feeling well? Should I check your water for poison?" She made a show of sniffing the Captain of the Guards water skin.

Vallyn rolled her eyes and continued cleaning their equipment. "Don't make me say it again."

Deming ducked her head to hide the smirk tugging at her lips.

She did feel stronger, quicker. She may not be a prodigy with a sword, but she felt confident in saying her skills were competent. And as pathetic as that sounded, the thought filled her with pride. It felt good to do this for her body, for her.

"Princess Deming."

The heir turned. A guard had appeared at the corner of the ring the pair of them had been sparring in. He held out a tightly rolled, very small scroll.

"A priestess arrived at your chambers not long ago, asking for a private audience. When denied, she scrawled this note and left. She was in quite a hurry."

Deming's brow furrowed. She walked to where the guard stood and plucked the parchment from his hand. "Did she say what this was in reference to?"

"No, Your Highness." The guard sketched a bow, then turned sharply on his heels and exited the pit.

Vallyn's feet shuffled closer. Deming didn't have to look to know the woman was peering over her shoulder, intrigued to see what a priestess had to say to the heir this early in the morning with as must haste as the guard alluded to.

Deming slid her thumb under the open end of the scroll and pulled. The parchment crackled as it unrolled.

A brief but perfectly complete silence settled like a cloud over the room as they read. Then Deming said, "Well this is vague."

Vallyn considered the short phrase haphazardly written on the note before them. Her countenance immediately falling from interested to on edge. "It's actually very specific."

Deming leaned closer. "Are we looking at the same thing? All it says is Swallow Street."

Vallyn ran her finger underneath the penned street name. "No, it's a time, too. See?" She tapped the note twice, once under the fifth letter in swallow and once under the sixth. "Both are darker, more pronounced."

Deming did so, tilting her head unconsciously, and gasped softly as the poorly hidden code rammed into her. "She wants to talk to me at ten."

After notifying Dresden, the pair found themselves stalking down the streets of Arsaela while its residents slept off their drunken stupors. The location the priestess had scrawled on the note, Sparrow Street, was only a few blocks away.

A sharp yowl from around the corner drew their attention.

Vallyn held out an arm to stop Deming and was halfway through drawing her sword when a pair of mangy cats darted across the cobblestones, spittle and hair flying.

The warrior muttered a string of curses and sheathed the weapon.

As they began walking again, Vallyn commented, "Seems odd that she needed to meet you in such a secluded place, no?"

Deming shrugged, "I don't think it's that odd. Temple is hardly the place to keep a secret, the shadows sing to Xiomara. I think it's quite easy to understand why she might want to meet somewhere she can speak freely."

"You don't trust the High Priestess." Not a question.

"It's not that I don't trust her, though I don't. It's more that whatever is said inside Temple walls has a way of finding the ear of the High Priestess. Perhaps our informant wanted the crown to hear what she has to say first."

Vallyn nodded, considering.

The city was quiet in the wake of Midwinter. The only sounds were the slaps of their shoes on the wet ground and the occasional ping and clatter of a rat or other small animal knocking a leftover stein around. The glass and paper lanterns that wreathed the city in iridescent color only hours before now hung limply from windows and wire strung across the sky, the candles inside melted to waxy puddles. Even the fog seemed to have taken advantage of the sulky, sleepy mood that had settled over Arsaela. It crept around corners, licking stone and gravel with intimate hunger as if the lack of life beckoned it to crawl deeper into the belly of the city. The morning held enough warmth that the ice it had caused to coat the city had melted, but the grayness remained ominous all the same.

Deming kicked at a tendril as she turned the last corner.

Without warning she was sharply yanked backwards by the fur lined collar of her jacket. Her attempt to choke out an exclamation was suffocated by Vallyn shoving a gloved hand over her mouth.

The warrior pulled the two of them quickly to the alleyway. The song of steel echoed through the morning air as Vallyn's sword was drawn and raised in front of them.

"Keep quiet," she hissed in Deming's ear.

Deming made to quip that whatever sound that had alerted Vallyn was likely just another cat, but stopped at the realization that the air suddenly felt charged with malicious intent.

Panic coursed through Deming, blood pumping through her veins so hard it felt like it was pounding against her skin. She swung her head around, trying to find the threat that Vallyn had picked up on.

Nothing from where they came from. Nothing aerial from what she could see, though the tall building walls limited her sight. That left only the long expanse of the alleyway to their—

Her stomach muscles contracted violently.

Her mouth filled with the taste of bile and vomit.

Crumpled in the middle of the alley like a rag doll, limbs bent at vile angles and skin flayed from flesh, lay the corpse of the priestess.

Stars flooded Deming's vision. Her peripheries turned pitch black. The cold stones threatened to rise up to meet her face as she lost her balance. Only Vallyn's steadying grip kept her from fainting.

Only an utterly grotesque semblance of a human remained where the priestess once existed. Had it not been for the temple robes and the fact that the left side of her facial features had been left intact, there was no way she would have been recognizable. The skin on the right side of her face had been scorched off. Black char flaked off into a pile on the street. Most of the skin on her extremities had been peeled away. Likely while she was still alive.

What remained of her mouth lay agape. It was a particular type of horror to see a human mouth without a tongue. Rows of chipped teeth peered out behind chapped lips. The column of her throat laid bare. A bloody tear across where the base of what would be her tongue connected to the hollow of her jaw.

The thought sent a fresh wave of nausea rolling through her. Deming retched.

Vallyn hissed and shook the warm bile from her hand, wiping the rest on her thigh.

"How..." Deming's voice shook uncontrollably. "How could some-one..." She gulped down air, wishing she had something strong to settle herself.

"Be quiet," snapped Vallyn.

She guided Deming down the brick wall to a sitting position, tucking her into as small a space as possible, before thrusting a small, sleek, silver dagger into her clammy hands. She then placed two hands on the hilt of her sword and stalked the perimeter of the alleyway. Smooth and efficient, the warrior cleared the corners nearest the body then circled tightly around the blocks immediately surrounding the scene of the crime.

Deming squeezed her eyes shut. She willed her heart rate to slow.

Deep inhale. Rust and tang coated her senses. Blood.

Slow exhale. A shuddering breath escaped her.

Deep inhale. Blood.

Slow—

"Deming."

She moved so quickly the muscles in her back seized. Her palm slapped and slid against the rough brick, opening small, stinging wounds on her palms. Her terror-filled eyes shot open.

Only Vallyn.

Slow exhale.

Deming leaned her head against the wall. All she could manage was, "Yes."

"We need to move. The area is clear at the moment but whoever did this is not far away. She is still bleeding."

Deming leaned to the side and heaved up whatever was left in her stomach. Slick remnants spattered onto her hand and soaked into the silky smooth velvet of her shawl.

She wiped the bile and froth from the corner of her mouth and stood on shaky legs. "What do we do with the body?"

"We'll have palace officials retrieve it immediately and bring it back to the castle." She kept a hand hovering near Deming's waist, not trusting the princess to stay upright. "We'll be able to take a closer look and determine the cause of death there, without risk of citizen interference."

"Leaving her here is risking citizen interference."

"You are my priority. Always. I need you far away from whoever did this. Once I am not the only person between you and certain death I'll be able to focus a bit more on whatever the fuck happened here. Now, go before I throw you over my shoulder."

Deming nodded and deliriously stumbled out into the main street, Vallyn's one hand firmly on the small of her back and the other grasping tightly to her still drawn sword.

Time morphed strangely as they made quick work of the walk back. It was all Deming could do to put one foot in front of the other. Was she blinking too much? Why were her fingers twitching? She distantly heard Vallyn say something but she couldn't remember if it was directed at her or someone else walking by. One second she saw a Fae male with lavender hair on the street corner the next he was gone. Had her palms always been bloody?

They made it to the last winding road with the castle looming high above when Vallyn whistled sharply and beckoned something in the sky with her sword.

Not something, someone.

Nikita landed in a flurry of black and white feathers.

"What happened?" Death would have had a warmer whisper.

"There's a corpse in the south quarter. Young priestess."

"Give her to me." At Vallyn's hesitation Nikita hissed, "She's mine."

"She is no one's but her own." Venom laced her response, but Vallyn released her grip. "Keep your territorial Fae bullshit on the other side of the continent." Despite her words, she passed Deming's barely standing body over to Nikita. "I'm reporting to the High Steward and then will meet you in her room." She glanced at Deming. "A bath will help. Eucalyptus essence. Respectfully." The weight of the last snarled threat lay heavy in the air.

Deming had the vague sense that someone was talking about her. And then the peculiar sense that she was no longer tethered to the earth. The priestess's death was a rip in time. Her decimated body a beacon that sound and light swirled towards.

Strong arms set her down on something plush with a feather soft touch. The light in the room went out. No, that wasn't quite right. The light in the room was blocked. Shrouded by a feathered shield that shimmered like oil. Deep shades of indigo and copper surrounded her. Piercing gray eyes cut through the chaos in her mind. They tilted. She cocked her head to match.

Blinked once. Twice.

On the third flutter of her lashes Nikita's voice broke through, quiet and muffled at first like it was traveling through an ocean to get to her.

"…to talk to me. Do you understand?"

"What?" The word croaked out. She cleared her throat.

Visible relief flooded his features at her response. He hung his head and exhaled sharply.

Brought back from the dead, sensations rushed up to Deming. His broad wings cocooned them tightly. Light filtered through only at the very edges where his feathers were downy and thin. Both hands, impossibly large, cradled the sides of her face. The tight space was filled with the warm, cardamom smell of him. She was sitting on a green velvet lounge chair. They were in her bathroom, then.

Nikita lifted his head. "You scared the shit out of me, you were catatonic with shock. What happened? Talk to me, please." His wings relaxed, hands slipped off her cheeks. He leaned back on his heels, staying at the same eye level as her as she recounted in a whisper why she and Vallyn had been in the city and what they had found.

Who they had found.

She couldn't bring herself to describe the mutilation the priestess' body had gone through. Nikita didn't ask. He would almost certainly see it for himself later.

Instead, he looked at her curiously and, with complete softness and immediate understanding, said, "You've never seen a dead body before."

Deming shook her head, emotion thick in her throat once more. "Not many. The attackers you… In the alley this fall. And my parents. Both times were at a distance."

He only nodded and sighed solemnly. After a moment, "I'll draw you a bath." He rose and brought flame to life in the fireplace, heating the large vat of water above it.

Deming watched silently as the Fae male paraded around the room, gathering all the tinctures and soaps for a bath.

When the water was hot but not scalding, he filled the basin and put a few drops of eucalyptus essence in, letting the oil mingle with the heat and fill the room with a calming scent.

He turned to Deming, running a hand through his loose, black curls and leaving it to rest on the back of his neck. He opened his mouth to say something but before he could, the room was flooded with overlapping voices as three bodies appeared in the open doorway.

Paris was the first through, broad shoulders edging out even Vallyn who was quickly followed by the slim form of Colette.

"Deming, I heard what happened. Are you—" The rest of the sentence died in his throat as Paris beheld who else was in the room. "What are you doing here?"

Nikita's lips pulled into a snarl but a pointed look from Vallyn had him remembering what she just told him. He seemed to debate pointing out that Paris was being just as territorial but ultimately decided it wasn't worth his time.

"I was just leaving," he ground out before swiftly exiting the room without looking back.

Though she was loathe to collect herself without Nikita present, it was a relief to not have to deal with a confrontation between the two.

In his absence the weight of the morning settled more heavily on her shoulders. She felt achey, tired. As if she could fall into a deep slumber. He had pulled her out of a deeply dissociative experience. The winged male was a better balm for the ever present panic in her bones than any medicine she'd tried over the years. When had that happened?

Paris turned back to Deming. "Are you okay?" He looked back, following her line of sight as she stared at the now empty doorway.

He stepped to the left, taking up her field of vision. "Vallyn filled us in."

"Unwillingly," she growled from the corner, arms crossed.

Colette trilled lightly, head poking out from around Paris's shoulder. "I noticed her going to my father's study. It seemed urgent. And since she's usually with you, I was worried you were in trouble."

"They eavesdropped on private state business like children."

"Deming," Paris pulled her attention back to him, "are you okay?"

"I'm fine. Just in shock."

He waited for her to say more. She found she couldn't.

Colette, Goddess bless her, put a hand on his shoulder. "Let's let her bathe. We can talk more later."

Pain filled his eyes. "I don't understand, Deming."

"I just need a moment to breathe."

Paris made a move towards her, as if to take her hand in his and comfort her with more than words. But he halted, his motions stiff when the fact that they were no longer more than friends came barreling back to him.

"I'll see you later, I promise. Thank you for checking on me."

He nodded and reluctantly headed towards the door.

Colette blew a kiss as she followed. "I love you."

"Love you too."

Deming took a deep breath with their departure. Still, she trembled.

"Vallyn?" Instantly the Captain of the Guard was at her side. She bit the inside of her cheek, focusing on the pain to keep the wobble out of her voice. "Can you get Miriam? Please?"

A curt affirmation and the guard swept out of the room.

Deming kept her mind occupied by lathering her skin with soap. The methodical motions soothed her just as much as the eucalyptus scent wafted from the water.

Calves and thighs, shoulders and arms. The soft plane of her stomach. The scarred tissue on her back.

She cupped water in her palms and splashed her face.

Only when the layer of death that she had felt coating her lifted slightly did she rise from the bath and wrap herself in a luxuriously thick towel.

Padding to her room, she pulled on soft linen pants and a matching shirt. She grabbed a warm, oatmeal colored shawl and threw it on.

Miriam walked through the door just as the wool settled into place on her shoulders.

The sight of Miriam snapped what little resolve Deming had left. The sob that escaped her was mangled and harrowing.

Miriam crossed the room in seconds, sweeping Deming into her arms and murmuring softly against her skin. "You're okay, my love. You're safe. I won't let anyone hurt you. Vallyn won't let anyone hurt you." Each sentence accompanied by a stroke of her hand through the wet tangles of Deming's hair.

"It's not—me—it's not—my safety—I—" There was no more air in her lungs to speak. Deming curled deeper into Miriam's arms and cried and cried.

"Come here, love." Miriam pulled her to the bed, nestled her in with the pillows and blankets. She leaned over to the nightstand, one knee on the bed, one hand still protectively on Deming, and grabbed a brush. Then, without jostling the princess too much, Miriam settled behind her and began brushing out the knots.

She was patient, waiting for Deming's body to stop shaking when waves of fear and adrenaline hit her anew. Her touch was masterful, each pull from root to tip eased a small bit of the knot in Deming's chest.

Slowly, Deming's sobs subsided until she was only hiccuping softly.

"I'm not worried about myself," Deming said quietly.

Miriam didn't push. She combed through the last swath of hair,
set the brush aside, and began braiding with nimble fingers.

"It's my fault she died."

There it was.

It wasn't only the sight of the priestess' corpse that caused Deming
so much pain, though that was gruesome. It was the knowledge
that she was responsible for the blood that painted the alleyway
pavement. She was responsible for the flayed muscle decorating the
walls. She was responsible for the shards of bone jutting out from
the flesh like knives.

"That isn't your burden to bear."

"Yes, it is. She wanted to share something with me and got killed
for it."

Miriam sighed and shifted so she could look at Deming. "Then let
me help carry the weight. You are not alone. You never have been
and you never will be."

CHAPTER THIRTY-SEVEN

A CHORUS OF CREAKING wood filled the chamber as each council member took his or her seat, echoing off the high ceilings and putting Deming more on edge than she already was.

Dresden rose, bejeweled crown twinkling brilliantly in the candlelight. "Thank you for joining us on such short notice. We are yet again faced with a grave crime." He held everyone's gaze with rapt attention. "Early this morning, Princess Deming and Captain of the Guard Vallyn, ventured into the South Quarter in pursuit of information offered up by one of our temple priestesses. The content of the information was not clear. When they arrived at the meeting location, they found the priestess flayed and brutalized."

Everyone had the good sense to gasp even though many of them had heard the news through their own personal information networks.

The High Steward continued, "I have dispatched members of the royal guard to retrieve the body. We will be establishing cause of death in the following hours. We don't know if there is a connection to the attempt on the princess' life and the fog, or if it was an isolated incident. Though," he sighed, weary and troubled, "the repetitive nature of these attacks lends itself to one of two solutions. Either they are interconnected and purposeful, or the fog is an anomaly and someone is taking advantage of the situation to destabilize our queendom."

The room was silent, everyone mentally running through scenarios and coming to no conclusions. Whoever was behind the murder this morning knew what they were doing. Seeds of doubt had been planted and sowed in the minds of the council, in the minds of the entire city, surely, when the news broke to the masses.

Though tendrils of panic still licked at the corners of her consciousness, Deming felt steady enough to consider how the recent events fit together with everything else that had happened in the past few months. The timeline was clear, though any sort of reasoning was not.

If they were to be trusted, which Deming thought they were, Nikita, Ilysse, and Hartford arrived in Arsaela in the midst of fall to scope out the city for evidence of this supposed impending war. Shortly after, the fog collapsed on Arsaela, isolating the city from the rest of the continent but not harming anyone. Deming winced at the recollection of what followed. The terror of being drugged and kidnapped by the two men at Firebrand's was easy to remember.

She pushed past the memory.

The thugs were killed by Nikita, who had been watching her at the bar and who also had found evidence in the escaped horses saddlebags leading to the arrest and conviction of Sasha. No chaos happened for weeks, then the priestess asked to meet with Deming. The priestess was murdered.

They had to be connected, didn't they? The priestess must have known something about Sasha or the fog that someone didn't want known.

The little food Deming had managed to keep down this morning curdled in her stomach. This wasn't over. Someone was still out there, hunting.

A pointed, quiet question from Lady Brittan broke the contemplative, concerned silence that had gathered in the room. "How do we know who to trust? Whoever murdered the young girl clearly knew her connections to the princess. They must have seen her in the castle. Are we to suspect our own, now?" Her voice wavered at the last half.

Eyes began flitting about the chamber, sizing up the lords and ladies trying to determine if one was more capable of murder than the other.

From the end of the table Lord Nolett spoke. "In light of the information we are now privy to and the events of last night, I would like to make a formal motion to place the visiting Fae delegation under arrest."

Deming's stomach dropped, her eyebrows furrowed in confusion. What?

Apparently she had said that out loud. "I know our princess has grown quite close to the Fae prince," Lord Nolett inclined his head to Deming, who was now sitting straight and stiff in her seat, hands balled tightly into fists, "however, the evidence against them is increasingly difficult to ignore."

Miriam put a hand on Deming's shoulder and squeezed, silently commanding her to reign in the bubbling emotions that were written across her face.

The High Steward responded. "That is a hefty accusation, Lord Nolett. Indulge us, please."

The lord stood, lithe and tall. The warm tones of his buckskin vest and emerald pants did nothing against the chill in his voice. The words came out confident but soft, as if even he didn't want to believe what he was saying. "The delegation has always been vague about their intentions. They claim to desire strengthening diplomatic relations, but where have any of them been this fall? Their liaison, the female with the antlers, has sparsely attended court sessions. And the threat of war? The prophecy? They could provide no tangible support for this. We all assumed the fog was a sign their seer was correct, but what if it was all a manipulation to worm their way into our court?

"We all seem to have conveniently forgotten how suspicious their arrival was. They were doing goddess knows what for two weeks before presenting themselves to court and were at the scene of the crime when the princess was attacked the first time. Perhaps the prince saved her in order to build in a level of plausible deniability later on."

Lord Nollet began pacing the room, his words rushing out faster and with more fervor as if the more he spoke, the further he convinced himself of the Fae's crimes.

Deming whipped her head around, looking from council member to council member. Lady Brittan was nodding solemnly. Duke Lowell was twirling his mustache with fingers full of too tight rings, his flesh bubbling up around the sides of the metal. Miriam looked worried, but convinced. And her uncle. Dresden's gaze was hyper focused on Nolett, hanging on to every word like the accusations were a savior in the night.

Nollet stopped at the head of the table. He placed his hands on the wood, leaning over slightly. "And last night. We were told they would return to the castle after the ceremony. However, I have been told by multiple sources that they were instead roaming the city unwatched.

Princess Deming was even seen dancing with the prince. Her and the Captain of the Guard can confirm the foreigners location."

Lowell's dark eyes shot to her. "Is this true?"

"Well, yes," she stuttered, caught off guard, "but both Vallyn and I were with them the whole time! The murder happened this morning, it isn't connected at all." She looked to the warrior for confirmation.

Vallyn shot her an apologetic look before stepping forward and addressing the room. "Princess Deming was indeed with Prince Nikita the whole night, and I remained with their liaison for the majority of the evening, but the lioness warrior was unaccounted for in the city."

Betrayal sank solid and deep in her gut. She didn't understand. Vallyn had reciprocated Deming's own feelings of trust on multiple occasions. Why turn her back on them now?

Vallyn offered a single shred of opposition to the accusation hanging heavy in the air. "I'd like it to be known that I have come to trust the delegation. However, it is possible that they are responsible and were using half their party to distract the princess and myself while the others strategized about removing the priestess from play. Even last night they were cagey when directly asked about their intentions."

The whole conversation took less than a minute. Concise. No nonsense. And to Deming's chagrin, extraordinarily convincing to the rest of the chamber. She sat, shocked into silence with her mouth hanging open like a fish, and watched as member after member nodded and mumbled their agreement. Slowly at first, then with more vigor. In a matter of seconds the fickle chamber was collectively demanding Dresden to send royal guards to the Fae's tower immediately.

Fortunately, Deming finally found her voice. Unfortunately, the protest that came was childish and unconvincing. "You can't!"

"The safety of the queendom comes first, Deming." Soft words from Miriam whispered only to her. "They will have a fair trial. The truth will reveal itself."

Tears pricked her eyes. "They didn't do anything! I know it in my bones. I know it like I know myself."

Miriam stroked her hair. "Then they will have nothing to hide."

"Give them a chance to prove themselves, force their hand!" Her voice increased in pitch and desperation with every word. If they knew the options were to divulge the full truth or be brought to the dungeons, she was sure they would offer exonerating evidence.

Although, would Nikita actually do that? Her heart hammered in her chest. He only just last night shared about his Rider's Mark in confidence. He was so stubborn and closed off there was a chance that whatever else he was hiding was worth rotting in a dungeon for.

Dresden didn't even look at her. He stood and spoke with conviction into the tense air. "I agree with the proposed course of action." He motioned to the wall of soldiers lining the outside ring of the chamber. "Place Crown Prince Nikita and the rest of the delegation of Runne under arrest immediately."

Chapter Thirty-Eight

THE TENSION WAS PALPABLE inside the tower where Deming and Vallyn stood. The open windows allowed an icy breeze to whisk around the stoic group, though the flush on the heir's cheeks was not from the temperature. No one had said a word since they began the climb to the viewpoint on the east side of the castle.

Deming had not been allowed to be present for the arrest. A liability, Duke Lowell had said. A sympathizer, he called her.

Renewed anger heated her from the inside out at the memory. She ground her teeth, biting back the scream that threatened to rip out from her throat.

Across the garden, she could see six members of the royal guard enter the North Tower. She shook her head imperceptibly. Two to one human guards to immortal Fae? Even if one was not a trained warrior? Laughable odds. If the Fae didn't want to go amicably, they wouldn't. If Deming was a betting woman, she'd go so far as to say that Nikita could take all six guards by himself. The memory of his scimitar gleaming in the moonlight dashed through her mind.

Yeah. The Arsaelian guards with their plumed helmets didn't stand a chance.

One by one they filed into the stone archway and disappeared into the spiraling staircase.

Deming crossed her arms and waited, counting the minutes.

One minute. Two.

After three minutes and thirty six seconds, the solid door at the base of the tower reopened. Six guards and all three Fae exited single file, though the guards quickly flanked each member of the visiting delegation. A ridiculous rectangle of pomp and circumstance for what looked like willing suspects.

Deming sent a silent, grateful prayer up to Kielle that no one was in chains, no wings were pinioned.

The Crown Prince was last to emerge. He immediately looked up at Deming, as if he was attuned to her presence at all times. Too far to say anything, he winked instead. An ember of warmth kindled in the expanse of winter air between them.

Her chest tightened. Her whole body condensed itself in an attempt to stave off the emotions coursing through her veins.

Wrong, wrong, wrong.

The feeling was overwhelming as she watched the winged male tuck his head, breaking eye contact with her.

Being so helpless was infuriating.

They made their way across the gardens and, far too soon, dipped again inside the castle and out of sight. Deming knew they would be heading through the smaller, less traveled paths to the stairs that led to the dungeons, rather than the direct route that passed by both the library and Grand Hall entrances.

She stood vigil for a handful of silent minutes after they had disappeared from view, needing the stillness to collect her emotions.

The Captain of the Guard behind her read the room correctly and continued to keep her comments to herself.

The moon hung high in the sky, silver glow misting through the fog. Only the flutter and chirping of bats echoed through the night. For all intents and purposes, this side of the world was fast asleep.

And yet the princess lay wide awake, ember and rose petal and snow streaked hair tossing back and forth as she shifted from one side of her pillow to the other.

Knowing this would be the case tonight, she had even requested peppermint and chamomile tea in the hopes of lulling herself to sleep. The dregs had sat in the teacup on her side table for hours now. Judging by how high the muted light of the moon was through the fog, it was nearing midnight.

Three hours of staring at the ceiling. Fantastic.

All she could think about was Nikita laying however many levels below her. His shoulders likely aching from trying to keep those beautiful, pristine feathers off the grime coated ground. She looked to where his gifted one lay on her night stand, delicately curved with glancing streaks of color. Would the copper shimmer be visible in the darkness below?

Deming muffled a sharp yell into her pillow then flipped over and rubbed her eyes. This was ridiculous. They would be fine. They were stronger and healed far faster than humans. No man made cell would do any lasting damage to them. Especially for only a day or two.

Right?

And so it went. On and on, over and over. The seconds ticking into minutes ticking into hours. The cycle of worry was beginning to make Deming feel insane.

She placed one hand on her stomach and one on her heart and closed her eyes. Deep breaths that let her feel the movement of air filling her stomach to the brim and then releasing through her nose. The beat of her heart slowed marginally.

They would be fine. Physically and mentally. She was overreacting and she knew it.

Her eyes opened. Hands remained resting on her loosely.

She may be overreacting about their safety, but that didn't change the fact that they did not belong there. How she knew their innocence so fiercely, she wasn't sure.

And the fact that she couldn't pinpoint a reason for their innocence cracked the door just enough for doubt to sweep in.

Maybe she was only seeing what they wanted her to see? Maybe she had fallen into the trap everyone else seemed so sure they had laid for her?

Could every placating word, every delicate interaction, truly have been for show?

It made her sick to think there was a possibility that she was as naive as everyone thought she was.

Deming pulled herself out of the anxious spiral she was in, slid into the slippers by her bed, and went to talk to the only person who was ever able to consistently give her comfort.

The hinges of her bedroom door creaked as they pried open. No amount of oil had ever been able to fix them, they had been the bane of Deming's existence when she was a child.

Vallyn's second in command, Fredrick, swung his head to the sound. He took in Deming, who had exchanged her sleeping gown for a more appropriate, albeit still casual, outfit. "Princess, it's late for a walk."

She forced a nonchalant smile. "Yes, it is. I have an urgent need to speak with Miriam." Asking for privacy would be futile, she didn't even try. "Will you accompany me?"

His brows furrowed in confusion. He stood rigid, hand firmly on the pommel of his sword. "I doubt the Lady Miriam will be awake at this hour." Not a direct reproach, but as close as he would dare.

"Perhaps. But let's try anyway, shall we?" She left no room in her tone for argument, extending an arm as punctuation. Fredrick took it hesitantly. The pair left her chambers and the guard whistled at the guards posted by her door to follow. One would remain to ensure no one entered while they were gone, but everyone else was to be within sight of the princess at all times.

Additional guards as a precaution, given the recent murder.

Deming strained against the urge to roll her eyes and instead set a brisk pace down the corridors silhouetted in silver moonlight.

The thick heels of the boots around her echoed, the only sound except for their breathing. There were so many of them Deming got the distinct impression of being surrounded by a band of clydesdales.

Up two flights of stairs and backtracking down the mirror of her own hallway, she finally arrived at Miriam's door. Two of her own guards stood on either side of the unimposing oak door. From the outside, it looked the same as any entrance in the castle. Inside, however, was a different story. Miriam's suite was a testament to the inhabitants of Reynes Castle's history with lavish and decadent interior decorating tastes.

"Princess Deming," said one of the two posted guards, "to what do we owe the pleasure at this late hour?"

She pressed her shoulders back, straightening her spine and lifting her chin. She knew she was backlit against the moonlight streaming in from the window across the hall. "I need to speak to Miriam."

"I'm afraid she is sleeping."

"Then wake her." The command was not unkind, simply firm. Confident. Royal.

Like a puppy, he obeyed.

It was strange what you could accomplish when you wielded the power in your blood with conviction.

The door swung open, revealing the immaculate sitting area where Miriam often took her afternoon tea. Two plush couches faced each other, a highly decorated table sitting low between them on a detailed, woven rug that covered most of the floor. The floor to ceiling window at the far end of the room faced out towards the city. They were high enough that all of Arsaela sprawled visibly below, the fog wrapped around the winter city like a cloak. Built in bookshelves, filled to the brim, flanked either side of the window and a small, round desk with an accompanying chair nestled nearby. Stacks of letters and a well of ink lay scattered on top.

As with Deming's own chamber, Miriam had posted a female guard just outside her bedroom door. Tall, imposing. A lot like Vallyn at the end of the day. Perhaps that should come at no surprise given the woman standing before her reported directly to the Captain of the Guard. She was older than Vallyn, but not by much. And just like her superior, she had never let her age or gender hinder her ability to be a terror to oppose.

Deming walked purposefully towards her. "Good evening, Rochelle. I require an audience with Miriam."

Rochelle arched an eyebrow but thankfully refrained from questioning the heir and merely stepped aside.

Deming reached for the handle. The guard from her own room took a step forward and without turning around she said, "Privately," then eased herself into Miriam's bedroom, closing the door quietly behind her. Creaking hinges didn't exist here, apparently.

Miriam's bedroom was, to put it simply, beautiful. An open concept, something Miriam had recently renovated, allowed the bed and bath to flow into each other seamlessly. A clawfoot tub with gold and silver engravings sat atop a tiled mosaic of the map of Laey in the far corner. Tile bled into hardwood floors that covered the rest of the room. Rugs overlapped atop each other and made the room feel cozy and warm even in the middle of winter. The coals of a once roaring fire burned red and amber in the brick fireplace along the far wall. Five tall windows were set into the city facing wall, each curtained with a deep mauve fabric hung from bronze rods.

And front and center, the first thing you see as you enter the room, was the massive, four poster frame topped with a duvet so thick and fluffy and white it looked more cloud than blanket.

"Miriam?" Deming whispered into the darkness, tip-toeing lightly into the sitting area in front of the bed.

Nothing. She must be deep asleep.

Deming walked around the side of the bed, right hand curving around one of the sleek pillars, wood smooth and cool in her palm. She pulled the gossamer material draping from the tips of the frame away. "Miriam? I'm sorry to wake you—"

She stopped mid step, alarm bells ringing in her head.

The bed was empty.

She turned slowly, careful to prevent making any noise, and quickly assessed the room. Minimal light shone in through the curtained windows and the fire was only emitting mild warmth from the coals, no light or flame, so it was very difficult to see anything.

Deming glanced once more at the windows. Closed and locked from the inside.

Back to the bed. Tentatively, she reached her fingers out to feel the silken sheets. Still warm. Wherever Miriam was, she hadn't left long ago. And if the windows were secure and Rochelle believed her to be sleeping, then she had to still be in this room.

Deming began pacing the room, looking for anything amiss. She had been in this room countless times, she was bound to recognize something out of the ordinary.

After her third time circling the room and fifth time looking under the bed as if Miriam was playing some kind of childish prank and would spring out from under it any second, Deming growled in annoyance and plunked herself down on the oversized chair in the center of the room.

She buried her head in her hands, elbows perched on her knees, and sighed deeply. When the balls of her palms were pressing hard enough into her eyes to make her see stars behind her closed lids, she pulled up and shook out her hands. She was just about to approach the bedroom door and alert the guards on the other side to her conundrum when she saw the armoire standing flush against the wall opposite her.

She cocked her head.

Her heart skipped a beat.

Was the door ajar?

As if she thought a sudden movement would spook the armoire away, Deming walked slow and steady towards it. The closer she got the more sure she was.

One of the winged doors was cracked open slightly. Only a hair's breadth, barely visible. How she caught it in the dimness of the room only Selene knew.

Perhaps the Goddess of the Moon wanted her to be here.

With a feather soft touch, Deming opened the armoire.

A wall of dresses met her. Evening gowns and dressing gowns. Gowns for court and gowns for strolling the gardens. Long sleeve and cap sleeve and some with straps so thin Deming wondered how they didn't snap with the weight of the fabric. Tulle bled into organza melted into crepe.

The only aspect that was unanimously shared between every dress was color. Sorrowful, deep, black as far as Deming could see. It took her only a moment to realize these were the gowns Miriam had worn during the mourning period after Silas, Samira, and Khalil died.

Emotions swelled in her heart. She had kept them all. Even Deming hadn't been able to bear the thought of seeing the depressing reminder of their shared trauma. She had Noreen and Julia unmake every piece after public mourning had concluded and reuse the fabric for other projects.

Her fingers twisted into the soft sleeve of a conservatively cut ball gown. It was easy to forget that she wasn't the only one to lose family that night.

Taking a deep breath to reset herself, she reached her hand deeper into the dresses. Sure enough, when she parted the sea of fabric and stepped into the armoire it was far larger than it appeared on the outside. A minute of pressing gently against the back wall and something clicked into place.

She hesitated, hand hovering over the wood panel, then pushed.

It swung open on silent hinges, revealing a small pathway lit with candles.

Deming peered down the corridor. Not far ahead lay a set of stairs.

She chuckled under her breath. Leave it to Miriam to have a hidden passageway in her bedchambers. And to think, all this time Deming thought her guardian to be a straight laced rule follower.

The candles hung on the walls were recently lit. Waxy pools had yet to form at their base.

Deming took a step into the hallway, glancing back to ensure the wardrobe door was left open. Rochelle and the rest would likely only give her ten or so minutes more before checking on the room. She hoped to be back by then, and she hoped that whatever lay in the darkness ahead was friend not foe, but in case trouble awaited her in the bowels of the castle, it was best that the guards had an inkling of where to come searching for her.

She arrived quickly at the base of the stairs and, having already decided on pursuing this to the end, began the climb down without hesitation.

It was difficult to gauge in the cloistered environment of the spiral staircase, but Deming guessed she had descended roughly seven flights of stairs when the path leveled out and yet another hallway stretched out before her.

Her thighs burned and she sent up a silent thank you to Vallyn for pushing her as hard as she did in training because the Deming of mere months ago would have no shot of climbing up the stairs to leave this place.

Catching her breath, Deming looked around. This hallway looked much the same as the one she had just come from. Candles hung sporadically along the walls, casting the stone in a warm yellow light. She had expected a multitude of doors down here, a labyrinth of passageways. But there was only one, solitary door at the end of the hallway.

Long strides brought her to it. Old, wooden, rusted hinges. About what one would expect from a secret hiding place that likely no one other than Miriam knew about and therefore was not part of regular castle upkeep.

Deming reached for the handle, then paused. She leaned forward instead, pressing her ear as quietly as possible to the crack between door and wall.

Nothing for many seconds except her soft breath and the pounding of her heart.

Then.

A pained cry.

Muffled, as if coming through a cloth muzzle.

Deming gasped and instinctively thrust open the door and rushed forward and immediately got smacked in the face with heavy fabric. She pawed it out of her way and burst into the room.

Raw fear shot through her at the sight of Miriam sitting in a rickety chair, cloth wrapped around her face binding her mouth shut, pain seared onto her face.

Deming whipped out the dagger hidden on her hip. She wielded the glinting metal defensively in front of her, spinning around to locate the threat.

Cabinets full of multicolored vials to her left. A large workbench in the center of the room. Three floor to ceiling shelves haphazardly full of books to her right.

She visually cleared all four corners within seconds and when the panic settled and she returned her gaze to Miriam she choked on a cry.

She knew this room. Should have known where she was heading based on the direction of the hallway. Should have recognized it the second she walked in.

The second apothecary.

The tunnel she usually came through was carved into the ceiling in the far corner, ladder spilling out of it.

The door she just came through... Deming spun backwards to look. The tapestry of Arsaela. A trap door. The edges blended so seamlessly into the stone it was impossible to pick out from this side unless you knew it was there.

Fear had also clouded her initial assessment of Miriam, whose eyes were no longer holding any pain, only surprise. She was not mute due to a cloth gag, in fact, the bundled fabric now lay discarded in her lap. Discarded because her mouth was now agape, and it had been used to bite into. Deming could still see teeth marks in the white fabric.

And held in Miriam's hand with the carefulness one holds a child, was an exact replica of the cylindrical mechanism that had been hand drawn in the notebook they found all those weeks ago.

The replica whose needle-like end had just been extracted from the crook of Miriam's arm. A drop of clear fluid fell from the tip and dampened a small circle on the tile below.

"Deming, what are you doing here?"

She blinked and countered, trying and failing to keep the accusatory tone out of her voice. "What am I doing here? What are you doing here?"

"I know what this looks like—"

"Well I don't. How do you know how to build..." She fumbled for the right word, landing eloquently on, "That thing? How did you know what it was used for?"

Miriam's eyes dropped imperceptibly to what she held in her hand. She opened her mouth, then closed it. Honeyed eyes flitted from her arm to Deming's eyes and back again.

"I swear on my place in Dothrum's eternal glory," Deming said, throwing a finger back towards the damp hallway behind her, "if you don't start talking I'm going back up those stairs and alerting every fucking guard in this castle."

"There's no need for that, my love—"

"I'd hold off on the niceties," hissed Deming through barred teeth.

Miriam sighed. "Fine, I deserved that. Please, sit." She straightened her shoulders and rolled her neck, then leaned back into the chair with both hands gently folded in her lap. A mixture of blood and whatever liquid she had injected into her arm dripped from the inside of her elbow. She was the picture of eerie elegance. If Deming hadn't known better, she would've believed the woman in front of her was more wraith than human.

Deming wondered absentmindedly if she should bandage the wound before continuing her story, but instead decided on a protest. "I don't particularly feel like sitting at the moment." She cringed internally at the childish tone her statement held. Then realized she was still gripping her dagger and sheathed it, swapping the weapon for crossed arms.

"Fair enough." Miriam waited for a long moment before shattering Deming's reality in a matter of seconds. "Khalil is not dead."

The words went in one ear and out the other. She couldn't possibly have heard right.

"What?"

"Khalil. My brother. He did not die in the fire that killed Silas and Samira. He is very much alive."

Deming tried to blink away the confusion. "But," she stuttered, "we found his body."

Miriam shook her head solemnly. "We found a body. We assumed it was his because of the height and build but... it was so charred we had no way of knowing for sure."

Deming stared at her blankly.

"He was, is..." She swallowed hard and looked up at Deming with more pity in her eyes than the heir had experienced in years. Especially from her. "He is responsible for your parent's death."

Time stopped. Deming could see Miriam's mouth continue to move but she heard nothing except a dull ringing. That was impossible. She had caused the fire. The fire had killed her mom and dad. It was her burden to bear. It had been for years.

"I know, my love," Miriam said, tears flowing freely down her cheeks. Apparently Deming had spoken out loud. "And I am so, so sorry that you have lived with that knowledge for so long. And I am even more sorry…" Her voice broke. She held a hand over her mouth, holding in a sob. "I am even more sorry that I've withheld the truth from you for these last few months. You deserved to know right away. I couldn't risk it though, not with everything at stake."

Shock made speaking in any sort of coherent sentences difficult. Deming managed a single word, mangled and layered thick with emotion. "How?"

Miriam stood and walked to the nearest bookshelf. She pressed against the wood paneling on the back and it popped open slightly, just as the wardrobe had. Inside lay a handful of books and a multitude of unbound parchment.

How many secrets did this room hold?

She pulled a folded piece of parchment from in between two books.

"There had been unsettling reports coming from deep within the Telaciens. Descriptions of experiments, cruel and vile in nature. Rumblings of an insurrection growing that had its sights on Arsaela, on the queendom. Based on the reports I…" Her voice faltered, shame filled her eyes. "I recognized my brothers style of exploring theory. You were too young to understand or notice, but my brother's tactics often prioritized results over ethics. It was the one thing he argued with your parents about. Him and I fought over it too. I know he felt cornered sometimes, like it was him against the world."

Deming could feel her brows furrow. Khalil had been best friends with her parents, he had been a legend with his ability to heal and create. He wasn't a bad person, someone whose experiments would be described as cruel and vile. She would have known if he was tampering with dark arts. Her parents wouldn't have let her spend so much time with someone dangerous.

"Don't believe me, that's fine. But it does me no good to lie now." Miriam grabbed a threadbare cloth from the table and dabbed the inside of her elbow. The injection site was inflamed, red and angry, though it no longer trickled blood. "Once I caught wind of what was happening in the Telaciens, I started screening as many letters that came to the castle as possible. I eventually intercepted a coded letter in Khalil's handwriting. I'm still not sure who the intended recipient was, but it was clear that he had been communicating with this person for at least a few months. He alluded to many things."

Miriam paused to collect herself before continuing. Each word seemed harder than the next to push out from her lips. "Including that the death of your parents was a set up. I don't know all the details, but it sounds like he believed your parents stood in Laey's way to greatness. When they disagreed with his methods so ferociously, he decided they needed to be removed from the picture."

Deming's breath caught in her throat. No one was that cold hearted. People didn't kill their best friends in cold blood.

Her fingertips were numb. Her whole body was trembling slightly.

"He fed you stories about the possibility of human flight, knowing you would eventually try to create the impossible miracle yourself. He watched you until you stole off in the middle of the night to do so and woke your parents, telling them he saw you sneaking off to the apothecary so they would be on the scene. Then staged the explosion and fire. I don't think the candle you knocked over ever played a part." Tears streamed down her face. "It was just an unlucky coincidence that caused you more guilt.

"He stole a corpse from the morgue to burn as his own body and slipped out of the castle unnoticed in the chaos of that night. I don't know why he never returned." Her head dipped low, hair falling off her shoulders in waves. She spoke the next words into her chest so quietly Deming could barely make them out. "I think, maybe, it is because he couldn't bear to kill me. I stood in his way, too, but he couldn't spill family blood." She inhaled deeply, steadying herself and her voice. Deming saw her hands were trembling, too. "We may never know."

Miriam seemed to rally herself. She pushed her shoulders back, wrangled the emotions on her face into something stoic. "I needed to cut off any further communication with Khalil until I could figure out who he was communicating with."

The hair on Deming's arm stood on end at the direction the conversation was heading. Every nerve ending from her toes to her fingertips felt lit by lightning. This woman raised her, knew her better than anyone in Deming's life. More than her uncle, her cousin. More than Paris.

And she had lied, repeatedly. By omission, perhaps, but that did nothing to lessen the blow of betrayal. How was Deming supposed to know to ask specifically about the race of Miriam's parent's? What reason would she have to suspect they were anything other than human?

She knew the answer before she asked.

"Who are you?" whispered Deming.

Miriam began fountaining off a slew of excuses. "I'm the same person I've always been. I love you so much and everything I have done is to protect—"

"Who. Are. You." Deming let the anger flow out of her. Surprise had simmered into rage over the course of the conversation. Her hands were balled into fists at her side, shaking right alongside her voice. She knew what was coming, but Miriam's answer hit her like a sack of bricks regardless.

"I am a mage. My father was a Fae male from a small town in Runne. The immortal magic from him manifested in me as shadow magic. As it did with Khalil. I raised the fog to hide Arsaela while I figured out what to do. To hide you."

Every syllable was a punch to the gut.

Yesenia herself had confirmed that the fog was likely created by a shadow mage who had found a way to amplify their skills. A shadow mage whose magic leaned into the dark and hidden aspects of elemental magic.

Little had they known the shadow mage in question walked among them.

That two shadow mages had walked among them once.

Who had known? Her parents? Anyone?

And hadn't Miriam retracted her arm in pain in the week leading up to Midwinter when Deming looped her own arm through Miriam's? She had said her joints ached because of the correspondence she had been working through. Deming's eyes drifted to the crook of her elbow. To the cylindrical tube that now lay discarded on the table. To the eyes that watched her grow up.

She collected every emotion raging through her. Time would come later to sort through everything Miriam had dumped onto her just now. But in order to do that, she needed every piece of information the woman in front of her was hiding.

Her voice echoed strongly off the dimly lit stone walls. "What is that." No lift in her voice, no uptick to signal a question.

To her credit, Miriam offered the explanation immediately. "The realization of a prototype that Khalil had worked on. You saw it yourself in his journal." A curt nod from Deming was all the confirmation given. "It allows me to supplement and enhance my magic by injecting myself twice a day with a serum made of a collection of natural stimulants." As an afterthought she added, "It lets me guard and protect the city."

Deming scoffed. "Protect?"

Miriam shook her head, knowing whatever she said would not be received well. "I know you feel as though I've lied to you, but I stand by my decisions." She lifted her head and stood, marking the most movement from her since Deming barged into the room. "Khalil wants something within the castle walls. Needs it more than he's needed anything. I couldn't allow him to access it. I couldn't allow him to convince someone to help him access it."

"What does he need?"

Full lips curved down ever so slightly. They trembled.

Deming pressed, grinding out the question once more. "Have you found what he needs?"

"Yes." A whisper so quiet, if Deming hadn't been staring intently at Miriam's mouth she would have missed it.

"So why haven't you destroyed it?" Deming spun around and grabbed a vial from the nearby shelf. "Is this what he needs?" She threw it to the ground. Glass shattered against stone. Shards glittered in the candle light. A vaguely purple substance exploded across the floor. "What about this?" Another vial. Another layer of glass littered the ground.

On the third vial Miriam raised her hand. "No," she exclaimed sorrowfully. "What he sought was far more precious."

"Too precious to destroy? To tell anyone about?"

Curls, disturbed from sleep and dishonesty, bobbed as she nodded. Long moments hung in the air as Deming waited for Miriam to say something, anything.

Then.

"You. The blood of the Reynes-Elychar line."

It was as if the entire world froze. As if even the gods themselves knew this moment was one that Deming needed more than the time nature allotted to process Miriam's words.

Khalil wouldn't hurt her. He loved her like a daughter. He stoked her imagination and gave her something bigger than herself to believe in. He... loved her, hadn't he?

She didn't feel connected to her body.

"I have a prickling suspicion that Khalil believes you to be the key to unlocking a power this world has never seen before. It is the only answer that makes sense."

Said banally as if everything else divulged tonight made sense.

Deming didn't register the fear that crept in at the thought of her blood being collected and foraged. A fog of dissociation had settled around her.

"I..." Deming couldn't find the words. Something deep within her shattered like the glass vials littering the ground. "I need to leave. I need to help my friends. I can't..." Her voice cracked. She swallowed hard.

Was she destined to have everyone she loved betray her? Was she not allowed to have comfort and peace? The gods had a penchant for punishing her, for digging the grave further with every new revelation.

All she wanted was to live and, recently, rule her people with grace and kindness and humility.

Was she not supposed to want those things? One horrible incident could be marked up to chance. Two, an oddity. But the string of blood and death and deception that spread like mold to everything she touched?

The gods did not want her on the path she was walking.

Deming turned to exit the apothecary the way she came but a gentle grip pressed something cool into her palm.

She unfurled her hand. A small brass key lay there.

She said nothing to the woman standing before her and pivoted towards the opposite side of the room and the ladder that offered an alternative to returning to the guards outside Miriam's bedroom door. There was nothing for her here. Swift feet took her far away from chilling revelations and toward that which felt like home.

Chapter Thirty-Nine

THE JOURNEY TO THE dungeons was a blur. One moment Deming was rushing away from the hidden apothecary and the next she was leaping to the floor of the underground cells, having taken the stairs by two on the way down in her haste.

The speed with which her legs carried her through the night-cloaked castle mirrored both the beat of her heart and the thoughts racing through her mind.

Khalil, alive.

Miriam, responsible for the fog.

Mages, both of them.

Adrenaline was the only thing keeping her afloat.

Adrenaline, and the inherent need to control something, anything. Her life may be falling apart around her, but she was not completely helpless.

She clutched the brass key tighter. Her palms sweaty and slick against the metal. Her lungs ached, her thighs burned.

It was all she could do to push the plethora of questions that came with everything Miriam shared to a small corner in her mind and beg them to be quiet for now.

She needed to accomplish one more thing tonight before contemplating which threads that wove her life were real and which were lies.

Apparently the Fae delegation hadn't warranted the furthest suite of cells in the dungeon.

It took Deming only two corners before she found herself face to face with Nikita and his companions.

"Took your sweet time, didn't you, princess?" Swirling gray eyes peered out from behind bars that cut Nikita's profile into ribbons. He smirked. Instead of aggravating her further, the familiar sight settled her nerves.

Curved around their prince, creating a half moon of immortals, Ilysse and Hartford eyed her carefully. All three Fae remained immaculate. In fact, there didn't seem to be a thread out of place or a speck of dirt or grime in sight.

"Tell me something, anything, about why you're really here." Deming didn't pause to catch her breath. Her voice came out in heavy pants. Rushed, tight syllables in between sucking air desperately into her lungs. "Just a sliver of honesty. Like you gave the other night, please. I..." Her heart cracked with her voice, the weight of the evening's events suddenly too heavy for her to bear. The walls she dutifully erected to keep Miriam's revelations at bay began crumbling, the information too impactful to be shoved into a corner of her mind. "I can't bear the thought of you down here and I want to believe you and trust you and I think I do regardless of how little you open up which is naive of me, I know—"

"Deming." Nikita cut her rambling off and stepped closer to the iron bars. They were close enough that his angular face took up nearly her entire field of vision. "Take a breath."

She obeyed.

Shakily, she pulled air into her burning lungs and exhaled into the dampness of the dungeon.

He looked to his second. Ilysse nodded curtly. Whatever silent question that passed between the two of them was lost to the rest of the room. Or to Deming, at least. Hartford's spine straightened as Nikita turned to face Deming once more.

"If you need proof, we can provide that."

Deming leaned in closer, waiting for him to say more.

"The preserved prophecy. We lied before, about leaving it behind. It's at our safe house near the port."

Conflicting feelings of relief and confusion clashed in Deming's mind like waves crashing against the shore. "Why did you lie?"

Nikita licked his lips. "It's complicated."

"Make it uncomplicated." Her grip tightened on the key. They were running out of time.

"It didn't mention a war revolving around Arsaela. It..." He sighed, his fingers knotted into the hair at the nape of his neck. His feet shifted. "Please, just let me show you. It will be better if you hear it yourself."

Deming wished she still had the dagger she left in the apothecary to point at him. "Tell me, now."

He shook his head, muttering something unintelligible under his breath, then met her eyes. "It mentioned you, specifically. The war doesn't revolve around Arsaela, it revolves around you. We came here to learn about you, to protect you."

Deming took a step back. She blinked. Once. Twice. "Seers don't have visions about specific people. The magic is general, overarching."

"Exactly," he said slowly. "We didn't feel it would be strategic to mention that the prophecy was about you. Arsaela is general enough for it to be believable."

The guards would be checking on Miriam's room soon. They needed to leave, but... "What does the prophecy say?"

Without skipping a beat Nikita quoted the seer. "The uncrowned queen is the key." His gaze seared into her, the intensity of it rattled her soul. "There is more, you can listen later. But that part is why we're here. The uncrowned queen. You. There is no other monarch waiting to ascend their throne on the continent. You are the key."

Deming tried to still her mind, to quiet the thoughts screaming at her, but she couldn't. A painful pulse began throbbing in the back of her head. "Why does your seer think I'm special enough to be that important in any battle, let alone a war?"

Hartford stepped forward. "It doesn't work like that, Deming. You were right before, seers divine swaths of the future, arcs and generalities, but not the details. Most seers never even are gifted with a true prophecy, let alone one that calls out one person with such clarity."

"We don't know what you'll do or why you're important," Ilysse said, "just that you are."

Every bit of growth Deming felt she made these last few months, every choice that carried her towards more responsibility, more acceptance of the path laid out for her, vanished. Suddenly she was a scared little girl again. More lives to care for. More emotional weight to shoulder. More expectations to live up to.

Deming stumbled backwards. The ground rose to meet her quickly, the uneven ground biting hard into her tailbone. She had lost her balance. Her vision fogged. Her breathing felt ragged.

Get it in control.

Deep inhale. Deep exhale.

One crisis at a time.

She pressed two fingers to the inside of her wrist, finding her pulse. It beat out of rhythm, chaotic and fast, like hummingbird wings. She took precious seconds to regain control of her heartbeat.

Miriam's words came floating back to her.

Those who hunger for power should never be the ones to have it.

She certainly didn't want power. She never had and likely never would. But maybe this is what she was meant to do, lead her people through wartime, not peace. Maybe she was not meant to have a little life with cushioned edges but a wild one with uncertainty that cut to the bone. It was not the life she would have chosen for herself. But maybe it was the life she was given.

She would stop running towards an idyllic future. That did not exist for her.

She had thought only moments before that the gods did not want her on her current path. Maybe this was confirmation of that theory.

If this was the path she was destined for instead, she decided on a whim but with conviction, she would learn to walk it with grace, however painful that may be.

In the next life, perhaps, she would be granted respite.

The air warmed as Deming rose, as if in welcome. As if even the wind could sense the shift in the fabric of the world.

Deming was thankful all three sets of eyes staring at her held no pity.

She knew the response Nikita would give before she said, "Your seer could be wrong."

He attempted to move towards Deming, reaching through the bars of his prison to touch her hand. She let him. His skin was warm against hers. "Yes, she could be."

The words held no conviction, as hers hadn't.

She brandished the key. "Let's get you out. I'll never get to hear the prophecy if you're rotting in a cell. We have a stop we need to make on the way." The key slid into the lock easily and a sharp snap sounded when she twisted it, opening the gate. As she freed them, she explained how Miriam was behind the fog and the reveal about Khalil as concisely as she could. Details would come later, when they were all alive and far away from here.

"If you are unwilling to share the prophecy at the trial," she said as the three immortals walked out of the cell, "they will convict you. I doubt they would sentence you to death." She nodded towards Nikita. "But the rest of you would be in danger. We need to get you out of the city. Soon."

Ilysse spoke, contracting and retracting her claws from her knuckles. "I assume you have a plan for lifting the fog barrier?"

Wicked intention danced in Deming's eyes. "Yes. We're going to destroy her store of serum. She needs to inject herself twice a day so if we get rid of it all tonight, the fog should disappear by noon tomorrow."

Ilysse voiced her approval. "All we need to do is hide away until the current serum wears off, then dip into the forest."

Deming said, "She knows how to make more, and I'm sure she will if she's so worried about Khalil. But we don't need the fog to be lifted forever, only for a couple hours. I'll deal with how to break the news to the council once you are all safely across the border."

Nikita eyed her carefully. "We should stay." Ilysse's nostrils flared but she respected her prince enough to not say anything. "The three of us are better fighters than the entire royal guard, even with Vallyn. We could be the tipping point if it came to a battle with Khalil."

Red monochrome hair shook ferociously. "No. I mean," Deming corrected, "yes, you are all better fighters than our guards. But you need to leave. Even if you stayed, you wouldn't be allowed to do anything except sit in this cell. Who knows how long a trial would take? And if the city gets attacked I would be secluded in a safe room, leaving you all down here to rot. This is our best chance at getting you out."

Nikita nodded curtly. His lips were pursed tightly, as if holding back more, but he remained silent.

"Besides," she pacified, "the city won't be attacked. Miriam will make more serum, remember? The fog will rise again before you've even reached the Laey-Runne border. If you can, help from that side of the fog."

And they would likely never see each other again. For a long while, at least.

Fear jolted through her at the thought, making her fingertips tremble.

Nothing to do about that inevitability right now.

"The city won't be attacked," he echoed.

"The city won't be attacked."

A hint of cardamom and salt, even this far underground, wafted to her as he shifted. The beat of his wings in time with the beat of her own heart.

A warm hand settled on her shoulder. "Thank you," said Hartford.

"There is nothing to thank me for. This is the right thing to do."

The female dipped her head. The gold adornments on her antlers swung and glinted softly in the dim light of the dungeons.

Nikita cupped her face in his hands. "I will never forget the choices you have made for my court. For me." Every piece of his tattered soul was laid bare in his eyes. Sorrow for having lied to her, fear of the unknown, terror at the idea of leaving when someone with the intent to harm her was trying desperately to reach the castle.

Warmth. A softness that only graced his expression when he looked at her.

Deming saw it all and more.

Her heart swelled. She opted for levity rather than acknowledgement of the truth. She pushed a hand into his broad chest. "Don't make me look a fool by turning out to actually have committed the murders. I'd drag you right back to that cell."

"I'd give you the lock and key myself."

She nodded towards the stairs. "Let's go."

They met the rest of the delegation at the top of the stairs, where Ilysse got right to the point asking for direction on next steps for the apothecary sabotage.

"We'll enter through the current apothecary," Deming said in a hushed voice. Now that they were back in the main portion of the castle they were at risk of being seen or heard at any moment. "Since Yesenia has taken up residence, its stores have been stocked. We'll take flint and kindling, maybe some alcohol for good measure, and duck into the second apothecary through the hidden door in the floorboards. Once we light the serum on fire, we'll leave through the passage that connects to Miriam's room. The explosion will likely draw everyone from the higher floors down to investigate."

"And if it doesn't?" Hartford arched an eyebrow.

"You gracefully climb out the window." She paused briefly, waiting for a protest. When none came, she continued. "There won't be guards in her immediate bedroom. If we hear anyone on the other side of the door we don't even attempt to exit, you just leave through the window. There's a trellis you can use to climb down."

The four of them looked around their crowded circle. Three Fae and a human. A castle shrouded in darkness. They could pull this off.

Deming pulled away from the group and peered around the corner. She sent a prayer of thanks up to Selene for keeping the midnight hallways quiet and then beckoned the Fae behind her to follow.

They stole down the castle hallways on near silent feet with the exception of Hartford's hooves clipped sharply on the stone. Even Deming with her human footfalls managed to keep her disturbances extraordinarily quiet.

Adrenaline coursed through her, but not in the panicky way she was accustomed to. This was life buzzing in her veins. She had a plan, a purpose. Her actions tonight would have consequences, yes, but more importantly they would be a match to her newly uncovered moral code. For too long she had avoided what was asked of her, never questioned what she wanted to do. What she believed in.

This was right. A complete alignment of body and soul.

A jolt of realization hit her mid-stride. She had felt more alive only once, high above the city skyline in the arms of the male running right on her heels.

She looked to her side.

Nikita's eyes sparkled with intent. Strong thighs propelled his lithe frame through the air like a hot knife through butter. Each iridescent feather wavered in the wind. Shades of copper and indigo flashing so quickly the changes were almost imperceptible.

Deming swallowed hard and faced forward. She led them around the last corner and they exploded into the main courtyard. In seconds they crossed the cobbled path in front of the ancient tree, forever marred from the last fire lit within these walls, and skidded to a halt in front of the imposing apothecary doors.

She looked back, breathing heavy.

Three sets of eyes looked back. Not one of them out of breath.

Fucking immortals.

"After you, princess," Nikita's lip pulled into a smirk.

She opened the door slowly, careful to not open it past the point where the hinges would alert others to their presence, and slipped inside. Three sets of feet, piercing canines, prominent stag antlers, and a pair of wings followed.

On instinct, Hartford went to the correct cupboard and pulled out a vial of incendiary fluid. She waved the clear contents in Deming's direction.

"Grab all that's there."

The freckled Fae gathered two more vials and a larger jar, tucking the smaller bottles into her emerald robes.

Deming turned her attention to the rest of the room.

Ilysse meandered through the room, opening drawers and cupboards aimlessly. Nikita just stood with arms folded staring at her.

"Not sure what you're looking at, prince, but find some kindling before I use your hollow bird bones instead." The title, while accurate, felt playful rolling off her tongue. How many times had he called her by her court title in lieu of her real name?

His eyes widened with dark pleasure, but he began collecting wood scraps nonetheless. "You've got a twisted mind hidden beneath that pretty face."

Deming walked to the far wall without responding, rolling her eyes once her back was turned to him. A dark chuckle from the winged male let her know he hadn't missed a thing.

A string of piercing cracks echoed suddenly through the room.

Her heart nearly leapt out of her chest.

"Quiet!" She spat, spinning around to find Nikita standing over a pile of wood that had once been a rickety rocking chair.

He shrugged unapologetically. "You said to find kindling." When her expression didn't soften he added, "Oh, unclench your jaw, princess. We're setting off an explosion in a few seconds, I think we'll be fine."

"Ilysse," she ground out, choosing to address the warrior female rather than the imbecile in front of her, "did you find the flint?"

The lioness lifted a dark stone in response, then fanned out two small knives from her other hand. "Lucky find. You never know when you'll need to stab someone."

Content that they had everything they needed, Deming kicked the rug off the trap door and pried it open. "Down we go."

Nikita began the climb down the ladder first, followed closely by Ilysse.

Hartford peered hesitantly down the damp tunnel.

"It's not that far down and it's not as dirty as it looks," Deming reassured.

Her curled, cropped hair blended in seamlessly with the darkness slowly enveloping her as she stepped down one rung at a time, leaving only bone white antlers looking like spiderwebs against the black background. "If you say so."

Deming pulled the rug back over them as best she could before closing the trap door.

They made short work of reaching the second apothecary despite the tight squeeze of the shaft pressing in on feathers and fur and wings and antlers and soon everyone's feet were on solid ground once more.

Empty.

Miriam vacating the premise already was the one stroke of good luck to happen to Deming in a long while.

Ilysse pushed past her, nose twitching as her feline sense of smell perked up at the new location.

As it turns out, it takes very little time to prepare a room to be blown to smithereens. Within minutes the kindling had been appropriately strewn about and Hartford had doused it all with every last drop of the incendiary fluid.

"Smells terrible," Ilysse said offhandedly as they moved towards the entrance that would lead them to Miriam's bedroom.

"Yeah, well," shrugged Deming, "it's about to smell a lot worse."

Not knowing what ingredients Miriam needed to make the serum meant they had to set fire to everything—including the vials of horse hair and stacks of animal pelts. It was about to smell like burnt fur and melting skin.

"Ready?" She took the flint from Ilysse. They all nodded. "Okay, back up." She pulled the door as close to closed as possible while still being able to reach her hands inside and pulled out the flint and steel.

Hartford had trailed the fluid from the largest pile of drenched kindling in the center of the room to where they now stood. Hopefully the flame would take enough time reaching the explosive pile that they could lock the door behind them and get far enough down the hallway to avoid the worst of the blast.

A creeping fear of being crushed under the weight of the stone ceiling weaseled its way into Deming's mind as she began striking the flint, trying to get a big enough spark to bring a hint of fire to life.

Far too late to worry about that particular consequence.

Especially because on her third strike, a spark flared through the darkness, igniting into flame quickly and ripping towards the treacherously soaked pile.

The race was on.

"Go, go, go!"

They had no time to think as Deming slammed the door shut and locked it.

Nikita pulled her away swiftly and tucked her gracefully into his chest as he flew down the hallway, everyone else fast on his heels.

Every beat of blood pumping through her heart felt enhanced. Each breath felt like her last.

The stairwell approached fast. Nikita slid into the turn chaotically and—

BOOM.

One moment she was in Nikita's arms the next she was flying through the air and colliding solidly into the curved stone wall of the stairwell.

Ringing, ringing, ringing in her ears.

The air was gray with dust. Motes of debris particles whipped through air in droves, circling and circling each other ferociously, the wind from the explosion propelling them until they eventually began to slow.

It was difficult to see anything, the air was so clouded. It brought memories of riding into the fog rushing back. Gray, as far as the eye could see. Gray, shrouding everything.

Deming blinked away the remnants that fell heavy on her lashes. Nikita filled her vision, his face was gray too. Ashy, covered in soot and dirt. He swayed back and forth as she tried to get him into focus.

His lips were moving but all she could hear was ringing, ringing, ringing...

"Deming?" His voice crawled through her senses.

"Mmm?"

"Deming, we have to keep moving. Can you walk?"

He reached down and braced her as she rose on shaky legs.

Around her, destruction.

The entire hallway was a mass of rubble. She couldn't even see the door at the end of the corridor, it had completely collapsed. The consequences of their actions had been swift, loud, and far more dangerous than they anticipated.

"What the fuck was in that bottle?" Ilysse said under her breath to Hartford, who merely shrugged as she kneeled in the rumble and spat out gravel.

"Something more potent than oil, that's for sure."

Ilysse grunted in agreement, wiping grime away from her eyes and mouth.

Other than a plethora of cuts and bruises, they seemed all in one piece.

As if reading her mind, Nikita spoke quietly into her ear. "Fae durability. You are the most at risk here, physically anyway."

"Thanks for reminding me."

"Can't have you getting an ego on me."

Deming's lips pulled into a snarl but she lacked the energy to actually quip back. She opted to pivot towards the stairwell, looking up to where the glow from the candles at the top of the stairs were barely visible.

"The only way out is up."

Ilysse chuckled and murmured something Deming couldn't quite make out but thought sounded a lot like a dig at the obviousness of her statement.

Regardless, the lioness trailed up behind the pack as they rose, and rose, and rose from the dark bowels of the castle to the living.

By the time they reached the top of the stairs Deming was panting like a dog and her thighs burned as if on fire. She swallowed her complaints though, knowing they were so impossibly close to pulling their plan off.

Ahead of them, she saw the carved out stone archway and thin wooden panels that made up the back of the wardrobe. And beyond that, she explained to the three Fae walking beside her, Miriam's bedroom and the large wall of windows that led to freedom.

Deming pressed a hand, black with soot and dust, against the wardrobe panel and hushed her companions. She heard nothing, but asked for confirmation. "Ilysse?"

Pointed ears flicked beneath golden braids. Ilysse shook her head and whispered, "Nothing immediately outside. Sounds like one or two pairs of boots, but from what I understand about the layout they seem to be in the gathering chamber, not the bedroom. Guards, likely."

Deming bounced lightly on her heels, steeling up her nerves to open the wardrobe's back panels. She pushed her breath out forcefully through her teeth and lifted a hand to press the wood.

The panel slid to the side as easily as it had from the other side. The layers and layers of black fabric still hung in swaths. Deming parted them carefully and stepped fully into the wardrobe. The actual wardrobe door was slightly ajar. Deming leaned in as close as she dared and peered through the thin crack.

Nothing.

She couldn't hear anything, either.

Maybe their distraction had proved large enough. Could the guards on the other side of the bedroom door really be their only obstacle?

She pushed the door open with her fingertip and paused.

When no noise of alarm or surprise greeted her, she stuck her head out and surveyed the room.

As suspected, there was no one. Miriam too, had been pulled to the site of the explosion.

Deming stepped into the bedroom and motioned for the immortals behind her to silently follow.

The guards, for now Deming too could hear the soles of their boots scuffing the floors a room over, must have been asked to remain in the suite for security purposes. The Fae would have to use the window rather than walk out the door, but Deming realized with a bang of relief that not racing through the castle would likely be quicker and easier anyway. It was well past midnight, most guards and likely a few of the more nosy members of court would be investigating the apothecary. By climbing down the trellis it would only take them moments to get outside the castle walls where they could wait the hours it would take for Miriam's most recent serum injection to wear off.

Hartford and Ilysse were already waiting by the window, the latter working on opening the delicate, golden locks as quietly as possible. A soft click sounded through the room as the glass panel swung open.

Hartford swung a furred leg over the windowsill and began shimmying down the trellis. Within moments her hooves on the stone floor could be heard.

Ilysse looked at Nikita.

Nikita looked at Deming.

Her eyes burned with tears. She wiped them away ferociously, not willing to let her last moments with him be marred or blurry.

"Promise me one thing, princess?" A rough thumb ran across her cheek and under her chin, lifting her eyes to his.

"Anything."

"Stay safe." His velvety voice wavered. "I couldn't bear to lose you so soon. Not after I just found you."

Deming threw her arms around Nikita, burying her head into the crook of his neck. Instantly his arms were around her. She knew if she looked his wings would be curled delicately around them, too. A protector, always.

"Safe, I can do safe." They shared a soft laugh, more nervous than anything. Breath mingled in the space between their lips.

Nikita pressed a kiss to her forehead.

"I'll find you," she whispered so quietly only he could hear the vulnerability in her voice. "Once everything settles down here, I'll find you."

A broad hand cupped the back of her head and stroked her tangled hair softly. "This isn't goodbye, princess. I could be thrown across worlds and still find my way back to you. All I need you to do is stay alive while I'm gone."

To her core, she knew he meant it.

She pulled back and looked up at him. She found eyes wild with storms of emotions already on her. Her mouth opened to vocalize what she had known for a while now but had been too scared to acknowledge.

Before she could, a cold, familiar voice breached the air instead.

"It really is such a shame to have my doubts about your treasonous behavior confirmed."

Deming whipped around in Nikita's arms to find the bedroom door open on silent hinges and her uncle standing directly in the archway, grinning with wicked glee.

Chapter Forty

Deming stared at her uncle, mouth agape.

The song of metal on metal echoed through the air as Ilysse drew the knives she stole from hidden sheaths on her thighs.

"Oh, let's not escalate to violence, my dear."

The knives remained.

"Uncle," Deming stammered, "what are you doing here?"

He opened his arms wide, like he was inviting a malicious embrace. "Isn't it obvious?"

He seemed to be waiting for an actual answer. Deming looked from his piercing eyes to his wide smile. He practically oozed glee.

Finally he brought his arms down and clapped his hands piously in front of his stomach. "Fine, if I must." He stepped into the room. Deming swore a chill washed through the room at his movement. "Bolton. Marist." He raised a hand and beckoned two hulking soldiers Deming had never seen before from the adjoining room. A complex crest of knots and swirls shimmered on their uniforms in the moonlight as they crept closer.

Who were they? How had they gotten here?

And why did that crest look so—

She unconsciously pressed herself further into Nikita's body. Sweat beaded at the nape of her neck. Her skin felt on fire and frigidly cold at the same time. "The bar," she whispered. "The alleyway."

"Crown Princess Deming, you have conspired to aid and abet enemies of this queendom and as such, I pronounce you a traitor to the crown."

The two were speaking over each other. One with shock, one with conviction.

"The men who attacked me this fall," Deming went on, "they wore that same crest."

Dresden spoke as stoically as if he was announcing what he had for dinner and not accusing his only niece and the sole heir to the throne of treason. "Any and all informants that aided you in your endeavors will be held equally accountable—"

"It was you all along, you tried to kill me."

"—including but not limited to," he continued as though he hadn't heard her, "Vallyn Morgan, Paris Chastain, and Miriam Hawthorne."

Deming pried herself away from Nikita's embrace, though his hand still clung tightly to her forearm. She held a shaky finger pointed straight at her uncle's chest. The guards flanking her uncle didn't so much as twitch. "You had men from your estate kidnap, drug, and attempt to murder me!"

At that, finally, Dresden paused his own proclamations. "Now, now my sweet niece. I very clearly told my employees to bring you to me alive. It's not my fault they went rogue." He shrugged nonchalantly. "I was going to kill you myself." Deming couldn't tell if the growl behind her came from Ilysse or Nikita. Maybe both. "Those in power need to stay in touch with the consequences of their actions. Only I wield the sword for my executions."

Executions, plural. Deming thought she might be sick. "The priestess?" She hated how small she sounded.

"I made an error, using the crest." His face soured, the idea that he could make a mistake was revolting to him. "I thought it would be fun to use a long dead symbol of rebellion within my inner circle. The girl wouldn't stop digging around the archives. She found one too many pieces of the puzzle and connected the dots. She was a loose end that needed to be snipped, an open wound to be cauterized."

He looked off in the distance, as deeply unconcerned with the three bodies before him as he was with his admissions of murder. He spoke about death as one might speak about a loved one.

Deming shivered. Gone was the man who helped raise her, whose knee she bounced on as a babe. The malice shining in his eyes now held no resemblance to the kindness she associated with him.

Her uncle tapped a finger absentmindedly in the air, as if just remembering something. "I'll have to make that waif of a woman's execution public."

Sasha, he was talking about the extremist who was wasting away in a cell. The woman who he had clearly framed somehow.

Guilt gnawed at Deming like a starving wolf on a bone. She had just been in the dungeons, she could have found her and released her had she known.

Too late, she was always too late to do anything.

And now another innocent woman would die.

"Why?" The only word she could manage.

"Why?" He looked genuinely confused. "What do you mean why? You were never going to lead our queendom in the direction it needs to go. Clearly." He glanced at the Fae in the room, lingering on their pointed ears. He had the good sense to take a step back as Ilysse hissed and lunged at the insinuated insult. "You lack the conviction to do anything meaningful. The gods don't even think you're worthy of the crown." He waved impatiently at her streaky hair. "We've been working behind the scenes for years to destabilize your reign. We needed to rid ourselves of you so that a more competent bloodline could take your place."

The ambiguous mention of a coconspirator was lost on Deming in the wake of betrayal that crashed into her.

A more competent bloodline.

The only bloodline Laey would recognize other than her own.

His.

Colette's.

Nausea won this round. Deming spilled the contents of her stomach all over the tile floor. She made to wipe the bile dripping from her lips away but another round rolled through her, sending her to her knees. When she finally rose, disdain dripped from her uncle's face.

"See? This is what I mean. Weak. In every sense. The reign of the Reynes-Elyachar line is at its end. The dominion of the Reynes-Penrose line has begun."

She could barely hear his words, could barely comprehend him tearing the royal surname from her.

Colette. Her confidant. Her friend. Colette with her brilliant ruby-red hair. One of two last remaining blood connections to her family. Colette had been in on it all.

A coup for her throne. Her crown. Her queendom.

Had she been naive? Missed clear signs? Or had her friend simply been that good at deception?

Deming almost hoped it was the first option.

Not concerned with Deming's impending mental crisis, her uncle steeled his face once more and motioned for the guards to take her. "Goodbye, Crown Princess," he cooed with saccharine sweetness. He drew a fine sword from his hip.

Oh, he intended to do this now.

Deming turned to Nikita, they could still make a break for the window. If they were lucky they could still escape.

He wasn't looking at her. Not in her direction at all, actually. He was eyeing Ilysse intently. The warrior stared back and then nodded imperceptibly as if they were having a conversation between minds.

Before Bolton and Marist could take another step, Ilysse launched herself at the encroaching soldiers.

Exclamations of surprise from her uncle and the two brutes heightened the instant chaos. Then two screams of pain in quick succession as Ilysse's knives found their home in the shoulders of the guards, buried to the hilt in muscle.

When the lioness appointed Fae jerked both weapons out, blood spattered and flesh tore.

That was all Deming saw before Nikita pulled her tightly into his chest and leapt out the window.

She barely had time to brace herself as they plunged through the air for the brief moment before his wings snapped open.

"Ilysse!" Deming reached a hand towards the quickly diminishing window. Nikita snapped her hand back into the folds of her body.

"She'll follow. She can hold her own." Sharp. To the point. A warrior in combat.

Sure enough, just as Nikita dove out of sight of the castle, Deming spied a wisp of golden hair scrambling out the window and sliding down the edge of a nearby trellis so fast she was sure her hands would be instantly red with blood and burns.

"But the guards at the gate... Hartford! What about Hartford!"

"Ilysse will find her. As for the gate, your uncle won't want this to explode any more than it already has. He wants control. I would bet my reign he has pulled everyone to the interior of the castle to contain panic around the blast and begin the smear campaign."

He must have sensed her disbelief. "Trust me," he added, "I've seen enough men like him. He isn't as unique as he thinks he is."

Wind ripped away whatever remaining hold her hair tie had. The ribbon disappeared into the night, causing her strawberry blonde hair to whip against her cheeks, fully loose at last.

She felt Nikita curve his head down just enough to press a chaste kiss on the crown of her head, then another. She twisted in his arms just enough to see his face. Worry lined his eyes and brow, but his words were assured.

"Everyone will be fine. You are the priority, you always have been. Hartford and Ilysse know this. We'll regroup at the safe house."

"Everyone will be fine," she repeated, more for herself than anything else.

"Yes," he murmured softly into her hair.

Steady wingbeats brought them lower and lower into the city. Deming thought they would touch down somewhere in the South Quarter, somewhere shadowy where no one asked questions because everyone had secrets, but Nikita flew them over the dubious quarter and banked left towards the Shipping District.

The port of Arsaela was even more enthralling than usual under the cloak of near dawn and with the lapping waves disappearing into the fog, Miriam's fog, not far from shore.

They circled the oceanside road once, twice, while Nikita scanned the adjoining streets for threats, then touched down on a small dock at the far end of the road.

The second Deming found her feet, the warmth of Nikita's hand left the small of her back and enveloped her hand instead, pulling her towards the row of apartments on the other side of the street with purpose. They rose up a small set of concrete stairs to a door painted white and embellished with shimmering gold stars.

"Isn't this a bit public?"

Nikita pulled a short, plain key from his boot and unlocked the door. "It's not compromised yet, don't worry. We realized someone was tracing our steps a while ago and have moved around every few days since then."

"You were being followed? Why didn't you say something?"

Nikita shot her an incredulous look. "Who would we have said something to?"

She frowned, then looked over her shoulder.

The edge of the water glowed with the warmth of the sun rising from the other side of the world. Dawn was approaching. In only a handful of hours the fog would fall and the Fae, and herself, Deming realized with a pang, would no longer be in the city limits. The realization that she wouldn't have to say goodbye to the immortal entourage after all was soured instantly by the circumstances, by the betrayal from her family by blood.

Traitorous pieces of shit, the both of them.

Once inside the building, they were greeted with a narrow corridor completely filled by a sweeping spiral staircase. On every floor, a walkway connected the stairs to various doors painted in the same eclectic style as the front door. A wall of stained glass windows rose from floor to ceiling, roughly eight floors up, directly behind the stairs. A glass chandelier so expansive it rivaled the one in the Grand Ballroom hung from the ceiling.

They climbed up and up, twirling around the spiral stairs so quickly Deming wobbled and nearly toppled backwards when they finally came to a halt at the second to last door.

"Welcome to the safe house," Nikita said as he opened the door and swept into the room with open arms and long strides.

Deming's first thought was how unassuming the space was.

There were two, tall windows against the far wall that let in some semblance of natural light, which was pleasant. The beds were well appointed with intricate quilts and plentiful pillows.

"Well, it's nothing to write home about but—"

The rest of the sentence died in her throat. Her head cocked.

"What's that?"

Nikita followed her line of sight to the desk along the far wall and a slew of expletives immediately flew from his mouth.

Deming walked tentatively towards the desk, and the expansive chart that lay sprawled on it. Curiosity melted into dread.

Her hand floated above the parchment. She pressed one yellowed edge between her forefinger and thumb and twisted.

It ripped.

She could hear blood pounding in her ears.

An intricate map of the continent was drawn in the top left corner, with an expanded section just below of Laey's capital city. The quarters, the streets, the docks. The apartment they were currently in was marked with a small gold star.

Red marks dotted the rest of the map, decorating her favorite haunts. Firebrand's. Temple. The castle. Colette's seamstress.

Her gaze drifted to the right. Detailed descriptions of her schedule were marked in a neat column. Times. Locations. The people she met with and their schedules.

Every other inch of the parchment was littered with her family's history. Notes scratched here and there in slanting pen.

And pinned in the middle, mud still speckling the velvet, was what had initially drawn her eye. The missing half of her sash that had torn off the night of her attack. She had assumed it was long lost to the bar floor, or more probable, a urine soaked gutter somewhere between Firebrand's and the alley Nikita intercepted them.

But no, here it was.

"What is this?" she asked Nikita again, not looking up from the evidence before her. Confusion edged the anger swelling rapidly within her.

"I told you, we came here to protect you. To learn about you." He spoke cautiously, moved slowly in the room so as not to startle her further or set her off.

An uncomfortable, sticky feeling crept up her spine. The same one she felt when the journal was recovered at Sasha's apartment. The feeling of having eyes on you at all times, no privacy.

That journal may have been forged, but this display... This was real.

Her body didn't feel like her own. Her memories didn't feel like her own. So many moments this fall, violated.

"Learn about me? You were stalking me!" Deming spun around, hair snapping in the air at the same time as her patience.

Ilysse, filthy but unharmed with Hartford right behind her, walked through the door at the exact moment the princess threw the words in Nikita's face. "Seems I'm interrupting."

Deming didn't take her eyes off Nikita.

He didn't take his eyes off her.

Ilysse whistled.

"What you have to understand—"

"Don't take that condescending tone with me."

Nikita held up his hands and took a step back. Wariness weighed heavy in his eyes.

She could feel the thorns begin to crawl their way back around her heart. Trusting anyone, after everything that had happened tonight, suddenly felt immensely difficult. Had anyone in her life spoken an honest word to her this fall?

Vallyn had, surely. She was steadfast.

Vallyn.

"We need to leave."

"Do you want to hear the prophecy?" Nikita's question sounded more like a peace offering than anything else.

Deming's gaze flicked to the delicate, pink conch shell that sat on one of the bedside tables. "No," she said firmly. After a moment she amended, "Later. For now we need to get back to the castle."

Ilysse's ears flicked as if she thought she heard wrong. "I'm sorry," she said with no attempt to hide the annoyance in her voice or the canines showing themselves through her lips, "I didn't just kill two soldiers, cut my palms to shreds on a gods-forsaken trellis, climb through rose bushes to escape out the garden, and sprint through the bowels of this disgusting city just for us to traipse back in there." She near spat the last insult.

"There are innocent lives in the castle."

"There are innocent lives everywhere."

"Innocent lives who will be killed directly for their involvement with me! Vallyn. Paris. Miriam." Her heart gave a pang as she forced out the last name. "My uncle specifically said they would be punished simply for their connections to me. We can't leave them."

Ilysse scoffed. "Vallyn can handle herself. Paris is protected by his father. And Miriam is not innocent."

"No. But she has fulfilled the role of a mother for longer than my birth mother had the chance to. And while I have my issues I need to sort out with her—" she swallowed hard. "—she does not deserve to die. And die she will if she stays in that castle. They all will." She turned to Nikita. "You heard my uncle. He would do anything to ensure Colette sits the throne. Everyone close to me will be targeted."

"We'll go back for them." Nikita, soft and sure.

Ilysse mumbled frustrated complaints under her breath but otherwise stayed silent.

"It doesn't make sense for all four of us to return," Hartford pointed out.

Nikita shook his head. "No, especially knowing we'll pick up Vallyn on the way. She'll be an asset in battle, not a hindrance like I suspect that blonde to be. Ilysse and I will go. You need to collect waterskins and as many horses as you can find and meet us at the edge of the wheat fields to the east. The fog will lift in a few hours, we need to be ready to leave immediately."

"What about me?" Deming asked.

"You stay here. Hartford will pick you up after she grabs supplies."

Deming was protesting before he finished. "I'm not staying behind. I'm sick of being treated like I have no agency of my own. This is my queendom, these are my people. I will not stand on the sidelines while my reign is under attack. Besides, Vallyn may believe you, but Paris will not. I need to go or he won't leave. I won't abandon him to the whims of my uncle. You heard him. Paris is as good as dead when the sun rises."

Nikita looked at her intently.

Deming did not back down. Her heart pounded, she tasted blood from a cut on her lip.

There was a moment where Deming was sure he would fight her on it, but eventually he nodded curtly.

He scanned their faces, all eyes on him. "In and out, quick as possible. No bloodshed."

"No bloodshed." Three voices echoed in unison.

Not a soul in the room believed it.

CHAPTER FORTY-ONE

DEMING SLID OUT OF the last cell in the dungeon, frustrated, annoyed, and anxious. She brushed her hands against her thighs but the tattered skirt was so filthy it did nothing to clean the muck off her palms.

They had turned over every stone, looked under every cot, pressed against nearly every wall looking for another hidden passageway in light of the fact that the castle was seemingly teeming with them.

No sign of Paris, Vallyn, or Miriam.

"They know we're here." Ilysse adjusted the sword on her hip.

They had come prepared to fight. The Fae had stockpiles of every manner of weapon you could imagine at the apartment. Nikita now wore twin scimitars that shone even in the darkness, begging to be used.

Deming had strapped as many daggers as she could fit to her thighs and waist. As much as she wished to wield something more thrilling, it was a simple matter of her only having a few months of swordplay training. Neither her technique nor her strength were at a level to compete with any of the royal guards. Daggers were easy. Thrust. Stab.

Ilysse opted for the more traditional approach. The hilt of her sword was plain, the leather worn, but a blade needed only to be sharp and sharp it was. "Or at least," she added, "They are expecting us."

"Where else would they be kept?"

Deming sifted through every corner of the castle in her mind. There wasn't another obvious place her uncle would have kept them. Unless. What if they were assuming wrong? "You said it earlier," she addressed Nikita, "he wants control. He wouldn't want to send the castle into any more of a panic than it already is with the explosion." Could it really be so simple? She looked towards the stairs. "He never sounded the alarm on us. He's using his personal guards, not the royal retinue, so no one would have to know you all had even escaped. Everyone would have been instructed to stay in their rooms while the explosion was investigated."

"They aren't under arrest at all."

"No," she breathed deeply, feeling the truth settle in her bones, "they're all in their rooms. Paris and Miriam, anyway. Vallyn could be on rotation anywhere in the castle."

Ilysse shouldered off the wall and clapped her hands. "Alright, team. Up we go."

"Do you always charge into situations with no plan?"

Nikita answered for her. "Yes."

"How did you ever become captain?" Deming scoffed, appalled.

"The same way anyone gets anything in this life. A healthy combination of skill and luck."

"And growing up alongside the prince, however disgraced I may be." Nikita tossed the words casually over his shoulder as he walked towards the stairwell.

The lioness stalked a step behind and hissed, "I said luck, didn't I?"

Deming, still standing deep in the dungeon, threw up her hands. "Hello? What's the plan?"

Nikita spun around mid stride. "We'll figure it out, princess." Without missing a beat he turned around again and began leaping up the steps.

The depths of his confidence knew no limits. Deming didn't know if she admired or despised him for it.

With a disgruntled sigh she left the reeking cells behind.

"Paris is closer," she whispered as they clustered together at the top of the stairs. "Miriam is in the other wing."

Ilysse looked to Nikita. "We should split up."

"Unless you want a scene I wouldn't do that. Paris hates us and won't go quietly. Or believe us at all. He will undoubtedly alert the entire castle to our presence."

Deming winced but couldn't deny the claim. "He's not a bad person."

"Didn't say he was, princess."

She chewed her lip, debating defending Paris more, but decided against it. "This way." With a nod of her head they were off.

The path to Paris's quarters was simple and direct. He and his parents both resided on the ground floor of the East Wing. This meant their rescue mission of three only had to traverse a handful of hallways and the smaller courtyard in order to reach him.

They made short work of the first half, Deming's heart only skipping a beat once when they heard a pair of guards walking near the corner ahead of them. She abruptly pulled Nikita and Ilysse into a linen closet, the former's wings making the already small space feel incredibly crowded, and waited, cramped and not daring to breathe, while the armored men passed along the perpendicular corridor.

They waited silently until the footsteps could no longer be heard, and then collapsed out of the closet.

Deming coughed and plucked a downy feather from her mouth. She held it up with concern to Nikita.

"Couldn't have been me. That was one of the pillows, for sure."

She didn't give him the satisfaction of a response.

They approached the courtyard from the shadows. For once Deming was thankful for the presence of the fog for it masked the beginning of dawn's light that tried to edge its way into the open air grassy knoll.

She looked down the row of doors across from them and swore softly.

"Death is the price we pay for justice."

Deming whipped towards Ilysse. "Absolutely not. They are innocent."

"We don't know that."

"They are members of the royal guard. Some of these men and women have protected me faultlessly their entire lives."

"And with the revelation of your uncle's betrayal it would serve us well to question the allegiance of every single person in this castle."

Far calmer than she felt, Deming pointed at the two guards posted stoically across the courtyard, one outside each door. "There has been enough harm committed within these walls tonight, and more to come I have no doubt. If it is in our power, we will not add to the toll. You are not to kill any member of the royal guard. Is that understood?"

Ilysse crossed her arms. Tilted her head. Looked at Nikita who held up his hands.

Deming narrowed her eyes. "I said, is that understood?"

"Yes, yes. We'll knock them out instead. I can control myself. Probably."

Deming growled at the last word. Ilysse blew her a mocking kiss and then darted beyond reach, weaving in and out of the columns faster than humanly possible.

Nikita opened his wings and flew directly across the open expanse of grass, scimitars out and glinting menacingly.

Deming opened her mouth to protest blowing their cover but before words could escape her lips, he and Ilysse were at their targets. Solid metal pommels met skulls and both guards hit the ground with a thud.

Neither had a chance to draw their weapons or voice alarms.

Threats neutralized, Deming walked across the grass, raised her hand, sighed deeply, and rapped on the door thrice with her knuckles.

The world was quiet.

Then three things happened in rapid succession.

Ilysse spun towards the corner to their left, blonde braids slicing the air and dagger held firmly in her dominant hand. "Someone's coming."

The door opened, revealing Paris rubbing sleep away from the corners of his eyes.

And a figure shrouded in shadow appeared at the end of the corridor.

Deming caught a glimpse of white hair, a wink of gold. But all she could do was yelp as fear swallowed her voice and Ilysse's dagger went flying through the air with deadly accuracy aimed directly at Vallyn's chest.

Deming saw white then stars then nothing at all.

Clang!

Metallic ringing echoed.

She blinked away the veil fear had thrown over her, gasping for breath.

The dagger hit its mark but ricocheted sharply away off the armor, skittering across the slabs of stone on the walkway. The tip had crumpled with the force of metal on metal and left a dent directly over the warrior's heart.

"That was rude," Vallyn quipped then immediately glared at the Fae with a look that walked an odd line of curious and wrathful. "Don't they teach you not to break out of cells and abduct princesses in Runne?"

Ilysse snarled back. No curiosity, just wrath. "Don't they teach you not to falsely accuse guests in Laey?"

Ignoring the female, Vallyn walked straight up to the heir. "Deming, are you okay? What are they doing here?"

"Yes. Well, no, not really." She heard a scuff of slippers on the floor and turned to see Paris standing, jaw agape and frozen in the doorway.

"Oh, for the love of the Goddess," Nikita gestured Paris to move over and ushered everyone into his room. "Let's not stand out in the hallway where anyone can see us while we very, very quickly explain what's happening and why we all need to simmer down immediately." He shot a pointed look at Ilysse, who did nothing but bare her canines back at him.

Paris's rooms were, expectedly so, well appointed and immaculate. Decorative pillows, perfectly fluffed, perched in the corner of each couch circling the moderately sized rectangular tea table in the center of the room. The curtains adorning the windows were pleated crisply. Through the open doorway to his bedroom Deming spied a singular row of shoes lined up in color order, not a lace out of place.

As much as Deming knew he hated to admit, so much of his father's military adherence to detail had passed down to him.

Nikita cut the tension. "Let's all sit."

No one did so. Vallyn moved to position herself closer to Paris and Deming. The former looked to the latter.

Deming rubbed the back of her neck. Best to dive right in, she supposed. "The Fae have been falsely accused. They were used as a convenient option to cover up my uncle." That snapped any lingering slumber away. Paris's eyes widened. "He's been working behind the scenes for months to get me out of the picture and put..." Her throat choked up with emotions. Gods-damned why was it so hard to say this? "To put Colette on the throne instead. He believes I'm not worthy of the responsibility and that my coloring is proof the gods believe so too." The last words trailed off softly. Deming pulled her fingers away from her hair, not realizing she was twirling a brilliant white lock around and around and around a red lacquered nail.

Nikita tried once more to address Vallyn and Paris directly. This time they met his gaze. "He admitted this all to us earlier this evening. Deming had broken us out of the dungeons, even before knowing the truth." He gave her a tender smile.

"I knew the truth. Not his involvement. But I knew enough."

"Before we could escape, he and his personal guards confronted us and attempted to take Deming with the intent to kill."

The revelations settled like a thick blanket around them.

"I never liked him," Vallyn said.

Relief washed over Deming. Short lived, however, because Paris spoke next, wariness coating every syllable.

"Colette wouldn't do this. She's our best friend, Deming. Your cousin."

Deming tried to pour as much of her soul as she could into her next words. "I know, Paris. I feel... so betrayed. So heartbroken. It feels like I've been living a lie. My whole life, a lie." She bit her lip, trying to focus on the pain instead of the tears pricking at the corners of her eyes. She couldn't cry now. If she started, she felt like she would never be able to stop. "I don't know why…" Her voice trembled, the words choked off as emotion surged and her throat tightened. She tried again. "I don't know why she's doing this. All I know is that I played right into their hands. They needed a reason to turn Arsaela against me. When the Fae arrived, one fell into their laps. They needed me to get close to Nikita and Ilysse and Hartford in order for everyone to doubt my intentions. And has the court not seen me training with them? Dancing with them? Engaging in conversation openly with them? I gave them all the evidence they needed to pin me as a traitor when the time was right."

She took a breath. "Now, you and Vallyn are in danger, too. My uncle won't keep either of you alive. Not when you both have such strong connections to me. He knows you wouldn't honor the coup he's throwing. Please," She took his hand in hers. Flashes to those hands on her hips and waist and thighs billowed through her memory like clouds. "I need you to be safe. I need you to come with us."

Paris opened his mouth to speak.

Crash!

The door behind them flew off its hinges and three armored guards with Dresden's crest emblazoned on their chest burst through.

"On your knees!"

Nikita and Ilysse whirled into motion before the bearded man could finish his command.

The lioness leapt into the air and landed a blow from her heel to the face of a haggard looking man, hair slick with grease. The man was thrown against the wall with the force of the impact. His head cracked against the stone but still he did not fall.

He rose, growling obscenities and slurs through his teeth, and met Ilysse blow for blow as they parried one another's attacks around the sitting room. Ilysse leapt with lethal grace to the back of a couch, claws fully extended from her knuckles and leaving deep grooves in the leather, and then immediately sprung over the man and landed light as air behind his back. She plunged her sword in for the kill but narrowly missed as he spun away.

Wrenching the sword from the couch, she stalked towards her prey, cornering him near the window.

At the same time, Nikita's curved blades slashed through the air, meeting an already raised broadsword wielded by the original speaker. The clash of metal on metal reverberated through the air, echoing so deep Deming's teeth felt their song.

A second man, thin and wiry but seeming deft on his feet, charged towards Nikita's back with two daggers, unique in their length and serrated edges. A jolt of panic surged through Deming as she realized why the man hadn't gone for a killing blow to the neck. Serrated edges for cutting through sinew and bone. Serrated edges designed to saw off extremities.

His wings.

They didn't plan to kill. They planned to capture, then torture.

Deming unclasped the dagger from her hip and made to enter the fray.

A bruising grip held her forearm in place. "Absolutely not," snapped Vallyn. "You are not remotely close to competent enough."

The Captain of the Guard wrenched the dagger from Deming's unwilling grip and flung it with deadly precision at the man cornering Ilysse.

Deming watched the blade soar through the air and sink into the wood behind the dueling pair. Vallyn had been a sliver of a second too late to land the blow.

Nikita leapt over a slow swing from his attacker and rolled smoothly off the ground, springing back to his feet in time to match the thinner man swing for swing. He twisted to the side, then with his elbow struck up with the force of a thousand men directly into the chin of the attacker.

His jaw cracked and his head snapped back so fiercely Deming wondered how it possibly remained attached to his neck.

With an inhuman sense of awareness, Nikita sidestepped the bearded man who had run forward, grunting with the effort and raising the menacing, serrated weapons again. Nikita kicked at the base of the man's spine, sending him crashing to the ground. He reached to recover his sword, but Nikita kicked it forcefully away and used his heel to stomp his hands. The man swore in pain as the frail bones in his fingers snapped like twigs then was immediately silenced with a swipe of a scimitar to his neck.

His last words gurgled out wetly and then the life left his eyes forever. The only remaining movement from him was the blood rapidly seeping from the cleanly sliced wound. It bled onto the rug, staining the fabric maroon.

Nikita turned swiftly. His feet coated in the pool of blood from his kill as he exploded forward and pounced on the other guard who lurched forward on shaky legs, clearly seeing two or three of Nikita as the Fae roared towards him.

Nikita barreled directly into the man, leading with his shoulder and slamming the both of them back into the wall. The impact knocked both knives from the attacker's grip and knocked him out cold, head lolling to the side, but only caused Nikita to lose his grip on one of the scimitars.

He grabbed the man by his hair with his now free hand. With the other, he drew the razor thin edge of the scimitar across the unconscious guard's neck. It cut neatly through the muscle but got caught on the bone. Nikita flung the scimitar to the side, wrapped the definitively dead man in a chokehold, and twisted.

The headless body fell lifelessly to the ground.

Every head in the room turned to the window just in time to see Ilysse wheelhouse kick the sword out of the guard's grip, ball her fists, and punch him square in the face.

Bone cracked, muscles ripped, and both eyeballs squelched as her claws sank knuckle deep into his skull. He fell in a crumpled pile to the floor, gravity releasing his mauled face from Ilysse's fists.

Ilysse stomped a boot into his nose, shattering it further, then spat on him for good measure.

Across the room, Nikita dropped the lifeless head.

The severed neck thudded against the tile and splattered blood over his boots.

He rolled his shoulders. Tensing and relaxing his hands trying to come down from the high.

There hadn't been a moment the entire time they'd been here that he'd looked more like the immortal warrior he was. He was not to be crossed.

A Fae Prince.

Deming exhaled and tried to still her shaking fingers. Not from fear. Never fear.

Ilysse wiped the blood dripping from her claws on her leg, smearing the blood of the fallen guard with her own. Battle fog lay heavy in her gaze. Through panting breaths she looked at Deming and said, "You said not to kill your men. Nothing about these pieces of shit."

"Yeah," Deming agreed breathlessly, "yeah, I did say that."

Nikita looked to the woman still shielding Deming. "Vallyn, go with Ilysse and meet us at the rendezvous point."

"I don't answer to you. I protect my own."

Frustrated, Nikita balled his fists. "We need to get you all out of here now."

Deming cleared her throat. "It's fine, Vallyn. I'll be fine. Besides, Paris will feel more comfortable if you're there." An afterthought, but a truth nonetheless.

For a moment it looked like she was going to protest further, but eventually she cupped Deming's chin with a hand that smelled of sweat and blood, kissed her forehead, and stepped aside. "Be careful."

"You," Ilysse jerked her chin to Paris, who was standing so still against the wall he might have been a statue, "with us."

He looked to Deming instead, an action Ilysse seethed at through barred teeth.

"If these fucking humans don't stop ignoring me, I swear I'll kill them all." No one bothered to respond.

The world quieted for a moment as Paris's eyes met her own. Here was a man who loved her with everything he had to offer. A man who, Deming knew intimately, would lay his life down for her even after everything she put him through. A man who still trusted his future queen utterly and completely.

"You're sure." Not a question and not solely about the dead men laying around them or the ferocious Fae female he was to leave with. Just a quiet confirmation before choosing to leave everything he knew behind for a woman who would never be able to return his love in the way he wanted.

"Yes," she whispered, "more sure than I could possibly express."

Crystal blue skies in those eyes. "Okay." He reached out and squeezed her hand. "Okay. For you, Deming, anything." Before she could respond he turned on his heels. "There will be fewer guards if we go through the library. There's an external door on the archival level only the servants use."

Ilysse sheathed her sword. "Get Miriam and then get the fuck out," she called over her shoulder, jogging to catch up with Paris. "If you aren't at the trailhead in thirty minutes I'm coming back and laying this castle and everyone in it to waste."

"Come on." Nikita gently pulled her away from the blood pooling at her feet and the ever growing distance between her and the person she had always envisioned spending her life with. "That wasn't an idle threat."

Deming let him turn her around.

"You'll see him soon."

"It's not like that—"

"I know," he interrupted. "And it would be fine even if it was. Now let's get Miriam and leave. We've clearly lost the element of surprise, this needs to be quick."

She steeled her nerves. Miriam. "Okay. North wing, fifth floor. Quickest path is through the main courtyard but that's risky, there's more likely to be guards."

"We don't have the time to be stealthy." He rubbed the pommel of his scimitar he had retrieved from the floor.

Deming groaned. Half the royal guard would be waking up with cracking headaches tomorrow at this point. "This way, then."

Side by side they raced out the door and down the hallway. Pain stitched in her abdomen, but Deming pushed herself faster. No time to waste, no time to waste, no time to waste.

She skidded around a corner and slammed into an immovable stone wall. "Fuck!" That was going to bruise. She'd be surprised if any part of her skin wasn't mottled blue and purple when they woke up tomorrow.

If they woke up tomorrow.

Don't think that.

Run, run, run.

Footfall after footfall they pounded through the castle. A shriek and immediate clatter of silver on stone came from behind them. A servant with platters for breakfast.

They shot up the stairs, near flying they were scaling the steps so quickly.

Rounding the corner at the top, they came face to face with two guards patrolling the hallway. Nikita, double fisting the scimitars, hit them both in the temple before they could even think to draw their weapons.

Frantic footfalls echoed from ahead.

Someone else approached, someone in a hurry.

Smooth waves of beautiful, red hair filled Deming's vision.

Colette's mouth moved, her eyes scared and confused, but Deming heard only the roar of betrayal.

With speed she didn't realize she possessed, Deming closed the space between them and pinned the false queen against the wall with her forearm. She brandished a knife to her throat so tightly that when she opened her mouth to speak the blade cut into her pale, freckled skin.

"There's no time, Deming! She's not worth it!" Nikita yelled from down the hallway. He hadn't slowed his pace at all.

Deming snarled and bit out a curse. She shoved her cousin harder into the wall then pushed off, not taking care with the knife and nicking the traitor on her cheek.

"You'll get what's coming to you."

She left her coughing and sputtering for breath, falling to the floor grasping at her neck as if to reassure herself it was still attached to her body.

They tore down the fifth floor hallway.

"Deming! Please stop! He'll kill you!" Colette shouted after them, her voice ragged.

Deming didn't spare her cousin a backwards glance.

Her legs burned something fierce. Her lungs were on fire.

Finally, they slid to a halt outside Miriam's door.

It was open.

Deming's stomach fell, hard.

Not trying to be quiet, they entered the suite of connecting rooms. Nikita was on edge, weaving beside her like a snake. She knew he was itching to get them both out of the castle.

As they approached Miriam's closed bedroom door, they saw the crumpled bodies of Rochelle and Dorian laying limply on the ground.

Deming's whimper was quickly followed by a rising panic that they were clearly too late.

A muffled cry sounded from beyond the door.

She shouldered through the bedroom door so forcefully it rebounded off the stone wall and hit her bruised body again.

The pain didn't register.

Not when the sight in front of her hurt so, so much worse.

CHAPTER FORTY-TWO

ON THE BED, BOUND and gagged, lay Miriam.

Bruises littered her face. What skin wasn't colored by burst blood vessels was pale and ashen. Her eyelids hung heavy, the iris's underneath seemingly unable to focus on anything.

She remained clothed, but the fabric was tattered and torn to make room for the rope binding all four limbs to the mahogany bed posts. The rope was tied painfully tight, stretching her body to its limits, and blood dripped from each extremity where it dug into her skin. The white linens of her bed were soaked ruby.

Despite all this, what made Deming stop dead in the doorway were the injuries sustained on her forearms.

Long, clean cuts sliced from her wrists to her elbows. Thin though they were, they were deep. Blood flowed like a river from them, collecting where her hips sank into the mattress.

And standing beside her, wearing a sinister smile that would carve itself into Deming's memories until the day she died, was her uncle.

"So kind of you to join us."

Nikita lunged forward, wings flared, but rage and exhaustion made him sloppy. Dresden dodged easily and before Nikita could counter, pulled a carving knife from beneath his robes and held it against Miriam's throat.

"Now, now," he whistled, "let's not be rash. We wouldn't want Miriam to die any sooner than she has to. Drop your weapon." He was apparently unworried by the small dagger clutched in Deming's hand.

The male snarled, but stood down. His sword hit the ground with a clang, the echoes sounding through the room melodically, like a bell.

"Over to the window." He jerked his chin to the windows they had escaped from less than an hour before.

Unwilling to risk the knife cutting any further into the delicate skin of Miriam's neck, Deming rushed to the spot her uncle indicated.

Nikita hesitated, glancing at the distance between himself and Dresden.

"Nikita."

The desperate plea from Deming snapped his concentration. He stalked to the window.

"That's better." He turned his attention to Deming. "I'm so thrilled to have you back in the castle, niece. Though I heard you've taken out a few of my prized soldiers. What a shame." He clicked his tongue.

The tsk, tsk grated on Deming's frayed nerves. How long could someone survive that kind of blood loss? If they managed to get her out of here, who would weave her arms back together? Was it even possible?

Auburn hair swished as Dresden removed the knife and slowly walked towards Deming. Out of the corner of her eye, she saw Nikita tense.

"Although," her uncle said, "it did provide a stunningly perfect opportunity for me." He held the knife loosely in his hand, then pricked a finger with the tip. Blood welled. He frowned, then wiped it away. "You see, I wanted desperately to get rid of Miriam here, she was going to be such a problem for me and Colette. And when you returned to the castle so loudly, knocking guards out here and there, killing my people in the East Wing, I knew exactly who you would end up attempting to collect.

"Poor Miriam." He pouted at her sarcastically. "Even if she was trained to fight, the poison on my knife incapacitated her quick enough that it wouldn't have mattered. The second I heard you all barreling through the castle I slit her wrists. She'll be dead in minutes. Poetic that you will get to see her last breath when she watched you take your first."

That couldn't be true. She wouldn't allow it to be true. Deming ached to go to Miriam's side but she didn't dare move. "You will never get away with this."

"Oh, my sweet child. I already have." He left the side of the bed and walked towards the door.

Deming raced to kneel by Miriam's side. She scoured the limp body in front of her, taking in every cut, every bruise. Her injuries were...

A sob escaped her lips. She didn't take her eyes off Miriam as her uncle began speaking again.

"You were seen by myself and my guards aiding in the escape of the accused. You were present at the death of three soldiers. You stood by while he knocked out a multitude of royal guards. And if that shriek I heard echoing through the halls was any indication, you were even seen by the help. It won't even matter this poison is famously only found in Runne. You'll be labeled as a traitor by your own before I even have to open my mouth. I don't even have to kill you now and risk you becoming a martyr. It will be so much sweeter to see your kingdom turn against you. I can see it now. The troubled heir, seduced by Fae vermin, turned conspirator as they murdered her people." He closed his eyes momentarily, soaking in his victory. "Just goes to show how utterly nonsensical you would have been on the throne. Incapable of protecting yourself. And tragically, yet again incapable of protecting those you love. I hope Miriam rots in the underworld with your father and my darling, darling sister."

Wrath erupted in Deming. She hurled the dagger at her side at her uncle. It flew through the room and she reveled in the panic that flashed across his smug face as it glanced by his cheek, missing him by a hair's breadth.

With a thud, it buried itself in the door.

"Best get back in the training ring. Your aim is off." He vanished through the lounge and to the hallway door, slinking out like a sewer rat.

Nikita stepped towards him in pursuit but halted at the sound of his name keening from Deming's lips, begging him to help.

There was no choice to be made. He rushed to her side.

"Miriam, Miriam, Miriam." Deming murmured her name over and over, stroking her cheek and gently rubbing away bits of dried blood. Nikita made quick work of the restraints, cutting through the rope in seconds. Where rope had been, raw, bloody skin now lay bare to the world.

Though her limbs were free and her gag removed, Miriam said nothing. Moved nowhere.

"Miriam, please," Deming whispered, voice shaking. "We can fix this. We can get you help, it isn't that bad." She choked on the last word, releasing a fresh wave of soul wracking sobs. "I can't do this without you, please. Please don't go. I'll be good, I promise. I won't complain, I won't skip council, I won't—" Her voice broke. "Just don't leave me. You can't leave me, too."

Deming crawled into the bed. Miriam's blood soaked into her skirts, staining it like wine. She curled into her neck, balling herself up as small as she could. "Please."

"Deming?"

Quieter than breath.

Deming bolted upright, her hand shot to Miriam's face, brushed back the tangled mess of hair that was trapped beneath the pillows. Searching, searching, searching for light in those hooded eyes.

A hint of recognition.

The noise Deming made was animalistic and unintelligible, relief and joy and terror wrapped into one exclamation. "Yes, yes, I'm here. I'm here."

"Deming." If at all possible, Miriam seemed to sink further into the bed, as if she, too, was relieved that the pair of them were once again in the same room.

"It's okay, don't worry we're going to get help. Nikita is here, he can bring you somewhere safe. Right?" She looked to the male. He opened his mouth, then closed it without saying anything. Tears blurred her vision. "Right, Nikita? We can get her help. You can fly her somewhere... To Ilysse and Hartford? Somewhere?"

"Deming." His voice as delicate as lace.

"No," she moaned, guttural and wild. "No, no, no..." Over and over she protested, pressing her face into Miriam's chest.

Nikita approached slowly. With the care one usually reserves for a hurt child, he caressed her shoulder. "You should say your goodbyes. She may be beyond saving, but you are not. I know that she would want you to live, Deming."

"Don't say that!" She wrenched herself away from his touch. "She'll be fine. We just need some bandages and..." She looked at

Miriam's arms. Her skin was ashen and cold to the touch. The blood pouring from the cuts had slowed to a trickle. "We just need some bandages," she whimpered uselessly.

Miriam's eyelashes fluttered. Her breathing slowed to a drip.

Tears of terror and grief carved canyons in her skin so deep the scars would never fade. Deming pressed her forehead to Miriam's. "I love you. I'm sorry I didn't say it more. I love you and I forgive you and I love you and I love you."

How do you survive saying goodbye to a mother twice in one lifetime?

One last inhale, so shallow there could hardly be any air in her lungs at all. On the shaky exhale Miriam closed her eyes for the final time and left the world with what she treasured most on her lips.

"My love."

CHAPTER FORTY-THREE

 Quiet.

Serene and full of light like how she imagined it must have felt when the world was new.

Full of light.

That was different.

Indeed, from where she was floating above it all she saw light streaming in from the window. In the distance, the sun gorged on the skies above Arsaela like it had been starved of its taste for months. Buttery yellow, peony pink, fuchsia, lavender, orange as rich and stimulating as the peel of a clementine danced across the horizon. The ocean lay clear as day to the south. Crystalline blue depths swelled and crashed and foamed frothy and white. The pine forests of Fairhaven rose tall and endlessly to the east, stretching out as far as the eye could see.

A woman was dead and Arsaela was free.

She knew that somewhere, far away, she was screaming.

She knew that somewhere, far away, she was ripping at drenched sheets, smothering her fingers and caking her nails in the spilled life blood of her mother.

She knew that somewhere, far away, she was collapsing on top of the dead woman's body and wailing into her cold skin.

But all of that was so... distant.

As if watching someone else, she saw the winged male collect her limp frame. She saw herself flail and cry and beg to stay, beg to die with the woman laying motionless in the bed because how could she possibly live without her? She watched as she writhed in his arms, reaching back for something, anything.

She watched as the male tried and failed to keep himself together, shoulders and wings shaking as sobs wracked his own body. Grief for both the woman laying dead on the mattress and for the woman in his arms proving too heavy to suppress.

He set her down, his attempt to let her lean on the bedpost for support failing instantly as she sank to the floor, legs no longer seeming to work, and went back to the dead woman. He lifted her neck and parted the matted curls. He unclasped the delicate gold chain and lifted the necklace away. He knelt beside the broken heir and clasped the last physical connection she would have to the lost soul laying on the bed around her own neck. The heart shaped locket rested against her tear stained chest.

And then he gathered her limp frame up in his arms once again, walked to the window, and leapt into the brilliant dawn sky.

Acknowledgements

Literature has always been a home for me, reading specifically. Where some kids had to put their phone away at night when they were younger, my parents made me put my books outside my door before bed so I wouldn't stay up till dawn with my nose buried in whatever story had caught my attention that week. I loved writing too, but it wasn't until my friend wrote her debut novel that I truly began believing that being a published author could be more than a pipe dream for me.

Neena, the courage and authenticity you bring to my life is un-paralleled. I was, and still am, in awe of you when you set out to publish your first novel. Thank you for your unwavering support through every part of this process. From fielding endless questions about writing and formatting programs, to beta reading this story with nuanced commentary, to working beside me in coffee shops, you have been a wealth of knowledge. You are an inspiration and the reason this book exists. There will never be enough words to properly thank you for paving the way.

Nick, my soon-to-be husband and the love of my life, thank you for believing in me when I struggled to believe in myself. Thank you for letting me bounce ideas off you, incessantly, from the inception of this story to the very end. Thank you for the time and effort you put into helping make this the best reflection of my work it could be. You have read this story more than anyone else, save myself, and I am forever grateful for your support. There will never be adequate words to describe what you mean to me. You are the perfect compliment to me in every way. I cannot imagine life without you.

To my beta readers—Chloe, Kate, and Beth—thank you endlessly for reading this story in its roughest form. Your insights and commentary were instrumental in taking it from something chaotic to something I am proud to share with the world.

To all of the wonderful professionals that worked on this book, thank you for sharing your time and effort with me. Laura, this cover is a whimsical dream. You took my idea and brought it to life like no one else could. Gin, the map of Arsaela is one of the most beautiful things I've ever seen in my life. Seeing the realization of my world through your eyes is an honor. Kay, your copy edits and proofreading polished this story until it glowed. Thank you immensely for being not only a wonderful editor, but a steadfast cheerleader for me and my work.

To my parents, thank you for raising me to be a woman who takes chances, speaks her mind, and cherishes the written word.

And to you, the reader, thank you from the bottom of my heart for taking a chance on me. I have found so many parts of myself reflected in these characters and this world, I hope you were able to find a bit of yourself within these pages too.

About the Author

Jessica Santi is a YA/NA Fantasy author. She holds a bachelor's degree in Elementary Education from the University of Michigan and a master's degree in Social Foundations and Community Education from Eastern Michigan University. Jessica lives in southeast Michigan with her loving husband, rambunctious dog, and quietly conniving cat. In her spare time she enjoys supporting other indie authors, exploring local coffee shops, and rewatching shows she's seen a million times before.

Veiled Skies is her debut novel. For information on upcoming sequels, including ARC opportunities and early access to content, follow @authorjessicasanti on social media.

www.ingramcontent.com/pod-product-compliance
Lightning Source LLC
Chambersburg PA
CBHW031827310726
48972CB00005B/1194